the
cruellest
game

Hilary Bonner is a full-time author and former chairman of
The Crime Writers' Association. Her published work includes
nine previous novels, five non-fiction books: two ghosted
autobiographies, one biography, two companions to TV pro-
grammes, and a number of short stories. She is a former Fleet
Street journalist, Show Business Editor of three national newspapers and Assistant Editor of one. She now lives in the West
of England where she was born and brought up and where most
of her novels are set.

BY HILARY BONNER

Fiction

The Cruelty of Morning
A Fancy to Kill For
A Passion So Deadly
For Death Comes Softly
A Deep Deceit
A Kind of Wild Justice
A Moment of Madness
When the Dead Cry Out
No Reason to Die
The Cruellest Game

Non-fiction

Rene and Me (with Gorden Kaye)
Benny: The True Story (with Dennis Kirkland)
It's Not a Rehearsal (with Amanda Barrie)
Journeyman (with Clive Gunnell)
Heartbeat: The Real Life Story

the cruellest game

HILARY BONNER

PAN BOOKS

First published 2013 by Macmillan

This edition published 2013 by Pan Books
an imprint of Pan Macmillan, a division of Macmillan Publishers Limited
Pan Macmillan, 20 New Wharf Road, London N1 9RR
Basingstoke and Oxford
Associated companies throughout the world
www.panmacmillan.com

ISBN 978-1-4472-1873-9

3 5 7 9 8 6 4 2

A CIP catalogue record for this book is available from
the British Library.

Typeset by Ellipsis Digital Limited, Glasgow
Printed and bound by CPI Group (UK) Ltd, Croydon, CR0 4YY

For Shirl
With love always

acknowledgements

Grateful thanks are due to:

The indomitable Heather Chasen for reminding me I should also be so, Doctor Rudy Capeldeo; Doctor Paul Bevan; Patricia May LIB, Barrister-at-Law; former Detective Sergeant Frank Waghorn; Devon coroner's officers Cath Lake, Jean Timms, and Leigh Bass; super-clever mechanic Robert Andrews; Alex Broadbent; my agent Tony Peake for his enduring support; and, of course, my inspirational editor Wayne Brookes and all the team at Pan Macmillan for the faith they have shown in me.

one

Do you know that feeling when you walk into a house and you're instantly absolutely sure that it's empty? That no one is there. Even if someone should be.

That's how it was the day it happened. The day my life, my nice comfortable ordinary life, changed for ever.

I'd recently gone back to teaching, just one day a week, every Thursday, at Okehampton College, our nearest community school. I liked to keep busy when my husband Robert was away working. Not that looking after our home and our son wasn't quite enough most of the time.

This was a Thursday. The 3rd of November 2011. After work I'd gone to the supermarket. We grew most of our own vegetables at home and this was a mild and gentle autumn, so we still had lettuces in the ground along with leeks, carrots and young Brussels sprouts. Our spinach would keep going through the winter, and we had potatoes and apples in store. I'd intended just to shop for more of the things a good mother should try to feed a growing teenager, like fish, chicken and wholemeal bread. But I'd also picked up several of my son's favourite pizzas, a rich chocolate cake and a block of clotted-cream ice cream. I could never resist spoiling Robbie.

I'd been the same ever since he was born. After all, I'd

1

thought I was going to lose him and I knew almost straight away I would never have another child.

Robbie, named after his Scottish father, Robert, and always known by the Gaelic abbreviation, was fifteen years old, tall, black-haired, pale-skinned, and beautiful. Just like his dad. At least I thought he was beautiful. I thought they were both beautiful.

He'd just begun his mock GCSEs, and I'd left him at home in his room studying. His school believed in making the mocks as much like the real thing as possible. They suspended the usual syllabus and allowed students to work in the library, or at home if they were day pupils, when they didn't have exams.

Robbie was a quiet studious boy. A little too quiet and studious some might think. He'd led a pretty sheltered life really. His father in particular had seen to that. But Robbie always seemed content enough. He did have his swimming, at which he excelled. He swam for his school and the county. And so far we'd not experienced with him the teenage nightmares so many other families seemed to have to deal with.

The traffic was heavy on the road heading home. We lived in an isolated old farmhouse with an acre or so of land on the edge of Dartmoor. Our nearest village, Blackstone, was almost eight miles away. It was not the pretty chocolate-box kind of moorland village which attracted tourists in the summer. Indeed, it was rather a bleak place. A string of ill-assorted housing – a couple of quite grand thatched places, several rows of small cottages, a line of 1930s pebble-dashed semis and a smattering of modern bungalows – ran along a single narrow road up one side of a hill and down the other. But it was quiet and peaceful and we liked it.

Highrise Farm could also be bleak in the winter. Even more so than the village. But by God, it was splendid. On this orange early evening, at the end of what had been an unseasonably sunny day, I was eager to get back home before darkness fell. Although there was a winterish nip in the air, threatening a frost that night, the sky was clear and glorious.

It was the location, of course, and the house itself, dating back to the seventeenth century and retaining many original features, which made the place so special. But our home was, quite frankly, gorgeous in every way. The kitchen and the bathrooms had all been stylishly refurbished by my husband Robert, who worked pretty much non-stop on Highrise when he was at home.

He was in the oil industry and spent far too much of his time away on the rigs. But we both agreed that it was worth it. He was a senior drilling engineer employed by Amaco Limited UK. It was an important and challenging job, and Robert talked to me a lot about the responsibilities and the stress of the post he held. He was involved in the most advanced aspects of the extraction of oil from the North Sea, and the generous salary he received for both his expertise and somewhat antisocial working arrangements enabled us to enjoy an excellent lifestyle.

When he was on leave he said that nothing gave him greater joy than working on our home. 'All I want to do, Marion, is to create a personal paradise for my family,' he often said. 'It just makes me so happy.'

He had even, virtually single-handed, built a long, narrow swimming pool so that Robbie, who we at any rate believed to be potentially an international swimmer, could train at home.

Robert loved our garden, which was mostly laid to shrubs and lawn so it wouldn't need too much attention when he was away. But the vegetable patch and greenhouse, his pride and joy, did need attention and, as this had been another in a succession of dry and relatively warm days, might well require watering in spite of the time of year. I cursed silently as yet another set of traffic lights demanded I stop at roadworks on the A30.

One of the two lanes on my side of the dual carriageway was closed. Speed camera warnings lined the roadside along with 50-mile-an-hour limit signs. Chance would be a fine thing, I thought irritably, as I was forced to slow almost to a standstill.

There seemed to be major works going on involving resurfacing and the widening of lanes and it looked as if this lot was going to last well into the Christmas holidays. I texted Robbie to tell him I was going to be a bit later than I'd expected. We always kept in touch, usually texting and calling several times a day when we were apart, but that day we hadn't been in contact since late morning. I'd not had my normal breaks between classes because I'd been standing in for another teacher who was off sick, and I realized Robbie was probably buried in his revision, and would remain so until I returned home, as he had two exams the following day. Actually, I'd been told by his teachers that he was expected to fly through his mocks. He was very bright. He was also conscientious.

I told him there was pizza for supper. Lots of it. Robbie had an enormous appetite. It never ceased to amaze me how much he ate and how thin he remained. But then, he was still growing, and fast. It looked like he was going to be even taller than his father, who stood a good six foot two inches.

I kept glancing at my phone in case he texted back. I half expected him to do so because he almost always did. But I reminded myself again of how hard he worked when he had an exam looming, let alone mock GCSEs.

As I drove along I could so clearly imagine him at the desk Robert had built for him in his room, custom-made to fit into the awkwardly shaped corner to the left of the ancient chimney breast. He'd be sitting, totally preoccupied, hunched over his keyboard, in just the position I kept telling him he ought to avoid, particularly as he was such a tall boy, in case he damaged his back. He'd have his left elbow propped on the edge of the desk, lower arm arranged so that one side of his face could rest on a splayed hand. His eyes would be screwed up in concentration and he'd probably be chewing a pencil, shredding the end with his front teeth and spitting out occasional splinters of wood onto the floor.

I was smiling as I pulled in to the yard and drew our four-wheel-drive Lexus to a halt. Thinking of Robbie always made me smile.

It was almost 5 p.m., and the sun had very nearly set behind Highrise, but the old house, with its tall chimneys and angular roof formation, still remained in quite spectacular silhouette.

Our dog Florrie, a Border collie, loped from the direction of the house to greet me. She pretty much had the run of our home, though we did try to keep her out of the bedrooms as she shed hair for England. But in any case she had farm blood in her and, particularly in decent weather, often preferred to roam the garden – and sometimes a little further afield, I feared – then lie on the squashy cushion in a box we'd installed in the porch.

She wrapped herself around my legs as I climbed out of the car, and whimpered appreciatively when I scratched the back of her neck. Laden with my shopping, I stepped onto the raised paved terrace which Robert had built right along the front of Highrise. Florrie followed close to my heels.

The door to the adjoining shed where we kept our bicycles was ajar and I pushed it shut with one foot as I walked past.

The front door was unlocked and I managed to open it, without having to put down any of my shopping, by leaning my shoulder against it and pushing the handle with my elbow.

Florrie squeezed past me heading for the kitchen. It was her dinner time, and Florrie had a tummy like an alarm clock. She had only one thing on her mind now. Food.

As I stepped into the flagstoned hallway I called out to Robbie, like I always did.

No response, so I called again. Louder. His room was at the top of the house. He may not have heard me. But somehow I didn't think that was it. I paused. Uneasy. The shopping heavy in my arms. No, that was not it at all.

It was then that I began to feel the emptiness of the house. That I was overwhelmed with the certainty that Robbie was not there.

However, when I'd closed the door to the shed I'd seen his mountain bike propped against the far wall and, unless Robert or I were around to drive him, Robbie's only means of transport was his bike. The house was too far away from anywhere for walking to be a reasonable option.

In any case Robbie rarely left the house without one of us, and he certainly would not do so without telling me. He would have called or texted.

No. He was upstairs in his room, too engrossed in his computer or his books to have been aware of the sound of the car pulling into the yard or to have heard me calling him.

I told myself off for having an overactive imagination and carried the shopping into the kitchen. I dumped it on the worktop, handmade by Robert from Dartmoor granite, and stretched my aching arms. Then, with a small moan of relief, I kicked off my shiny black 'school' shoes. They were nearly new, had heels I was no longer very used to, and did not feel entirely comfortable at the end of a long day. Gratefully, I thrust my feet into my well-worn old slippers.

The kitchen felt chilly and I realized when I reached out to touch the Aga that I certainly wasn't imagining that. The range was barely warm. Perhaps unusually nowadays, ours was a solid fuel version. We fed it with wood, mostly gathered from our own land, on which grew sycamore, ash and pine regularly culled by Robert. And, certainly not unusually, Robbie seemed to have forgotten to stoke it. I opened the door to the fire compartment. There was just a faint glow at the bottom. I swiftly gathered up handfuls of small pieces of wood from the box which stood alongside the stove, piled them in, closed the door and hoped that Aga magic would ensure that its energy revived without my having to empty and relight the thing. I also made a mental note to chastise Robbie, not that I expected that to do any good.

Meanwhile Florrie pushed her wet nose against my leg and gazed at me imploringly. She had me exactly where she wanted me, that dog. Obediently, I emptied the best part of a tin of dog meat into her bowl along with some dried mixer.

Then I flicked the switch on the kettle to make tea, and began to unpack my shopping. But I was still battling with that inexplicable and overwhelming sense of unease. I walked to the bottom of the stairs and called up at the top of my voice.

'I'm back, Robbie. Cup o' tea?'

Still no reply.

I put one foot on the first stair and was just about to run up to the top of the house. That was what I wanted to do. But I didn't. Instead I told myself to pull myself together. I was just being silly. Extremely silly.

The kettle would have boiled by now. I went back into the kitchen and made two steaming mugs of strong English

Breakfast. I didn't finish unpacking the shopping, though, nor did I put any of it away. I was, by now, in too much of a hurry. None the less, I kept telling myself I would soon be drinking my tea while sitting in the old cane rocking chair in Robbie's room, quietly watching him at work until he was ready to come down for his supper.

I quite often did that. He never seemed to mind. From what I gathered from the few other mothers I spoke to, most boys of his age would hate it. But Robbie was different. Our relationship was different. And, after all, I never interrupted. I just sat in silence, unless he spoke to me first, looking out over the view of the moors or maybe thumbing through one of his biking or swimming magazines.

There was a sharp angle on the landing from which a second narrower staircase led up to Robbie's room. Florrie had finished her dinner and was now able to take an interest in matters other than filling her belly. She came tearing up the stairs after me and pushed past just as I was trying to manoeuvre the awkward angle. I spilt some of the tea, a generous slug of which slurped out of both mugs, and swore under my breath.

I'd been trying to climb the stairs too quickly, of course, considering that I was clutching mugs, which, with the benefit of hindsight, I probably should not have filled to the brim.

It might have been irrational, but I remained so anxious to reach Robbie's room, to see him there in his familiar surroundings, to watch him turn and smile at me, warm and welcoming, the way he always did, that I hadn't been able to help hurrying.

Once more I told myself to pull myself together, and slowed to a more sensible pace as I climbed the last few stairs.

The door to Robbie's room was open just a foot or so, probably pushed ajar by Florrie whom I could hear whimpering on the other side. Later I came to believe that somewhere in my subconscious I registered that the sound she was making was not her normal 'pleased to see you' noise. But, to be honest, I don't really know whether I did or not.

I usually knocked before entering Robbie's room. Even though I knew I was always welcome, even though there were no locks on any doors in our house, not even the bathrooms. Nobody had ever shown me much respect when I was fifteen, as far as I could remember, but I tried to treat Robbie with respect as well as love and all the other mother stuff.

I could not, however, knock while carrying two mugs.

Instead I called out.

'Tea's up, Robbie. Hands full. I'm coming in. OK?'

I pushed the door with one foot, aware as I did so that my son had still not replied. There hadn't been a sound from him since the moment I had entered the house. The house I'd felt so sure was empty. The house which still felt empty of any other human occupation.

The door swung easily wide open on its well-oiled hinges. Everything in our house was well maintained. Robert saw to that.

I took just one step into the spacious attic room with its high vaulted ceiling and ancient blackened beams.

I am not a tall woman. The first thing I saw was Robbie's feet. He was wearing the trainers I had given him for his birthday the previous May. They were black Adidas Originals with a narrow red and white trim. At first I think I looked only at the trainers, before allowing my gaze to travel upwards.

My son was suspended from the central beam stretching across the room, his back towards the mullioned windows which presented such a spectacular view of the countryside beyond, his face, his poor distorted face, directly towards me.

Florrie sat below him, staring up. She was still whimpering and now I could quite clearly detect a note of distress. Also, perhaps, of fear.

Robbie was hanging from a rope tied around his neck. Bizarrely, I recognized it as one of the lengths of extra-strong nylon cord, startlingly yellow and shiny, which we had bought, along with all manner of other new equipment, when he and his father had taken off on their bicycles for a few days' camping on the moors during the summer holidays.

The cord had embedded itself deeply into the flesh beneath Robbie's chin, and two puffy circular ridges of skin had risen around it. His face was already swollen and had turned an unnatural greyish purple and his tongue lolled obscenely from his mouth. His eyes, his lovely pale-blue eyes, were wide open, bulging only slightly and staring straight at me.

There was an unpleasant smell in the room. I recognised what it was at once, and registered, in a distracted sort of way, that Robbie must have lost control of his bowels.

Behind him his computer, his treasured iMac, lay on the floor, the glass of the screen shattered into pointed shards, as if it had been swept carelessly and with some violence from the desk. That desk, so lovingly constructed by his father, must have been moved across the room. It was now positioned directly behind the spot where Robbie was hanging.

It seemed logical that Robbie had stood on the desk, in order to attach the rope to the beam and to his neck, and had then jumped off. His head was at an acute angle, almost resting on one shoulder. I knew at once that his neck was broken. This was somehow quite abundantly clear even to a woman like me who had never before witnessed anything remotely like it.

Indeed, I took in the whole terrible scene in a matter of seconds, absorbing it, at first, in a curiously clinical fashion.

The implication of what it actually meant took some seconds more. The fact that my beautiful boy hung dead before me was, perhaps, almost too much for me to grasp.

When the brutal reality finally hit me my whole body slumped into a state of muscular collapse. My fists, clutching the two mugs of tea, involuntarily opened. The mugs fell to the wooden boarded floor, smashing into many pieces. Scalding tea gushed onto my feet, burning my instep and toes through the felt material of my slippers.

I could hear myself screaming, though. Not from pain, but out of pure unadulterated desolation. Florrie ran right through my legs and raced down the stairs at even greater speed than she had ascended. She could not possibly have understood what she was witnessing but was suddenly quite desperate to get away.

I just screamed and screamed and screamed.

My life, my world, was over. Hanging from a beam which I knew had once formed part of the hull of a ship that had sailed to America, attached by a length of rope which had anchored a tent against the winds of Dartmoor, swaying grotesquely in the cross-draught caused by my opening a door opposite windows already flung asunder to the unlikely mellowness of a sunny autumn day.

My boy was dead.

two

I have no idea how long it took me to stop screaming. When I did, I used Robbie's iPhone to dial 999. It too had fallen onto the floor, and lay there alongside his broken computer. I had to reach past him to get it, and in so doing I brushed against his body, making it sway a little more. My hand touched his deathly cold one. I felt sick.

I tried to bend down to pick up the phone but my legs gave way. I was kneeling when I made the call. Later, that always seemed appropriate somehow.

My voice when I spoke to the emergency services sounded as if it belonged to someone else.

'Ambulance,' I said, 'I need an ambulance. It's my son. Please. Come quickly, quickly . . .'

And yet I knew there was no need for speed. I was already aware that Robbie was beyond help.

I continued to kneel as I waited for them to come. I wanted to leave that room. And I wanted to cut my son down from that obscene hanging position.

I couldn't do so. The emergency services operator had told me not to touch anything, but I didn't care about that. I just didn't have the strength to move. Barely a muscle. I closed my eyes. I could not look at Robbie's body. It was almost as if by shutting out the image of him I thought I could make the whole thing go away. But even with my eyes shut I could still see him hanging there.

I was aware now of burning pains in both my feet where the hot tea had landed. I didn't care about that either. It really didn't matter. Nothing mattered much. In fact, I doubted anything would ever matter much again.

However, there was something I knew I had to find the strength to do.

I had to contact Robbie's father. I had to give Robert the terrible news and I had to do so swiftly, even though I knew he would be destroyed by it. Perhaps more than I already had been. If that were possible.

I couldn't phone Robert when he was on a rig – there were no mobile signals – but all the Amaco platforms had Wi-Fi. Robert and I spoke frequently on a Skype video link, his laptop to our computer in the office downstairs, or sometimes my iPad. And if I needed to get in touch with him unexpectedly, the routine was that I sent an email and he called me as soon as he could, either on my mobile or our home number, via Skype.

Ironically, Robert was actually due home at the weekend, two days later. Meanwhile, I had little choice but to email him. I was still holding Robbie's phone in one hand. I hesitated for just a moment or two, trying to find the right words, which was, of course, impossible. I could not tell the man his son was dead by email. Instead I settled for tapping out a brief message asking him to call me urgently and giving no further information.

An ambulance crew arrived within about half an hour, I think. I heard them knocking on the front door and calling out. I did not move from my crouched position on the floor. I still couldn't do so. Without any response from me the crew entered the house. I hadn't locked the front door; we rarely did until bedtime. I could hear their footsteps on the stairs. I had been asked on the phone where in the house my son was. The crew must have been given that information. They climbed straight up to Robbie's room and found me there, half kneeling, half lying by then, on the floor at my son's feet.

I was vaguely aware of reassuring voices and someone putting a blanket around my shoulders. Strong arms helped me upright and I was led, limping as the pain from my feet began to hit me, out of the room. I complied meekly, but I think I cried out as I looked again at Robbie's body. I'm not sure.

Two police officers, a man in plain clothes and a uniformed woman constable, turned up just as we reached the bottom of the stairs. I was by then leaning quite heavily on the shoulder of a small female paramedic, who'd told me she was called Sally and I wasn't to worry about anything. Whatever on earth that meant.

I hadn't asked for the police when I made my emergency call, but apparently they always attend a sudden death. Particularly of such a young person.

I vaguely heard Sally the paramedic tell them, yes, the boy was dead all right. And the body was upstairs. Then the male officer muttering about the SOCOs being on their way. Better get everything checked out before moving the body, just in case, he said.

I knew what 'SOCOs' were, of course. Didn't everybody nowadays? Scenes of Crime Officers. Brought in to collect and evaluate forensic evidence. But why were they needed here? Surely Robbie's death was suicide. A hanging like that always is, isn't it? Even in my state of total shock I'd just assumed my son had killed himself, although, in my wildest imaginings, I could think of absolutely no reason why he would have done such a thing. But I'd read about unexplained suicides among young people. They seemed frighteningly common. Anyway, I wasn't thinking straight. Far from it. But, perhaps surprisingly, I was just beginning again to at least think.

'What's going on?' I heard myself ask. 'Why are you bringing the Scenes of Crime people in? You don't think a crime has been committed here, do you? Surely we know how my son died, don't we? Don't we . . .'

I knew I was babbling. The man in plain clothes interrupted me quite kindly.

'Just routine, madam,' he said. He introduced himself then as Detective Sergeant Paul Jarvis.

'I'll be in charge of this case,' he went on, shocking me all over again somehow by referring to the death of my only son as a case.

Then he gestured to the uniformed woman officer. 'This here is PC Janet Cox, and you must be Mrs Anderson. Is that right?'

I nodded. He murmured something I didn't quite catch to PC Cox.

'Look, Mrs Anderson, you must have had the most terrible shock,' she said. 'Why don't we go into the kitchen? Make a nice cup of tea?'

If my brain had been functioning more sharply I would have shouted out that I didn't want a nice cup of tea. Indeed, I couldn't imagine there being anything nice in my life ever again. Or anything that I'd ever want, come to that.

But I had no fight left.

Sally the paramedic told PC Cox she really should do something about my burned feet, they could turn quite nasty if they weren't given some attention. So the three of us went into the kitchen where I sat at the big old scrubbed pine table in the middle of the room, as instructed. Sally crouched by my side and removed, as carefully as she could, my slippers and beneath them the black pop socks which I almost always wore on school days. In spite of her obvious care shreds of skin came away with the socks. Sally made soothing noises, told me to sit as still as possible, and that she was off to the ambulance parked outside to fetch the right dressings. Then she left the room. Meanwhile PC Cox busied herself filling the kettle, finding mugs, milk and tea bags.

She didn't ask me where anything was, and it didn't occur to me to assist by telling her. When she put a mug in front of me I obediently sipped from it.

The contents tasted as if at least six spoonfuls of sugar had been added. That old chestnut about sugar being good for shock. I hated sugar in my tea. Even at that moment, the most terrible of my life, I remembered that I hated sugar in my tea.

PC Cox pointed to my abandoned shopping on the worktop and asked if she should put the food in the fridge before it spoiled, and clear away the ice cream which had started to melt and form a gooey puddle. I didn't bother to answer, but she did so anyway.

Sally returned carrying a red and black bag from which she removed some packets of assorted dressings, and began covering the burned areas of my feet with practised efficiency.

'You'll need to go to your local medical centre in a few days, have that lot checked,' she instructed.

I nodded vaguely. I actually had no interest whatsoever in the state of my feet.

PC Cox also made tea for Sally the paramedic and for herself, mumbling something about the boys being big and ugly enough to get their own when they came downstairs, and then sat at the table opposite me.

'You must call me Janet,' she said. 'And I'm just here to help as much as I can. If there's anything I can do, just shout.'

I stared at her. *Yes, you can bring my son back to me,* I wanted to scream. *You can bring my beautiful boy back to life.*

She wriggled a bit under my gaze. Bizarrely, I wondered what it must feel like to be in her situation with a complete stranger.

She asked about my husband. I explained that he was away working in the North Sea and that I had so far been unable to contact him directly. But I had emailed him an urgent message.

'Look, you should have someone with you,' she said. 'Someone close. Is there a relative you could get round, or a friend?'

I shook my head again. My mother had died when I was a child, the grandmother who had more or less brought me up had also died many years previously, and I had no brothers or sisters.

The only relative I had left really was my dad, who lived in the village of Hartland, on the North Devon coast, more than an hour away. He worshipped his grandson, and was notoriously bad in a crisis. The next nightmare on my agenda would be to tell him about Robbie. Having him anywhere near would be even worse.

There were people in the village I vaguely knew and passed the time of day with, and the parents of some of the other pupils in Robbie's school, but none of them could remotely be regarded as friends.

We were a tight-knit happy little band, our tiny family. At least I had always thought so until that dreadful evening. Even Robbie had few friends, as far as I knew, anyway, and certainly none that he brought home with him.

Robert did not encourage visitors, not when he was at home certainly, although he tolerated occasional visits from my father

17

with reasonable grace. And he didn't lay down any rules for when he was away or anything like that. He just wanted us to be busy and happy, he said.

'But when I'm home I do like my family all to myself,' he would tell me and Robbie repeatedly. 'In our own bit of paradise.'

'A neighbour, perhaps?' persisted Janet Cox.

I continued to stare at her and gestured out of the window at the far end of the kitchen, where the lights had not been switched on. You could still see through it quite well. Although darkness had fallen, the sky remained as clear as I had earlier thought it would. Dartmoor stretched before us, silver and black, lit now by the moon and the stars, its distinctively jagged tors bisecting an eerily bright night sky like something out of the Tate Modern.

'Our nearest neighbours are five miles away,' I said. 'We're not exactly in and out of each other's houses.'

PC Cox, whom I somehow could not even think of let alone address as Janet, looked perplexed.

'There must be someone . . .' she said. 'We can't leave you on your own. The whole team will be going soon. I suppose I may be able to stay for a bit, I'll have to call the boss . . .'

There was something annoying about Janet Cox, her incongruously fluffy blonde hair brushing the stiff collar of her uniform, her eager determination to help. She had rather more the manner of a harassed social worker than a police officer.

It was strange, perhaps, that I could even be aware of such stuff at such a time, but I was.

'I'll be fine,' I said. 'Honestly. I'm sure my husband will soon be in touch.'

'But he's in the middle of the North Sea, isn't he? He still has to get to the mainland.'

'They'll chopper him back. They'll get him here fast. They do in an emergency. Look, he'll call any minute, I'm sure.'

Actually, I wasn't sure at all. Robert and I had spoken early that morning, before I left for school, via Skype. I thought he'd mentioned something about being on a late shift, though I wasn't sure of anything that day. He would probably only be able to check his emails at the end of his shift, or perhaps on his break, though that was less likely. The reality was that I had little idea when he would call.

'Don't you have some kind of emergency contact number?' asked PC Cox.

I glanced at her in surprise. She had her uses after all. I did have an emergency number for Amaco Limited UK. Indeed, it was me who'd insisted Robert gave me one. Just in case I ever really needed him in a hurry. I couldn't believe I hadn't thought of it, but then, I was barely capable of any kind of thought. And, of course, I'd never used it before. Nor indeed envisaged any kind of emergency as extreme as this one.

I stood up. Robert had written the Aberdeen number on a piece of card and I'd pinned it to the cork noticeboard on the kitchen wall by the house phone. As was my habit. It was more or less buried by other more recently attached bits of card and scraps of paper. I retrieved it. Head office, human resources department. A direct line, Robert had told me, with a link to a 24/7 duty officer, and they can always get through to us on the rigs if they need to.

He'd joked with me that the riggers called them inhuman resources. I wondered if Robert and I would ever share a joke again.

I dialled the Aberdeen number. All I got was the number unobtainable tone. Janet Cox looked at me enquiringly.

I shrugged. 'It was probably five or six years ago when Robert gave me this,' I said. 'Maybe the number's changed.'

'Yes,' agreed Janet Cox vaguely. 'It was Amaco you said, didn't you?'

I nodded.

She used her mobile to dial directory enquiries, asked for Amaco UK in Aberdeen, scribbled the number on the shopping list which I'd earlier dropped onto the worktop along with my bags of shopping, and began to dial again.

'It'll be out of office hours now,' I said.

'Yes, but this is the oil industry . . .' she began, then stopped to listen.

'There's a recorded message giving a number for a duty officer,' she said, as she wrote that number down.

I used the house phone again to dial the new number, explained briefly to the duty officer who I was, that I had a terrible family emergency, and that I needed desperately to get through to my husband Robert Anderson.

There was no urgency at all in the young male voice at the other end of the line. Indeed, it seemed to me, not even much interest.

No, I didn't know which platform Robert was on. I hadn't realized it mattered. I'd never had reason to ask, not before. Anyway, as a drilling engineer didn't he move from rig to rig?

I was pretty certain the voice sighed.

'Anderson, did you say? I'll need to go through our lists and cross-refer. It may take a minute.'

I thanked him, though for what exactly I was unsure.

'Oh here, I have him,' said the voice, returning quite quickly. 'Anderton, Rob. A derrickman. He's out on Jocelyn, that's Moray Firth—'

'No,' I said, the frustration of it all adding to my distress.

'Anderson. A N D E R S O N. And it's Robert. He's never called Rob. He's one of your senior engineers.'

'I'm sorry, I can't find an Anderson at all—'

'But he's been with your company for nearly twenty years,' I interrupted, wishing I could reach down the phone line and slap the owner of this still disinterested-sounding voice.

'All right, hold on then. I'll have to check the complete database . . .'

I waited for what seemed like for ever. Then my mobile rang. Robert's Skype number flashed at me from the display panel.

I ended the call to Amaco without bothering to explain or even to say goodbye. In any case, once again, there was no one on the other end of the line.

'Robert,' I said. 'Oh, my darling Robert . . .'

I stopped speaking abruptly simply because I was unable to continue. I just could not find the words. I glanced across at PC Cox. She was looking down, fiddling with her mobile phone, unwilling, I thought, to meet my eye. Distancing herself. I didn't blame her. There was, in any case, no way she could help me with this.

Down the line I could hear Robert's anxious voice.

'What is it, Marion? Whatever is wrong? Marion? Marion?'

'I-I don't know how to tell you,' I said eventually.

'Tell me what?'

'I-I c-can't, I don't know how to—'

'Just tell me.' There was already a desperate note in his voice.

'It . . . it's Robbie,' I said.

I heard his sharp intake of breath.

'Yes?'

I think Robert knew before I spoke again. Finally I just blurted it out. There were, after all, no words in the English language that could soften the blow.

'Our beautiful son is dead,' I said. 'Robbie is dead.'

There seemed to be a very long silence.

'What? B-but how, what . . . what happened?'

'It's just so so awful—' I began.

'Was there an accident? Was it his bike? The car? Are you all right?'

'Yes, I'm all right. But no, no, worse than any of that. So much worse. I came home and found him . . .'

I stopped again.

'What do you mean, you found him?' queried Robert. 'I don't understand.'

'H-he was hanging, hanging from the beam in his room.'

'Oh my God,' Robert said.

I told him all of it then, in a jumbled burst.

Robert seemed as unable to take it in as I had been.

'Suicide?' he asked eventually, his voice high and squeaky, not sounding like him at all. But then, I already knew I didn't sound like me.

I mumbled something incoherent.

'It can't be suicide, it can't be,' said Robert, suddenly stronger, almost authoritative. 'Why on earth would Robbie want to kill himself?'

'I don't know.' I half whispered the words. 'I don't know. It's all so awful. And then I couldn't get you. And I so needed you. I called Aberdeen. They didn't even seem able to find you. Why couldn't they find you, Robert?'

'Oh, Marion, our business is like every other – they've sacked half the proper people and taken on children for a fraction of the wages. Especially in areas like human resources. They're all worse than useless nowadays . . . Dammit, Marion, does it matter?'

'No, no, of course not. Just come home, Robert. Come home quickly.'

'Yes. Oh God, yes. Straight away.'

There was a pause. I could hear Robert's voice, as if in the distance, and other people talking, but I couldn't understand what they were saying.

Then Robert spoke directly into the phone again.

'Look, Marion, it's dark already. You know the new regulations. They don't fly from our rigs after dark. Health and safety. Plus one of the transporter choppers is out of action at the moment and the other one's on some op for head office. I don't think I'll be able to get out until the morning. Anyway I've already missed the last flight from Aberdeen. I'm so sorry . . .'

I hadn't thought it possible to feel any more desolate than I already did. But I realized that even now I was looking forward to the comfort of having my husband with me. Robert was a calm man. A typical dour Scotsman my dad had once said, though that had been when Robert had done something, I could not remotely remember what, to annoy him.

I didn't know if Robert would be able to be his usual calm self, nor indeed whether he would have the inner strength to be able to offer anyone any comfort right now, even me. But I did so desperately want him with me.

'Please, just get here as fast as you can,' I said.

'I'll do my absolute damnedest and I'll call you as soon as I have some news,' he replied.

We said an awkward goodbye, almost like strangers, and I clicked my phone off.

PC Cox had unfortunately got the gist.

'Probably won't be able to get back tonight, then?' she said.

I nodded, feeling numb.

23

'Are you sure there's no one else who could come over? Just to be with you until he arrives?'

She wasn't going to give up, was she? I racked my brains.

Suddenly it dawned on me. There was Bella. She seemed to have become fond of Robbie too. She had often actively sought out his company and, unusually, as our son had inherited his father's lack of interest in outsiders, Robbie had seemed to quite like having her around. Not that she had been to the house many times. But more than anyone else, that was for certain.

Bella was, I suppose, what people nowadays call 'my new best friend'. I'd only known her for just over six months. We'd met on Exmouth beach at the end of April just before the summer dog-walking restrictions came into force. I'd had to take Robbie into Exeter to buy some stuff for school which we couldn't get locally, and as it had been a decent day we'd loaded Florrie into the back of the car and driven on to Exmouth to take her for a run. She was not a young dog, but she still loved to scamper about on the sand and play in the sea, jumping over the waves.

Bella had been throwing a ball for her own dog, a spaniel cross-breed called Flash, and at one point had accidentally thrown Flash's tennis ball straight at Florrie. Florrie had gratefully accepted the gift, taken it in her mouth, lain down on the sand and done her best to chew it to pieces, while Flash ran around her in frantic circles.

Bella had tired eyes, but a smile that changed everything. On the beach that day she'd stood by laughing while I'd tried to extricate her dog's ball from Florrie's enthusiastic jaws. We'd walked along the sands together for a bit. Chatting. Just ordinary stuff. But I was someone who didn't often find strangers, or indeed anyone outside my immediate small family circle, easy to talk to. Yet I was somehow comfortable with Bella from the start, even though, on the surface at least, our backgrounds, apart from us both being mothers, seemed so different. My life was really quite privileged, whereas Bella told me that she was a single mum living in Exeter, struggling to bring up two children alone since her husband had walked out on her some years previously.

Just to make conversation really, I'd told her how I'd taught at the Bodley School in Exeter before I was married, and she'd said that was a coincidence because Bodley was her kids' school. Then we'd made those remarks you do about what a small world it was.

Before I knew it we'd exchanged names and phone numbers and arranged to meet again with our dogs. One way and another, it seemed Bella was now the nearest I had to a friend.

I called her on her mobile. The phone seemed to ring for ever and I was sure it was about to switch to voicemail when she finally answered.

After I'd told her what had happened, just like Robert she didn't say anything for what seemed like an age. Well, what did you say, exactly, to the mother of a fifteen-year-old boy who has just killed himself?

Eventually she spoke, quietly and slowly.

'This is unbelievable. Are you all right?'

Of course I wasn't bloody all right. What a stupid question. For a moment I thought it had been a mistake to call her. Then she spoke again. Somehow cutting straight to the chase without my having to ask.

'Look, who's with you? Is your husband there?'

'No. And he doesn't think he can get back until tomorrow. The paramedics are still here, and the police, they're checking everything. It's awful. But they're going soon, I think, and then . . .'

'I'll be right over,' said Bella. 'As soon as I've sorted something out for the kids.'

I hadn't met her children, but she'd told me they were aged eleven and twelve, and I remembered then that Bella also had a part-time job, working on the till in a supermarket, I think it was. But I hadn't given any of that a thought when I'd called her. I was, perhaps understandably, totally wrapped up in my own devastating situation. I suppose I just expected her to drop everything and come to my aid. Which she more or less did.

'You'll need me to stay the night,' Bella went on.

'Th-that would be wonderful,' I stumbled.

'Right,' she said. 'And I'll be as quick as I can.'

I thanked her and pushed the end button. Curiously, I'd only just met the bloody woman and hardly knew her really, but I suddenly couldn't wait for her to arrive.

DS Jarvis, a thin man with an incongruously fleshy face, came into the kitchen a minute or two later. He didn't look comfortable and was fiddling with the cuffs of his anonymous grey suit.

'I should tell you that the paramedics have formally pronounced your son dead, and the SOCOs have nearly done, Mrs Anderson—' he began.

'I'd like to see my son,' I interrupted him. 'I'd like to see him, before . . . before he's taken from here.'

Jarvis nodded, not looking at me but at the cuff of one sleeve which he seemed to be finding particularly fascinating.

'Of course,' he said. 'And you may want to take the opportunity of formally identifying your son for us. It has to be done sometime . . .'

Still not really taking anything much in, I agreed to do so.

The detective sergeant led the way up the stairs. I limped

behind him. Just before we reached the top a thought occurred to me. I reached out and touched his arm. He stopped and glanced back at me over his shoulder.

'Is . . . is Robbie still . . .' I began.

He understood at once and shook his head. 'No, he's on a stretcher.'

Jarvis continued up the stairs and led the way into Robbie's room. My son lay with his legs straight and arms by his side. Someone had closed his eyes. At first glance he looked quite peaceful until you noticed the discoloration and swelling of his face and neck.

It was a shock all over again seeing him like that. I reached out to touch him. He was stone cold. I knew, of course, that he would be. None the less, that was another shock. I had planned to kiss him goodbye. I couldn't do so. Already this was no longer my son, no longer my beloved boy.

I burst into tears and ran from the room, hurrying down the stairs as quickly as my damaged feet would allow me, and into the kitchen. Janet Cox made more tea and more soothing noises while I struggled to regain control. I really didn't want to weep in front of strangers. Gradually I calmed down, super-ficially at any rate.

DS Jarvis appeared in the kitchen again and looked relieved that at least I wasn't still having hysterics. He handed me a form to sign confirming that I had formally identified Robbie's body. Then he announced that he'd done all he could for the moment, adding, with not a lot of sensitivity, that he had another big job on and couldn't stay any longer.

'But we'll be getting back to you, and any time you want to be in touch with us, any time at all, I'm your man, just call me,' he said, handing me a business card.

'There will have to be a post-mortem, of course,' he told me.

'Just routine, Mrs Anderson, routine you see, with a sudden death. Especially in the case of one so young.'

I nodded. I hadn't thought of that. Of Robbie being examined after his death, of his pale flesh being sliced into on a mortuary slab. Would they use one of those circular saws I'd seen on TV to cut into his skull and expose his brain?

I was numb. I just nodded. Then something else occurred to me. Something so obvious I couldn't believe it hadn't struck me straight away.

'Was there a note?' I asked. 'I didn't think to look. Did Robbie leave a note? Did you find anything?'

DS Jarvis shook his head. 'No note, I'm afraid,' he said.

'But isn't that unusual? D-don't . . .' It was hard for me to say the word. 'Don't suicides always leave a note? Some sort of explanation?'

DS Jarvis shook his head again. 'That's a common misconception, Mrs Anderson,' he said, as he headed for the front door. 'The vast majority don't. We're taking your boy's computer hard drive away just in case there's anything on there, and to check it out generally. His mobile too. But I wouldn't expect too much, if I were you.'

The paramedics left soon afterwards. Then the coroner's undertakers arrived, and Robbie, his beautiful body zipped into an ugly black bag, was carried out to a waiting vehicle which would, I was told, take him to the mortuary at Barnstaple's North Devon Infirmary.

I watched him go. Watched him leave our lovely home, where I had thought, maybe just assumed, he had been so happy, for the last time.

That was the worst bit. My God, that was the worst bit. The tears ran down my face, much as I tried to fight them back. They were the first I had shed since discovering him hanging there from the beam in his room. Funny that. I would have expected to have been fighting back tears ever since. But I hadn't been. Not until I saw Robbie's body leaving.

The SOCOs finally finished their work and also left the premises.

PC Cox remained for a few minutes more, and I tried not to break down totally in front of her because I so wanted her to go. Eventually she seemed to accept that I wasn't going to do anything silly, as they say, and she actually did say that. She patted my arm in what I supposed was intended to be consolation. There could be no consolation. Not ever.

At long last she left.

I wished desperately that Robert was already with me. I do not know if anything or anyone could have brought me comfort at that moment, but I may not have felt quite so desolately alone if my husband had been by my side.

Strange, the circles your mind turns in at such times. I couldn't help thinking that the entire entourage which had more or less taken over my home that dreadful day had seemed as relieved to be leaving me behind and getting on with their lives as I'd been to see them go.

It was only then that I allowed my tears to fall freely, and once they'd got properly going, they would not stop. I was still crying when Bella arrived.

She didn't say anything at first. Just took me in her arms.

I found myself holding on to her. Clutching her. Even in the midst of my shock and my grief there was this flash of the old conservative me. You shouldn't behave like this with strangers. But I couldn't help myself.

She held me until I stopped crying. For another ten, or maybe even fifteen, minutes, I think.

Then she began to lead me upstairs. Speaking, certainly in

terms of anything more than an occasional murmured word of attempted comfort, for probably the first time.

'Look at your poor feet,' she said. 'You must tell me what happened.'

I just said I'd spilt some tea. I couldn't go into the details.

She expressed concern, and told me she was going to run me a hot bath.

'You mightn't think you want one, but warm water is one of life's great restorers—'

'I'm not sure I can, my feet are quite badly burned,' I interrupted.

'We'll keep them out of the water, don't worry, I'll help you,' said Bella. 'And let's get you into a dressing gown first. I'm sure you have a lovely warm fluffy one somewhere? In this house, eh?'

I did. It was hanging behind the door of the master bedroom. I realized, even then, that she was treating me like a child. Telling me what to do. I didn't mind. I gladly allowed her to do so. Anything as long as someone else was doing my thinking for me. I didn't want to think at all, because all that filled my mind was the horror of what I had seen within the walls of my own home.

On the beach, on the very first day we met, Bella had told me she'd been a nurse before she'd married. Maybe that had something to do with the way she was. She had a professional air about her, and seemed to instinctively know the right thing to say, and when it was best not to speak at all.

I entered the bedroom which had always been something of a dream room to me. It was probably the first time ever that its pink and white prettiness and the magnificent Dartmoor views offered from both its windows failed to give me joy. Gazing sightlessly out into the moonlit night, I let my clothes fall to the floor, a lined linen jacket and smart black trousers also bought specially for school, and put on my dressing gown. Bella stepped out of the room while I undressed. Normally I was an obsessively private person, but I wouldn't have cared a jot if she hadn't done so.

She waited for me to join her on the landing. The door to the main family bathroom, the only one with a bath as well as a shower, stood ajar and I could see steam already wafting through the gap.

'You've got good water pressure,' Bella said. 'Bath's almost ready.'

Meekly I followed her into the bathroom. She'd found my favourite evening primrose bath oil. I breathed in the musky perfume of it as I undid the tie of my dressing gown.

She leaned over the bath, tested the temperature of the water with one hand, and turned off the taps.

'Just about perfect,' she murmured. And again she began to move away to give me privacy, heading towards the bathroom door.

I restrained her. 'It's all right,' I said. 'Anyway, you have to stay. I need your help. Remember.'

The throbbing pain in my feet had certainly reminded me that getting into the bath was not going to be straightforward. However, displaying both strength and efficiency, Bella, a substantially built woman, helped me lower myself into the bubbling tub without too much trouble, and in such a way that I could keep my feet dry, propping them on the rim by the taps.

There was a chair by the window and a DAB radio stood on the window ledge. She sat on the chair and gestured towards the radio. 'Some music?'

'Yes,' I said. 'I'd like that.'

She switched on the radio and the sounds of a Classic FM

evening concert filled the room. She turned the volume down just a little.

I leaned back in the bath. The next thing I was aware of was the touch of Bella's hand lightly on my shoulder. I jumped.

'You've been asleep,' she said. 'The water's getting cold.'

Indeed, the bath was now lukewarm and when I glanced at my hands and my legs I saw that my skin was wrinkled.

'How long did I sleep for?' I asked in surprise. I wouldn't have thought it possible that I could have slept at all, indeed perhaps ever sleep again. Let alone fall asleep in the bath.

'About forty-five minutes,' she said, holding out a big white bath sheet. 'I think you should get out now.'

With her help I stepped into the softness of the towel. It felt warm. And that was a welcome sensation, even in the state I was in. Or maybe particularly in the state I was in. I glanced at her enquiringly.

'I warmed it on the Aga,' she said.

'It's still alight then.'

'Yes, I fed it some more wood.'

I nodded my thanks.

'Don't hurry,' she instructed me. 'And don't get dressed. Just come downstairs in your dressing gown when you're ready. I'll try to find us some food.'

'Oh, there's plenty of food,' I said. 'I went to the supermarket on the way home from work. There's chicken and fish, and several of Robbie's favourite pizzas – they're quick and easy . . .'

I stopped. Saying Robbie's name hurt physically like I was being stabbed in the heart. The pain was just so much greater than the pain of my burns.

Tears threatened again. I so needed Robert. I would have expected him to have phoned again by now. But maybe he had whilst I was asleep. I asked Bella if there had been any calls.

She said not. Then she asked me when I thought would be the latest he would get home.

'Sometime in the morning, for certain,' I said.

'Good,' she replied. 'I'll have to be off quite early for work, I'm afraid. I can't really afford to risk my job by not turning up on a Friday. But I don't want to leave you here on your own for long.'

'I'm sure I won't be,' I said, with a confidence I didn't entirely feel.

Why hadn't Robert called? I couldn't understand it.

I'd left my mobile, a BlackBerry, in the bedroom. I hurried to find it to double-check that I hadn't missed him. I hadn't. So I sent him another email.

'I just want to talk to you, to hear your voice,' I wrote.

But surely he would know that already, wouldn't he?

Bella, who had not followed me into the bedroom, tapped on the door and sort of half leaned into the room.

'Look, why don't you have a bit of a lie-down on the bed,' she said. 'Close those eyes and maybe you'll have another sleep. You never know. You think you couldn't possibly but the body looks after itself at times like this. I'm sure Robert will phone you soon, and the ringing will wake you. Meanwhile I'll put some food together and give you a call when it's ready.'

Again I did as I was told. And again to my surprise I drifted off into a this time uneasy, rather unpleasant sleep, disturbed by nightmare visions of bodies with distorted faces and twisted or even missing limbs.

Eventually Bella woke me and led me downstairs. She'd heated a pizza in the oven and made a tomato salad, warmed a loaf of bread and put some cheese on the table.

I couldn't touch the pizza. I'd bought it for Robbie. Just looking at it made me want to cry again. But this time I managed to hold the tears back. Perhaps there were no more tears to come. Not yet anyway.

I put some salad, some bread, and some cheese on my plate and began to eat mechanically. I ate quite a lot. There was a big empty hole inside me. It was almost as if I were trying to fill it. But it was, of course, impossible to fill.

I kept checking my mobile. Like a teenage girl waiting for a call from her boyfriend, or a woman waiting for one from a married lover, more than once I picked up the house phone just to make sure there was a dialling tone. Still no call from Robert. I was both bewildered and desperate to hear from him.

Bella had opened a bottle of red wine which I presumed she had selected from the rack in the kitchen, where we kept some of our stock, so that we didn't have to scramble continually through the funny little door under the stairs which led to the cellar Robert was so proud of. Even at that moment I noticed that it was one of his best clarets. The bottles he would never share with visitors, not that we had many visitors. Our home was for us, not for showing off to other people, he said.

Bella's hand shook as she began to pour for me and she knocked over my glass, the stem of which snapped as it fell sideways onto the tabletop. Bella, too, was suffering from the stress of that dreadful day, I supposed. She muttered apologies as she mopped up the precious liquid and replaced the glass. I barely noticed. Of course, if Robert had been with us, under normal circumstances he would have been furious. But these were certainly not normal circumstances.

I downed the first glass of wine in almost one swallow, hardly tasting it, and found myself also reflecting automatically on what Robert's reaction to that would have been. The expensive mellow red liquid hardly touched the sides.

We were still sitting at the kitchen table when the grandfather clock in the hall struck once. It was one in the morning. Bella had a little earlier muttered something about it being time for bed, but I was afraid of going up, afraid of being alone, afraid of attempting to sleep in the room which was directly below the place where I had found my son hanging. And I was afraid that if I did sleep the nightmare images would return.

Also, I was still waiting for the phone to ring.

I suggested to Bella that we open another bottle of wine. As she moved to do so I heard the handle of the kitchen door behind me begin to turn. Florrie was lying under the table by my feet. She did not bark. Instead she jumped up and ran towards the door, her feathered tail wagging frantically.

I swung round in my chair just as Robert stepped inside. He always made his way round to the back door if he arrived home late, as he liked me to bolt the one at the front at night, even though, or maybe because, we were so far from anywhere. He was unshaven, ashen-faced and dishevelled-looking. His thick black hair, which he wore long, needed washing. Greasy curls flopped over the collar of a filthy denim shirt. He had not been expecting to be coming home and, in order to have reached Highrise by now, wouldn't have had time to change or to shave. Even if he'd given such matters a fleeting thought after the news I had given him. His appearance still shocked me, though, even at that moment. Was this how he really lived out on those rigs, I wondered obscurely?

'Oh, Marion, Marion,' he said. Then again. 'Marion.'

Just my name. Over and over. But there was such pain in his voice and in his eyes, which filled with tears as I rose from my chair and rushed towards him.

'I c-can't believe it,' he stumbled. 'Is it really true?'

35

I nodded, once more searching for words that wouldn't come.

'But why, why would he do such a thing?'

I had no words with which to answer that, either. I wrapped my arms around him and just clung to him. I could feel his weight. He seemed to be leaning on me.

Then I saw his glance shift. He had seen Bella standing behind me, a bottle of his wine in her hand.

His face seemed to turn even more ashen. His eyes widened. I could not detect quite what I saw in them. My first thought was that it might be anger. It was probably just a mixture of grief and distress, and the horror I know he would have of being forced to share any of this painfully private time with an outsider.

'What the hell is she doing here?' he asked quite quietly.

'Somebody had to be with me,' I burbled. 'The police insisted on it. This is Bella. You know, Bella whom I told you about. I met her on the beach with the dogs . . .'

I stopped. He couldn't be about to go into one of his tirades about unwanted visitors, surely. Not now. I wasn't going to let him.

'Robert, what does it matter?' I asked. 'You're here now. That's all that matters.'

I looked up at him pleadingly, although I had absolutely no idea really what I expected of him. I was clinging to him, but he made no move to touch or hold me. His arms hung limply at his sides. His face was so grey and so still. Frozen almost. I supposed it was the shock. I had never seen him look anything like it before. This almost wasn't my Robert. Even his accent, usually very light, was far more Scottish than usual. Through stress, I assumed.

'You're here,' I said again. 'Thank God. But how did you get off the rig? You seemed so sure you couldn't until morning.'

'The boss pulled out all the stops,' Robert replied in a distant kind of way. 'He managed to borrow a ride from BP. He and the pilot decided the regs didn't apply in an emergency. They choppered me straight to Glasgow airport. EasyJet do a 9.45 p.m. flight to Bristol. I didn't even know that—'

'Why didn't you phone?' I interrupted.

'It all happened so suddenly. I only usually bother to recharge my mobile just before I'm about to go on leave and I didn't realize the battery was flat until I reached the mainland. Then when I got to Bristol I just hired a car. I couldn't wait to . . .'

His voice tailed off. What did it matter, I thought, how he'd got home so quickly? Why was I even bothering to ask? He was here. That was all that counted.

He still seemed to be looking at Bella over my shoulder. I knew him so well, knew just how much he would not want her or anyone else there with us.

'I'll be off then,' said Bella, as if reading both our minds. She put the bottle of claret down with a bump on the table.

'Now you're home, Mr Anderson, there's no need for me to stay,' she continued. 'You'd rather be alone, the pair of you, I'm sure. I'll just clear this lot away and put the plates in the dishwasher—'

'No, I'll do it,' Robert interrupted, rather curtly I thought. But surely neither of us could be expected to remember our manners. I managed to find a semblance of them.

'I just can't thank you enough, Bella,' I said. 'I really don't know how I would have got through this evening without you—'

'Bella,' said Robert, interrupting. 'Bella,' he repeated. His eyes were still looking in her direction but I could see he was off in some other world inside his head. So was I. A shattered world which had once been made whole by a truly beautiful boy.

Bella backed away out of the kitchen towards the front door. Robert and I stood together silently as she left the house, and stayed like that until we heard the engine of her car start.

The expression on Robert's face remained one of total despair. And he seemed rooted to the spot. I reached up to kiss his face. It was damp. I saw then that tears were rolling down his cheeks, but he wasn't sobbing. It was as if he had no idea that the tears were falling.

He was still staring straight ahead.

As I kissed him he switched his gaze, with what seemed to be a considerable effort, and looked down at me, his troubled eyes meeting mine for the first time. He kissed me on the forehead. Just as he so often did. Only this time it was different. I supposed it would always be different in future. Now that we shared this terrible loss.

'Oh, Marion, what has happened, what has happened to us, to our wonderful little family?' he asked. 'What's going on?'

I was fleetingly puzzled. That was a strange question. He knew what had happened well enough. Our family had been destroyed by an inexplicable tragedy.

'What do you mean, what's going on?' I asked falteringly.

Something flickered in Robert's eyes.

'What? What? Did I ask that? I don't know what I'm saying. I don't know what I'm doing. I rushed here to comfort you and now I'm talking gibberish.'

Only then did he at last enfold me in his arms and hold me tightly. He began to kiss me all over my face. To my utter astonishment I felt my body react to him the way it always did. Even though the stubble of what must have been several days of beard scraped my skin and he smelt of stale sweat and something else I didn't quite recognize. The stench of the rigs perhaps, which he had never brought home with him before. I didn't care. I just wanted him close. As close as possible.

Robert and I had always had a wonderful sex life. He was, I thought, a truly fabulous lover, not that there'd been many men in my life for me to compare him with, but I just knew he was special. My body had always known that.

'I'm so very glad you're here,' I said. 'So glad you got here so quickly. I don't know how I would have got through the night without you. As long as you're with me, as long as you love me, I feel that maybe, just maybe, I can survive anything, even this.'

He kissed me hard on the mouth then, and I could feel the sheer power of his love, just the way I always did.

'You will always love me, you will always be with me?' I asked when he stopped kissing me, knowing as I did so that this was a question far more stupid than anything he'd asked. Robert and me. Mr and Mrs Robert Anderson. We were cast in stone together. Had been from the day we met and would be until the day we died. Even the death of our beloved only son could not change that. Surely it couldn't.

'Always, my darling,' he said. 'I will always love you and I will always be with you. Always, always.'

As he spoke he picked up the as yet unopened second bottle of wine, two glasses and a corkscrew. Then he led me upstairs to the bedroom and I could feel in him a determination greater and indeed grimmer than I had ever felt before. I didn't quite understand it.

But then, we had never lived through a day like this before.

three

Robert wanted to shower and shave. I was clinging to him again and wouldn't let go. In the end he just discarded his clothes on the floor where I'd dropped mine earlier, and we climbed into bed, me still in my dressing gown which I couldn't bear to remove because I was shivering so much. I felt chilled to the marrow even though the day had been warm and I had stepped out of the bath not long before.

Robert wrapped his arms around me inside the dressing gown and eventually his body and the bedclothes covering us warmed me at least to the point where the shivering stopped.

We did not make love. It might have brought us comfort, but I don't think either of us were capable. Neither could we sleep. Instead we talked, going over what had happened again and again, asking the same questions repeatedly. The same unanswerable questions.

After a bit Robert sat up in bed, opened the wine, without any of the care he usually applied to the task, and poured us both large glasses. We drank deeply then clung to each other again.

'I want to know why, Robert,' I said. 'We both do, don't we? Why would our beautiful boy have taken his own life?'

After all, hadn't he had everything that he could possibly

have wanted? A loving family, a wonderful home, the brightest of futures?

Yet I recalled how Robbie had once responded when Robert and I had been discussing a teenage suicide case reported in the press. I had wondered aloud how anyone so young could find life so hopeless. Robbie had enquired what difference age made, if life no longer felt worth living.

'Do you remember that, Robert?' I asked. 'We were quite taken aback. It was when he didn't seem happy at school. We even thought he might be being bullied.'

'Marion, that was nearly three years ago at his old school,' said Robert. 'Everything changed when we moved him.'

I nodded. 'But he was always such a sensitive boy. Maybe even more so than we realized . . .'

Robert made no further reply. At first he seemed content to let me do most of the talking. We were both in shock, of course, him every bit as much as me in spite of it having been me who had found our son's body.

However, when he started to ask questions, in some detail, about exactly how I'd found Robbie, exactly what the police had said, exactly what conclusion they had come to, and so on, it was as if the floodgates opened. He talked and talked. We both did.

'They don't really think there's anything suspicious about his death, do they?' he enquired.

'I don't believe so. I don't know. There will have to be an inquest apparently.'

'An inquest?' Robert sounded alarmed. 'Why does there have to be an inquest?'

'Just routine, the CID man said. He said that about everything.'

'Will we have to appear in court?'

'I don't know. I shouldn't think you'd have to. I might. I found his body. Doesn't that make me what they call a material witness?'

'I have no idea.'

'No.'

'I just don't understand it, any of it.'

'How will we ever be able to understand it?'

'Your friend. Bella? Has she been to the house before?'

'Yes. Two or three times. She came here and then we took the dogs up over the moors for an hour or so. She's barely a friend. Though she was tonight, that's for sure.'

'What about Robbie? How did they get on? Did he go with you on the walks?'

'Only the once, I think. He seemed to like Bella actually. But to him I suppose we were just two old biddies nattering on. He wasn't very interested in our company. Who cares about that, Robert?'

Suddenly I felt irritated by him. That was unusual. But then, this was an unusual and horrible night.

'I was just trying to think of anything that was new or different in his life, anything that could have caused him to . . . to want to do such a thing. What about school? Maybe things weren't as perfect as we thought. You've always been much more involved than me. Could there have been something wrong at school?'

'I don't think so. I'm almost sure not.'

Robbie had been a day pupil of Kelly College, the famous Devon public school just outside the Dartmoor market town of Tavistock, about thirty minutes' drive from our home. He'd won a swimming scholarship there a couple of years previously, which had halved the fees, thus making it possible for us to remove him from Okehampton College, where we had felt he was unhappy. There was nothing much wrong with our local community school, as I knew well enough first-hand now that I taught there part-time, but it had probably been a tad too boisterous for our Robbie. However, he seemed to have fitted in smoothly at Kelly, one of the country's top swimming schools. He was not remotely interested in any other school sport and hated team games, but he loved his swimming, and had successfully represented Devon County on several occasions.

'Robbie had so much to look forward to all round,' I went on. 'You know his coach was trying to get him trialled for England youth? He was on cloud nine about that.'

And we had been so proud. Had we pushed him too much? No, I was sure we hadn't. Yet something had pushed him over the edge.

'He had his GCSE exams looming, though,' Robert countered. 'He'd already started his mocks, hadn't he? Was he worried about the results? Was he having problems?'

'Not that I knew of. And why would he have been worried? He was clever. You came to the college open day last time you were home. Don't you remember how all the teachers said Robbie would sail through?'

'Yes I do.' Robert was thoughtful.

'Robbie always seemed to find everything so easy, didn't he?' I continued. 'He was an athlete and an academic. The tote double. I'm sure he didn't have any problems at Kelly. I know he didn't seem to make many close friends, if any, but that's how he was, wasn't it? That's how we've always been as a family, I suppose.'

'Yes. And maybe that's what was wrong. I blame myself for this, Marion. The life I forced him to lead. I will always blame myself.'

I sighed. 'You didn't force him do anything. Robbie was a happy boy. He liked his life, I'm quite sure he did.'

'Apparently not,' said Robert grimly.

We kept going over the same ground. And always we came to the same conclusion. Robbie could not have taken his own life. It wasn't possible. He had no reason to. No reason at all. And yet he had. There could be no rational alternative to that. Could there?

I felt as if all my insides were tied in one big knot. And the more we talked, the more I had to accept that it wasn't just Robbie's death that had shocked and bewildered me so. I was also anxious about my husband and the manner of his homecoming. I had uncertainties. I couldn't help it. There were concerns I needed him to satisfy, but feared to raise. In the end I could not stop myself.

'Robert, which rig have you been on?'

'Jocelyn. Why?' Robert sounded puzzled, as he might. A rig had always been a rig to me. It had never mattered which one he was on, only that he was away from home.

'It's just that when I called Amaco and they couldn't find you on the list, well, they mentioned a man called Rob Anderton. And he was on Jocelyn.'

Robert made no comment. Did I feel him stiffen as he lay by my side? Or did I imagine it?

'So who's Rob Anderton?' I went on.

'He's a derrickman, I barely know him,' said Robert evenly.

'Yes, they told me he was a derrickman. That's a crewman, isn't it? Someone who helps maintain the drill—'

'A senior crewman, yes,' Robert interrupted, his tone indicating that he had no wish to continue with this topic.

'Quite a coincidence, isn't it?' I carried on doggedly. 'Rob

44

Anderton and Rob Anderson on the same small platform in the North Sea?'

'Is it? I suppose so. I don't know. And aren't I Robert? Since when did you ever call me Rob? I don't want to talk about Rob Anderton, Marion. Actually I don't want to talk about anything more tonight. I just can't. We really need to try to get some sleep. I don't know if it's possible, but if we're even going to begin to get through this, we must try.'

He turned away, wrapping his arms around his pillow instead of me. I lay on my back staring at the ceiling. I had slept before, but I feared sleep was not going to come again that night.

Robert tossed and turned by my side. Eventually he began to snore intermittently, so I knew that he at least had finally managed to find some brief respite. Or had he? Once or twice he cried out as if in torment. I hoped his dreams were not as bad as mine had been earlier.

At about five o'clock in the morning I crept out of bed and groped my way from our bedroom without switching on the light. My burned feet had stopped throbbing while I lay in bed but started to hurt again as soon as I put weight on them. Moving cautiously, I closed the door as softly as possible behind me and, on tiptoe, or as near to tiptoe as my damaged feet would allow, climbed the second staircase to Robbie's room.

It was the first time I had been in it since the police and the ambulance crew had left and Robbie's body had been removed. The nylon noose had thankfully also been removed from the central beam.

Other than that nothing much had been touched, or at any rate altered, from how I had seen it when I had kicked open the door, clutching those two mugs of tea, to be confronted by my son's body hanging before me.

The desk was still in the middle of the room where I'd presumed Robbie had dragged it. The shattered computer screen still lay on the floor. I picked out the shards of glass and put them in the bin. There were sheets of paper, pens and pencils, and a couple of books on the floor too. I picked them up and piled them neatly on the desk. Unusually for a teenage boy, Robbie had always been tidy. So I set about tidying his room, making it look, as much as I could, the way it had always been before.

I didn't move the desk, though. I was afraid that dragging it across the wooden floor would wake Robert. And although I had been so desperate for his return, and thankful that he'd arrived so much earlier than either of us had expected, I just wanted to be alone for a bit in my boy's room with all his things around me.

I did move the chair, carrying it across the room from where it had been left by the chimney breast, and placing it carefully in front of the desk so that I could sit there, just as Robbie had spent so much of his time sitting before that same desk.

I ran my hands over the smoothly finished wood in front of me.

I wondered what sort of things the police looked for when they checked out a death like Robbie's. I found, now that I was confronted by such an unimaginable situation, that I had little or no idea. I had no experience of these matters other than watching the odd detective show on TV.

This was different. This was for real.

I supposed that in a case like Robbie's they would routinely look for anything that might indicate that his death was not as it first seemed. Anything which indicated that there was something suspicious about it. That another person might be involved, presumably. Although DS Jarvis had more or less suggested that they weren't considering that option very seriously. 'Routine, just routine, Mrs Anderson.'

I slid open the top drawer on the right-hand side of Robbie's desk. I knew he'd always kept his diary there. I was mildly surprised to see that it was still there. I'd somehow expected the police to have taken it away.

Perhaps they'd read it on the spot and decided it wasn't relevant. I'd never read Robbie's diary. I wouldn't have dreamed of doing such a thing. Even though Robbie and I were so close.

Things were different now, though. Very different.

I lifted the diary from the drawer. It was a rather smart shiny black leather job, with Robbie's initials on it, which Robert and I had bought off the Net for him the previous Christmas. I suppose a lot of young people nowadays kept an electronic diary, if they did so at all. But there'd been an old-fashioned side to Robbie. He'd said he much preferred the traditional version, a bound book.

I opened the diary towards the back, and turned to the most recent entries. The dates of his mock GCSEs had all been neatly entered. I flipped backwards. Our birthdays were marked, Robert's and mine, and the date of his own late spring birthday, the 28th of May.

He'd indicated it with a cross and added a comment. 'Mum and Dad arranged for me to have a flight over the moors in a glider. FANTASTIC!'

I felt the tears welling up again. I could see his face when we told him about the glider trip. I could so clearly remember his enthusiasm both before and afterwards. He hadn't stopped talking about it for days.

I flipped a few pages further on and the diary fell open at random to that weekend in late July when he and his father had gone on their biking trip over the moors. Robbie's entries there also burst with enthusiasm. 'Coolest time ever,' he'd written. 'I'm going to make Dad do this again.'

There was quite a lot about school. And his swimming, of course. All pretty positive. A few schoolboy jokes, including one really obscene one which he credited somewhat gleefully to another boy.

He'd been invited, it seemed, though I didn't remember him ever mentioning it, to a classmate's rather smart-sounding black-tie birthday bash just before Christmas. I hadn't known about that, but I suppose he would have told me eventually. For a start Robbie hadn't owned a dinner suit and he'd doubt-less have expected me to acquire one for him.

He hadn't been a bit interested in clothes, and had always relied on me to sort out his wardrobe. One of so many tasks I would never have to perform again. I swallowed hard and read on.

'I suppose I'll have to go, Jack is a really good bloke,' he'd written. 'I do hate those kind of things, though.'

He always had too. He was so like his father in that regard. At his happiest in his own home. Or so I'd always thought.

He went on to mention the name of a girl I'd never heard of before.

'It would be OK if I could persuade Sue S. to go with me. I wonder if she might?'

Girls. He was beginning to show an interest in girls. And he hadn't told his mother. It was all so normal. I was fleetingly glad of that somehow. Of course he was showing an interest in girls. He was fifteen, wasn't he? TV and the papers seemed full of tales of fifteen-year-old dads, for God's sake.

I vaguely wondered who Sue S. was. Another pupil at Kelly? Someone he'd met through his swimming? I might never know

now, and probably would never meet her. She could have become his first girlfriend. Maybe she had been.

I flipped through the pages again, looking specifically for a mention of her name. I found it just once more, part of a frustratingly brief entry in mid-September.

'Sue S. so well fit. Wicked!'

I wondered what that meant, but the diary offered no further clarification. Indeed, Robbie seemed not to have shared too many intimate thoughts at all with his diary, keeping it principally for factual entries, reminders of dates and appointments and so on. Just like his father, I thought.

I felt the tears welling again and only just forced them back. It's difficult to think clearly through a haze of tears, and I was trying so hard to think clearly.

Another entry did supply a little more insight into his life. It referred to him and a couple of mates managing to successfully order a few beers at a pub in Tavistock where the landlord either hadn't noticed or didn't care that they were under age. It made me smile. I had no idea he had ever done anything like that and again was rather glad he had.

'Everybody keeps going on already about what they're going to do in their gap years, and which uni they want to go to,' Robbie had continued. 'I suppose I'm going to have to think about that one day. But I don't want to. Certainly not yet. I don't like to think about leaving home.'

I felt a pang of the only anxiety Robbie had ever previously given me, really. I'd worried about his leaving home. He'd certainly displayed none of the usual desire to spread his wings that might be expected of a young man at the beginning of his life. And I'd always feared the experience might ultimately be traumatic, both for him and for us. I'd sometimes even thought that maybe Robbie would just stay at home. Find work nearby.

Or attend a local college. Was it mandatory nowadays for a young person to fly the nest so irrevocably at a tender age?

I closed the diary and put it back in its drawer. As far as I could see there was absolutely nothing in it to indicate that Robbie had any worries at all, let alone anything serious enough to make him want to take his own life.

Perhaps he was the sort of boy who kept his true feelings bottled up to such an extent that he quite simply could not cope with them any more. I hadn't thought he was like that, but I no longer knew. I didn't know anything. That was the trouble. Perhaps he'd had concerns, worries, fears that he'd never shared with us or his diary. With anyone.

And perhaps these had driven our Robbie to such a point of despair that he'd felt that he could not carry on.

Could that be? It kind of had to be. I still could not accept it.

I sat there for a while, elbows on Robbie's desk, my chin resting in my hands, staring out of the window. It had become pretty much completely light outside by then. Or as light as it was probably ever going to get that morning. Appropriately, somehow, dawn had broken dull and wet, in sharp contrast to the previous day. The night must have clouded over eventually. It was drizzling and there was thick mist over the moors. Actually, you couldn't even see the moors. They were concealed by a dense grey curtain. This was typical November weather. On Dartmoor anyway.

I felt close to Robbie sitting in his room like that. I thought back over his all too brief life. Robbie had been born prematurely twenty-nine weeks into my pregnancy. For several weeks he was in an incubator fighting for survival and at first we were told his chances were not good. Fearing that we were going to lose him made him all the more special. That and the fact that complications during the birth meant I would have no more children.

But that didn't matter one jot, because Robbie, a little fighter, got through it all, grew into the fine young man we were so proud of, and from the beginning was more than enough for his father and me.

He had been all either of us wanted. He'd meant absolutely everything to us both. And now he was gone.

I had no idea how much time passed before I heard noises from below. Robert was moving around down there. I heard him go into the bathroom.

I stood up, preparing to go downstairs. Before doing so, and now that Robert was awake, I decided to move the desk back to its rightful place by the chimney breast. It was somehow important to me that everything in the room was once again as it should be.

I grasped one end of the desk with both hands and dragged it across the room, finally pushing it, with some difficulty, to fit flush again in its corner.

Standing back to check that it was correctly in position, I noticed the floor. There were two crooked grooves in the highly polished wood clearly marking the path the desk had taken when I pushed it back. The floorboards were ancient, but when Robert had refurbished Robbie's room he'd put a finish on the floor which had produced a wonderful deep glow that looked as if it had evolved with age rather than out of a bottle, but had turned out to be rather more fragile than he'd expected. I remembered him telling Robbie to take care, and how the two of them had attached little patches of green felt to the legs of Robbie's chair. The desk however, had not been designed to ever be moved, and no such protective measures had been taken.

I stared at the floor, slowly taking in the significance of what had just happened. There were no other noticeable marks on the floorboards. Just those I had caused by dragging the desk back to its place. No other marks at all.

I ran down the stairs to Robert, making my feet throb badly again. I shouted out to him before I even got to the bedroom, eager to share my discovery. The door to the en-suite bathroom was open. Robert was standing naked at the basin, his mouth full of toothpaste. His hair was wet. He'd obviously showered, and he'd shaved off his stubbly beard. Funny how the routine of life goes on even on such a day. Although his distress showed clearly in his eyes, he looked like my Robert again and not so very different from how he'd been when we'd first met. His face, long and narrow with angular cheekbones, was a bit more lined and leathery and not quite so pale, down to all those years of exposure to North Sea air probably, but his hair had yet to show any trace of grey and he was still in quite good shape.

'Robert, Robert, there was someone there with Robbie when he died,' I cried. 'I'm sure of it. I don't think he did kill himself, I really don't.'

As I said the words they brought me relief. It seemed crazy, but I realized I would prefer my son to have been murdered rather than to have taken his own life. It was totally selfish and all to do with guilt, I assumed.

While Robert rinsed the toothpaste from his mouth I explained what had just happened in the room upstairs. How I'd moved the desk on my own, leaving nasty jagged grooves on the polished floor and how these were the only marks on the floor.

'Don't you see, Robert, don't you see? The only way that desk could have been moved to the middle of the room in the first place without marking the floor would have been if two people had carried it, one lifting each end. Robbie couldn't have carried it on his own. You made it out of solid oak. It would have been far too heavy for him. Anyway, you wouldn't try to lift it, would you? Not if you were going to . . . going to . . .' I didn't want to say it.

'No, if he'd been on his own he'd have dragged the desk across the room,' I went on. 'Just like I did.'

Robert wiped his mouth with a towel.

'But he was always very careful with that floor,' he ventured tentatively.

'Not when he was planning to kill himself, surely,' I blurted out finally. And saying it hurt me terribly again, physically as well as mentally.

'I don't know, Marion. I just don't know. What alternative could there be? Anyway, he was alone here, wasn't he? While you were at work. Who would have come here? And who could possibly have wanted to harm our Robbie?'

Robert had said the last words in a very distracted sort of way. I could see he was still having difficulty taking anything much in. Or else he was just trying to blot everything out. Or maybe a bit of both.

'I'm going to call the police,' I said. 'This changes everything. I'm sure of it.'

'It's only just gone half past seven,' said Robert. As if that mattered a damn.

'Since when have the police worked office hours?' I enquired.

'Look, you're clutching at straws, Marion,' Robert persisted.

'Am I? There aren't any straws to clutch. Our son is dead.'

'I know. But it's the guilt, isn't it? Don't you see? I understand exactly how you feel. I told you. I feel so guilty. If our boy killed himself, we must be responsible. Surely? Me mostly.

It was me who created this life we have here. Me who cut us off so much from the rest of the world. I reckon that's what he couldn't take.'

He was right about the guilt, but I hadn't invented the marks on the floor. I was just about to tell him so, when I noticed that tears were rolling down Robert's cheeks.

My heart melted. I went to his side. How could I ever doubt him, or anything about him?

'You created a wonderful life for us, Robert,' I said. 'Robbie thought it was wonderful too. I've just been reading his diary. Our boy didn't kill himself. I'm absolutely certain of it. The police have to listen to me. And I'm going to make them. I promise you that.'

four

I found the business card DS Jarvis had given me. It was in the pocket of the jacket I'd been wearing the previous day, which now lay in the middle of our bedroom floor tangled up with the rest of my clothes and Robert's. It seemed the detective sergeant was stationed at Exeter's Heavitree Road Police Station.

I dialled the mobile number he'd written on the back.

While I was doing so Robert dressed quickly in jeans and a clean shirt and went downstairs. I loved him dearly, but he'd disappointed me by being so apparently unimpressed by what I considered to be my big discovery, and he seemed to have no wish even to listen to any conversation I might have with the police.

As it turned out there wasn't much of a conversation to listen to.

I had been vaguely reassured and perhaps a bit impressed to find that Jarvis had supplied me with the number of his mobile phone. I was not so impressed to be patched straight through to a duty officer at Heavitree Road.

He said DS Jarvis was not immediately contactable and all he could do was take a message. Unless he could help at all.

'Perhaps you would like to tell me what you are calling DS Jarvis about, madam?' he enquired.

'No, thank you,' I said. I knew about duty officers who answered calls to police stations nowadays. They weren't even police officers any more.

'Just ask him to call Marion Anderson as soon as he can, will you?' I said. 'He has my number, I think. But I'll leave it again.'

I followed Robert downstairs, still wearing my dressing gown.

Vaguely I wondered why he'd been in such a hurry to dress, on the day after our son had died.

I went into the kitchen, expecting him to be making tea. That was our usual routine. He was the morning tea-maker when he was at home. Though my first cup was normally brought to me in bed.

But Robert wasn't in the kitchen at all. The Aga was still alight – I could feel the heat from it. However, the big old kettle, almost always simmering away on top when Robert was at home, was not in place. Robbie and I were inclined not to bother with it. That day it seemed Robert hadn't bothered either. I touched the electric kettle gingerly. It hadn't even been switched on. But then, this was no normal day. Why on earth should either of us be following any kind of normal routine?

I heard a noise in the hall, and called out.

'Robert? Are you there, Robert?'

He didn't reply. I stepped into the long passageway. I could see Robert standing by the front door. He was now wearing outdoor shoes and a waterproof jacket over his jeans and shirt. His hand was on the door handle.

'Are you going out?' I asked in surprise.

'Uh, yes. There's something I have to do.'

'What? Today? Now?' I studied him. The way he was

standing. The slightly sheepish manner. He seemed unwilling to look me directly in the eye.

'Were you going out without even telling me?' I asked incredulously.

I thought his face, not as ashen as it had been when he returned home but still on the pale side, coloured slightly.

'No, no, of course not. I was just waiting for you to come down.'

I didn't think he was telling the truth.

'Where on earth are you going? What is it you have to do on this morning of all mornings?'

'I have to take the hire car back.'

'What? Won't they pick it up from here? Anyway, does it matter if we keep it another day?'

He stood silently for a moment looking at me.

'I have to go out,' he said. 'I have to be on my own—'

'But you've only just got back. I need you with me. Here. In our home.'

'You must understand. I just have to have a few hours on my own. And this way I'll be able to leave you our car in case you want to get out too. I can drop the rental in Okehampton later and get a cab home . . .'

'But why don't I come with you? Follow you in our vehicle. Then I can give you a lift straight back.'

'Look, I thought I might take a walk up over the moors to Meldon Reservoir, or maybe Yes Tor. I need to clear my head.'

'Robert, you'd drown.' I gestured out through the hall window. The rain was still pouring down. 'It'll be blowing a gale up there, too. What are you thinking of? And where are your heavy-duty waterproofs, and your boots?'

I knew where they were well enough. In the boot room by the back door. We were standing at the front door. Robert was in no way dressed for a tramp over the moors, not even on a much better day than this.

Suddenly he yelled at me.

'You really don't understand, do you?' His voice was not only loud but very Scottish again. He sounded furious. He'd never spoken to me so roughly before.

I took an involuntary step backwards.

'I have to go out, Marion,' he continued in the same loud and angry tone of voice. 'And I have to be on my own. Just trust me, will you, woman?'

I thought I was going to break down and cry again. He saw it in me, I think. His manner softened as swiftly as it had become so harsh.

'I'll be back in a few hours, Marion. I promise. I just need a bit of time to myself, that's all.'

He reached out and touched me on one shoulder. I half waited for the kiss. We never parted, Robert and I, even for a few hours, without kissing. No kiss came. Instead he swung around and left the house.

I found myself shuffling backwards until my heels hit the staircase, jarring my burned feet, and then I just sat down. I was shocked to the core yet again. The death of a son could make any man or woman behave strangely and in a totally out of character way, I told myself. None the less, I was further traumatized by Robert's behaviour.

After a while I hoisted myself up off the stairs and wandered distractedly into the kitchen. I switched on the kettle but never quite got round to making myself the tea I had half planned. I just sat down at the table, my back to the door, in the same chair I'd been using when Robert had arrived at one in the morning, unexpected in every way. Neither looking nor sounding like the husband I so loved. And now he had walked away from me, when I needed him most.

I began to wonder again what it meant. One half of my brain and certainly my heart told me that it meant nothing at all. Robert was a terribly bereaved father. I couldn't expect him to behave logically. I couldn't expect him to be his usual self. No doubt I was not my usual self, either. The other half began to relive the events of the last twenty-four hours. To dissect them meticulously. And even to look further back into our shared past.

I thought about the Amaco emergency number he had given me being unobtainable.

The piece of card upon which he had written it all those years ago was still on the kitchen table in front of me, alongside the discarded shopping list upon which PC Cox had scribbled the main number of the Amaco head office in Aberdeen after she'd got it from directory enquiries.

I checked my watch. It was now just after 9 a.m. I dialled the head office number and asked for human resources, telling the operator that I was the wife of an Amaco employee.

'Oh, and just before you put me through I wonder if I could check with you the direct-line number my husband gave me in case of an emergency,' I said. 'I can't seem to get it to ring.'

The operator obligingly did so. Just one digit was wrong in the number Robert had supplied. A simple careless mistake, easy to make, or a deliberate one designed to present an obstacle, albeit not one that couldn't be overcome with persistence, should I ever try to contact Amaco? It could have been either.

I ended the call before being put through. If the situation had not been so dire, and if PC Cox had not been with me, I mightn't have persisted the previous evening, mightn't have sought out an alternative out-of-hours number for Amaco.

I didn't know what to think. I didn't know anything any more. I didn't even know why I was torturing myself like this.

My son was dead. That was all that mattered in my life. What was I doing doubting my husband at such a time? I hadn't doubted him in sixteen years. He had shown me and our son nothing but kindness and generosity. What was wrong with me? Why was I doubting him?

It was perhaps odd, but my brain seemed overly active at a time when I might have expected it to be anaesthetized. If I suddenly had all this mental energy, then surely I should be concentrating on Robbie's death, the manner of it, and what might lie behind it, rather than questioning my husband.

Anyone was entitled to behave strangely in such circumstances, I told myself.

I went up to Robbie's room again and spent an hour or so there, checking everything, looking around the place, once more studying those marks on the floor.

Then I made my way down to the kitchen to call DS Jarvis again and for the second time was patched through to Heavitree Road.

This time I didn't even bother to speak. I just hung up.

I opened the back door. Robert had fashioned a kind of lean-to gazebo, wooden uprights and a slate roof, beneath which we could shelter on wet days while still enjoying the garden. I breathed the Dartmoor air deep into my lungs and stood there watching the rain fall.

A song kept going through my head. Robert was a bit of a jazz buff, and it was one of his favourites, sung by Dinah Washington – 'What a Difference a Day Makes'.

Could it really be only a day ago that I'd set off cheerily for work at Okehampton College, leaving Robbie in the kitchen tucking into the bacon sandwich I'd made him? Crispy, on naughty white bread. Just the way he liked it.

I tried to remember our last words to each other. And I couldn't, which made things even worse somehow.

I was quite sure, though, that there had been nothing to give cause for concern. But had I missed something? No, I was sure of it. It had all been so ordinary and inconsequential.

I thought he'd just said: 'Bye, Mum, see you tonight.' Or something like that. He wasn't a great talker in the mornings. What teenage boy was?

I couldn't even remember what I'd said to him. Vaguely I recalled telling him I'd be stopping off on the way home to do some shopping, and then I'd just said 'goodbye'. Or 'cheers' maybe. I said that sometimes.

I shivered. It was a cool morning as well as wet. I was still wearing only my fluffy dressing gown. And I'd never fully warmed up from the unnatural chill I'd experienced during the night. I stepped back into the kitchen. I really should eat and drink something. I needed energy. I needed strength. I toasted a couple of slices of bread and, using our fancy coffee machine, made a double espresso in a bid to wake myself up a bit, to hopefully become just a little more alert.

Then I switched on the TV in order to provide a diversion. It didn't work.

I waited until nearly midday before I tried to call DS Jarvis again, with exactly the same result. I cursed under my breath. Perhaps I should speak to somebody else. Perhaps I should get dressed and just drive to Exeter, to Heavitree Road.

But that could so easily prove to be a total waste of time and effort. It would be better to be patient for a bit. I'd call again later.

I paced around the house. In spite of my throbbing feet I

just couldn't sit still anywhere. One half of me was drawn to Robbie's room again. The other half wanted to stay as far away as possible.

The house phone rang and I rushed to it hoping the caller would be Robert, offering an explanation, apologizing for his behaviour, saying he was on his way home. Anything. I could see from the display panel that it wasn't him. I had no wish to speak to anyone else so I waited for the answering machine to kick in. The caller was the bursar at Kelly. The school wanted to know where Robbie was, and why he hadn't turned up for his mocks that day.

I didn't pick up. I couldn't pick up.

I made more coffee. Just to give myself something to do. On top of my shock and grief I was now just so bewildered and troubled by Robert's behaviour. It hadn't occurred to me that he would leave me for anything that morning. I had assumed, once he had made his so welcome middle-of-the-night arrival, that he would just want to cling to me as I'd so wanted to cling to him while we tried to make some sense out of the terrible tragedy which had befallen us.

Instead he had gone off on his own. And in anger, it seemed.

I thought back to our first meeting sixteen years previously. I'd been twenty-four and had just started teaching at Exeter's Bodley School. I'd taken a break after finishing my training when the grandmother who'd brought me up became seriously ill. I'd looked after her until her death the previous year. Work and independence were still new to me and I didn't find Bodley easy. As an English literature specialist I had been attracted to the school because it had been named after Thomas Bodley, founder of Oxford University's famous Bodleian Library, who was born in Exeter. The school was situated in a leafy residential road to the north of the city, and I'd imagined it to be a civilized, rather bookish seat of learning in this predominately rather middle-class old county town. I was, however, to discover that much of Bodley's catchment area covered the Bridge Estate, a 1960s-built council development already way past its sell-by date, which, by West Country standards anyway, was quite notorious. And Bodley turned out to be a far tougher school than I'd expected.

Perhaps preoccupied with the assorted problems I had to deal with on a regular basis at Bodley, I was riding my bicycle through the city centre on a wet November day, unaware of any danger, when, as he was passing me, a BMW driver swung in too tightly to take the approaching corner and just caught the rim of my front wheel, which folded right round. The bike collapsed, and me with it. I fell to the ground, raking one arm right along the edge of the pavement and knocking my head. I was momentarily stunned.

Robert was my good Samaritan. A kind stranger at my side in a flash. The BMW driver did not stop. Robert, loudly and colourfully Scottish, cursed him as he tended to me. He seemed to know at least the rudiments of first aid – making me count the fingers he held up in front of me to check if I was concussed, and so on – as indeed, I was later to learn, did all Amaco rig workers. He wanted to take me to hospital, but I insisted that I was fine.

'In that case I'm taking you home,' he said.

We padlocked my buckled bike to a railing, to be collected some other time, and picked up a taxi from a nearby rank to take us to the little studio flat I rented near the station in Exwick, less than five minutes' cycle ride from Bodley School.

Robert found some vaguely appropriate ointment, tore up a tea towel to fashion bandages, and dressed my grazed arm. Then he made us both tea. And I began to notice that striking

Gaelic colouring, the black hair, the sharply contrasting pale skin, the light-blue eyes. And his big capable hands. I thought he was an attractive man. Obviously a kind man too.

We began to talk. I told him about my grandmother, whom I'd adored, because she was still so much on my mind. And he said that he too had been brought up by his grandmother who'd also recently died. Wasn't that a coincidence? He was in his early thirties, some years my senior. He'd decided to move from his Glasgow home to Devon, where his gran had taken him on holidays as a boy, after the irrevocable break-up of a long-term relationship a few months earlier. He also told me about his work in the oil industry, which meant he could make his home, such as it was, pretty much anywhere he wanted.

I don't know if it was love at first sight. Or lust. Or the shock of my accident, minor as it was. I do know I had never done anything like it before in the whole of my rather sheltered life. But we ended up in bed together that very night. It seemed the most natural thing in the world. Not to mention unexpectedly and wonderfully exciting. It somehow never occurred to either of us to take any precautions. We had unprotected sex, at the time quite oblivious to all that might lead to.

Rob, as he called himself then, stayed the whole night but in the morning told me he had to leave for his scheduled spell of duty on a North Sea rig. He would call me as often as he could and be back to see me as soon as he returned on leave right after Christmas. He said he usually offered to work over the festive season to allow the married men time off at home, but he could spend New Year with me, if I liked.

I shared a quiet Christmas with my father in North Devon, as previously arranged, feeling as if I were in a kind of limbo. And even though Robert did phone several times, from one of the land–sea payphones used on the rigs in those days, I couldn't help wondering, of course, if I would ever see this man again. He was, however, as good as his word, which was just as well, because I soon realized that I was probably pregnant. Tests confirmed this to be the case. I had fallen for Robbie that very first night.

I told Rob – whom I'd already begun to call by what he'd told me was his full name, Robert, because it seemed to suit him so much better – with some trepidation.

He was overjoyed. I couldn't believe it. He didn't seem fazed at all to be having a child with a young woman who was more or less still a stranger.

'That's it then,' he said. 'We have to find a home together and we have to get married.'

And that is what happened. That was the beginning of our life together. I just allowed myself to be carried along by him, to be swallowed up in his plans.

Robert told me he'd been renting a room close to Exeter city centre, because his work kept him away so much and he'd had nobody to make a home with. He went out one afternoon, just a couple of days after I informed him I was pregnant, saying he had some business to attend to, and arrived back at my little studio flat mid-evening carrying a large suitcase. He said he'd given notice and paid off his landlady. I never even had a chance to see where he'd been living. In any case, he said he hadn't really been living there at all. The room had just been some-where to keep his stuff, not that there was much of it, and a place to stay when he was on leave.

A few weeks later we married at Okehampton Register Office. It was a quiet occasion, which Robert had made clear he wanted from the start, and, with the benefit of hindsight, convinced me I did too. My father came up from the coast and was my witness, and I invited a couple of friends from college and a fellow teacher I'd become matey with.

We'd already found and were trying to buy Highrise, which even in considerable disrepair was a much more impressive home than I'd expected us to be able to afford. But Robert had explained how well rewarded his job was, as it should be too, he'd said. The estate agent who helped us find the place turned out to be Robert's witness. An unlikely choice perhaps, but Robert had an easy explanation.

'He's the most important person in my life right now apart from you,' he said. 'Thanks to him we have our dream home.'

There was nobody else. He had no relatives left, he told me, and he'd moved on so far from his old life in Scotland that there wasn't anyone from his past he wished to be present.

I just accepted it all at the time and indeed had accepted it for sixteen years. Robert was a loner after all. Only now did I begin to wonder, to wonder about so much.

The photographer Robert told me he had booked failed to turn up. The only photographs of our wedding were taken by my father with his ancient camera, and the film seemed somehow to have become damaged, so that the images were mostly just a blur. I'd been disappointed, of course, to have no pictorial record of our big day, and Robert had professed disappointment too. Only now did I reflect on how he had so often throughout our marriage avoided having his photograph taken, saying merely that he was camera-shy.

I thought again about a derrickman called Rob Anderton. A derrickman working on Jocelyn the day my son died. On the same rig as my husband, Robert or Rob Anderson. I had tried to put it out of my mind without success. I didn't know how many people Amaco employed. I didn't know how big or small the coincidence was. But it continued to bother me.

On an impulse I dialled the direct line I now had for Amaco's human resources department. Rather to my relief a different, female, voice responded.

'I'm trying to get hold of my brother, Rob Anderton,' I said, surprised by the ease with which the lie rolled off my tongue. 'It's a family emergency. His wife called me late last night and left a garbled message about some sort of tragedy, and now I can't get an answer from either of their phones. Rob was working on Jocelyn. I don't know if he's still there. Or if . . . or if he's hurt or something . . .'

'Just let me check,' said the voice.

There was silence. I was just beginning to wonder if I'd been cut off when the voice returned.

'Could I ask who I'm speaking to?'

'I told you. I'm Rob's sister. Marion Jackson.'

I used my maiden name.

'Well, I can tell you your brother is no longer on Jocelyn, Mrs Jackson. He was transported back to the mainland last night.'

'But is he all right? What's happened?'

'Look, Mrs Jackson, we're not supposed to give out information like that over the phone. I know you're a relative but—'

I interrupted. 'Please help me if you can. I'm about to get in my car and drive to Rob's home. It's all I can think of. But neither he nor his wife are answering their phones and I don't even know if he's back there. I mean, has Rob been taken to a hospital? Is he still in Scotland?'

There was another pause.

'I can tell you that your brother is fine,' said the voice, sounding, I felt, more than a little awkward and uneasy.

'Then it's his son, Robbie. I thought that could be it. Only my sister-in-law didn't actually say what had happened. Is Robbie hurt? Is he . . . he's not, not dead? Is that it?'

I tried to make myself sound as hysterical as possible, which wasn't difficult.

The voice on the other end was being very calm.

'Mrs Jackson, it's your family that you should be speaking to, not me.'

'But, I've told you. I can't get through to them. Look, please help me. It is Robbie, isn't it? Something terrible has happened to Robbie. Hasn't it?'

There was an even longer pause.

'Well, yes,' said the voice eventually. 'Something has happened to Robbie, I'm afraid. But you must get the details from your family, I can't possibly—'

I hung up, cutting her off in mid-sentence.

She had told me all I needed to know.

five

In spite of everything I could not wait for Robert to return. I hadn't quite worked out what I was going to do or say. I just wanted him with me. I needed him more than ever and I loved him to bits. And I knew he loved me. Surely he did. There had to be some simple explanation for what I had discovered. There had to be.

However, that was my heart speaking. My head reminded me that, following the death of our beautiful boy, I had uncovered a dreadful secret about my husband. I still didn't know quite what it was, but I knew I was already afraid of it.

And yet I had to find out.

I sat in the sitting room for a few minutes trying to make some sense, any kind of sense, of the telephone conversation I'd just had. Then I went upstairs, showered as best I could after wrapping my burned feet in plastic bags sealed around my ankles with Sellotape, and dressed in jeans and a warm cashmere sweater. The big old house felt cold again. The oil-fired central heating never really did the job, not when it was cold and wet anyway, without being supplemented by the Aga which somehow radiated heat throughout the place. And that day, that terrible day, I had been responsible for allowing the range to go right out. More wood needed to be brought in from the shed outside and I'd had neither energy nor inclination to do so. That day it had not been Robbie's fault. It would never be his fault again. How I longed to be able to chastise him for it. Just one more time.

My head was full of desperate questions. I couldn't believe that Robert had left me alone to face this first day without our boy. It just wasn't like him. Not like the man I had thought I'd known anyway.

My imagination ran riot as I considered what he might be doing. Whatever could it be that was important enough for him to have left me alone? Even when he had behaved so aggressively towards me that morning, and perhaps half because of that, I'd realized that he had not wanted to leave me. But for some reason he had been unable to stay.

Therefore, in spite of myself, I still longed for him to return.

I spent most of the rest of the afternoon watching out for his return, sitting, with Florrie at my feet, on the wide sill of the landing window which provided a more or less uninterrupted view of our lane. The weather cleared after a bit, the change as swiftly dramatic as it so often is on Dartmoor. I watched the warm orange glow form over the yard as the sun began to sink in the sky behind Highrise. This was not the finest vista the old house provided, offering only a glimpse of moorland over the roofs of the little cluster of outbuildings across the yard, but I was struck possibly more than ever before by the beauty of the place. It brought a lump to my throat, and made the memories all the more poignant.

I waited in an almost trance-like state, barely aware of the passage of time. Darkness had fallen before I heard the sound of a vehicle approaching down the lane. I was jolted into some sort of awareness. I checked my watch. It was nearly seven o'clock.

The automatic security lights flashed on in the yard, and I recognized the approaching vehicle to be the rental car Robert had arrived in during the night. It was him then. And he still had the rental car. He had not even managed to return it in spite of having insisted that he must do so. I wondered yet again exactly what he had been doing all day. It was almost as important for me to know that as to learn the truth about the Rob Anderton scenario. This had been a crazy, muddling day, and remained so.

I stood up and stepped back from the window. I didn't want Robert to know I had been watching there, waiting for him. I turned and ran, as fast as my injured feet would allow, downstairs to the kitchen, with Florrie at my heel, and closed the door behind me. I would wait for him there in silence. I wanted him to wonder if I was in the house, or what might have happened to me, just as I had wondered about Robbie, with so little apparent cause, when I'd returned from school yesterday.

Was it really only yesterday? My throat was tight and I felt as if I had to fight to get air into my body.

I sat down at the table and tried to control my breathing which had taken the form of short sharp gasps. And my thinking. Again I told myself how important it was that I kept a clear head.

I had deliberately placed myself with my back to the door from the hall, and I hadn't switched on the lights. I did not want Robert to be able to see my face. Not at first anyway.

I'd been so angry when he left me that morning. Even angrier when I had made my revelatory call to Amaco. Since then I'd descended into a state of sheer misery. I was distraught, and I was totally confused.

This would not do. It would not do at all. But I could feel

the world Robert and I had so meticulously built for our little family, the world that now seemed to have always been so fragile, disintegrating around me. Indeed, with the death of our son it had more or less disintegrated already.

I slumped in my chair, still fighting to contain my emotions.

I heard Robert open the front door, then close it again after he had stepped inside. I knew the house would seem cold and empty to him. Just as it had to me the previous day.

He called my name. Once. Twice. 'Marion, Marion, are you there? Are you all right? I'm sorry, Marion.'

And so you should be, you bastard, I thought. Enormously, unimaginably sorry. Not, I feared, that any amount of remorse could ever help now.

Florrie trotted to the door and began to whimper. She also loved Robert and, unlike me, had no reason to have begun to question not only that love but the entire basis from which it had evolved.

I could hear Robert's footsteps in the hall. Florrie barked a couple of times. Then I heard them right outside the kitchen. He called out again. I still did not respond.

I heard the kitchen door open behind me, and light from the hall flooded the room. Florrie's whimpering turned into doggy cries of joy. I didn't need to look round to know that she would have become just a wriggling, whimpering furry mass wrapping herself around her master's legs.

I remained slumped, motionless, in my chair. My back to Robert.

He cried out in anguish. 'Oh, my darling,' he said.

I sat up at once, very straight.

'Thank God, my darling,' he said, his voice heavy with relief.

'Am I?' I asked, turning in my chair so that I was looking directly at him over one shoulder. 'Am I really your darling?'

He didn't seem able to take in what I was saying, and indeed appeared only barely able to speak.

'My darling,' he repeated. 'I thought . . . I was afraid. When I saw you like you were, just s-so afraid . . .'

He stumbled over the words.

'Were you, Robert? Afraid of what exactly? And what exactly did you think?'

'I-I don't know. I just don't know anything any more. It was just the way you were slumped there . . . so still, I—'

I interrupted him. 'You thought I'd taken my own life too, didn't you, Robert? Like our son?'

'No. No. Well, maybe. I can't think, Marion . . . But I was afraid. I was certainly afraid. When I came into the kitchen and saw you—'

'And why did you think I might do that, Robert?' I interrupted again. 'Because our only son is dead? Or because of what I could have found out about you today?'

He switched on the kitchen light, making me blink at the brightness, and walked around to the far side of the table so that he was facing me. His eyes were red and swollen, as I am sure mine were. His face was ashen. He looked a broken man.

'What do you mean by that?' he asked.

His body language suggested that he was about to say something more. I wouldn't let him do so. I rose to my feet and held out my hand, palm vertical, obliquely aware that I probably looked like a policeman stopping traffic.

'Did you think maybe I'd decided to do away with myself because I'd found out you'd deceived me throughout our married life? Is that it, Robert? Is that what you were afraid of? That I'd discovered the truth about you?'

Robert stared at me for a moment as if unsure what to do or say. Then he seemed to make a decision. Blinking furiously, he thrust back his shoulders, pulled himself upright, and did his best to deflect my onslaught.

'Is this what our wonderful, magical marriage has come to?' he demanded. 'My wife, the woman I adore, no longer trusts me. What exactly is it that you have found out? Or, what you think you have found out, more likely.'

Fleetingly, I admired his devastating cheek. But then, if I was right, and surely I had to be, then he had been lying to me for sixteen years. And I supposed that old habits die hard.

'You know, Robert, you know what I've found out,' I said. 'Please don't treat me like an idiot.'

'I have no idea what you are talking about,' he replied.

I stood up and took a step towards him. Suddenly I found myself overtaken by a strange sense of composure, a sort of icy calm.

'You're a lying bastard, Robert Anderson,' I said in a cool, level voice. 'Or should I say Rob Anderton?'

I tried to display no emotion. Nothing to give away what I was really thinking. Except that I found to my annoyance I could not quite control just the merest flicker of my eyelids and an involuntary twitch to one side of my mouth. The mouth he knew so well and had kissed so often. Would I ever feel able to allow him to do so again? I wondered.

Robert remained silent, a desperate look in his eyes. It was easy to recognize. It was the look of a trapped animal.

'Just don't deny it any more,' I said, trying to keep my voice low and forceful. 'Do not deny anything. Do not lie to me any more. Tell me the truth. Tell me what has been going on all these years. If you don't, I shall walk out of this house and you will never see me again. I didn't think there could be anything worse than finding our son dead. But then to learn that our whole marriage has been some kind of sham . . .'

I paused, interrupting myself.

'No, nothing could be worse than finding Robbie like that. But this, this is some new impossibly mad nightmare. Just tell me the truth, Robert. Now.'

'Our marriage has never been a sham, Marion,' he began. 'I love you more than—'

'Please, Robert. Stop it. This is your final chance.'

I felt his eyes bore into me. Finally the trapped look turned into one of resignation. He nodded.

'Yes,' he said. 'You are quite right. I have to tell you everything and just hope you can understand. But first, let me take my coat off and make us a cup of tea.'

I studied him. He was extraordinary. He was still prevaricating, still seemed to be playing for time. Though what he thought he could gain now, I had no idea. He shivered, and glanced around, aware as I had been the previous evening of how cold the kitchen was.

'The Aga must have gone out,' he continued. 'Perhaps we could light the fire in the sitting room and sit by it, it's a long story and—'

'No, Robert. No!' This time my voice was not calm. I shouted at him with full volume. 'We will not have a nice cup of tea by the fire. Those days are fucking over. Just tell me what's been going on. Fucking tell me.'

I don't think I had ever sworn at him before. Indeed, I don't think I'd sworn at all really, not out loud anyway, since my days at teachers' training college when everybody did. As a matter of rite of passage. During my life with Robert and Robbie it would not have been expected for me to use bad language, and neither did I ever seem to have cause.

I saw him flinch. Then he sat down at the table opposite me, still wearing his waterproof, and began to speak. Everything about him indicated that he really had finally accepted that he had no choice.

'You're right, of course,' he confessed. 'Rob Anderton and Robert Anderson are one and the same.'

I sat down again too. With a bit of a bump. It was almost involuntary. I more or less lost the use of my legs.

I had not thought it was possible for me to feel any worse than I already felt. But I did. I realized how much I hadn't wanted Robert to admit what he just had, even though I had, of course, already known it, really, beyond any reasonable doubt. I'd still hoped, however foolishly, that he might have some other plausible explanation. That he might have been able to tell me he hadn't kept a bloody great secret from me throughout our marriage, that the pair of us had not been living a lie for sixteen years.

'Why, Robert, why?' I asked. 'What has been going on all this time?' I felt absolutely defeated. My heart ached.

I watched him take a deep breath.

'Let me start at the beginning, with meeting you,' he said, looking not at me but at his hands, which were trembling slightly, spread out on the table before him. 'It was the most extraordinary day of my life. I loved you from the second I first set eyes on you, lying there on the pavement, in the rain, after being knocked off your bike, not quite sure even where you were for a moment or two. All that wonderful curly bright brown hair of yours in a damp tangle.'

He glanced up at me. Fleetingly, I thought he might try to stretch across the table to touch those curls, still brown but only thanks to the attentions of a skilful hairdresser. Like my mum and my gran before me, I had begun to go grey in my mid-thirties. I leaned right back in my chair. We had always enjoyed reliving the joy of our first meeting and would smile and laugh about it endlessly. Not this time. Not the hint of a smile touched my lips. I would not give him that satisfaction.

'I thought you were so lovely,' he continued. 'The smattering of freckles on your forehead, the colour high in your cheeks, that perfect little mouth, and those yellow eyes. Like a cat's.'

He paused as if waiting for me to respond. I still had no intention of doing so. My eyes weren't yellow, of course. They were a mottled light brown. I didn't think any bit of me was perfect and I hated my freckles. However, I had never before minded Robert's romanticizing; indeed, had rather liked it. Now he was just annoying me.

'You were so plucky too, even though there was nothing of you,' he carried on after a bit. 'But, most of all, you were just in a different class, a different class to any women I had known before and, of course, a different class to me. You were a schoolteacher, educated, quite sophisticated in a way. Compared to me anyway.'

He paused again.

'Just get to the point, Robert,' I snapped.

'All right. I know it's crazy, but I didn't want you to know I was just a common rigger. A roustabout I was, back then. So I promoted myself. Told you I had a much better job than I actually did. And, of course, once I'd started, the whole thing kind of snowballed.

'One thing I told you that was the truth was how much I wanted to escape my past. But I left out just how disreputable it had been at times. I'm afraid I even have a criminal record for assault following a brawl in a Glasgow pub. I didn't want you to know any of that, I didn't want to be Rob Anderton any more. You remember that I told you I wanted to start a whole new life? Well, that was absolutely the truth.

'It might seem stupid now, wrong even, but I wanted to

appear to be as well educated and middle class as you seemed to be. I wanted a lovely home and a proper family. Things I'd never really had before. I'd never had much luck in my life, but suddenly a wonderful opportunity seemed to have opened up for me. And when you told me you were expecting Robbie, that was it. You and our unborn baby were my dream and I just grasped it.

'Robbie made everything complete. Our beloved only son. So handsome, so clever, and just so nice. And I was able to give him an education way above anything I'd experienced. I told myself that whatever else I'd done or omitted to do in my life I was giving my boy the kind of start a man like me could only ever have dreamed about. The world would be at my boy's feet, I thought, so that he could pick and choose which bits of it were for him.

'I'd had another stroke of luck, you see, and when I met you it just seemed like fate. I was able to finance the kind of lifestyle which would previously have been quite beyond my reach, not because of a fancy job, but because I'd just had a lottery win. Unbelievable though it might seem, I'd heard only the day before we met. And I was wandering around Exeter trying to take it in and think about what it could mean. It was not one of those huge wins, certainly not enough for me to give up work – not the way I wanted us to live, anyway – but enough to be life-changing – if I chose it to be.

'And my God, did I choose. I was determined that my life was going to be so different to how it had been before. You and Robbie were everything to me, from the start, you see.'

I could see the tears forming in his eyes again. He half reached out towards me. I flinched away.

'But why the lies?' I asked. 'Why the subterfuge? For sixteen bloody years. Why couldn't you just tell me all of that? I don't understand why you couldn't tell me what you really did. Do you think that would have made any difference to me? And I certainly don't understand why you couldn't have told me about the lottery win.'

'Look, I wanted a whole new life, I wanted a whole new identity, I didn't want to be the person I was before. Not when I was with you anyway. I wanted to be the same sort of person you were.'

I was bewildered.

'Surely you didn't have to go to the lengths of changing your name. What was that all about?'

'Well, I thought otherwise you might find out I was just a roustabout, I suppose . . .'

'I don't even know what a roustabout is,' I said.

'The lowest form of rig labourer, more or less. I just wanted to become a new person for you, don't you see?'

'No, I don't see,' I said sharply. 'It can't be just that. There must be more to it than that.'

I made myself speak with terrible certainty. I hoped I was wrong but I strongly suspected that he was still lying to me. His story didn't yet make complete sense. It seemed incredible that he would dare to do so, but he had to be still lying. He had to be.

He seemed to give in.

'All right, all right,' he blurted out. 'If you really have to know, well, I've been married before. There were no children, and it was a disastrous marriage. My wife was unfaithful to me from the start. After a few years she fell heavily for an Aussie backpacker and ran off to Australia with him.'

I stared at him. Shock and disbelief overwhelmed me.

'And why couldn't you tell me that?' I asked, my voice quiet again and as calm as I could make it.

He shrugged, then dropped the final bombshell.

'I may still be married.' His eyes were fixed firmly on his trembling hands.

'What?' I cried out in disbelief.

He looked up at me again, eyes pleading.

'I just don't know, Marion, I just don't know,' he said. 'I never heard from her again. I don't even know if she's alive or dead. When I met you I had no way of contacting her, let alone asking her for a divorce. And I was desperate to marry you. So I changed my name. By doing that I felt I would be more likely to get away with marrying you, and that was just the most important thing to me at the time, particularly when I learned you were carrying our baby.'

The shock washed over me.

'Do you realize that almost certainly makes you a bigamist, and our marriage illegal?' I asked. 'Are you aware of what you have done? Are you aware that I am almost certainly not and never have been your wife?'

He nodded apologetically.

Bizarrely, I found myself wanting to hear the details of what he had done, the mechanics of the lie he had lived for so long.

'Why did you change your name so slightly?' I asked. 'If you wanted a new identity, why didn't you go the whole way and call yourself something completely different?'

'You don't want to know all that.'

'Oh yes, I do.'

He sighed and continued, again seeming resigned to more or less having to.

'I thought it would make things easier and it pretty much did. By changing just one letter in my name I was able to alter the documents necessary to construct a new identity, setting up bank accounts and so on, without too much difficulty. Sometimes I used genuine unaltered documents in the hope that the tiny difference in name would not be noticed. And I pretty much always got away with it. People weren't quite so hot on identity fraud sixteen years ago, either. And computers weren't what they are today. Quite soon I had two more or less complete identities. I was still Rob Anderton at work, for tax purposes, National Insurance and so on. But I owned this house as Robert Anderson and everything concerning our life together was in the name of Robert Anderson.' He paused. 'I also thought that if you ever did come across stuff in the name of Rob Anderton, that tiny one letter difference might mean you either wouldn't notice or could even dismiss it as a mistake.'

I lowered my head into my hands.

'My God, you've been devious, Robert,' I said. 'And cruel too. Don't you see that?'

'I do now,' he said. 'I am so desperately sorry, Marion. But you are my wife whether the law says so or not. I've been such a fool. I just hope you can believe I've been guilty only of loving you too much. From the start.'

I heard him begin to sob.

I looked up. The tears were rolling down his cheeks and his shoulders were heaving.

It was hard even to see in him any part of the man I had believed him to be.

The past flashed before me. It was all beginning to fall into place. I remembered how I had never met anyone at all from Robert's earlier life and how he always avoided getting close to outsiders and liked to stay at home, indeed hidden away at home, I now realized, as much as possible. Our years together had seemed to be so idyllic that I'd never questioned him about any of that. Now I could only think how stupid I had been.

'You bastard, Robert,' I stormed. 'You utter bastard. I

thought at least I still had you after losing Robbie. And in such a terrible way. Now I know I don't. In fact, I never really had you at all, did I?'

'You did, of course you did,' he mumbled ineffectively through his tears.

'No, I didn't. And neither did our son. Do you think that's why he killed himself? Do you think he'd found out about you and couldn't live with it? Do you think you're to blame for Robbie's death on top of everything else?'

His sobbing became more pronounced.

'No, no,' he wailed.

'Well, I think you might well be to blame; in fact, I'm damned sure of it,' I said.

'No, no,' he wailed again.

Once or twice earlier while Robert had been talking I'd been afraid I might myself break down and cry. But now the icy calm had descended over me again.

'And where were you today?' I asked coldly. 'What was so important that you left me alone on the day after our son's death? What was it, Robert? What were you doing?'

He was still sobbing, and again could only mumble through his tears.

'I just wanted to be on my own, I just needed to be on my own.'

I was sure he was still lying to me. I had nothing more to say to him. I stood up, swung round, and strode out of the kitchen, slamming the door shut behind me.

six

I couldn't stay in the same room with Robert. I certainly couldn't sleep in the same bed. I made my way upstairs and stopped off at our bedroom to gather up my night clothes, my dressing gown and the bottle of paracetamol I kept in the drawer of my bedside table.

We had two guest bedrooms at Highrise, even though we so rarely entertained guests, but I chose to go up to the top of the house to Robbie's room. I wanted to feel close to my son, even though I knew how painful it would be.

I pulled back the navy-blue-covered duvet on his bed and climbed in, without bothering to take off my clothes. The walls of Robbie's room were painted bright white and dotted with posters of his favourite musicians of the moment – Arctic Monkeys, Bombay Bicycle Club and Kasabian. A life-size blow-up of Adele, his long-time idol, took pride of place directly opposite the foot of the bed. There were also some photographs of him at swimming competitions, and one of him and me hugging each other and laughing hugely in the heavy snow of the previous winter. I had to look away from that one. Several rows of shelves at the far end carried his books, mostly reference. Robbie wasn't a great reader of novels, though I had at times tried to encourage him with gifts of my favourite authors. They were a catholic selection: Ruth Rendell, Steinbeck, Laurie Lee, Orwell, Sebastian Faulks. I wasn't sure if he'd even opened most of them. Indeed, the only disappointment in my life that Robbie had ever been responsible for was his lack of interest in literature. He was an academic, but he was a practical boy. He just didn't get fiction.

I lay in his bed looking all around the room which I knew had been so special to Robbie. His books stood in tidy rows propped up by swimming trophies which he was inclined to use as bookends. A pair of jeans and a tracksuit jacket had been folded neatly over the dark-red chair in the corner by the window.

A couple of businesslike speakers, linked to his computer, were mounted on the wall above his desk so that he could play his music at impressive volume. Even though his room was at the top of the house, the thud of the bass had echoed throughout Highrise, causing predictable outbursts of grumbling from his old-fogey parents.

How I longed to be able to hear the sound of Robbie playing his music now, I thought, as I snuggled down into his bed, burying my face in the pillows. I could smell him. Or I thought I could anyway. I was torturing myself.

I had lost my son for ever. And now it felt as if I had lost my husband too, certainly the husband I'd believed him to be.

I tossed and turned in Robbie's bed, then I sat bolt upright. What on earth did I think I was doing? I checked my watch. It was not yet nine o'clock. I felt totally exhausted and drained. All I wanted was the relief, the oblivion of sleep, but I was hardly likely to find it so early and on such a day, lying fully clothed in my dead son's bed. Not without assistance anyway.

I got up, undressed, put on my pyjamas then went into Robbie's bathroom, carrying my bottle of paracetamol. I filled the tooth mug with tap water and emptied it in one swallow. I was thirsty but not hungry. Even though I had eaten only two slices of toast all day, I had no desire whatsoever for food of any kind.

I filled the tooth mug with water again and washed down four paracetamol capsules. I was going to need all the help I could get for sleep to come that night. I paused for a moment, holding the paracetamol bottle in one hand and its cap in the other. It was possible that I held in my hand a means to the only ultimate escape from my misery.

I remembered, then, something I had read in a magazine interview with a famous actress who had spoken with rare common sense, I'd thought at the time, for a member of her profession. If ever you contemplate suicide, she'd said, you should wait until the next day before doing anything about it.

I knew she was right. I didn't feel that my life would ever be worth living again, but the man I had married in good faith and had loved so much was still there, downstairs in the kitchen of our fine home, proclaiming his everlasting love for me. I felt unbearably betrayed. Yet perhaps I would feel differently in the morning. Or perhaps I was clutching at straws. I didn't know.

In any case I'd also read somewhere that it takes considerably more than the contents of an average-size bottle of paracetamol to kill a human being, and that death comes neither quickly nor in sleep, but is ultimately caused in most cases by acute liver failure, agonizingly, and only after several days.

I replaced the cap on the paracetamol bottle and left it in Robbie's bathroom.

Then I crawled back into his bed and pulled his duvet over my head.

I began to cry. I couldn't stop. Eventually, aided no doubt

by my mild drug overdose, I cried myself to sleep. When I woke, rather to my surprise, dawn was already breaking. I checked my watch. It was 7 a.m. I realized I must have slept for almost ten hours. My gran would have said it was my body looking after itself. Giving me the rest I desperately needed to find the strength to cope with all that had happened.

I felt hot and sweaty. My forehead clammy to the touch. I badly needed to urinate. Indeed, without the pressure of my bladder I suspected I may have slept even longer.

I climbed out of bed and made my way into Robbie's bath-room again. His electric razor, a birthday present from his father, stood on the shelf above the washbasin. He'd taken to using it most mornings, I believed, even though he hadn't really needed to.

As I relieved myself the tears pricked at the back of my eyes again. I made myself take some deep breaths and splashed my hot flushed face with cold water.

Back in the bedroom I threw open the windows to the cool air of another wintery Dartmoor morning and did some more deep breathing.

What was I going to do? If I left Robert, where would I go? I had no money of my own. I supposed I could go back to teaching full-time, but in order to acquire a proper staff appointment I would almost certainly have to retrain.

In any case, was that what I wanted? Did I want to leave Robert? Or did I still love him and want to be with him, flaws and all? I really wasn't sure. And just how bad were those flaws?

Maybe what he had done was not so very dreadful. Cer-tainly his motives seemed to be good. But if a man were capable of such a massive deception over such a long period, what else, I asked myself not for the first time, might he have been keeping from me? What other secrets could he be holding?

I didn't know, of course, and I had to accept I might never know. But, just as I'd half suspected, I did feel slightly different about the whole thing in the cold light of morning. I knew I had to think very carefully before destroying whatever might still remain of the life I had once so enjoyed. But on the other hand, I was aware that I might just be kidding myself to even consider the possibility that any significant part of that life could really be salvaged.

I pulled on my dressing gown and made my way downstairs to the kitchen. I needed a cup of tea. I also realized, rather to my surprise, that I was hungry. In spite of having barely eaten anything the day before, I'd rather thought I'd never be able to face food again.

Robert was sitting in the big old leather armchair by the Aga. He was asleep when I opened the door but immediately awakened. He was unshaven and ravaged-looking again. It was pretty obvious he hadn't been to bed.

The kitchen was very warm. He must have fetched in more wood, stoked and relit the range. Indeed, the box which stood beside it was overflowing with logs. Florrie lay at Robert's feet, curled up on the mat. She rose and ambled sleepily over to me, wrapping her body around my legs and stretching her neck so that she could lick my hand.

Robert didn't speak. He just gazed at me. His eyes were imploring. Under any other circumstances I would have been overwhelmed with compassion for him. As things were, I really didn't know what I felt for him any more.

That morning I was empty of emotion.

The kettle simmered on the Aga's slow plate, as usual when Robert was home. I stood it for a minute or two on the fast hob and then took two mugs and a couple of tea bags, poured in boiling water and added a splash of milk to each.

I handed one of the mugs to Robert. He mumbled a 'thank you' as he took it from me. The first word either of us had spoken.

'Would you like some breakfast?' I asked.

He nodded. An expression almost of puzzlement flitting across his face.

I reached for the big old iron frying pan that hung from a hook above the stove, took some bacon and eggs from the fridge and began to cook.

'Make some toast, will you,' I instructed Robert. 'There's sliced bread in the freezer.'

I didn't really know what I was doing, and I don't think Robert did either. Whatever he had expected from me that morning, I doubt it was this kind of normality. It wasn't what I would have expected from myself either.

But it was, of course, just how people did behave when someone died. Even when that someone was their son. They just carried on. Only this was different. I still did not know if I would be able to carry on with a man who had deceived me so, nor if I really wanted to. I had decisions to make, that was for sure, but maybe the sensible thing to do was to defer deciding anything irrevocable until I'd had time to come to terms with all that had happened.

It was always said, was it not, that big decisions should never be made right after bereavement. Particularly an unexpected one. And I had an additional shocking dilemma to deal with.

I carried two plates of bacon and eggs to the table and set them down. In our usual places. In front of our usual chairs. I tried not even to glance at that other usual place. At Robbie's place.

Robert piled toast into a basket and put that on the table between us.

We began to eat. I was surprised at how good the food tasted. Strange. I hadn't expected to be able to taste anything. I'd thought I was totally numb.

We ate in silence. Robert, I think, was afraid to speak. I hadn't yet worked out exactly what I was going to say to him. Nor even if I wanted to say anything yet. But I did still have questions.

By the time I'd finished eating, and drained the last of my tea, I at least felt ready to ask some of those questions.

'You still haven't told me where you were yesterday,' I said.

'I did tell you. I needed to be on my own. I went walking. I'm so sorry I left you alone. Really I am. I wanted to be with you, but somehow I just needed time—'

'You told me you were taking the hire car back,' I interrupted. 'It's still here, parked at the front.'

'I'm sorry, Marion,' he said. 'I can't explain yesterday. I'll never be able to explain yesterday. I don't even know what I did for most of it, to tell the truth. I just walked . . .'

His voice tailed off. I glanced across the kitchen. His shoes lay where he'd presumably discarded them the previous night, alongside the leather armchair. There was no mud on them and they did not even look as if they had recently got wet, even though the previous day's weather had been so awful.

'I know I should have been with you,' Robert continued after a bit. 'I wanted to be with you. I'm just so sorry. All I can say is nothing like it will ever happen again. We are both grief stricken. I promise you I will be here for you one hundred per cent from now on.'

I looked at him, sitting in his familiar place at the table. My Robert. Except that this was a Robert I barely recognized. Unshaven. Eyes wild and swollen. Above all a man who was not what he had seemed to be for all those years. I'd caught him out in an enormous lie. A lie which rocked the very basis of our life together. Even his name was a falsehood. Yet he was all I had. That and our home, though suddenly even Highrise, wonderful Highrise, didn't mean much any more.

'How can I trust you?' I enquired in an almost conversational sort of way. 'I thought I knew you through and through, knew everything about you. It seems that I didn't. How will I ever be able to trust you again?'

'You can, Marion,' he said, his eyes and his whole body language imploring me now. 'I promise, promise you. You just have to believe me, you really do.'

'Do I?' The question was rhetorical. But he answered it anyway.

'You must,' he said. 'You cannot throw away all that we've had together. We've lost Robbie. We cannot lose each other, surely?'

I was afraid we already had. But he looked and sounded so anguished that, angry as he'd made me, I did not have the heart to say so. I remained silent. After all, whatever he may have done, this was my son's father.

'I'll put it right,' he continued eventually. 'I will, Marion. I'll find my first wife somehow. I'll get that divorce. We'll get married again, you and me, somewhere exotic, just the two of us. Mauritius, the Maldives. Somewhere like that. We'll have a ceremony on the beach as the sun goes down . . .'

His voice trailed away as if even he realized the nonsense of what he was saying.

I shook my head in exasperation.

'You're a fantasist, Robert,' I said. 'A romantic fantasist. Maybe that's partly what I fell in love with in you. But now, now, with Robbie dead and all this deception, this terrible deception coming to light, it's just . . .' I searched for the right word.

'It's obscene.'

Robert recoiled almost as if I had hit him.

'I'm sorry,' he said, 'but I will put things right.'

'You can never put things right, Robert. You can certainly never bring Robbie back.'

He slumped in his chair.

'No,' he said quietly. 'I can't do that.'

His eyes were focused on his empty plate. He obviously couldn't meet mine.

'M-Marion,' he stumbled. 'Can I ask you something?'

'I suppose so,' I said.

'Y-you, you don't really think I had something to do with our son's death, do you? I would never have harmed a hair on his head. Never.'

'I know that,' I replied a tad grudgingly. 'I don't think you actually harmed him, of course I don't. In any case you weren't even here. But, like I said yesterday, perhaps he'd found out about you, and was traumatized by what he learned. That has to be possible.'

Robert turned ever paler. He looked up at me.

'Does it? Traumatized enough to hang himself? You suggested that yesterday. It can't be what happened, surely.'

He paused, and shook his head quite ferociously before continuing.

'Oh, Marion, I have no idea if or how Robbie might have found out that I was not quite what I seemed. But I was still the father who loved the bones of him, for God's sake. Surely he wouldn't want to take his own life because my name was really Rob Anderton and I'm a derrickman who got lucky on the lottery instead of a highly paid big-shot engineer. Would he care that much?'

'I don't know,' I said.

'I just have to believe he didn't,' Robert continued, desperation in his voice. 'I just have to believe that even if he had discovered the truth about me it would not have driven him to take his own life. And I hope you will believe that too.'

I fixed my gaze on him.

'But perhaps there's more,' I continued. 'Perhaps there is more about you that I still do not know. Are you sure you've told me everything, Robert?'

'Of course I have,' he said. 'What else could there be?'

'I really don't know, Robert,' I said. 'But then, I don't know about anything any longer.'

He was silent for a moment or two.

'In any case I thought you didn't believe Robbie had killed himself,' he went on eventually. 'I thought you believed there was someone else involved, that he may have even been murdered.'

'I did think that. But that was when I could not imagine that there was anything in Robbie's life that would make him want to end it. Now that I've learned about you, about your deception, I'm not so sure. Robbie was at a vulnerable age. Teenagers are easily tipped over the edge, we all know that—'

'Not by me,' Robert interrupted almost fiercely. 'I just cannot believe that. It's too dreadful for me to accept. Look, you said you were going to look into his death because the police are obviously not going to take it any further. Let me help. Let us try to find out the truth together.'

I laughed humourlessly. 'Truth? You? Not really your specialist area, it seems, is it? In any case you just want to prove to yourself that you're not to blame.'

'I'll admit that,' he said. He looked so gaunt. Every so often I couldn't help remembering how much I'd always loved him. And, even now, the one thing I didn't doubt about him was that he loved me.

'Well, I suppose I can identify with that,' I said. 'I want to prove to myself that I'm not to blame too.'

He reached out a hand to touch mine.

'Of course you're not to blame,' he said. 'How could you be?'

I pulled my hand away. I had softened a little, in spite of myself, but I wasn't ready for that sort of contact yet. Far from it.

'The same way any parent of a child that kills himself is,' I said. 'How can you not blame yourself?'

He looked down at his shunned hand. Then up at me.

'I know,' he said. 'I know what you are feeling.'

And he did, of course.

'Marion,' he went on. 'You will stay with me, won't you? We need each other now more than ever, surely. There's nobody else in the world who could understand what we're going through, what we've lost. Only us.'

I nodded. That was the truth, of course. How could anyone else understand?

'So you will stay?' he asked again.

I wasn't ready to make any promises. Not to this man who had thrust a dagger into the very core of my soul at a time when I hadn't thought it possible to be more deeply hurt than I already was.

'We have a funeral to arrange,' I said. 'Our son deserves that it is done properly, without his parents waging war on each other. I will stay until after the funeral. Then we'll see . . .'

There was hope in his eyes then. At least I thought that's what it was. But this was a man I no longer knew, had perhaps never really known. So I suppose it could have been anything really . . .

seven

What a difference a day makes, I thought again. Yesterday I had so wanted my husband to stay with me. Today I did not even know whether or not he was my husband. I did know that I couldn't remain in his company.

Apart from anything else I was still sorting my head out. I realized I remained in deep shock. And I was afraid I might do or say something I would later regret.

I went upstairs to our bedroom, sat on the bed and tried to think straight. When someone died there were always so many things to be done. I knew that from the death of my grandmother, and could even remember further back to the busy comings and goings in our North Devon home after my mother died when I was child. Followed, of course, by the emptiness.

But Robbie's death had been so utterly unexpected, and the revelations that followed it so shocking. I had so far done none of the things that should be done. We couldn't make funeral arrangements until the post-mortem was completed and Robbie's body released. However, there were people who needed to be told what had happened, and I hadn't been in touch with anyone. Notably his school and, of course, my father. Robbie's grandfather. I knew it was unforgivable for me not to have already contacted him.

The school was the easy one, so I did that first. I assumed the office would be closed on a Saturday, which gave me an excuse to avoid actually speaking to anyone. I would send an email. My iPad was on the bedside table where it had remained since before Robbie's death. I'd almost always taken it to bed with me when Robert was away working. Robert had refused to have a TV in the bedroom, saying it would detract from the pretty tranquillity of the room and the stark beauty of the Dartmoor views through its big picture windows. I'd agreed with him, actually, but when he was away had been inclined to cheat with my iPad, using its catch-up TV and access to movies.

I wrote to Robbie's headmaster, briefly, and almost emotionlessly, telling him what had happened. As I pushed the send button I reflected fleetingly that the email looked rather tardy. It couldn't be helped. It was the best I could do.

I had to speak to my father. I could no longer put off making the call. How dreadful it would be if he found out about his beloved grandson's death from some other source, I thought suddenly. I couldn't imagine what the source might be, but one did see stories of teenage suicides in the newspapers. I had no idea who would or could be responsible for that sort of coverage, not before some sort of court proceedings anyway, but I could no longer take the risk.

However, just as I was about to pick up the bedside phone it rang. DS Jarvis was returning my call of the previous morning. I had almost given up hope of ever hearing from him again. I told him about there being no marks on Robbie's bedroom floor until I dragged his heavy desk back in place.

Jarvis was unimpressed.

'Robbie could have lifted the desk across the room, Mrs Anderson,' he said.

'It's made of solid oak, Detective Sergeant,' I told him. 'It's very heavy. I can't even lift one end of it.'

'You are a small woman, Mrs Anderson,' he responded. 'Your son was tall and strong, and a very fit young man. Besides, in extreme circumstances people are inclined to find extra strength.'

I tried to push the point, but got nowhere. It was as if DS Jarvis and the Devon and Cornwall Constabulary had made up their minds, and that was that. I ended the call, and before I had time to do any more thinking made the one I had been putting off.

I dialled Dad's Hartland number. He sounded so cheery when he answered the phone and heard my voice that I desperately wanted to have a conversation about nothing and then hang up. I knew I couldn't.

'I have the most dreadful news . . .' I began.

He gasped, in both pain and disbelief, I thought, when I told him what had happened.

'Oh my God, Marion, how? Why . . .'

Always that same question. Why?

'We don't have any answers, Dad,' I said. 'I can't give you any answers. I can barely talk about it at all, to tell the truth.'

'Of course,' he said. Then he asked me when Robbie had died.

'You should have called me before, I'd have driven right over,' he said.

I couldn't tell him that on the night Robbie died I would have been unable to bear his grief, that he had not been the person I'd wanted with me. And I couldn't tell him about the revelations of yesterday that had made me feel I'd lost a husband as well as a son and rendered me quite incapable of contacting anyone.

'I've just been too upset,' I said.

'Well, shall I come now?' he asked. 'I'll just get in the car and I'll be there in no time. I'd like to—'

I interrupted. 'No, no,' I said, a little too quickly, more than a little insensitively, I realized. I tried to soften it, probably not very successfully. 'Look, it's just so hard. Robert's with me. We need time.'

'Of course you do, I understand,' said Dad, sounding as if he didn't understand at all.

'Thanks,' I said lamely.

'But the funeral, when's the funeral? I must come to his funeral.'

I agreed that of course he must, explained about the post-mortem, and promised to let him know as soon as we were able to make the necessary arrangements.

I ended the call as quickly as I could. I knew that I was treating him shabbily. We had once been so very close. When I was a child, perhaps because of losing my mother so young, I'd always wanted to be with my dad, and to be like him, really. I used to try desperately to be useful, too. I don't know why because Dad never made demands of me, but I did think it pleased him. He called me his 'right-hand girl' in those days. As a loving father and grandfather he deserved to be included in all aspects of family life, even in the aftermath of tragedy. But I couldn't help myself. After all, my family had just been torn asunder and in any case we had never been what we seemed.

The call had been horrible to make. I didn't want to break down again. It would serve no purpose at all. I was so determined to keep what remained of my wits about me.

I needed to get out of the house. I shivered even though the bedroom was quite warm. The place just didn't feel right. I supposed it might never feel right again.

I called Bella, thanked her for her kindness, and asked if I could perhaps visit her in Exeter for a bit.

She hesitated momentarily. 'Look, the kids have got chums over,' she said. 'It's chaos here. But I'll get my neighbour to keep an eye on them, and why don't we meet on Exmouth beach? Usual place. Walk the dogs, get some fresh air. It's not such a bad day, dry anyway.'

I agreed.

'I can be there in just over an hour or so,' she said. 'Have to be back in good time for this evening, though. We've got fireworks and a bonfire down the road.'

I remembered then. Not only was it a Saturday and no school, but it was the 5th of November, Guy Fawkes Night. Robbie had loved fireworks but had ultimately forgone them because they frightened Florrie so much. He'd been that sort of boy.

I dressed in my dog-walking clothes – old jeans, sweater, Barbour jacket and boots – slung a thick scarf around my neck and pocketed gloves and a woolly hat. I called to Florrie. She whimpered at the kitchen door. Robert opened it. Florrie trotted towards me and Robert followed her into the hall.

'Are you going out?' he asked.

'I didn't think we bothered to tell each other that sort of thing any more,' I responded tartly.

'Oh, come on, Marion, I've told you how sorry I am about that. We had just lost our son, you know . . .'

I relented. Slightly.

'I'm going to meet Bella in Exmouth,' I said. 'We're going to walk the dogs. I just need some space. You should understand that, after all.'

He coloured slightly and shuffled from foot to foot.

'Please don't go,' he said. 'Please stay here with me. I really want you here with me—'

'Tough, Robert,' I said. 'From now on I make the rules.'

I opened the door straight away, called Florrie through and slammed it shut in Robert's face. I didn't even know quite what I meant by that last remark. I just knew things would never be the same again between Robert and me. And not only because we had lost our beloved son.

I drove to Exmouth far too fast. Normally I was a careful driver. That day it was almost a case of not caring what happened to me. Maybe even half wanting something to happen to me.

On the road into the seaside town there's a 30-mile-an-hour limit where you don't expect it, and the speed cameras that so often accompany such a limit on the approach road to a town. Easy pickings, I'd always thought, particularly in a tourist town. That day I didn't give a toss about the cameras, of course, but then a young woman stepped out into the road from behind a parked car. She was pushing a pram, presumably containing a child, and the pram came first. I braked hard and swerved, missing the woman and the pram by inches.

Florrie, in the back, was thrown against the dog guard which separated her area from the rest of the car. She whimpered in pain and protest. I could see the startled white face of the young woman in my rear mirror. What she was doing pushing a pram out from behind a parked car when she clearly would have been unable to see the road, I didn't know. But I did know I'd been travelling far too fast. I slowed down.

I found a parking space at the eastern end of the seafront where the sand dunes begin and there's no charge during the winter months. There were usually plenty of spaces at this time of year, and Bella and I were in the habit of parking as close as possible to the town end of the free parking zone. I couldn't see her Toyota, and was pretty sure I was the first to arrive.

I sat for a moment just staring into space. Now that I'd got to the beach I really had no idea why I'd made the arrangement to meet Bella in the first place. It was understandable that I'd wanted to get out of the house and away from the man who had caused me so much pain over the last couple of days, on top of the biggest blow of all, the loss of my son. But why I'd even considered meeting up with another person I had no idea. Particularly another person who I really did not know that well. I'd never even been to her home or met her children, for goodness' sake.

For a brief moment I thought about restarting the engine, turning the car around and just driving away. I might have done so, too, in spite of letting down this woman who had been so kind to me on the night of Robbie's death, if it had not been for Florrie's persistent whimpering. She was eager for her run.

I climbed out of the car and flipped open the rear door for her. She seemed none the worse for her close encounter with the dog guard and was merely in the throes of her usual paroxysm of excitement at the sight and smell of sand and sea.

I crossed the road and sat on the low sea wall opposite my car. It was cold but there was only a light breeze blowing in across the estuary from the Atlantic Ocean. Once I'd wrapped my scarf tightly round my neck and pulled on my gloves and hat I was not uncomfortable. Florrie ran happily onto the dunes in front of me and began sniffing and snuffling around. She also had a roll. As usual. Normally I would already be grumbling to myself about the job of brushing the sand out of her coat later. That was something else I couldn't have cared less about that day.

I just sat there gazing blankly out to sea. But after just a few minutes I heard the sound of a vehicle approaching and drawing to a halt. I turned around just in time to watch Bella open her car door and climb out.

She looked rather grim. I hadn't really noticed before the deep lines which ran down her cheeks and curved around her eyes. Her bobbed reddish-brown hair displayed prominent grey roots. I was reminded that her life had almost certainly been far harder than mine. Until now that is.

She spotted me, and smiled. It was that already familiar wide, warm smile.

'I'm glad you came,' she called, zipping up her blue anorak and slipping the hood over her head.

'I nearly didn't,' I replied. 'I nearly couldn't . . .'

She crossed the road, Flash bounding away from her and straight past me to join Florrie on the dunes.

'I know,' she said. 'I mean, I did wonder. I wouldn't have minded. But I'm glad.'

The tears pricked again. This woman had a way of hitting the spot. She seemed to really know me, to really understand me.

'C'mon,' she said. 'Let's get on the beach and give those dogs a good run. You don't have to talk unless you want to.'

I nodded and swung my legs over the little wall. She clambered over it alongside me. We shuffled across the loose sand of the dunes and through a gap in the breakwater onto the beach proper. Two miles of golden sand. That was Exmouth's tourist commercial. And pure joy to any self-respecting canine.

Florrie and Flash duly took off at full speed, scattering seagulls and crows.

We watched them in companionable silence for a while, as we strolled vaguely in the direction of the town, past the Octagon, the eight-sided building on the Esplanade which houses a snack bar and a shop, and on along the sand towards the marina.

A white wintery sun darted in and out of fast-moving clouds. The breeze seemed to be getting up a bit. Bella thrust her hands deep into her anorak pockets.

'Should have brought my gloves,' she muttered. 'Didn't realize it was this cold.'

It was an inconsequential remark, but it somehow prompted me to say something I felt needed to be said.

'I'm so sorry Robert was rude to you the other night,' I told her.

'Oh no, you don't need to apologize,' she responded with what seemed to be her customary kindness. 'He'd just had the most terrible news, after all.'

'Yes, but there was no call for . . .'

I let the sentence trail off lamely.

We did not talk a lot at all. I told her, as I had my father, how we were waiting for Robbie's body to be released by the police, and that I would let her know when we had set a date for the funeral.

'I would really like you to come, and I know Robbie would have done too,' I said, trying not to break down as I spoke his name.

She said nothing. I glanced at her. In spite of my distress I realized that she didn't look too keen.

'But, I mean, I'd understand if you don't wish—'

'It's not that,' she interrupted. 'I just hate funerals, that's all, particularly when it's someone so young. But of course I'll come. Robbie was a fine lad. I'd like to be there for him. And for you.'

I touched her arm, fleetingly. Had I been a different sort of person I would have given her a hug.

'Thank you,' I said. 'Just thank you, for everything.'

She shrugged.

'It's been nothing. I can't imagine what it must be like to lose your child so young. And in such an awful way. I mean, if there's anything else I can do. You only have to ask.'

I nodded and mumbled more thanks. My feet, although I'd worn extra thick socks over my bandages, were starting to pain me, and Bella noticed that I was limping a bit. We turned back towards our cars and made our way up to the Esplanade where the walking was easier. I quickly attached Florrie's lead to her collar, and when I saw Bella struggle to do the same with Flash offered to help and, in fact, managed the snap clip quite easily.

'Numb fingers,' said Bella, by way of explanation, as we continued walking. 'Really could have done with those gloves.'

I managed a small smile. I was not used to disclosing my innermost thoughts to anyone except Robert. But I suppose I just needed someone right then to share certain things with.

'Bella, you know, you'll probably think I'm mad, but I'm not sure about the way Robbie died,' I blurted out suddenly. 'I don't entirely believe he killed himself.'

She half stopped in her tracks and turned to me, asking me why not.

'I mean, do the police have any doubts?'

I shook my head. Then I explained about the desk and the marks on the floor, and the conclusion they had led me to.

'That was clever of you,' she said, giving me what seemed to be an appraising sort of look. 'Have you told the police?'

'Yes. But they're not really interested. I can't believe it. They just seem to have made up their minds.'

'Ummm.' She looked and sounded thoughtful. 'What about Robert? What does he think?'

'I don't know what he thinks.' I realized I'd rather spat the words out and sounded quite bitter.

She shot me another appraising look.

'Nothing wrong between you two, is there?' she asked. 'I mean, you're going to really need each other to get through this.'

I paused before replying. A big part of me wanted to tell her all about the events of the last two days, to share with another human being the whole barrel load of shocks I had received. To tell her that the man I so loved, the husband with whom I had shared everything, had in fact deceived me throughout our marriage.

I wanted to tell her that I no longer felt I could trust Robert, and how that had devastated me. I wanted to tell her how I did not know whether I could stay with him or not. But that I was afraid to leave him.

I didn't, though. I didn't tell her any of that. I just couldn't.

eight

The rest of the weekend passed in a fog of unreality. Robert and I coexisted on tenterhooks. I couldn't trust myself to have anything more to do with him than I had to, in case I just exploded, and he seemed afraid even to speak to me.

I knew I could not face another night in Robbie's room. I would drive myself quite mad with grief. But neither could I countenance sleeping with Robert. I moved into the guest room at the back of the house. Robert accepted my decision regarding sleeping arrangements without question. He did offer to be the one who took the guest room, but I declined. I didn't want to sleep in the room we had so happily shared for so long, even if he wasn't there.

On Monday morning the *Western Morning News* carried a front-page report of Robbie's death. There were quotes from an anonymous school friend, and a photograph of him in his school uniform which looked as if it might have been lifted from a group picture, possibly also obtained from the school friend. Certainly I had not supplied a photo to anyone, Robbie had been far too private a boy to be on Facebook, and as far as I knew there were no pictures of him on the Net.

In the afternoon PC Cox called to tell us that the post-mortem had been completed, and Robbie's body would now be released for burial. She explained that a preliminary inquest, just a paperwork formality at this stage, she said, had already been opened and adjourned. Rather to my surprise, it seemed we would have to wait five or six months for the inquest proper.

''Fraid the coroner has a bit of a backlog,' said PC Cox.

Not that an inquest was likely to make much difference to anything whenever it was held, I thought, judging from the lack of interest shown by the police.

Over the next two or three days we received a number of cards and notes of condolence, some of them from local people whose names I barely recognized. Dad phoned every evening. The headmaster of Kelly College also phoned, and so did Robbie's swimming coach.

Tom Farley, the village's capable jack of all trades, and the only man Robert had ever wanted to work with him on Highrise, called round to ask if there was anything he could do. He brought with him a large steak and kidney pie, made by his wife Ellen, he told us, adding by way of explanation: 'Missus says you won't want to cook, but you'm to make sure you keep your strength up.'

Our local weekly paper followed up the *Western Morning News* story about Robbie, publishing the same picture, and one of the nationals carried a thankfully quite small piece, focusing on an alleged increase in the number of unexplained suicides among young people.

We organized the funeral for the following Friday. Or to be honest, as Robert barely seemed capable of doing anything, I organized it with the help of the local undertaker and the vicar's wife. I was glad to be busy. I didn't want to think any more.

None of the three of us in our little family had ever had any religious beliefs at all. I certainly didn't, Robert had always been an equally emphatic non-believer, and Robbie had seemed to embrace our lack or faith effortlessly. Indeed, just like us, he had sometimes expressed wonderment at how, in the modern world, anyone with a modicum of intelligence could accept the mumbo jumbo of any religion. I therefore did wonder if it was hypocritical to involve the church. But it meant that Robbie could be buried in Blackstone's little churchyard at the foot of the Dartmoor hills, a place I knew he so loved.

The secular options seemed so bleak by comparison. I'd been to a humanist funeral of a school friend's mother when I was a teenager. It had been most unusual, and considered really not quite the thing in those days. Even then I hadn't cared about any of that, but I'd been aware, as I suspected my friend had been, of an added sense of emptiness about the occasion. A feeling that all was not as it should be. Whatever one thought about religious institutions, funerals were probably what they did best.

Robert just nodded everything through. He seemed numb. Also, almost pathetically afraid to offend me in any way. He agreed with everything I said.

I first attempted to contact our local vicar, who gloried in the name of Gerald Ponsonby Smythe, straight after getting the go-ahead from PC Cox. My call was diverted to an answering service, so I left a message.

Within the hour there was a knock on the front door. I was taken by surprise because I'd been at the back of the house and hadn't heard a vehicle approach. Outside stood a woman I immediately recognized as the vicar's wife, Gladys Ponsonby Smythe.

She was pretty unmistakable – a big woman, both in longitude and latitude, with ferocious grey hair apparently quite determined to defy her attempts to tie it back from her face.

She was wearing no make-up except for a prominent and slightly askew streak of vermilion lipstick. Her clothes, which were more like robes, multicoloured and hippy-like, ebbed and flowed with every roll of her ample curves.

I hadn't met her before, but I'd seen her photograph many times in the press. I'd always somewhat dismissed her, both from her demeanour and the nature of her press presence, as a somewhat flamboyant churchy do-gooder, intent on being a tower of strength, and probably rather bossy and pleased with herself.

She introduced herself and expressed her deepest sympathy over Robbie's tragic death. The first surprise was the way she spoke. Gladys Ponsonby Smythe had a strong Liverpool accent.

'We didn't know anything about your awful news until you called,' she said. 'I just had to come straight away. I hope you don't mind, Mrs Anderson.'

I did rather, but I could hardly turn her away. In any case I needed the woman.

The Reverend Gerald Ponsonby Smythe was old-school high church, and steeped in classical Latin. Again, something I'd learned from the local press. I'd also spotted him once or twice walking round the village in a long black frock. All right, a cassock. But I didn't think it was very usual for clergy to wear that kind of garb any more, certainly not outside their churches.

I remembered when I'd first seen both their names in a local paper how I'd thought that nobody could really be called Ponsonby Smythe, and that at the very least they had to be clichés on legs. I still didn't know about him. But she certainly wasn't that. Gladys, as I was instructed to address her, swiftly proved to be not at all what I had expected. Except, of course, in the tower of strength department! More than anything else, Gladys Ponsonby Smythe was a Scouser with attitude.

I found myself apologizing for not having met her or her husband before, and for asking to arrange a funeral in their church when I'd previously never been inside it. The Church of England was surely well accustomed to that sort of behaviour, as for so many people churches were only for weddings, christenings and funerals. But it was somehow as if I needed to clear the territory ahead before burying my beloved son.

'I hope you don't think I'm a hypocrite,' I said.

'You don't need to worry about that, chuck,' Gladys responded swiftly. 'Not half as hypocritical as a considerable number of our regular congregation at St Andrews, I can tell you. Only I never said that.'

She had me smiling in spite of myself. For a start I didn't think anyone, from Liverpool or anywhere else, actually said 'chuck', except Cilla Black.

I invited her in, trying not to let my reluctance show. After all, I really did need her.

She stepped into the hall but made no attempt to move further into the house.

'Look, I'm not staying, not this time,' she said. 'I just wanted you to know that I'm here to give you all the help I can with the funeral and anything else. I'll come back to sort out the details.'

I thanked her and said I appreciated having a bit more time.

'If you'd rather pop out for a bit and come to the vicarage or go to the pub or something, just let me know,' she said as she left.

I didn't believe in anything that she stood for, but I did feel very slightly less bereft after her visit.

Ultimately I called her the next day to say I was ready to talk about the details of the funeral, or as ready as I'd ever be, and I would like to meet at the vicarage. I just wanted a break from the sheer bloody misery of Highrise.

Blackstone Vicarage, built right next to the church, was an ugly Victorian pile in dire need of a major facelift outside and in. It boasted few of the comforts of life which I took for granted. The Reverend Gerald, a distracted man several years older than his wife, I thought, who wore wire-framed spectacles balanced crookedly on a large pointed nose, greeted me in the hall before retreating to his study, saying he would 'leave Gladys to it, then', which I somehow thought was his habit.

Gladys made instant coffee in an orange Formica kitchen dating back to the 1970s, I guessed. She sat me at the Formica-topped table, plonked half a packet of chocolate digestive biscuits before me, then got down to business. First she asked what hymns I would like. I didn't think I knew any appropriate hymns, except 'Abide with Me', which I definitely didn't want because it would be sure to cause me to totally break down. Other than that I had only a distant memory of hymns I used to sing at school and I couldn't even remember what they were.

'Would you like me to choose, luv?' she asked.

I nodded my agreement. She suggested 'All Things Bright and Beautiful', which, of course, even I had heard of, and 'Be Not Afraid', originally an American Catholic hymn, which I hadn't.

That hymn began with the verse: *You shall cross the barren desert, But you shall not die of thirst, You shall wander far in safety, Though you do not know the way.* It's chorus was: *Be not afraid, I go before you always, Come follow me, And I shall give you rest.*

I was moved by the words. It made me think of Robbie not knowing the way and seeking rest, and it reminded me of how I had almost always been moved by the Bible whenever I encountered quotations or readings. Even though I didn't actually believe a word that was in it.

'But can you have a Catholic hymn at a C of E funeral?' I asked.

'Oh, Gerry doesn't worry about stuff like that, chuck,' responded the vicar's wife cheerily. 'In any case he's so high church there's some round here think he secretly is RC!'

I smiled and told Gladys those two hymns would be fine.

She then asked if either Robert or I would like to speak about Robbie at the service. I shook my head vehemently. I knew I would not be able to do so, and I really didn't feel I could sit and listen to the husband I now knew had deceived me for so long eulogizing about the son he had also grievously deceived.

Gladys suggested that if I told her a little about Robbie then her husband could give a short address.

'He's surprisingly good at that sort of thing, is Gerry. Still, plenty of practice, I suppose,' she remarked.

She also said that if I wanted to lay on a little 'do', as she called it, after the service, I might prefer to use the village pub, the Lamb and Flag, rather than have a load of people descending on Highrise.

I agreed to that with alacrity. I would have preferred nothing at all, but if there had to be a 'do', and I supposed that there did, then the pub was definitely the best alternative.

'But I doubt there'll be a lot of people,' I said. 'We've never mixed much in the village, you see, and we don't really have many friends . . .'

I finished the sentence lamely, letting it trail away. Of course we didn't have friends. Robert had seen to that. Friends might have found him out, I supposed.

Gladys had begun to speak again. I tuned in halfway through.

'. . . and you can be quite sure there'll be more than you think. There's a tradition in this part of the world to turn out for the funeral of one of their own. All the regular congregation will be there, you can be sure of that, and goodness knows who else . . .'

I drifted off once more. The very thought made me feel sick. Would I be expected, then, to make polite conversation with total strangers? Was this the price I had to pay for ensuring my son had a decent burial and was laid to rest somewhere that was special to him?

Gladys did have a bossy side, as I'd suspected, and a conviction that she was in the right. Although I also suspected that she probably was, more often than not, I considered challenging her. Or even just backing out of the whole thing. But I didn't. I just went along with it.

On the day of the funeral, Friday the 11th of November, eight days after Robbie's death, it was tipping down with rain. From the windows of Highrise only a veiled curtain of water and mist could be seen, effectively masking the moors from view. It seemed appropriate.

My father drove up from Hartland that morning. I had managed to keep him at bay until then and I'd asked him if he'd mind driving home again after the service as we didn't feel able to cope with having anyone to stay right then, not even him. I felt guilty but I had no choice. Apart from anything else, the more time he spent with us the more likely he was to pick up on the atmosphere between Robert and me and to start asking questions I couldn't deal with.

I dressed in the navy-blue suit I'd bought for my gran's

funeral all those years ago, navy chosen because she'd so hated funereal black. Rather miraculously, it still fitted me, more or less, but I knew I had already lost some weight since Robbie's death. There was a navy hat, a kind of trilby, to match, and, coincidentally, my best raincoat, which was certainly needed that day, was also navy. I couldn't wear the black patent court shoes which would have been my first choice because my burned feet continued to pain me, but in any case sensible brogues were rather better suited to the weather.

The service was scheduled to begin at 2 p.m. At 12.30 Robert was still sitting slumped at the kitchen table, unshaven and dishevelled, looking every inch the rough and ready rigger I now knew him to be.

'You're going to be late,' I told him sharply.

'I wasn't even sure that you wanted me to come,' he mumbled.

'What, to our son's funeral?' I snapped. 'Have you completely taken leave of your senses? Whatever happened last week, that boy worshipped you. Though, with what I now know, I rather wish he hadn't.'

Robert winced, as if in pain.

'Of course you must come,' I commanded. 'Just go and get ready. Quickly.'

He left the room and reappeared half an hour later, clean-shaven, hair washed and slicked down. He was wearing the beautiful black suit he'd bought for our wedding. That still fitted him pretty well too and, of course, had barely been worn since. He was carrying his Burberry raincoat over one arm. His shirt was bright white and crisply pressed. I'd always enjoyed looking after Robert's shirts and presenting them to him in the best possible order. Not any more, I thought. He could iron his own damned shirts.

114

Then I noticed his tie. It was Robbie's county swimming tie, of which our son had been so proud. Indeed, the only tie he had ever really wanted to put around his neck.

I felt a lump in my throat. In spite of myself I was affected by Robert having thought of and chosen to wear that tie.

I reached out and touched it lightly. He lifted a hand towards mine, and I knew it was his intention to wrap his fingers around my fingers. The way he'd always done before. We both withdrew at the same time. Those days were over. For now anyway.

'Shall we go?' I asked. He nodded.

Dad was waiting alone in the sitting room, as if unsure what to do. He glanced up as I put my head round the door. Robert had let him in when he'd arrived earlier, and Dad had quite obviously been shocked by his appearance and demeanour. He looked relieved when he saw Robert now, smartly dressed and reasonably composed, standing by my side.

'We're ready if you are, Dad,' I said.

If he'd noticed that Robert and I were not as we should be together, Dad had so far made no comment. But then, we'd just lost our only son and Dad his only grandson. Amidst the grief and despair of that one dreadful reality he was probably unlikely to have noticed anything much else that might be amiss.

'I thought you'd like some time on your own,' he said. Dad was not a big man and he seemed to have become smaller since I'd last seen him. He was in his mid-sixties, and the thin hair which barely covered his head had turned grey many years previously. His face also seemed grey that day. He too had loved Robbie dearly. Yet he could still be thoughtful and considerate. Which is more than I had been able to be in my behaviour towards him since Robbie's death.

Even then all I could manage was a brief 'Thanks'. Followed by: 'The funeral car is here.'

Gladys had arranged that too. I'd said I'd drive. There were only ever going to be the three of us setting off from Highrise, and I'd told her we didn't want any fuss or ceremony.

'You won't want to drive, though, you really won't feel able,' she'd said. 'Trust me, luvvie.'

I'd thought she'd been showing her bossy side again. But, of course, she'd turned out to be absolutely right. As our sad little threesome left Highrise on that terrible day, the day when Robbie was to be buried and reality could no longer be denied even for a second, I didn't feel as if I could have unlocked a car door and started its engine, let alone actually driven the thing.

Gladys was also right about the turnout.

The church was packed.

Dad, Robert and I walked in behind Robbie's flower-strewn wicker coffin. It had been made not far away by craftsmen on the Somerset Levels, the undertaker had told me.

I'd thought Robbie might have liked that, and that it would seem less grim than a wooden box. But I couldn't even look at his coffin. I knew if I did I would break down.

To me, the congregation was just a sea of faces upon which I could not properly focus, but I did become aware that there were a lot of young people in the church. Robbie's schoolmates and fellow swimmers, I assumed. Although it was obvious, I had not even thought of them being present.

Gladys had told me that there would be someone taking down names and I would be given a list of mourners so that I would know who'd attended.

'You'll not be able to take it in on the day,' she'd said.

At the time I hadn't given a damn. Now, even before the service began, I found that I really wanted to know who had

116

bothered to come out on this dreadful wet and windy November day to mourn my beautiful boy.

I began to think about him, which I had tried not to do all morning. The tears welled up behind my eyes. I felt myself stumble.

A strong arm grasped mine and gave me support. It was Robert. I turned and looked up at him. There was such anguish etched on his face.

'I loved him so much,' Robert whispered. 'And you, Marion. Whatever else you doubt, never ever doubt that.'

He grasped my arm a little tighter. For the first time since I had learned about his double identity I did not pull away. He was my man and Robbie's father. Whatever might come next, I told myself, on this day of all days, that was all that mattered. If I needed to cling to anyone, then it would be to Robert that I would cling. There was, after all, no one else.

The funeral itself was a blur. I was only vaguely aware of the hymns being sung. I didn't really listen at all to Gerald Ponsonby Smythe's address. After all, that man had nothing to do with my Robbie. He'd never even met him as far as I knew. But people told me later that the vicar had done Robbie proud, whatever that meant.

When we gathered at the graveside I could hold myself together no longer. The tears began to flow. I was aware that Dad was crying too, and that made me worse. When Robbie's body, in its quite flimsy-looking wicker casket, was lowered into the ground I broke down totally. I would have collapsed onto the mud and wet grass surrounding the newly dug grave had Robert not held on to me.

'Come on, girl, we'll get through this together,' he whispered in my ear. Just the way he'd always done whenever we'd had any kind of problem. But, of course, we'd never really had any bad problems before. This wasn't a problem. This was Armageddon.

I found myself holding on to Robert, my tears staining the strip of white shirt exposed where the raincoat he'd slipped on as we'd walked through the churchyard had fallen open. He seemed strong again, grateful, I supposed, to be allowed to look after me. Just as he had always done before, or at least as I'd thought he'd always done before.

We both threw clods of earth onto Robbie's coffin, me half carried by Robert to the edge of the grave. The rain still poured from a leaden sky, swirling around the churchyard, and a good strong gust of Dartmoor wind hit me full in the face as we moved forward. My hat was blown from my head and would probably have landed in Robbie's grave had not a young man I vaguely registered to be one of the village lads leapt forward like a limited-overs cricketer and taken a smart catch.

Robert took the hat from the boy and helped me replace it, then he led me away to the far end of the graveyard, dabbed at my eyes with his hanky, told me again how much he loved me, and asked me if I was sure I wanted to go to the 'do' at the pub.

'It's your choice. If you want us to go straight home that's fine with me,' he said.

I thought about how determined I'd been that Robbie should have a good send-off and be laid to rest in the right place. I had Gladys Ponsonby Smythe to thank for making that happen, and even at that moment my innate good manners kicked in and I felt I shouldn't let her down. Nor the 'load of people' she'd promised, who had indeed turned up. They'd come to pay their respects to Robbie. Now I had to show my respect for them. He would have wanted that. He'd been a polite boy. We'd brought him up that way.

I blew my nose loudly.

'I want to go,' I said. 'I can't explain, really, but I do.'

'Fine,' he said. 'We'll go then. And I shall be by your side, right through it, and ready to take you away just when you want.'

I nodded. It felt good, even on this day, or maybe particularly on this day, to lean on Robert again, to let him take over.

The funeral car took us to the Lamb and Flag. Robert held my hand as we drove through the village, and I didn't stop him from doing so. Just this day at least, I told myself, just this day it had to be right that we, Robbie's parents, were together, were united. Outside the shop a farmer, or perhaps a farm worker, I didn't even know by sight, was climbing down from a tractor connected to a trailer full of ewes. He removed his cloth cap as we passed and bowed his head. I was touched. He was just a young man. But Blackstone was that sort of place, as were its people: old-fashioned and steeped in the traditions and ways of some bygone age.

The pub was full of people I didn't know, or knew only vaguely, coming up to me and offering their condolences. I peered around me, remembering suddenly that I hadn't seen Bella at the church. I switched on my phone. There was a text from her waiting for me: *So sorry, Marion. Daughter fallen off bike. Concussion and prob broken arm. Taking 2 hospital. Sorry not to be with u. Send love and thoughts. X.*

I found that I was curiously disappointed and was about to tell Robert, but he was talking to the landlord about whether or not extra food should be provided as even more people than Gladys had expected had turned up. In any case he wouldn't have been interested.

He was certainly attentive to me, though. Throughout the afternoon, just as he'd promised, Robert barely left my side.

And Gladys continued to be a tower of strength, right from the moment she'd greeted us at the pub door to say she'd reserved a little corner table so that we had somewhere to sit where we hopefully wouldn't be too overwhelmed by the gathered throng.

I introduced her to Dad, then remembered she and Robert didn't know each other either and introduced them too.

'Oh, so this is your husband,' she responded quickly. 'We have met, of course.'

I glanced at Robert. Had he turned even paler than usual again, or was that my imagination?

'Perhaps, but just in passing,' he said.

I studied Gladys. Was she looking puzzled? Or was that my imagination too?

I was considering questioning her when a young woman, who looked as if she had only recently stopped crying, approached us.

'I just wanted to introduce myself,' she said. 'I'm Sue Shaw . . . Robbie and I, uh . . .' She hesitated. 'I . . . we swam together.'

Immediately I forgot all about Robert and Gladys. After all, this was a small village and there could have been many innocent occasions when Robert might have encountered the vicar's wife, even though he had always been reluctant to leave the house any more than he had to.

I stared hard at the pretty blonde standing before me. Could this be Sue S., the girl Robert had written about in his diary? The one he had wanted to take to his friend's birthday party. The one he'd described as 'well fit'. I felt sure it must be her. But I didn't want to admit that I'd been reading Robbie's diary. Not even after his death.

So I merely said, 'Hello,' and 'Thank you for coming.'

'Yes, thank you for coming,' repeated Robert without a lot of interest. But then, he had not read Robbie's diary.

'I'm so sorry . . .' she told me, half turning away. Then she turned back, a determined look on her face, as if she had made a decision.

'I just wanted to tell you, I don't think you know, I was Robbie's girlfriend,' she blurted out.

'I didn't know,' I said.

She blushed.

'He was going to tell you,' she said quickly. 'We'd only been going out for a few weeks. He said he was going to tell you and he wanted me to meet you. And his dad . . .'

'Girlfriend, but he was only fifteen . . .' began Robert.

'Well, I never,' said Dad.

'Don't,' I said, sensing that Sue Shaw was already uneasy.

I touched her arm. I could find no words. So this had been Robbie's girlfriend. I wondered what the term meant for them. Had they been lovers? She looked so young and fresh-faced. I found myself rather hoping that they had been lovers. That my son had at least known the joy of sex with someone he cared for before he had died, even though he had been so very young.

Sue Shaw began speaking again, oblivious it seemed to Robert's and Dad's interruptions.

'He was always talking about you, you know,' she continued. 'Some of the boys don't even mention their parents. They think it's soft. But Robbie did. He was so happy, you see, at home and everything . . .'

She stopped as if realizing what she was saying.

'So you thought he was happy too?' I asked.

'Of course he was happy,' said Robert.

I ignored him. So did Sue Shaw. She nodded.

'But do you know anything, anything at all, that might have made him do . . .' I paused. 'Do what he did?'

She shook her head. 'No,' she said quickly. 'Of course not.'

'Of course not,' I repeated.

Her colour deepened, and she began to back off again.

'It's my dad, I have to go, he doesn't know I'm here . . . he didn't approve, you know, of Robbie and me . . .'

I put a restraining hand on her arm.

'You mean he knew about you two?'

Her face was quite red by then.

'Yes, well no, not until . . . until just before Robbie died. I have to go. He'll kill me.'

She seemed to realize she'd made an inappropriate re-mark. 'I mean . . . I mean, he wouldn't approve,' she tailed off lamely.

I tried to reassure her with an attempt at a smile. Then I asked if she'd be kind enough to give me her phone number.

'I would just like to talk about Robbie sometime,' I said. 'That's all.'

She nodded and rattled off the number, but I could tell that my request had made her even more uncomfortable. She scur-ried off in the direction of the exit. I found a pen and an old petrol receipt in the front pocket of my handbag and scribbled the number down, hoping my short-term memory remained as good as it always had been.

Most of the rest of the time at the Lamb and Flag was a blur pretty much like the funeral itself. I stood up to thank Gerald Ponsonby Smythe and managed to knock red wine over Robert's pristine shirt. I'd cried all over it and then thrown wine at it. It was as if I were determined to destroy it.

He said not to worry, he'd give it a scrub down in the Gents, and left my side for the first time since we'd arrived at the pub.

Dad had gone off wandering around the bar looking at the old Dartmoor prints which hung from almost every wall. Just for something to do, I imagined. Gladys was still with me. And, even though I'd told myself it was of absolutely no consequence, I continued to wonder how she and Robert had met. So I asked her. As casually as I could manage.

'I'm afraid I know he's never been to church, that's for sure,' I said, with another attempt at what passed for a smile.

'Oh no, not this church anyway. It wasn't here, not in Blackstone,' she replied. 'Curiously enough, I've never seen your husband in the village, and I do get about a bit, as you're probably aware.'

Not as curious as you might imagine, I thought.

'So?' I prompted.

'Oh, it was some years ago when Gerry and I had an Exeter parish. He used to sing in the choir.'

I felt as if an ice-cold hand had been placed on the back of my neck, the touch of freezing fingers seemed to be running down my spine.

Robert did have a fine baritone singing voice. The woman must be mistaken, though. Surely. I tried to make myself believe that. And to make her believe it too.

'He used to sing in a church choir?' I queried. 'But he hates religion. Right through our married life he's never gone near a church even for a wedding or something if he could help it. I'm sorry. I don't mean to be rude, and you've been so helpful. But that's the truth.'

She looked doubtful.

'Well, I'm pretty sure it was him, although, of course, I didn't really know him. You see, it was . . .' She stopped abruptly as if about to say something she'd thought better of. 'No, well, I'm sure you're right.'

123

'He'd lived in Scotland right up until just before we met,' I said.

'I see.' Gladys definitely looked puzzled now. 'I've usually got a good memory for faces, but—'

'What about names?' I interrupted, suddenly not quite so sure of myself after all.

'Names?' she queried.

'Yes, what was his name?'

She hesitated for a moment.

'Well, obviously, if it was your husband, his name was Robert Anderson, I assume.'

'But do you remember that?'

Now she looked plain bewildered.

'Well, I'm not sure, I hadn't thought . . .'

She paused again. I waited a moment before deciding to take the plunge. 'Or could it have been Rob Anderton?'

'Do you know, I think that might have been the name . . .' There was yet another pause. 'No. How silly of me. That makes no sense. It must have been Robert Anderson, if it was him at all. And it was a very long time ago. Perhaps I've got the whole thing mixed up. Do you know, I used to trust my own memory with anything, chuck, but nowadays, I don't know, it's not what it was, that's for certain . . .'

Her voice was just a babble in the background. I felt sick.

I could see Robert walking across the bar towards me. His shirt front pink now rather than red.

I'd almost let him in again. It had been a relief on such a day to lean on him, to feel his love for me without drawing back from it. I think I might have subconsciously more or less decided to let the doubts and uncertainty go. Or at least to live with them. After all, Robert was still the same man. What did a name matter? And he was all I had. Now the doubt and uncertainty had become totally overwhelming again. I feared what Gladys's innocent remark might really mean.

'I've done my best,' he remarked ruefully, screwing up his face in mock embarrassment almost like the old Robert. He came very close to me and rested one hand on my shoulder, again almost the old Robert, the old proprietorial Robert.

I could tell that he thought he had got me back, or at least was in the process of getting me back. One thing I believed totally was that, like me, he would never get over Robbie's death. But suddenly he did seem to be coping. He even had a bit of a smile on his face as he looked fondly down at me.

He didn't know that I not only wanted to wipe that smile off, I wanted to slap him. Hard. Just as I had when I'd first learned of his deception.

And, of course, I so feared there was more to come. Gladys had made me remember that. What else had he not told me in spite of his promises? What other lies might yet be revealed?

nine

I didn't confront Robert straight away. Instead I just told him I'd had quite enough of the Lamb and Flag and all the doubtless well-meaning mourners who were filling it. The 'friends' I hadn't known any of us had.

'I'd like to go home as soon as possible,' I said. 'Don't forget Dad needs to pick up his car to drive back to Hartland.'

The funeral car was no longer at our disposal, but Gladys overheard and offered at once to take us back to Highrise.

As usual she chattered non-stop. And by leaving Robert and occasionally my father to make any necessary responses in the few gaps, I was able to shut my eyes, lean back in my seat and retreat into my own head. That was not, however, a happy place.

Back at Highrise, Gladys dropped us off without, thankfully, giving any indication that she expected to be invited in. Robert and I went through the rather stilted motions of sitting down in the kitchen and sharing a pot of tea with Dad. None of us had any conversation. It seemed like for ever before Dad stood up to leave, and I remember thinking he was probably still angling to stay the night. But I didn't offer. I just couldn't.

I kissed him goodbye, aware that his cheeks were damp with tears again, and we waved him somewhat shabbily on his way.

Even then I still did not trust myself to confront Robert with my new suspicions. Or maybe I just didn't have the energy.

Robert busied himself making even more tea.

I glanced up at the clock on the wall. It was only just gone 8 p.m. Too early for bed? I didn't care. I so wanted the day to end.

'I think I drank too much red wine,' I told Robert. 'I just need to lie down.'

'Of course,' he said. 'Would you like me to bring you anything up? Another cup of tea? Something to eat?'

I shook my head. At the pub I had eaten some of the food provided – a couple of sausage rolls and several sandwiches. I'd been on a kind of autopilot. And eating had given me something to do.

'Only some water, that would be good,' I said over my shoulder as I made my way up the stairs.

I hesitated outside the room which had been mine and Robert's for so long. I thought for a moment about the big comfortable bed and the goose-down pillows. Earlier in the day I'd thought I might return there that night. But, full of all that fresh doubt following Gladys's casual remarks, I couldn't face it.

I headed for the guest room again. My fluffy dressing gown hung behind the door. I undressed, put it on, and climbed into bed. I would have loved to have fallen into a long, deep sleep but I just knew that wasn't going to happen. However, when I heard Robert's footsteps on the stairs, with a pause outside the master bedroom while he perhaps checked if I'd relented and was inside, then further approaching footsteps followed by the sound of the guest-room door opening, I made sure that my eyes were tightly closed.

There was a kind of clinking noise which I knew must be

him placing a jug of water and a glass on the bedside table, followed by footsteps and the sound of the door closing behind him.

Only then did I open my eyes. I sat up in bed, poured myself a glass of water and drank gratefully. The water at Highrise came from our own well. It was cool and fresh and unadulterated by chemicals. Even at that moment it tasted great.

I lay back on the pillows and tried to rest, to regain my strength, and I had no idea, really, how long I lay like that, half awake, half dozing, submerged in my own misery and distress.

I must have been dozing when Robert returned. I didn't even hear him come through the door. I opened my eyes automatically, having become suddenly aware of another presence. And there he was standing looking down at me, concerned and kind.

'I thought you might like something now,' he said. He gestured to the bedside table upon which stood a steaming mug and a plate of shortbread biscuits. I could smell the unmistakable aroma of freshly made hot chocolate.

'W-what time is it?' I asked.

'A few minutes before ten,' he said. 'I thought I'd have an early night too.'

He reached to touch my shoulder. Only then did I take in that he was wearing his pyjamas.

'And I thought maybe you were ready for some company,' he said.

I jerked myself away from him.

'No, I am not,' I barked.

His face flushed.

'I didn't mean anything, I wasn't suggesting anything,' he said, stumbling over the words. 'Just somebody to hold on to.'

'No,' I said again, forcefully.

'I'm so sorry,' he said. 'I must have misread the signs. I

thought today I was giving you some comfort at last. That's all I want to do now . . .'

I sat up in bed, moving quickly and clumsily. I knocked against the bedside table. Hot chocolate spilled from the mug onto the pale oak surface.

'You were comforting me,' I said. 'Until I caught you out in another damned lie.'

'What do you mean?' he asked.

'You never told me you sang in a church choir, here in Devon. What the heck does that mean?'

'It doesn't mean anything,' he said. 'Because it's not true. I've never sung in a church choir anywhere. Not here, not in Scotland. Why would I? I hate religion. You know that.'

'The vicar's wife remembered you. You can't deny it. She told me all about it.'

'I can deny it,' he continued. 'Because it's not bloody well true. That woman's barmy, if you ask me. She's also an interfering old cow.'

It was his turn to sound angry now. I couldn't take any more.

'Oh, just go to bed, Robert,' I ordered him wearily. 'Anywhere you like, except here with me.'

I wriggled down into the bed again, turned over so that my back was towards him, pulled the duvet up around my neck and shut my eyes tight.

He did not persist. Without another word he left the room. Only when I heard the door shut behind him did I relax. And then the tears came again and just would not stop.

I must have fallen asleep at some stage. It was a bright morning and the sun was quite high in the sky when I woke. I checked my watch. It was gone nine. Much later than I would have expected.

I had a shower, put on the dressing gown again, picked up my funeral clothes and began to make my away across the landing to Robert's and my room in search of a pair of jeans and a sweater.

I could hear Robert's voice downstairs. He was on the phone. I didn't trust him any more. And I realized that I quite badly wanted to know who he was talking to and what he was saying without him being aware of my presence. I dropped my armful of yesterday's clothes on the landing floor and made my way as quietly as I could downstairs, avoiding the treads which I knew creaked.

Robert was in the kitchen. The door was open. I stood in the hall outside with my back pressed against the wall.

'Look, I just don't know when I can return,' I heard him say. 'It's far too early to decide. I can't leave my wife . . . Well, yes, thank you. If you could give me a couple of weeks before we talk again, that would be great. Really. I can't make any decisions right now. I just can't . . . No. Well, thank you anyway . . .'

He ended the call. I stepped into the room and spoke as if I knew nothing of his call, which had fairly obviously been to his employer.

'Who was that on the phone?'

'The Amaco personnel people,' he said. Surely speaking the truth for once, I thought nastily, even though it was a Saturday. But then, as PC Cox had remarked on the night of Robbie's death, this was the oil business. It didn't shut up shop for the weekend.

'They wanted to know when I could go back to work. I told them not for at least another two or three weeks—'

'I think you should go back straight away,' I said, interrupting. 'There's no point in moping around here. That won't help either of us. Just go. It'll be for the best.'

He looked surprised and hurt.

'Not yet, surely,' he said. 'I don't want to leave you on your own. Not yet.'

'I'll be all right,' I said. 'Call them back. Tell them you've changed your mind.'

He shook his head. 'No,' he began. 'It wouldn't be right—'

I interrupted him again. This time I screamed at him.

'Don't you understand, you lying bastard. I don't want you here. I want you to go. I want you to go anywhere, anywhere at all, and just leave me alone.'

I hadn't meant to fly out of control like that, but I couldn't stop myself.

He recoiled from me as if I had physically attacked him.

Which I was just a hair's breadth from doing.

Robert left for the North Sea less than forty-eight hours later, early on Monday morning, eleven days after our son had died. He hadn't argued at all after my near violent outburst. Instead he'd meekly called the Amaco people back and made the necessary arrangements to return to work as soon as possible.

He told me he'd managed to get a flight to Aberdeen from Exeter – sometimes it had to be Bristol from where the service was more frequent – and I drove him to the airport just as I always had. We'd only ever run one car as Robert was away so much and almost never wanted to go anywhere alone when he was at home.

We had little to say to each other on the hour or so drive, and he looked sad and beaten as he climbed out of the car and made his way to the terminal building. It occurred to me that I was suddenly the strong one. The decisive one. And that I'd never realized how weak the man I'd married could be, whatever his bloody name was.

As soon as I got home I called Gladys Ponsonby Smythe. I thanked her for all her help with the funeral arrangements and told her I'd never have got through it without her. Which was more or less the truth.

'Shall I pop over?' she offered at once. 'I could pick up one of Mrs Simmons's home-made cakes from the shop.'

I turned down the offer, a little too quickly probably, even though I knew only too well how delicious Mrs Simmons's cakes were.

'Robert and I need some time alone, just to be quiet together,' I fibbed by way of explanation. I was fairly sure that if I confessed that I was alone in the house a herd of Dartmoor ponies wouldn't have stopped her dropping everything and rushing to my rescue.

Gladys said she quite understood, and I was able to move on to the real reason I had called her.

'About Robert,' I began as casually as I could. 'You know when you said you thought he used to sing in the choir at your other church? I wondered how long ago it was, and if that would have been when he was with his first wife?'

Was there an almost imperceptible pause? I wasn't sure. But Gladys sounded clear enough when she did answer.

'Oh, Marion, luv, I feel such a fool,' she said. 'I don't suppose it was your Robert at all, chuck. After all, it was years and years ago. I couldn't tell you exactly how many, but Gerry and I have been in Blackstone over twelve years. The man I remembered must have looked then like Robert does now. Silly of me.'

'So you don't remember his wife?' I persisted.

'To be perfectly honest, I don't think I remember anything,

luvvie,' said Gladys, with a small snort of laughter. 'I got it all wrong, didn't I, and I have no idea what I thought I was doing sticking my oar in like that, and at your poor lad's funeral too. Typical, Gerry would say. I just hope you can forgive me, flower, that's all . . .'

She was prattling now, in true Gladys fashion, and absolutely determined to treat me to her full range of Northern endearments, it seemed. I knew I wasn't going to get any more sense from her, even assuming there was any to get. I let her voice wash over me until I could reasonably interject and end the conversation.

Afterwards I wondered if perhaps I had been wrong to attack Robert the way I had. If Gladys had made a genuine silly mistake, then I had not caught Robert out in another lie after all. But that was the terrible dilemma the two of us now shared. With even the slightest cause, would I ever again be able to stop myself becoming suspicious of him?

I also tried to call Sue Shaw. She didn't pick up. And I didn't somehow expect her to. Nor really did I expect her to respond to the message I left asking her to call me back for a chat, only a chat.

Then for the rest of that day, and most of several that followed, I just moped around the house, poking about among Robbie's things, periodically bursting into floods of tears. I ate and drank little, delving into the freezer only if I really needed food and not interested at all in the form it took. Any crockery and cutlery I did use was piled in the sink. I couldn't even be bothered to load the dishwasher. For the first time since we had moved in, Highrise looked grubby and uncared for, and I didn't give a damn.

Paracetamol were no longer helping at all with my sleeplessness. I visited my doctor to request some sleeping pills which he duly provided, prescribing zolpidem, apparently the UK's most popular sleeping aid, although I had never heard of it before. While I was there he insisted that I get my feet redressed. I'd neglected them totally since scalding them on the day of Robbie's death, but my wounds had stopped leaking and seemed to be healing OK, in spite of my lack of attention.

I answered the phone as infrequently and briefly as possible and then only to ensure that neither Gladys nor my dad nor Bella nor any other of my relatively small band of acquaintances descended upon me. I ignored Robert's calls and emails completely. I thought he deserved to suffer as I was suffering. The only time I left Highrise was when Florrie more or less forced me to take her for a walk, rubbing herself against my legs and whining pitifully.

Even with the aid of the zolpidem, I tossed and turned my way restlessly through most of each dark night, and endured each long day with lonely and harrowed anguish.

Then, six days after Robert had returned to work, on a particularly bright and beautiful Sunday morning, I decided I could take no more of it. I dug out my heavy-duty boots, put on extra thick socks to protect my feet, loaded Florrie into the back of the car, and drove up onto the moors past Okehampton Camp, the big army training centre where hundreds of cadets, including Royal Marines Commandos, are put through their paces every year. Fortunately no military manoeuvres were taking place and the track into the heart of Dartmoor, which cuts right through the camp's firing range, was open.

After a mile or so I parked. Only then did I wonder why I had bothered with the protective socks and why I had brought Florrie with me. Habit I supposed. But in view of what I was planning, both were irrelevancies.

I set off on foot, Florrie running circles around me, towards

Yes Tor, the second highest point on the moors, its peak more than two thousand feet above sea level. The air was cold and the sky impossibly clear. I could see for miles. Beyond that. Purple hills seemed to stretch to infinity. But not even Dartmoor at its best could lift my dismal mood nor alter my intention.

A life that had seemed so idyllic now appeared not to have been real at all. Robbie was dead. And I could see no future. Thinking of my son and how he would have loved to be up there with me on such a day, I climbed to the very top of Yes Tor, and stood trembling on its famous angular granite summit.

It seemed a very long time ago that I had stood in Robbie's bathroom contemplating a bottle of paracetamol while telling myself that it really was true that potential suicide cases should always wait until tomorrow. For me, there was no point any more in waiting till tomorrow. Every day was the same. Filled with total despair.

Florrie took off after a rabbit, winding, whirling and leaping her way through the heather and bracken at a speed that belied her age. I didn't call her back. I did not want her under my feet. I stepped forward to the edge of the top-most granite slab on the steepest side of the tor and prepared to jump. I could feel the sun and the wind burning my face with an unexpected intensity. It was as if all my senses and every nerve ending were more acutely tuned than they had ever been before in the whole of my life. And just as I was planning to end it.

A lone crow circled overhead, its grating *caw caw* quite deafening to me. The sun seemed blindingly bright. I shut my eyes against its glare and tried to force my body forward over the edge of the tor. But I couldn't get my legs to move. I wanted one more look at the world I was leaving behind. I opened my eyes again and, staring straight ahead over the purple peaks of

135

this place I so loved, made myself begin to shuffle towards the permanent oblivion I so sought.

It was then that I heard the voice. Clear as the day itself.

'No, Mum, no. Don't do it.'

It was Robbie's voice.

I threw my upper body back to safety just as gravity threatened to pull me irrevocably forward and down. I collapsed in a crumpled heap on the ground, and sobbed for England. I was a wreck. But I was still alive and I knew with absolute certainty at that moment that I intended to remain so.

I am not a fanciful woman. I do not believe in God or the devil. I do not believe in life after death or the supernatural. I knew even then that Robbie's voice was inside my own head. And only inside my head. It could be nowhere else.

None the less, his voice had been absolutely real to me. As was the message it had given.

No. Don't do it.

As far as I was concerned Robbie had spoken to me just as certainly as if he had been alive and standing by my side. I didn't fully understand it, but I knew I had experienced a road to Damascus moment from which there was no turning back.

Florrie bounded back towards me, panting, excited. She began to lick my hands and my face.

I pulled myself upright, called her to follow, and began the descent.

After a bit I turned and looked back up at Yes Tor. There is, on the side where I had positioned myself intending to leap, a short sheer drop from the very top, but by and large tors are not designed for suicide. I studied the terrain with a kind of detached interest. It would, I feared, have been far more likely that I would have just broken bits of me instead of killing myself. Suddenly the absurdity of it hit me. Along, I suppose, with the enormity of what I had so nearly done.

I began to laugh hysterically. Florrie trotted at my heels, looking at me curiously. An approaching couple walking a yellow Labrador, the only other people I had seen on the moor that morning, took a sharp turn onto another path. In order to avoid a woman who must appear to be quite mad, I suspected.

By the time I reached the car I had stopped laughing and felt more like crying again. But I still believed that something monumental had happened, and that I was going to be able to cope again soon. None the less, I had to return to a home I could barely stand being in.

Around mid-afternoon I forced myself to eat something. I tried to read and to watch TV. Both proved more or less beyond me. I remained determined that I would never again contemplate suicide, but the brief flash of optimism I had experienced in the car had been just that.

By bedtime I was preparing for another predominantly sleepless night. However, ironically, considering my purpose in going there, the sharp Dartmoor air seemed to have done me good. Or maybe I was just totally exhausted. But mercifully I fell into a deep sleep almost as soon as my head touched the pillows.

I was still using the guest room. Somehow I remained unable to return to the room Robert and I had shared. Florrie was in her bed in the kitchen. My gran had always taken her beloved Jack Russell to bed with her, but Florrie slept in the kitchen because Robert didn't believe in dogs being allowed in bedrooms and had convinced me I didn't either. After all, she did moult everywhere. Robbie and I had kept to the rule, whether Robert was away or not, without thinking about it, and it hadn't occurred to me to change the dog's sleeping arrangements. I had other things on my mind. In any case, that night I was out for the count.

It was perhaps because I had been deeply asleep at last that I woke so suddenly and with such a start. Something was wrong. I sat up in bed, shaking my head to try to clear the fog which filled it.

I'd been woken by something, and I didn't know what. Had it been Florrie barking? She wasn't barking now. Had there been some other noise?

I listened hard.

At first there was only silence and I began to wonder if I'd just been having a dream. I'd been taking sleeping pills after all.

Then I heard a scraping noise, like a chair being dragged across a floor. Still no sound from Florrie. My first instinct was that Robert had returned, and I very nearly called out his name. But then I stopped myself. If someone other than Robert had entered my house in the dead of night, I could put myself in danger by attracting attention.

Yet if there was an unknown intruder downstairs, I would have expected Florrie to bark. Or would I? She was such a soft, friendly creature, all over strangers usually. Any dog-savvy burglar who had brought her a meaty treat would probably have her rubbing lovingly against his legs in no time.

I switched on my bedside light, then wondered if that were such a good idea and switched it off again.

I climbed out of bed as quietly as possible, made my way out onto the landing and stood at the top of the stairs listening. There are always noises in an old house. Robert said Highrise was like a ship.

There was silence for so long I almost began to doubt myself.

Then I heard the distinctive creak caused by a footstep on the bottom stair. Then on the second stair.

I panicked, ran back into the bedroom, forgetting all about trying to be quiet, slammed the door behind me, and dialled 999 on my mobile.

The operator asked me if there was a lock on my bedroom door, which there wasn't. She then instructed me to stay as quiet as possible and wait for assistance. Whatever happened, I should not attempt to leave the room.

I sat on the edge of the bed with my ears pricked. I heard no further creaks on the stairs. Did that mean the intruder had retreated, perhaps even left the house while I was on the phone to the emergency services? Or had he or she climbed the rest of the stairs while I was distracted? Could someone be lurking outside my bedroom door right then?

I stood up and padded softly to the door, pressing my ear against it. Total silence. Upstairs and downstairs as far as I could make out. I thought about calling Florrie, but supposed that would not be very wise either. Fleetingly, I wondered if she was all right. You hear about burglars dispatching dogs that might cause them trouble. I decided not to dwell on that. In any case Florrie hadn't caused a human being any trouble in the whole of her life.

The police arrived in about forty-five minutes, which wasn't too bad when you considered how remote Highrise was. It felt like several days.

When I heard them knock, I opened the bedroom door cautiously. I could also hear Florrie barking in the kitchen, which was a relief. I made my way to that bit of the landing with a window overlooking the front of the house. The automatic security lights must have switched on as the police had arrived and I could see that a patrol car stood in the yard and two uniformed officers were at the door. I wondered if the lights had been activated earlier by the intruder. But in any case I would not have seen them from the bedroom I was using.

I went downstairs, unbolted, unlocked and opened the door, registering as I did so that it seemed unlikely the intruder had gained entry through it.

My first impression was how fresh-faced and young-looking the two officers were. I know it's a cliché but policemen really do get younger as you get older.

'Mrs Anderson?' queried the taller one.

I nodded. I realized for the first time that I was shaking. And it seemed just too difficult to speak.

'Don't worry,' he continued, his voice professionally reassuring. 'We'll check everything out for you. I'm Constable Jacobs and I just want you to stay here with Constable Bickerton, while I have a look round.' He gestured to the shorter officer who seemed to be wearing a cap that was a size or two too big for him, then he set off in the direction of the kitchen.

I found my voice. 'Our dog should be in there,' I called out.

'That's all right, I like dogs,' PC Jacobs called back.

'He does too, more than people if you ask me,' muttered PC Bickerton.

I glanced at him. Was he trying to make some kind of joke? Possibly not. It seemed PC Jacobs quickly made friends with Florrie. I didn't hear another peep from her.

Meanwhile Constable Bickerton busied himself with investigating the locks on the front door. He would have heard me turn the big old key and pull back the bolt.

With the door standing open he ran the bolt to and fro a couple of times and turned the key in its lock.

'Nothing has been tampered with here, I don't think,' he said. I nodded in agreement.

He also checked the gate at the side of the house, solid and about five feet high, which gave access to the back of Highrise and to the garden. We usually kept it locked at night, and it too seemed secure.

After a few minutes PC Jacobs returned.

'I've had a look in every room in the house, Mrs Anderson,' he said. 'If there has been an intruder, he's certainly not here any more. And so far I can't see any signs of any disturbance or of forced entry. But perhaps you'd have a walk around with us to make sure.'

I followed the two officers into the kitchen. They had both removed their caps. Jacobs was very dark, almost as dark as Robert, his hair slicked down and parted at the side like a 1950s schoolboy. Bickerton's head was covered only with closely shaven blond stubble. Perhaps that was why his cap seemed too big for him, I thought obliquely.

Florrie flew at me, wriggling her entire body around my legs. She was a picture of joy. Her tongue hung out of her mouth and she licked every bit of flesh she could find on my exposed legs and my hands. I did my best to calm her down.

'I've checked the back door and the windows in every room,' said PC Jacobs. 'But perhaps you'll make sure for us that every-thing is as it should be, as it was when you went upstairs to bed.'

I glanced around the kitchen. Nothing seemed to have been touched; everything did indeed seem to be as I'd left it. I turned the handle on the back door and pulled. It didn't budge. Still locked. I swung round to look at the hook on the wall by the fridge. The back door key still hung from it, just as it should.

I made my way to the sitting room, the police officers right behind me and Florrie running ahead. Once again it was the same story. Just as PC Jacobs had reported there was no sign of any disturbance to anything, and no sign of any windows having been tampered with.

Our state-of-the-art smart TV stood on the chest of drawers to the right of the inglenook fireplace. It was still there, and quite obviously no attempt had been made to move it. My iPad was on the granite-topped coffee table. I saw that PC Bickerton was also looking at the iPad. I knew what he was thinking. Surely no self-respecting burglar would leave that behind?

We moved into the dining room. Again, nothing seemed to have been touched, and certainly nothing seemed to be missing.

Upstairs it was the same story.

I felt my heart sinking. I didn't want there to have been an intruder in my house, of course, but I feared I knew only too well what both police officers were thinking. And I wasn't wrong.

'Is it possible you could have been mistaken, Mrs Anderson?' asked PC Jacobs eventually. 'Are you sure you heard someone in the house?'

'Yes I did and no I wasn't mistaken,' I responded, quite forcefully.

'But wouldn't your dog have seen an intruder off?'

'I shouldn't think so for one moment,' I said. 'You must have learned already, PC Jacobs, what a softy she is, even with strangers.'

'She did bark when we arrived, though.'

'Yes, and I think she did when the intruder arrived. I think that's what woke me. But you'd only have to make a fuss of her, or give her a treat, and she'd soon quieten down and be all over you.'

'So,' concluded PC Bickerton. 'You think the dog's barking may have woken you, but you didn't hear her bark at all after you were properly awake, is that correct?'

I shook my head lamely.

The PC coughed slightly, as if embarrassed.

'Look, we know you must be going through a very stressful time, Mrs Anderson. It is quite understandable that you would be on edge and that you might think—'

'I didn't think anything, Constable Bickerton,' I said. 'There was someone in my house. I heard him, or her, moving around. Quite definitely. And what do you mean about me going through a stressful time? What do you know about any of that?'

PC Bickerton coughed again. 'It is a matter of record that your son has just died under extremely distressing circumstances. There was, after all, a police investigation . . .' he began.

'Call that an investigation?' I snapped.

'Look, Mrs Anderson, you are clearly overwrought—'

I interrupted him again. I realized I had to pull myself together and fast or I would probably never get any help from the police ever again, although little help they'd been so far.

'Just let me have a proper look around, will you?' I asked. 'I think I'm in shock. I may have missed something.'

'Of course,' said PC Bickerton patiently.

I went through the bedrooms, opening all the wardrobe doors and the drawers, still without noticing anything amiss, and then downstairs to the little room next to the kitchen which we used as a study. The computer Robert and I shared stood untouched on the desk. I opened the top left-hand drawer of the desk first, rummaged around in it a bit, checked quickly through the others, then back to the top one again.

'My iPod is missing,' I said triumphantly.

'Are you sure?' asked PC Bickerton.

'Quite sure,' I said. 'I always keep it in the top drawer of this desk. It's gone.'

'iPods are so small, couldn't you have misplaced it?'

'Definitely not. It's been taken.'

'But why would a burglar take an iPod from a drawer and leave behind an iPad clearly visible on a table?' asked PC Jacobs, his voice a little sharper than PC Bickerton's.

I felt the colour rise in my cheeks. I had no answer and I didn't try to give one. Instead I turned my attention to the sitting room. I stood in the doorway just looking around me, trying to calm myself down in order to make sure I didn't miss anything.

Then I did remember something. I thought it through before I spoke. Yes. I was sure of it. Robbie's camcorder had stood on the sideboard, just where he'd left it, ever since his death. I'd not had the heart to move it, somehow. It too was missing.

I told the two officers that.

They did not look impressed.

'Are you sure your son mightn't have put it somewhere else?' asked PC Jacobs.

'Constable, it's been there on the sideboard ever since Robbie died.'

'Well, could you have moved it, put it somewhere you don't recall?'

I closed my eyes and opened them again. They really did think I'd lost the plot.

'I haven't been able to touch it,' I said. 'Have you any idea what it is like to lose your only child?'

PC Jacobs stared straight ahead, not attempting to respond. PC Bickerton, shuffling uneasily from foot to foot, shook his head slightly.

I stopped, realizing I was only making things worse, confirming the impression they already had of me as a middle-aged mother overcome with grief who had no idea what she was doing, nor what was happening to her.

'Look, I would remember if I'd moved it,' I said, making my voice as calm as I could.

'Of course you would, Mrs Anderson,' said PC Jacobs soothingly. Or was there a note of carefully veiled sarcasm there somewhere? I wondered.

He rather pointedly took a note of the items I had said were missing, laboriously naming them aloud as he wrote them down.

'Caaam-corder, iPooood.'

I watched in silence.

'I think we've done all we can for the moment,' said PC Jacobs, when he'd finished his note-taking. 'It's curious that there is no sign of any break-in. And your front door was still bolted on the inside when we arrived, wasn't it?'

I agreed that it was.

'Not the back door, though,' I said.

'But it was securely locked,' said PC Jacobs.

'And so was the garden gate,' interjected Bickerton.

'Well, you could climb over that,' I said.

Bickerton half smiled. 'Yes, but not without some difficulty and a deal of noise, I shouldn't think,' he said.

'Does anyone else have keys to your property, Mrs Anderson?' asked PC Jacobs.

I shook my head. 'Only my husband, and he's on an oil rig in the North Sea.'

PC Jacobs looked even more sceptical. PC Bickerton seemed to be trying hard to be understanding and behave appropriately, but was not succeeding very well. I was pretty sure both officers genuinely sympathized with my predicament. They also without doubt considered me, that night at any rate, to be neurotic and unreliable. I felt quite numb with humiliation and frustration.

'Well, perhaps you should change your locks just to be on the safe side,' said PC Bickerton.

I nodded. All I wanted now was for the two officers to go and leave me alone.

'To put your mind at rest and to make absolutely sure, we'll take a look round the yard and your outbuildings on our way out,' PC Bickerton continued. 'And if you have any further cause for concern, do feel free to call again.'

It was my turn to look at him as if I thought he was quite mad.

At that moment I felt I would rather take my chances with a mad axe-man at large in my bedroom than ever again call the Devon and Cornwall Constabulary.

ten

It was several minutes more before they actually left my property. I watched the tail lights of the patrol car fade as it proceeded up the lane, the two officers inside extremely pleased, I suspected, to be leaving the madwoman behind.

I checked the time on the hall clock. It was nearly five. No point in going back to bed. In any case there was absolutely no chance of my getting back to sleep.

First of all I walked all round the house again, scrutinizing each room, just in case there was anything else missing that I hadn't noticed before, and to check if, upon closer examination, I could see any signs of disturbance. There wasn't and I couldn't.

Florrie followed me eagerly. We ended up in the kitchen. I beefed up the Aga, made myself a cup of tea and pulled the old leather armchair closer to the stove, relishing the warmth.

Florrie lay half across my feet. I chastised her mildly for being such a useless dog. But was she really that useless or had she known and loved the intruder? That made me start to really think. To ask myself more questions.

Was I absolutely sure that I had heard someone downstairs? Answer: yes.

Could I possibly have been mistaken? Could the police be right about me? Could I have turned into the madwoman, deluded by grief, they obviously thought me to be. Answer: no, no and no.

In that case who could possibly have been in the house? Who could have effected entry without leaving any telltale signs? Who had keys? Who would Florrie welcome most into the house apart from me?

The answer to all of those questions seemed to be Robert. But he was at work on a North Sea oil rig. And this time I knew which one because I'd asked him, and made a mental note of it. But was he and did I?

I now knew that my husband was a very convincing liar. Just because he'd told me he was returning to Jocelyn did not necessarily mean that was the case.

I was still shaky and I had a headache. I needed to calm down and sort out my muddled thoughts. I switched on the TV to distract myself, hopping from channel to channel and not staying tuned to any of them long enough to really take in what they were broadcasting. Nothing could distract me. I switched the thing off.

My mind was whizzing around in circles, but I always reached the same conclusion.

The intruder had to be Robert. Surely. I had no idea why he would pretend, knowing that I was now aware of his long-time subterfuge, to be on a North Sea platform when he wasn't. And I had no idea why he would turn up surreptitiously in the middle of the night, at what was still his own home after all, and apparently take two such disparate articles away with him. The camcorder, yes, I supposed. It had a lot of footage of Robbie and me, in happier times, and even some of Robert too. I hadn't been able to bear to look at it. Not yet anyway, but I could understand Robert wanting it and maybe just picking it up when he saw it lying on the sideboard, not least because he had always so disliked being featured on any kind of film. And now I knew why that had been, too. But why on earth would he want my iPod? He had one of his own. He always said it was music that kept him sane on the rigs, particularly when the weather kicked up and the men were confined to their quarters.

I wondered if either of us was sane any more.

Could Robert have been trying to frighten me? Surely the one thing I still believed about my husband was that he loved me, and had never deliberately set out to hurt me.

But I could not think who else would have broken into my house and behaved so strangely. Indeed, I could not think who else would have been able to. After all, there was no sign of a break-in and, as I'd told the police, nobody but Robert and I had keys.

I tried to think logically. First of all I needed to ascertain for certain whether or not Robert was in the North Sea.

That shouldn't be difficult, but it would be simplest to wait until nine o'clock or thereabouts, and time passed very slowly. Almost as the grandfather clock struck in the hall I dialled the direct line of Amaco's human resources department in Aberdeen.

I put on a Scottish accent just in case I ended up speaking to someone I had spoken to before, and told the young man who answered that I was Rob Anderton's wife and that my husband had recently been home on compassionate leave following the death of our son. The young man seemed at least vaguely familiar with what had happened and expressed his condolences.

'Look. I need to speak to my husband urgently. Can you help? Please. I'm desperate.' As I did the first time I called, I allowed a note of hysteria to creep into my voice. Once again, given the circumstances, that wasn't difficult.

The young man responded almost without hesitation. 'Yes, of course, Mrs Anderton. I can patch you through on our VoIP line directly to Jocelyn. It isn't usual company policy, but under these tragic circumstances I'm sure we can bend the rules.'

I thanked him and waited.

After a minute or two another, older male voice, just a bit fainter, came on the line.

'Hello, Mrs Anderton, you're through to the manager's office on Jocelyn. We've sent someone to fetch your husband. It shouldn't take long. Just hold on.'

I held on. Until eventually I heard Robert's voice. 'Darling, what is it? Are you all right? Has something else happened?'

I didn't reply. Instead I hung up on him. I still had no wish to speak to the man. But now I knew that he was on Jocelyn for certain. As far as that was concerned he had been telling the truth. Or his version of it. And certainly he could not have been the intruder.

I made myself more tea. This was crazy. Maybe the police were right after all. Had I been having a nightmare, and had the noises I was so certain that I'd heard downstairs just been part of it?

Yet I was still sure of myself, really, and quite sure about the disappearance of my iPod and Robbie's camcorder. But I could make absolutely no sense of the events of the night before, and certainly nobody else was going to believe me.

My mobile rang then, and I saw Robert's Skype number flash up. I let the call go to 121, but I did listen to his message: 'Marion, you must tell me what's going on. Why did you call me here through the office? And why didn't you speak to me? If you don't pick up, I shall come home.'

That's what I'd been afraid of. Whatever happened, I couldn't face that. I hurried to the study, jacked up our computer and used Skype to call him back. He was waiting online as I'd expected him to be. He answered very quickly.

'It's OK, I just wanted to know exactly where you were,' I told him without prevarication.

'You mean, you were checking up on me?' He had the nerve to sound rather indignant.

'I suppose I was, yes. And can you blame me?'

He changed his tone at once.

'No, I suppose I can't, can I? But, look, I do so worry about you. I want to put everything right. I could easily get more leave again, you know—'

'No, Robert, let's just try to do what we normally do. We're used to time apart. Let's do what we're used to. And maybe we can get through this somehow.'

'Do you really think so?'

'Yes, of course, yes.'

There had been such hope in his voice that I felt almost guilty when I so easily lied in my reply. But all that mattered really was keeping him at bay. I knew I couldn't cope with having him home, and I certainly couldn't cope with how he would react if he knew about the night-time intruder.

After I'd extricated myself from the call I did something I'd been meaning to do ever since Robert had confessed to also being Rob Anderton. I searched the house from top to bottom looking for any paperwork in the name of Anderton, or any reference at all to a Rob Anderton, or to a lottery win or a bank account showing an appropriate balance. I found absolutely nothing. Robert had covered his tracks well, it seemed. But then, he had been my husband, if not absolutely legally, for sixteen years without ever raising my suspicions.

Frustrated and fed up, I made a snap decision. If I was going to hang on to what remained of my sanity, I had to give myself something else to think about other than the terrible chain of events that had engulfed me.

I called the headmistress's office at Okehampton College and when I was put through to Mrs Rowlands told her I was ready to come back to work.

She expressed concern and mild surprise, asking: 'Are you quite sure?'

But when I said I was, I thought I caught a sigh of relief.

'We certainly need you,' she continued. 'It's black Monday here. Some sort of autumn flu bug seems to have hit the staffroom. I have three people off sick today, including our new, regular part time English teacher. I don't suppose you could work every morning for a bit?'

'I certainly can,' I replied. And I felt mildly cheered for the first time since Robbie's death.

It was always good to feel needed. And I had to do something. I'd spent enough time sitting around an empty house all day torturing myself.

'Can you start tomorrow?' Mrs Rowlands asked.

'I certainly can,' I repeated.

Later that afternoon I briefly called everyone I knew – that small list again: my dad, Gladys, Bella, the Farleys – to tell them about my return to teaching. I hoped it might stop them fussing over me and, most of all, lessen the danger of any of them turning up on my doorstep uninvited. My calls to Dad and Gladys were both diverted to answer services, which suited me fine. I knew it was wrong of me in view of Dad being Dad and Gladys having been so kind, but I didn't really want to talk to either of them. Ellen, Tom's wife, answered the Farley phone, and I kept that call as short as I politely could. Bella also answered her mobile straight away. But it was she, after welcoming my news, who cut the call short.

'We're just walking back from school, had to go to one of those parent–teacher meetings,' she said. 'But why don't we try to get together next weekend? Take the dogs to the beach perhaps? And if there's anything I can do to help . . .'

I then emailed Robert for the same reason. I was still afraid that he might take emergency leave again, and if he knew I was back at work, full-time in fact, and apparently doing my best to return to normality, he would hopefully be less likely to do so.

Of course, nothing could take my mind off losing Robbie. Even though there can be few activities more diverting than trying to ram the wonders of English literature into the wandering minds of a class of thirteen-year-olds. However, Robbie's presence and the grim reality of his death were with me all the time.

One of my pupils, who I knew lived on the outskirts of Okehampton, was called Conor Shaw, and even though Shaw was not an uncommon name it seemed quite natural for me to ask if he was related to Sue Shaw.

'She's my sister, miss,' said the boy.

'But she goes to Kelly,' I blurted out stupidly, already knowing the response I would provoke. Like us, I didn't expect the Shaws would have been able to pay the full fee for a place at Kelly, and certainly not for two children.

'Got a swimming scholarship didn't she, like your Robbie,' he said, then coloured up. 'Sorry, miss, I didn't mean to . . .'

They all knew so much more about my family now, with Robbie having died in such a public way, his bright young face all over the papers, than they ever had before.

'That's all right,' I said. 'It's fine, Conor.'

It wasn't, of course, and never would be. But after a couple of days back at school I knew I was beginning to function almost normally again. You didn't get much choice when you were teaching. And I was well aware I wasn't properly up to speed, my previous regular one day a week having kept me only barely in touch with the curriculum, so I had to work all the harder.

Small things still threw me. I was just arriving at the beginning of my third morning back when I saw Conor Shaw emerge from an elderly Range Rover. The driver was a red-headed man I assumed must be his father, his and Sue's. I approached the vehicle, and the man wound down his window.

'Hi,' I said. 'I'm Marion Anderson, Conor's English teacher.'

The man smiled a greeting. 'Michael Shaw, his dad,' he responded easily.

'I'm also Robbie Anderson's mum,' I said.

The smile faded at once.

'Pleased to meet you,' said Michael Shaw, sounding and looking anything but. 'Unfortunately I'm in a hurry. Must go, I'm afraid.'

With that he started the engine of the Range Rover, slammed his foot on the accelerator, and took off at a considerably greater speed than was ever encouraged outside Okehampton College.

I'd only been able to see Michael Shaw through his car window. He had a broad, quite highly coloured face and looked as if he would be a big man when stood up. I remember what Sue Shaw had said on the day of the funeral. 'Dad will kill me.'

I wondered, watching the dust settle after his sudden departure in the big four-wheel-drive, if the man had a temper. And if so, just how bad it was.

I thought I would like to at least try to talk to both Michael Shaw and his daughter again one day soon. But not yet.

I still did not believe my son had killed himself, and I still wanted to find out the whole truth about his death. I also doubted that I yet knew the whole truth about the husband who had deceived me for so long.

But I'd put all of that almost deliberately on hold by returning to teaching. I felt that I needed to heal myself before I could proceed further with anything else. And my wounds were deep.

However, by the end of the working week, and of my fourth day back at Okehampton College, I felt pleasantly weary and certainly more in control than I had since Robbie's death. I'd stayed on in Okehampton for a Friday pub lunch with a couple of the other teachers, and almost enjoyed myself. On the way home I called Bella to see if she would like to set a time for that dog walk she had suggested over the coming weekend. There was no reply so I surprised myself somewhat by leaving a message which, while far from cheery, was at least fairly bright and positive.

But this very slightly better frame of mind was not to last for long. I arrived at Highrise to find Florrie running loose in the yard and the front door standing wide open.

Hesitantly, I approached the old house. My heart felt like Big Ben booming away within my chest. I was full of foreboding, but I just had to step inside.

The grandfather clock Robert had always been so proud of lay on its side on the flagstoned floor in the hall. Its lovely glass face had been smashed and its mechanism, its core, ripped from its casing.

The sitting-room door was open and I could see that the chairs and settees had been turned on their sides and the TV screen smashed. There was also a horrible smell in the house. It was all too familiar. The same smell which had greeted me when I'd found Robbie's body. The sour stench of human excrement.

I took a step back outside again. I could not enter any further. Not alone. I was afraid of what other terrible damage I might discover. But more than that, I was afraid of who might still be there.

I called the police at once on my mobile. I'd told myself I'd never trouble the Devon and Cornwall Constabulary again. This was different. I had no choice. And in any case, this time they could hardly conclude that I'd imagined what had happened, surely.

I loaded Florrie into the back of the car to keep her out of the way, and then sat in the vehicle myself, waiting, in a kind of trance, until a police patrol car arrived. The two uniformed officers who stepped out of it were regrettably familiar. They were the same young men who had been sent round when I'd reported my night-time intruder the previous Sunday.

Apparently I was on their beat.

It was the same routine too. PC Bickerton waited with me outside Highrise while PC Jacobs checked the place out. This time, though, it was several minutes before he returned, and when he did he looked shocked.

'Mrs Anderson, you may not want to go back into your house today,' he began. 'It's a bit of a mess. Is there anyone you can stay with? Anywhere we can take you?'

I shook my head vehemently. 'No,' I said. 'This is my home, I want to see what's happened to it.'

He hesitated just for a second. 'Of course,' he said. 'But you'd better prepare yourself. It's not very nice, not very nice at all.'

We walked up the steps to the front door together. PC Bickerton checked the lock and the bolt, just as he had before.

'Nothing wrong here,' he said. 'No sign of forced entry at all at the front. What about the windows and the back door?

Did you notice any signs of tampering when you were inside, Jim?'

Jacobs shook his head.

Bickerton leaned forward, studying the lock on the front door more closely.

'Doesn't look like you've had this changed, Mrs Anderson,' he remarked. 'Nor the other two, at the back and on the garden gate, I suppose?'

I agreed that I hadn't had any of the three locks replaced. I saw the two officers exchange glances.

'Bit surprised you didn't do so after the other night,' Bickerton continued quite casually.

I supposed that was surprising. And I couldn't explain it really. Except that after I'd ascertained that Robert really was in the North Sea and made the decision to start teaching again I'd just tried to put everything else out of my mind. Maybe even to make myself believe I had imagined that intruder. Crazily, perhaps, I hadn't even seriously considered any kind of repetition.

I pushed past PC Bickerton into the hall. Again, the first thing I saw was the poor broken clock.

I paused and turned to face the policemen.

'You're sure there . . . there's nobody i-in there, are you?' I asked falteringly.

PC Jacobs gave a little tight-lipped smile he presumably thought was reassuring. 'Of course I'm sure,' he said.

Highrise was a wreck. Every room had been rubbished. The sitting room, in spite of the human excrement which had been smeared over the soft furnishings, the carpet, and the walls, was not the worst. Robbie's room, at the top of the house, was the most affected. All his beautiful oak furniture had been attacked with an axe. The desk he and his father had been so proud of was little more than firewood.

In the kitchen, just about every piece of crockery I possessed had been smashed. And all my glasses. The best stuff, displayed on a Welsh dresser, had been swept onto the flagstoned floor, and every shelf and cupboard seemed to have been emptied. There were no longer any bottles in the kitchen wine rack. They had been smashed too, their contents forming predominantly red puddles. The room smelt of alcohol, and we had to pick our way carefully through fragments of china and glass.

The fridge-freezer that I so loved, one of those big American ones, had been disconnected and its doors left open. Ice cream was already dripping onto the floor. The table and all the chairs had been overturned. Predictably, the screen of the TV, even though it was fixed high on one wall so that it could be seen from every part of the room, had been shattered.

There was so much damage I couldn't take it all in properly. Everything that had been free-standing, including almost all of my kitchen utensils and electric items like the toaster, appeared to have been swept violently to the floor. Only the microwave and the espresso machine, which were built into the units, seemed to have survived. I also registered that the Aga was still burning. There wasn't much you could do to an Aga, however vicious you were. And suddenly I realized how cold I was. I supposed it had been cold waiting in the stationary car in the yard, although I hadn't really noticed. It could also have been shock again. The leather armchair had been knocked onto its side. I hauled it upright, moved it as close as possible to the big iron stove, and sat down.

PC Bickerton asked if I wanted a cup of tea. He was being quite sympathetic. I thanked him but declined. I reckoned he'd only want to load it with sugar.

'A glass of water,' he persisted.

I shook my head. I didn't feel I could swallow anything. Not even water. Anyway, I wondered, looking down at the floor covered in pieces of china and glass, whether it would be possible to find an unbroken glass or mug anywhere among the terrible mess.

PC Bickerton lifted another chair from the floor and stood it upright opposite me. 'Do you think anything has been taken from the house this time?' he asked.

'It's hard to tell,' I said, glancing around me at what was left of my home.

'Yes, I suppose it is,' he agreed. 'In any case, burglars do trash places, but I've never seen anything like this. Never.'

'So what do you think?'

'I don't know what to think, Mrs Anderson,' he said. 'Are you aware of anyone with a grudge against you or your husband?'

'No,' I said, realizing as I spoke that as I hadn't even known my husband's real name until three weeks ago, I might not be in a position to say who could have a grudge against him. But I didn't want to involve the police in that side of my life. Not yet, anyway.

There was a crunching noise as PC Jacobs, who had been making his own examination of the house while PC Bickerton seemed to have been delegated to looking after me, appeared in the kitchen, striding confidently over the mess on the floor in his heavy police-issue boots. I wondered vaguely about the wisdom of trampling in such a fashion on what was presumably evidence. But I supposed he knew what he was doing.

'I wonder if you'd mind coming upstairs with me again to your son's room, Mrs Anderson?' he asked. In spite of his courtesy I was aware somehow that he did not seem anything like as sympathetic as PC Bickerton.

'Of course,' I said.

I stood up, and followed him upstairs, PC Bickerton behind me. The old prints and paintings which lined the walls of the staircase and landing, mostly gathered by Robbie and me at car boot sales and the like, had been torn down, their glass and even, in some cases, their frames, smashed.

Once that alone would have been enough to reduce me to tears. Now the trashing of my home seemed to be just another in the series of blows I was enduring, and I had no tears left.

PC Jacobs led the way into Robbie's room and pointed to an object lying on the floor, curiously intact amidst the dreadful mess of his smashed belongings.

It was Robbie's camcorder. I was surprised I'd failed to notice it when I'd first entered his room earlier. But I suppose I just hadn't been functioning properly. The two officers presumably hadn't noticed it, either, first time round, and they also knew about the missing camcorder. But then, they'd probably been concentrating on my reactions, not to mention making sure I didn't collapse in a heap. Or else the camcorder hadn't been there earlier. Perhaps PC Jacobs had planted it.

I realized, as the thought presented itself, that this was beyond paranoid. It made absolutely no sense for me now to be the victim of a police set-up, on top of everything else. That was pure fantasy land. Worthy of Robert himself, I reflected wryly.

I glanced at PC Jacobs. He nodded sagely.

'Do you recognize that camera, Mrs Anderson?' he asked.

I agreed that I did, and confirmed that it was Robbie's.

'The one you told us was definitely missing?' he enquired.

I affirmed that it was.

'Stolen by the intruder you thought was in your house last week?' he persisted.

I found a bit of spirit.

'I didn't think there was an intruder,' I said. 'There was an intruder. And Robbie's camcorder was taken. It must have been. This is the first time I've seen it since before that night. And what about my iPod? That's still missing.'

'Is it, Mrs Anderson?' Jacobs asked, continuing to speak without giving me chance to reply. 'An iPod is rather a small object. Don't you think it may turn up?'

Suddenly I felt totally defeated.

'I have no idea,' I said.

'Neither have I, Mrs Anderson,' he replied. PC Jacobs sounded sad more than anything else. He tugged at the collar of his uniform shirt as if it were causing him discomfort.

We made our way back to the kitchen. My head was in a total daze. PC Bickerton hovered, and PC Jacobs said he would check the outbuildings.

After a bit Jacobs returned holding by the blade a large axe, the one we used to chop our firewood.

'I think we'd better get this off to forensics,' he said, looking straight at me.

Suddenly I was furious. And it gave me my fight back. This idiot now seemed to think I had trashed my own house. And he wasn't making much of a secret of it.

'Are you accusing me of something here?' I demanded as forcefully as I could manage.

Jacobs backed off a little. 'Certainly not, madam,' he said. 'Just pursuing our inquiries.'

'Do you really think I would do this to my own home?' I asked, throwing both my arms in the air, gesturing towards the wreckage all around me. 'Do you really think anyone would? Do you?'

PC Jacobs shrugged. 'I think you've been under a great deal of stress, Mrs Anderson . . .' he began.

'Not that hoary old chestnut again,' I interrupted. 'I can't believe that's all you can come up with.'

PC Jacobs glanced pointedly down at the axe he was holding. My axe.

'If you're going to look for my fingerprints on that, of course you're going to find them, you bloody fool,' I stormed at him. 'My husband is away from home more than half the time. Who do you think chops the wood round here?'

eleven

I suppose swearing at a police officer is never an especially good idea. PC Jacobs told me stonily that he would overlook my expletives under the circumstances. I knew I had been pretty stupid, however it's quite bad enough having your home destroyed without being accused of doing it yourself. As near as dammit, anyway.

Particularly after what I'd already been through.

I remained silent as he left the house. I didn't really trust myself to speak to the man.

'But you do really have to get help, Mrs Anderson,' he told me, over his shoulder, for what felt like the umpteenth time.

PC Bickerton held back a little. I didn't think he was quite so certain that I was mad enough to have wrecked the place.

'If you call the station tomorrow, they'll give you a crime number,' he said.

I looked at him blankly.

'Also, we will be checking your property for fingerprints, Mrs Anderson, and asking to take yours for purposes of elimination,' he went on. 'But as nobody has been hurt it's not top priority—'

'So when is it likely to happen?' I interrupted.

'Could be two to three weeks. Possibly more—'

'And what exactly will be the point of it then?' I interrupted again.

He shrugged. I noticed he was carrying at arm's length a transparent plastic evidence bag with a dark brown substance in it which I suspected had been removed from my sitting room, presumably as a DNA sample. They were going to do *some* checking, then, it seemed.

'Don't you also need a DNA sample from me for the purposes of elimination?' I went on.

'Well, yes, perhaps you could pop into the station sometime. I'll get someone to call you with an appointment.'

'As long as you're taking me seriously.'

PC Bickerton shuffled his feet.

'Look, are you sure you want to stay here tonight, Mrs Anderson?' he asked.

I nodded. 'Yes. Anyway, I have nowhere else to go.'

'There must be somewhere,' he persisted.

I shook my head. 'No, but it makes no difference. This is where I live and I'm staying here. Nobody is driving me out.'

'Well, you really shouldn't be here alone, you know. What if something else happened?'

'I thought you and PC Jacobs believed I'd done all this myself?'

Bickerton didn't respond to that.

'I could probably get a PCSO over.'

'What's that?'

'A Police Community Support Officer.'

I could think of little I would like less than the company of some sort of assistant policeman.

'No, thank you,' I said.

Bickerton shook his head sorrowfully.

'Well, Jim and I are on duty till the early hours, so we'll keep an eye.'

I was actually rather grateful for that, but I certainly wasn't going to show it.

As a child and a young woman I'd had a reputation for being stubborn. My dad used to say that I might have been small in stature but I had a big heart and a strong will. During all those years of my apparently idyllic existence with Robert and our son I'd had no reason to take a stand about anything much, and I suppose I'd become a fairly benign sort of person.

But that evening, amid the wreckage of my home and of my life, I could feel that indigenous stubbornness returning.

And I remembered my road to Damascus moment on the moors the previous weekend. There was no longer any question of me attempting to escape, by any means at all, including suicide, from the desperate crazy world I now appeared to inhabit. I was not going to be beaten. Somehow or other I was going to find out what was going on. I needed to know who could hate me and Robert so much that they would embark on a vicious campaign to further destroy lives that were already broken, probably beyond repair.

First I had to protect myself. And I didn't need PC Bickerton to remind me not to repeat the mistake I had made after the first break-in at Highrise. I needed to get my locks changed. Fast. I called an emergency twenty-four-hour locksmith company in Exeter. Rather to my surprise, they agreed to have someone at Highrise within a couple of hours. Apparently coming to the rescue of panicking householders really was their speciality.

While I waited for one of their employees to arrive I went out to the car to fetch Florrie. And as I led her along the hallway I remembered I hadn't yet fed her. I left her outside the kitchen door, aware of how much she could damage herself walking amidst all the debris inside, piled some tinned food into her bowl, thankfully made of stainless steel or I imagine that would have been smashed too, and carried it out into the hall for her.

Then, unwilling to face the horrors of even beginning to clear up the desecrated house that night, I sat on the bottom of the stairs cuddled up with Florrie until the locksmith arrived, actually only just over an hour later. He was a cheerful-looking chap, who told me his name was Billy, but his face registered a kind of bewildered embarrassment when confronted with the state of Highrise. Billy said little as he crunched about over broken furniture, shattered glass and smashed crockery, but he worked fast, taking little more than an hour and a half to change all three of my locks.

After Billy left I realized I was still quite numb with the shock of what had been done to Highrise. And all this on top of Robbie's horrible death. I didn't dare dwell on any of it. Not that night. What I needed was oblivion.

Automatically I began to lead Florrie to the kitchen, then I realized that I could not leave her there overnight amidst layers of broken glass and crockery. Indeed, it was a miracle she hadn't cut her paws already.

'You're going to have to sleep upstairs with me tonight, girl,' I told her. She wagged her tail gleefully. I swear that dog understood every word I said.

I also realized that while I had fed Florrie I had eaten nothing myself. But I still had no interest in food. Drink was a different matter. I stepped across the hall, wriggled my way through the little door leading to Robert's wine store in the cellar, which had mercifully and miraculously escaped the attention of whoever had destroyed so much of the house – presumably they just hadn't found it – and selected two of his finest and most expensive French reds.

I found a bottle opener among the wreckage of the kitchen and uncorked them both. Then, after checking the back door was locked and all the windows downstairs firmly closed, I carried the wine upstairs to the guest bedroom I had been using. The bedclothes, along with my beloved pink Turnbull & Asser pyjamas, had been pulled off the bed and tossed carelessly around the room, but otherwise the bed was undamaged and, most thankfully of all, unsoiled.

I undressed, picked up my pyjamas from the floor and put them on. The door to the en-suite shower room stood open and I could see that the tooth mug which lived there remained intact in its wall bracket. I collected it and filled it to the brim with red wine. I pulled the bedding back on the bed and climbed in.

Florrie, hardly believing her luck, jumped up straight away, snuggled close and lay her head on the empty pillow beside me. Robert would have been horrified. It had been so much more his decision, rather than mine, that she be confined to her bed in the kitchen at night. I'd never thought about it before but her warm furry presence was extremely comforting, and from now on one of many changes I intended was that Florrie should have bedroom privileges. Regardless of the hairy residue she would leave behind.

I stroked her head, picked up the tooth mug, downed its contents in almost one swallow, filled it again and emptied it just as swiftly. Even at that moment it gave me a kind of perverted pleasure to dispose of Robert's best wine in such a manner because I knew how it would have offended him.

The third mug finished off the first bottle and I drank it more slowly, washing down two zolpidem as I did so. Then, after a moment's thought, I swallowed another pill just to make sure.

For the first time since Robbie's death the only emotion I felt was anger, perhaps because I had no other emotion left. But I did need to block out the world. I was, of course, extremely anxious about being alone in Highrise in spite of the new locks and in spite of my show of bravado to PC Bickerton. The next day I planned to make it even more difficult for whoever it was to enter my property again. Meanwhile I just wanted to sink into enough of a stupor to get me through the night. And I did. After drinking slightly more than half of the second bottle, I slept soundly until about six o'clock the following morning.

Florrie, her head resting on my chest, seemed to have been waiting for me to open my eyes. She wagged her tail and licked my face.

My mouth felt uncomfortably dry and I had a dull headache. A hangover presumably. It was so long since I'd had one of those I'd almost forgotten what it felt like. This one, it had to be admitted, was well deserved. But at least I'd found the oblivion I had both sought and so badly needed, and I did now feel, in a strange way, able to begin to face the chaos that surrounded me.

I dressed in the jeans and sweater I now kept in the guest room and, remembering the debris all over the kitchen, dug out a pair of old trainers from the cupboard on the landing. Then I led Florrie downstairs, letting her out of the front door as I did not want to risk taking her into the kitchen again until I'd cleared up a bit.

I found a mug which was chipped and had lost most of its handle, and made myself tea. While Florrie was still outside pottering about I retrieved a spade from the garden shed, and a brush from the cupboard in the hall. I began sweeping up the debris that covered the kitchen floor and shovelling it into heavy-duty bin bags. I piled these outside the back door.

I switched the big fridge back on and replaced any food that could be retrieved from the mess. Like packets of bacon that had been frozen, now defrosted but surely come to no harm in such a brief period, packaged sliced bread, a tub or two of butter, packets of cheese and so on.

The rest of it, including the smashed remains of a box of half a dozen eggs (I was thankful that at least there were no more), I binned. I used my vacuum cleaner, which fortunately was one of those that dealt with liquid, to suck up the worst of the mess left by broken eggs and spilt milk and wine. Then I let Florrie back into the house, gave her a handful of her breakfast biscuits and checked my watch. It was still only just gone seven o'clock. Too early to begin the phone calls I wanted to make.

In spite of everything my stomach reminded me that I was hungry. I'd eaten nothing since a school lunch of dubious merit the previous day. And a lot had happened since then.

I opened a packet of bacon, and lay five rashers across the base of one of my selection of iron frying pans, something else more or less impervious to any sort of damage. When the bacon started to frizzle up I moved it to the side of the pan and added two slices of bread. After both bacon and bread were cooked to my satisfaction – I liked my bacon very crispy and the bread too – I let the pan cool a little then ate directly from it. But then, I didn't have a lot of choice. It seemed that there wasn't an unbroken plate in the kitchen.

By the time I'd finished, and made and drank a couple of double espressos, thankful at least that the built-in espresso machine had escaped the wrecker's attention, it was approaching eight o'clock, and certainly an hour that would be considered respectable by Tom Farley, to whom Saturdays I knew were just another working day.

Our number one local handyman was an unflappable sort of chap invariably willing to take on almost any job. Above all, he drove a large white van. Even Robert had liked and respected Tom, and sometimes, I'd thought, actually quite enjoyed his company when Tom had helped him with work on the house. On the very rare occasions when we took a few days' holiday – Robert always said there wasn't a better place in the world than Highrise so why would he want to go away? – it was to Tom we gave a key to the house so that he could keep an eye on the place and water the indoor plants. I couldn't help reflecting a moment on those days. In the summer we would occasionally rent a little coastguard's cottage virtually on the beach just outside Padstow in Cornwall, walk for miles along the cliffs, barbecue fresh fish, and bathe in the sea when the weather allowed. We never went abroad. Of course, I knew why now, didn't I? Robert's passport would almost certainly be in the name of Rob Anderton, wouldn't it? I suddenly realized I had never seen his passport and didn't even know if he had one. He really had been so duplicitous and I, it now seemed, had been so ridiculously trusting.

I shook myself out of my reverie and dialled Tom's number.

There was a distinct note of sympathy in his voice when I told him who was calling.

'What can I do for you, Mrs Anderson?' he asked.

I'd noticed that Tom had been at Robbie's funeral. He and his wife had briefly paid their respects as Robert and I had left the cemetery, awkwardly muttering condolences, though I didn't remember seeing either of them at the pub afterwards. But Tom worked all hours. He'd probably had a job to do.

I explained that Robert had returned to work, that our

house had been wrecked by a person or persons unknown, and that I needed help to clear up the mess, take irreparable items away and so on.

He wondered what the world was coming to, asked who on earth would do something like that to a woman in my situation, and said that under the circumstances he'd come round that very afternoon.

'I've got a job on this morning I can't put off,' he said. 'But I should be able to make it about one. And I'll 'ave our Eddie with me. Good as a man now, that lad.'

I thanked him, ended the call, and removed my iPad from my schoolbag, grateful that I was in the habit of taking it to school with me or it would surely have been destroyed or stolen. I knew I might be closing the stable door after the horse had bolted, and in a way rather hoped that I was, but I'd already decided that I wanted more security if I was going to stay at Highrise. I looked up burglar alarm companies which supplied systems linked to some kind of security service – an unconnected bell, however strident, would be no use at all, alerting only the birds and the beasts of the moors to any intrusion. I called the most likely looking one, Top Alarm Security, based in Exeter, hoping fervently that they operated on a Saturday. They did. I told them I needed my case to be treated as an emergency. They offered to send an advisor to give me an estimate later that day. I told them I just needed some sort of alarm system to be fitted straight away, and I would accept whatever their standard charges were. They warned there would be an extra charge for Saturday, and they might not be able to complete a full installation. Ultimately we agreed that two of their engineers would arrive at 4 p.m., thus giving the Farleys and me time to clear up the worst of the mess.

Then I decided to have one last crack at convincing the police that I was a victim of crime, not a perpetrator of senseless destruction as I thought they believed.

I called DS Jarvis to tell him what had been going on. I quite expected, however, to be patched through to Heavitree Road again, and was mildly surprised when the detective sergeant himself answered almost at once. I got the impression, though, that he had been expecting another call and had not looked at his phone's display panel before answering. But he seemed quite pleasant and helpful. At first anyway.

'Yes, I do know about it,' he said when I began to explain the events of the previous night.

'It is the second incident,' I persisted.

'I know that too,' he said.

'Right. So is anyone actually doing anything about it?'

'Of course, Mrs Anderson. Inquiries are proceeding, and we are doing all we can.'

'But the two policemen who came round yesterday gave every impression that they thought I imagined the first break-in, then trashed my house myself,' I said. 'It's ridiculous.'

There was a pause.

'I'm really not aware of that, Mrs Anderson,' he answered patiently. 'This force takes all incidents of burglary and damage to property very seriously indeed . . .'

There was another pause.

'Look, hold on a minute will you.'

I could vaguely hear him talking to someone else. When he returned he did not sound quite so patient.

'Look, Mrs Anderson, we have two officers investigating the incidents you have reported,' he said. 'It's their case, not mine now. I really cannot help you any further and—'

'Please listen to me,' I said. 'Something is going on that I don't understand. It's not burglary, that's for certain. Hardly anything's been taken. It's some sort of attack on me, and maybe my husband too. And I feel sure it must be connected to Robbie's death. I don't know how, but it just must be. Robbie's death is your case, isn't it? And you told me to call you any time.'

DS Jarvis sighed.

'Actually, to be honest, Mrs Anderson, we are, of course, awaiting the inquest and the coroner's verdict, but we feel it is unlikely that we can take your son's case any further,' he said. 'As for the other matter, the two incidents at your home, as I told you, our inquiries are proceeding and we are doing all that we can.'

He sounded weary. And no longer that interested.

'I don't believe that,' I said angrily. 'At the very least, and whatever you say, I don't think I am being taken seriously.'

'Of course you are being taken seriously, Mrs Anderson. But I have seen the reports of your two suspected break-ins and we do have to look at all possible scenarios—'

'I don't believe I'm hearing this,' I interrupted again. 'You don't believe me either, do you? I'm the victim here, for God's sake.'

'Mrs Anderson, I can assure you that no conclusions whatsoever will be drawn until our inquiries have been completed,' he said. 'Look, we do understand how upset you must be.'

'You have no idea how upset I am,' I replied. 'First my son dies, having apparently taken his own life – which I will never accept, by the way – then I hear intruders in my house while I'm in bed at night, and then my home is wrecked, my belongings trashed, excrement smeared over the walls, the floors, and the furniture—'

It was DS Jarvis's turn to interrupt me. 'Mrs Anderson, I'm

really sorry, I have assured you that everything possible is being done, and I really do have to end this call now. The entire force is at full stretch because of the Luke Macintyre abduction, as I'm sure you can understand.'

I was bewildered. Who the heck was Luke Macintyre and what did that have to do with me and my Robbie?

'I don't know what you're talking about,' I said.

'Then you must be just about the only person in the country who doesn't.' He rather spat that at me, then added: 'I'm sorry, Mrs Anderson, I didn't mean to be short. It's pretty obvious you wouldn't have been taking much interest in news of the outside world lately. When you do catch up I know you will appreciate why I'm not able to give you the time either of us might like right now.'

He ended the call without waiting for a response.

Straight away I looked around for the remote control to switch on the TV. Only then did I remember its shattered screen. I headed for the study. There was, I was pretty sure, an old-fashioned portable, with a built-in video player, stowed away at the back of the big cupboard in the corner. We'd kept it just in case. It was still there. I pulled it out, carried it into the kitchen and connected it to our Sky box, intact on its purpose-built shelf tucked under a kitchen cabinet. The TV was analogue, of course, but I believed that it would still work with the Sky system. I was right. I tuned into Sky News.

The main item, topping each bulletin and repeated again and again, was the story of a three-year-old boy, Luke Macintyre, who had been abducted from the front garden of his Exeter home. He had now been missing for almost two days.

There was footage of his distraught parents. His tearful mother explained that she'd been with the little boy in the garden, playing ball with him, until she'd run inside the house to answer the phone.

'I suppose I expected Luke to follow me, he follows me everywhere, only this time he didn't. I was only a minute or two, just a couple of minutes. But when I went outside again he was gone. The garden gate was ajar, I thought he'd trotted off down the road, I went after him straight away. He'd disappeared, just disappeared . . .'

She could not continue. Her husband led her away and DS Jarvis made the usual sort of police statement calling for anyone who might know anything about Luke Macintyre's whereabouts to come forward.

I found myself quite mesmerized. I knew how those parents felt, of course. They feared losing their son, their only child it transpired, just as I had lost my only child. The only real difference was that they still had hope. Hope that their little boy would be found alive and well.

I could understand, however, that in some ways that almost made the whole thing worse. The desperation in the eyes of little Luke's parents had been terrible to see.

It cut me to the quick. Oh God, I thought. The whole world is falling apart.

For a moment I lost my determination not to be beaten. The strength I had somehow managed to find, the will to clear up Highrise and even to begin to rebuild my life yet again, and my resolve to find out the truth about all that had happened evaporated.

I felt totally alone in the world. Abandoned. But was I? There was still Robert, wasn't there? Maybe he really was all I had left. And maybe I could not get through this without him, after all. I reached for the phone to send him a message, to share with him all that had happened, to ask him to come home to comfort me. To look after me. And he would come at once. I knew that.

Then I snatched back my hand. The Robert I wanted by my side no longer existed. Indeed, the terrible truth was that he had never really existed.

I slumped to the floor amid the wreckage of my home and the wreckage of my life. I wrapped my arms around my knees and sobbed my heart out.

twelve

Bizarrely, I was saved from myself by Tom Farley. He arrived a good two hours before the time he had given me, just before eleven o'clock. When I heard the doorbell ring I almost didn't respond, and may not have done so had he not shouted through the letter box.

'It's me, Mrs Anderson,' he called, obviously quite certain that I would know who 'me' was, and I did, of course. Tom had an unmistakably resonant voice, rich in its broad Devon vowels.

'I managed to get away early, couldn't leave 'ee in the state you be in, could I?'

'Oh, Tom, you're a saint,' I called back, fighting to keep my voice steady and wiping away my tears with the back of one hand. 'I won't be a minute.'

I picked myself up from the floor, quickly splashed my face with cold water from the sink, blew my nose in a piece of kitchen paper, did my best to straighten my hair and my apparel, and hurried along the hallway to let him in.

I knew I must look almost as much of a wreck as my house. But Tom made no mention of my appearance. He was a good practical Devon man, just the person, I felt sure, to bring order back to Highrise. But not all that hot, probably, on coping with

177

an overly emotional woman in a state of significant distress. If I wanted his help, and by God I did, I was just going to have to pull myself together again. And that was, of course, probably the very best thing for me.

As I opened the door the first thing Tom saw was our smashed grandfather clock lying in shattered pieces on the flagstoned floor.

'Oh, my good Lord,' he said. 'Now, who on earth would do that to such a lovely thing?'

'I have no idea,' I told him. 'But I intend to find out.'

And as I spoke I realized I did still intend to do just that. My emotions were all over the place. But I would not weaken again. I must not weaken again. There would be no more sobbing and breaking down. That was not helping anything or anybody – not Robbie and his desecrated memory, and certainly not me.

And if the police weren't going to offer any assistance, then somehow or other I had to get on with it alone. They may think that the case of the missing child completely overshadowed all else, but dreadful though that was, I had lost my child too. And I was damned well going to find out why.

However, first I had to work with Tom to restore at least some order to Highrise. The house could not be lived in as it was.

'Our Eddie's finishing t'other job,' Tom told me. 'Missus'll bring him up dinner time.'

Tom had been a manual worker of some sort all his life and had ended up with shoulders so wide he was almost as broad as he was long. His face, beneath still abundant white hair, had been well weathered by Dartmoor and could only have been the face of a countryman. He was able to lift large pieces of furniture alone and with animal grace. When Tom was about you knew you were in safe hands.

He suggested I continued to sort out the kitchen. He wouldn't let me near the sitting room where excrement clung to the walls, the carpet and the soft furnishings.

At about one o'clock Eddie arrived. His mother did not come into the house, merely dropping her son in the yard and driving away again immediately. I was relieved. I certainly didn't want visitors, and Ellen Farley, although the most kindly of women, was known to be one of Blackstone's premier gossips.

Eddie was now a strapping fifteen-year-old, the same age as my Robbie had been, but I knew I mustn't dwell on that. He was at least a couple of inches taller, surely, than when I'd last met him a year or so ago. Having said that, it suddenly dawned on me that he was the young man who had rescued my hat at the funeral, though, unsurprisingly I suppose, I hadn't recognized him at the time. I thanked him for doing so. He smiled awkwardly. A shy boy, but, as his father had promised, every bit as good a worker as any man.

Eddie brought with him a professional-standard upholstery and carpet cleaner and a couple of tins of antique white emulsion paint. Tom took his son, the equipment and the paint into the sitting room and shut the door on me.

I assumed they would wash the walls and then cover the nasty amendments with paint, but I could not imagine that they would be able to clean the upholstery or the carpet properly. Both had looked permanently defiled to me.

I was, however, proven wrong.

When I was eventually allowed back into the sitting room it really didn't look bad at all. The walls needed a second coat and I could still see a bit of a shadow on the part of the settee that had been most badly affected, but I didn't suppose I would even have noticed it had I not known what had occurred. The room was without a television, of course. The Samsung Smart, which Robert and Robbie had been so fond of, had been damaged beyond any hope of repair and now lay, its once super-shiny screen smashed to pieces, in the back of the Farley van, to be delivered later to the local recycling centre.

During the early part of the afternoon Dad phoned, and so did Bella, coincidentally within minutes of each other. I didn't feel up to taking either call, but I did listen to their messages. Dad wanted to know how I was and asked again if I'd like him to pop over and maybe stay overnight. I managed a wry chuckle. He'd be lucky to find a bed in one piece. Bella, returning my call of the previous evening, suggested the following morning, Sunday, for that dog walk. I told myself I would get back to both of them sometime the next day. But I certainly no longer felt like a walk on the beach with Bella.

The Farleys continued to load everything else that was irretrievable into their white van. Everything that could be saved they set to work cleaning and restoring. I helped as much as I could.

We concentrated on the ground floor first, making it as ready as possible for the alarm people, who arrived, as promised, promptly at four. There were two of them, both male, wearing pale-grey overalls proclaiming the initials of their company, TAS, in fluorescent yellow. One was young, thin, bespectacled and clever-looking, the other older, plumper and with that air of a man who's seen it all before. Or thinks he has, anyway. After tut-tutting at the state of Highrise and the state of the world in general, as Tom Farley had done, they began at once to fit alarms to the external doors on the ground floor and a beam system inside, as I had arranged with their head office.

While they worked Tom and Eddie and I disappeared upstairs to give them a clear field. They took just over three hours to equip the front and back doors and install motion sensors in each of the downstairs rooms. The control box was set up in a hall cupboard. Modern electronics, it was explained to me, meant that little wiring was called for and that speeded up the installation process. They would come back the following week, if I wished, to fit alarms upstairs.

After they had gone the Farleys and I just kept on working. While they painted, cleaned and repaired what they could, I swept and washed all the uncarpeted floors including the flagstones on the ground floor, which rewarded me by glowing even more than ever. Nothing could destroy those floors, I thought, and surely nothing could ever totally destroy Highrise.

I told myself firmly that the old house had badly needed decluttering. And my further needs were going to be few. I would have to acquire some new crockery and a few glasses, but I wasn't about to be doing any entertaining. Other than that I could manage with Highrise just how it was.

Once all the wreckage had been removed from the house, including the furniture from Robbie's devastated room, Highrise looked surprisingly clean and in order again, if a lot emptier than before. There was too much to be taken in one vanload, so Tom and Eddie piled the rest of the broken furniture and other debris in the yard. I would just have to try not to look at it until they could dispose of that too. They refused to leave 'till you'm straight, near as dammit', as Tom put it, and finally departed just before 10 p.m.

'Us'll be back in the morning to give the sitting room a second coat, and take away the rest of the ruined stuff,' Tom said. 'But at least you'm on the way to being straight again.'

I thanked them with all my heart. They'd been quite wonderful and done an amazing job, to a higher standard than I had imagined possible. I was cheered to be no longer sur-rounded by wreckage, and by the restoration of some degree of order.

But as I watched them trundle off up the lane, their van weighed down with the smashed remains of a life that had once seemed so perfect, the sadness of it all was overwhelming. I had lost so much. And the loss of so many treasured possessions, though, of course, totally overshadowed by the death of my son and the realization that my husband was not the man I had thought him to be, was another devastating blow. Indeed, very nearly the straw that broke the camel's back, I thought to myself unoriginally. But I was not going to let my back be broken. Absolutely not.

I closed the front door on the Farleys' retreating van and a cold and damp Dartmoor night and retreated to the kitchen with Florrie. Then I sat down at the table, with my chipped mug full of hot chocolate and a tooth mug full of malt whisky, and made myself think.

Someone out there was persecuting me. Or maybe trying to get to Robert through me.

I still did not intend to tell Robert about either of the break-ins. Or that I had suspected him of the first one. I don't think I ever seriously considered that he might have played a part in the second horrific violation of Highrise. I was pretty sure he was still in the North Sea and I could not imagine he would be capable of such desecration of the home he had so loved; there was surely no motive for him to have done so. It was almost as if he already was no longer part of my life nor of our home together. More than anything, I suppose I felt that I didn't trust him any more. He really wasn't my Robert. For a start, I had absolutely no idea whether or not I could believe anything he said.

I needed to sort out my own thoughts. I still felt the key to all that had happened lay in finding out exactly how and why Robbie had died. And although I had little idea how to set about that, I believed less and less that my son had killed himself.

I also needed to find out more about my husband, which was another reason why I didn't want to speak to him. Until a few days ago it had not occurred to me that there was any more to Robert than the man I knew and lived with. He was simply my husband, and a good, kind one, I'd thought.

That was no longer the case.

I had two telephones, my mobile and my house phone, and I had one remaining intact computer, my iPad. Our broadband system also remained intact. Surely that was all the equipment you needed nowadays to embark on almost any investigation?

I decided that the master bedroom, spacious and virtually undamaged, would be the least unpleasant and most comfortable place to be right now, and that I should overcome my aversion to it. I carried my iPad and mobile up there in my school bag, which also contained pens, pencils and paper. Florrie followed very quietly, probably not quite believing her luck at being allowed upstairs, and maybe into bed with me, for the second night running.

The pillows and the duvet in the master bedroom had been slashed and tossed on the floor, their stuffing spilled out everywhere. But the Farleys had removed them and cleaned up the mess. I carried in the bedding from the spare room I'd been using. The duvet wasn't quite big enough but it would do.

I wondered if it was significant that only the bedding in the room that was obviously mine and Robert's had been damaged. And I thought it probably was. But I was not going to indulge in any more unconstructive thoughts.

I would have liked some music to help blot out all the bad stuff, and reached instinctively for the digital radio, which usually stood on the wide window ledge. It had obviously been swept to the floor, where it still lay partially concealed by a curtain, its casing cracked in several places. It rattled as I picked it up and stood it upright again. More in hope than expectation I switched it on. The radio stuttered a bit, then, rather to my surprise, came to life. I tuned in to Classic FM.

As the sweet sounds of a Mozart piano concerto filled the room, I sank back on the pillows, Florrie draped over my legs, iPad on my lap, and set to work.

thirteen

Tom and Eddie arrived promptly at eight in the morning, just as they'd said they would, even though it was Sunday. It was undoubtedly the coldest morning of the season so far. There had been signs of a frost early on, now being washed away by freezing rain.

'Us 'ave 'ad our Indian summer all right, proper damned winter this be,' said Tom by way of greeting, rubbing his big hands together.

I was already dressed and ready to leave the house. I'd checked out Robert, both as Anderson and Anderton, on the Net the previous evening, but not really got anywhere. However, I had made some progress in other directions, and I did have a plan for my day.

My school bag was by the front door. In it were my iPad, my phone, Robbie's retrieved camcorder, my digital radio, all my credit cards and bank information, and a few other treasured items, like the diamond engagement ring which was just about the only thing I'd inherited from my mother.

I was taking no further chances. Even with my flash new burglar alarm system.

I told Tom and Eddie I just couldn't bear to stay in the house any longer.

'I need a break,' I said, pushing my arms into my best Barbour.

'I'm sure you do,' agreed Tom sympathetically. 'Look, if you want somewhere to go and someone to lend an ear, you could do worse than call in on my Ellen. Er's ever so good at thic gee sort of thing . . .'

I cringed inside at the thought. Tea and sympathy with one of the biggest gossips in the village, albeit that she may well be a kind woman, was the last thing I wanted.

'I don't know what I'm going to do or where I'm going to go,' I told Tom. 'But I think I need to be on my own for a bit.'

I handed Tom the key to the front door.

'Shut Florrie in the kitchen and make sure you lock up and set the alarm system when you leave,' I instructed him, adding my thought of the previous day. 'Even if it does appear that the horse has already bolted.'

I couldn't help feeling uneasy, but surely if there was anyone I could still trust, it had to be Tom Farley, I thought, as I jotted down the alarm code for him and showed him how to programme it so that Florrie wouldn't set it off.

I'd considered taking her with me. But even Florrie seemed like too much trouble.

'Us will, and don't you worry about nothing, Mrs Anderson,' said Tom, letting the sentence tail away a bit as he probably realized what a ridiculous thing it was to say to a woman in my situation.

I got in the car, switched on the engine and took a deep breath.

It was certainly true that I needed to get away from Highrise for a bit. But I was also on a mission. I had 192.commed Sue Shaw's family and found them quite easily. Because Conor Shaw was one of my pupils, I'd already known they lived in

Okehampton, but not their address. Sue's father had introduced himself as Michael Shaw. And he'd popped up on the Net in Manor Road. Other occupants Susannah J. Shaw, Conor H. Shaw and Susan P. Shaw. Quite obviously the family I wanted.

There was a company director's report too. It seemed that Michael Shaw was in the business of manufacturing garden sheds and summerhouses.

I'd decided I was going to confront him and his daughter. There was something they weren't telling me, I was sure of it. And I was determined to give it my best shot to find out.

I drove to Okehampton slowly through horizontal freezing rain. None the less, I arrived in the moorland market town well before nine, and even in my state of manic distress mixed with fervent impatience I realized it would probably be counter-productive to knock on anyone's front door uninvited at that hour on a Sunday morning.

A rumble in my tummy reminded me that it was probably the best part of twenty-four hours again since I'd eaten anything worth mentioning, so I found a cafe and ordered scrambled eggs, bacon, toast and coffee. Once more I was surprised by how good food tasted even though I had so little desire for it. Bacon and eggs anyway.

I dawdled over my breakfast, and by the time my satnav had found 14 Manor Road the rain had stopped and it was just gone ten.

I didn't allow myself to hesitate. I parked, marched up the short garden path to a neat semi-detached house, and rang the doorbell. Sue Shaw answered the door. She wasn't yet dressed. She wore a pink dressing gown over matching pyjamas and slippers pretending to be toy rabbits. Her fair hair, hanging lank and unwashed, framed a pasty yet still pretty little face. She looked shocked to see me.

'Dad's not here. He and Mum went early to take Gran her shopping. I can't let you in, he wouldn't like it . . .' she stumbled, spots of colour rising in her cheeks, just as at Robbie's funeral.

'Of course you can,' I said, sweeping past her in what I assumed to be the general direction of the living room. 'I'm your boyfriend's mum, after all.'

I was aware of her shutting the front door and following in my footsteps. I hadn't left her much choice.

A boy's voice called from upstairs. Almost certainly Conor Shaw.

'Who's that, Sue?'

'Mind your own,' she responded.

I rounded on her at once, aware that being able to confront her alone, at first anyway, could well work to my advantage. She looked vulnerable. She clearly was vulnerable. And I didn't care. I was going to take full advantage.

'You obviously wanted to tell me something more when you came up to me at the funeral,' I began. 'What was it?'

She shook her head and mumbled something.

'Sorry?' I queried sharply.

She repeated herself just a little more clearly.

'Nothing.'

'I don't believe you, Sue. You really wanted to tell me something, then thought better of it. Tell me now. You know you want to. Is it something you think I should know about? Something about Robbie?'

Sue looked as if she might burst into tears.

'N-no,' she stumbled. 'Well, yes. Sort of.'

'So tell me. You'll feel better. You know you will.'

'I can't. Dad said I mustn't. He said I'll ruin . . .'

Sue paused. I waited.

'He just said I mustn't tell anyone, that's all,' Sue continued.

Neither of us had sat down. We stood facing each other in the centre of a small square room, its very modern black-leather sofas and chairs lining cream walls scattered with reproduction oil paintings in big gilt frames.

The girl's lips were trembling. She didn't look well. There were dark shadows beneath her eyes.

Suddenly a bloody great light bulb exploded in front of me.

'You wanted to tell me you were pregnant, didn't you?' I almost shouted the words. She recoiled from me, and started to cry.

'It's all right,' I said, aware that it was anything but, making my voice as near to reassuring as I could manage. 'It's all right. That's it, though, isn't it? You wanted to tell me you were expecting a child and that Robbie was the father, didn't you?'

She just carried on crying, her shoulders heaving.

'Didn't you?' I repeated, still trying desperately to sound reassuring.

Sue Shaw nodded. 'Y-yes,' she said.

I found that my breath was coming in short sharp gasps. I hadn't expected this in a million years. Maybe I should have done, but I hadn't. After all, Robbie had been a quiet studious boy, though what I thought that had to do with teenage sex drives I had no idea. He'd also been a sensible boy. Surely he would have taken precautions? Obviously not.

I made soothing noises in the general direction of sobbing Sue Shaw, standing trembling before me in her girly nightwear and silly slippers, so young, so pretty, so distraught, and so bewildered.

I encouraged her to sit with me on the sofa, and put my arm around her. After a bit she quietened.

'Did you love him, my Robbie?' I asked softly.

'Oh yes,' she said, her blue eyes very wide.

'And did he – do you think he loved you?'

'Oh yes,' she said again.

'Did he know? Did Robbie know you were carrying his child?'

She nodded through the last of her waning tears.

'I told him that morning, the day he died . . .'

She sniffed hugely, and I was afraid the tears were going to start flowing again before they had even properly stopped.

'It's all right,' I repeated, wishing I could think of something better to say.

'Did . . . did you see him that day then?' I asked, wondering if the enormity of the question would hit her. It didn't seem to.

'No. I phoned him, right after I did the test. He was shocked, of course. I mean, we'd only done it about three times altogether, and only once without . . .'

She stopped. Colouring up again. Embarrassed by her own words. After all, I was Robbie's mum.

'Please tell me,' I coaxed. 'I want to know everything, everything you can tell me. It could be very important.'

She shrugged.

'We only ever did it once without proper precautions, the first time,' she went on. 'We hadn't meant to, you see. We hadn't meant to do it. Swimming was cancelled suddenly because there was something wrong with the pool. We went off for a walk over the fields. It was September. The weather was so warm then, do you remember?'

There was a faraway note in her voice. She looked directly at me.

'I remember,' I said.

She nodded.

Without actually having said so, she left me in little doubt that she had been a virgin when she and Robbie first made love, in the open air it seemed, and I rather surprised myself with my next question.

'Was it, was it what you expected, what you wanted?' I asked. 'Was it special?'

'Oh yes, it was special.' Briefly her face lit up, then clouded over again, as if remembering what had then transpired.

'So when you told Robbie, what happened?' I pressed. 'I mean, did he have any idea before your test? You obviously did.'

'I did, but he didn't,' she said. 'I didn't want to tell him, or anyone, anything until I knew for sure. I got one of those test kits from the chemist, you know, and that was it. There wasn't any doubt.'

'So what did he say?'

'I don't know really. Sounds silly, but I don't properly remember. He didn't say a lot, I don't think, he just sounded shocked, and, well, I was, too . . .'

'Didn't you arrange to meet? Surely you would have wanted to meet, to talk it all through properly?'

She nodded again. 'We did want to, of course we did,' she said. 'But, well, Dad overheard my call, you see, and once he'd heard enough he just marched into my room, grabbed my phone and switched it off. I was at home studying for the mocks, like Robbie. I didn't realize Dad was in the house. He'd come back from work because he'd forgotten something. I think he listened in deliberately. I knew he'd been suspicious; he'd kept asking me what was wrong with me. When he realized he went ballistic. He has such a temper on him, I thought he was going to hit me. He didn't, though. He just said that was it. I was going to do what he said and what he wanted.

191

And I was never to have anything to do with Robbie again.'
She paused.

'But Robbie didn't know any of that presumably?'

She shook her head.

'No. I'm sure he would have tried to call me back, but I didn't even have my phone. Dad took it from me.'

She turned away from me a bit as if she didn't want me to see her face.

'I keep thinking it must have been my fault that he . . . that he did what he did,' she said. 'Could learning I was pregnant really have upset him that much? Could it?'

'No, no, I don't believe it could,' I told her honestly. 'There had to be something more.'

'I wanted to speak to him, honestly, to talk about what we were going to do; us, not my dad. I so wanted to see Robbie,' she continued, almost as if not having heard what I'd said. 'But Dad grounded me. I had no phone, no money, no nothing, and he told me if I stepped foot outside the front door, he'd throw me out for good . . .'

She stopped, seemingly unaware of the impact of her words.

Another light bulb lit up before me, almost as spectacularly as the previous one.

'Sue, where did your father storm off to?' I asked.

'Well, I'm not sure, not really sure . . .' she began.

'I think you are, Sue,' I said. 'He went to see Robbie, didn't he? The father of your child.'

She nodded.

'Tell me, Sue, please tell me. Robbie is dead. Anything you know about what happened on the day of his death could be so important.'

She nodded again. 'He told me he was going to see Robbie, yes, t-to sort him out, he said.'

I felt my whole body trembling. Could this be it? Could this be what lay behind my boy's death? An angry dad berating the teenage father of his teenage daughter's unborn child? Could that have been enough to tip my Robbie over the edge?

Sue started to weep extravagantly again, her shoulders heaving, her face blotchy and distorted. I wanted the rest of the story, but first I had to calm her down.

'Hush,' I murmured gently. 'Hush. You must try to keep calm. You're pregnant.'

It seemed I'd unwittingly said just the wrong thing. Sue jumped to her feet, screamed once piercingly, and then yelled at me through her tears.

'Oh no, I'm not. No, I'm damned well not. Not any more. Dad saw to that.'

My jaw dropped. I was just wondering if I dare ask another question without sending her totally hysterical when the sitting-room door opened and in walked Michael Shaw with, I assumed, his wife.

Sue Shaw screamed once more then ran past her parents out of the room and up the stairs.

'Leave me alone, just leave me alone,' she yelled over her shoulder.

'What the hell's going on, woman?' Michael Shaw asked me angrily. 'What the hell are you doing in my house?'

'I would have thought that was pretty obvious under the circumstances,' I responded, not even entirely sure what I meant by the remark.

But Michael Shaw seemed to think about it for a moment or two. Then his belligerence fell away a little. His shoulders dropped and his voice was quieter when he next spoke.

'Well, you've really gone and upset our Sue now, haven't you?' he said.

'It seems to me you've already done that yourself,' I countered.

I felt a cold fury enveloping me. I rose to my feet and squared up to him. He towered above me. I'd guessed he was a big man when I'd first encountered him sitting in his Range Rover, and he certainly was big. I thought he was probably six foot four, or even five. Taller than Robert certainly, and far broader. I didn't care.

'After all, you're the one who forced her to have an abortion, aren't you?' I yelled at him. 'It was you who made my son's fifteen-year-old girlfriend abort his baby. You, you bastard. And it's quite likely you're responsible for my son's death too, as well as the death of his unborn child. You went to see him on the day he died. What did you say to him? What did you do to make my son want to kill himself? Or maybe I should be asking what you did to make it look as if he'd killed himself? I think you could have killed my son. Perhaps you're a murderer. You evil, evil bastard.'

My level of hysteria now left Sue Shaw's earlier outburst in the starting stalls. I was boiling with rage and despair. I was in a frenzy that was quite off the planet.

Michael Shaw, big as he was, looked as if he'd been poleaxed. He sat down with a bump on the edge of the sofa, long legs akimbo, thick arms hanging loosely.

'Whoa,' he said. 'Whoa. I didn't murder anyone. I didn't hurt your son. I never even saw him . . .'

'You lying evil bastard—' I began again.

This time he shouted over me.

'Will you just listen to me, Mrs Anderson. I went to your house, but I didn't see your son because he was dead when I arrived. The front door was on the latch. I thought the boy was avoiding me. I was angry, all right, yes. I stormed right through the place looking for him. And when I found him, in his room up at the top, well, there he was, hanging by the neck. I took off back home, trying not to touch anything, left the door on the latch again, wiped the handle with a tissue. I don't know what I was thinking about—'

'So why didn't you call the police?' I asked, my voice still raised. 'If that's how it was, and you found a dead body, the body of my son, why the hell didn't you call the police?'

Shaw shrugged. 'I – uh, I realized how it would look, I suppose. I just didn't think. I just wanted to get out of the place, back to my daughter.'

'Oh yes,' I continued at full pitch. 'The fifteen-year-old girl you then made have an abortion. An abortion at that age, for Christ's sake!'

'No, no,' said Shaw emphatically. 'My God, where did you get that idea from? What sort of a man do you think I am? I didn't make her have an abortion.'

'Well, she's not pregnant any more is she? And she's just told me it was your fault, you bastard. You utter bastard.'

'Mrs Anderson,' the woman with Shaw, whom I'd already assumed to be his wife, blonde and pretty like Sue, but shorter, indeed not much taller than me, stepped forward and spoke for the first time, 'I'm Sue's mum. And you really must calm down and listen to me. Sue hasn't had an abortion. She suffered a miscarriage on the night of your son's funeral. She was only just pregnant, of course, but that made no difference. The poor love's been beside herself ever since. We can't do a thing with her, to be honest. She blames her father because they had a such terrible row when she came back from Robbie's funeral. He'd forbidden her from going, you see. Sometimes, well . . .'

She glanced quickly towards Michael Shaw, who was sitting staring down at his feet.

'My Mikey's a wonderful family man but he doesn't always think things through,' she continued.

And that was what I was afraid of, I thought. But I made myself stay silent, albeit with some difficulty. I needed to hear the rest of this.

Mrs Shaw glanced towards her husband. He took up the story.

'I blame myself too, if you want to know,' he said. 'I felt it was the boy's fault my girl got pregnant. We blokes do. Him being dead didn't change that. And I didn't want our Sue to have anything to do with the lad's family, with your family. I thought she'd get mixed up with the suicide thing, that fingers would be pointed at her. Her life was suddenly in enough of a mess. So much promise. I was afraid it was all going to be ruined, and I didn't know what to do about it. When I realized she'd disobeyed me and gone to the funeral, I was hopping mad. We had a right shouting match, Sue and me, when she got back. Then, well, she just collapsed. And that was that. She lost the baby later that night.'

There was total silence in the room. I felt weak and drained. I sat down again in one of the leather armchairs and Mrs Shaw sat on the other. We were all sitting now.

I struggled to control my breathing.

'I don't know what to believe,' I said.

'It's the truth, all of it,' said Susannah Shaw.

'You don't know that,' I snapped back, recovering some of my spark. 'You weren't with your husband when he drove to my home to confront my son, were you? You weren't with him when he claims to have found my Robbie already dead, were you?'

'No, I wasn't with him,' said Mrs Shaw mildly. 'But I know my Mikey. He's telling the truth. He has a temper, but he's not a bad man. He'd never have hurt your son, not really, no more than he would hurt our Sue.'

I clenched my fists to stop my hands shaking. The revelations of the last few minutes had completely bowled me over. I wasn't angry any more. In a way I was deflated. I didn't know what to do or say next.

'I think the police had better decide that, don't you?' I said eventually. 'Obviously I shall pass on what you've both told me.'

Mr and Mrs Shaw exchanged glances again.

'You must do what you feel you must,' said Mrs Shaw. 'But I promise you that the results of any police investigation will be exactly as my husband has told you.'

'He discovered a dead body and failed to report it,' I said. 'I don't have any choice.'

Mr Shaw lowered his head and stared at his feet again. Mrs Shaw stood up. 'Go and put the kettle on, Mikey,' she said. 'I'll pop upstairs and see to our Sue.'

I should have left then, I suppose. But I didn't. It was as if I hadn't the energy to do so. I was running on empty. Michael Shaw obediently began to do his wife's bidding. I sat and waited while he clattered about in the kitchen next door and his wife got on with whatever seeing to Sue entailed.

The big man returned balancing an incongruously delicate china tea set on a tray: teapot, matching milk jug, sugar bowl, and proper cups and saucers.

He poured and passed me a cup, milk already in. I added sugar in spite of disliking sugar in my tea. If there was just a chance that there really was any substance to the old adage I had always been so scornful of, that sweet tea was good for shock, then this time I really had to give it a go, because I was quite numb with shock yet again. And I had to drive home.

Mrs Shaw returned as I was forcing down the first sickly mouthful. Michael looked at her enquiringly.

'She'll be all right. She's calmed down. Gone on her computer. Best leave her alone for a bit.'

Michael Shaw nodded. His wife stepped towards me, with surely genuine compassion in eyes that were so like her daughter's.

'You know, I really am sorry about your son,' she said.

I looked away from her. What did she expect me to say?

'And I'm even more sorry if my family has done anything to make it worse,' she continued, flashing a sharp look in the direction of her husband.

I still didn't reply.

We sat together awkwardly with little or no conversation. There was, however, one remaining question I needed to know the answer to.

'Where were you on Friday, Mr Shaw?' I asked abruptly.

'On Friday?' he queried, sounding puzzled. 'At work, of course. As usual. Why?'

'Because somebody broke into my home and wrecked the place,' I replied in a level sort of voice.

'And you're accusing me of that, now?'

'No,' I said. 'I just wanted to know where you were when it happened, that's all.'

'You've got no bloody right—' Michael Shaw began, his voice raised.

'No, Mikey,' his wife interrupted him. 'Mrs Anderson has just lost her son. That gives her the right to ask almost anything, in my book. And on top of that she says her home has been trashed. Just tell her you didn't do it. That's all.'

'Of course I didn't bloody well do it,' said the man. But his voice was no longer so harsh.

'I'm sorry you've had that to put up with as well, Mrs Anderson. However, I can assure you it's got nothing to do with this family,' said Mrs Shaw, managing to sound both gentle and assertive.

She was quite convincing. But I didn't know whether or not I was convinced. Not by so much of what I had heard. I did know I really couldn't stay with the Shaws any longer. I abandoned the remains of my sweet tea and left.

Mrs Shaw escorted me to the door.

'Are you going to the police?' she asked, as we stood together in the hall.

'What do you think?' I responded.

Once back in my car I started the engine immediately and drove to the end of the road and round the corner until I knew I would be out of sight. Then I stopped again, and slumped forward over the steering wheel. Had I already solved the mystery of my Robbie's death? And if so, if I really believed that Michael Shaw was responsible in some way, then why on earth had I sat in his house drinking tea with the man?

The truth was that I still didn't know what to believe. That scenario just seemed too simplistic somehow. And Shaw? He might well be the sort to lash out in the pub or on the street, but was it likely that he was a murderer? And was it remotely likely that he had the psychological make-up of a man who could effectively incite another human being to suicide?

I suppose that by staying with the Shaws for as long as I did, I'd perhaps hoped that something would present itself to answer those questions. It hadn't.

One thing was certain though. I was definitely taking this new information to the police. At the very least, surely, it was enough to make them conduct further investigations into Robbie's death. Then I thought about exactly how I was going to approach the Devon and Cornwall Constabulary. My two local bobbies seemed to think I was a lunatic. DS Jarvis had made it quite clear he was involved with a much more pressing case, and I could hardly disagree with that, if only on the grounds that little Luke Macintyre might still be alive and my Robbie was not. I considered driving into Exeter straight away and taking my chances with the front office staff at Heavitree Road. But, of course, that Sunday everyone on duty was likely to be totally preoccupied with the case of the abducted three-year-old. Nobody was going to have much time to spend dealing with someone half the force seemed to have already dismissed as a madwoman, were they?

I thought for a moment or two more. Then I made a decision. I would leave it until the morning, then I would drive to Exeter. On a Monday morning staffing at Heavitree Road would be at full strength, and surely not everyone would be assigned to the Luke Macintyre investigation. In any case, it was even possible that the little boy might have been found by then. Yes, I would go to Exeter's premier police station and I would ask to speak to a senior CID officer. And maybe, just maybe, I would be seen by someone who would listen to me.

Feeling very slightly better at having made even that much of a decision, I checked my watch. More time had passed than I'd thought, both at the Shaws and sitting in my parked car using my steering wheel as a pillow while trying so desperately to gather my thoughts. It was nearly midday. I didn't want to encounter Tom and Eddie again, or indeed anyone else, that day, but they should be well gone by now.

Just in case, as a further delaying tactic, I made myself stop at Waitrose, on the edge of the town. I loaded a much-needed starter pack of plain white crockery into a trolley – four mugs, four dinner plates, four tea plates and so on; and also a couple of packs of cheap glasses – four tumblers and four wine goblets. I also bought milk and fresh bread, more eggs and bacon, which seemed to be the only food I even half wanted to eat, and a couple of bottles of malt whisky, an even more effective anaesthetic than copious quantities of red wine, I'd found.

I shivered as I packed my purchases into the back of the car. It had stopped raining, for the moment, but this iron-grey day remained without doubt the coldest of the autumn. As Tom Farley had remarked, it had a real wintery feel. And there was a bleakness about it which totally matched the bleakness that now engulfed my heart.

I started the engine and headed for home. Or, rather, the place that had once been my home.

I turned into the lane leading to Highrise with caution, letting the engine of the Lexus slow to the point where the electric motor kicked in so the car made virtually no noise at all. Tom and Eddie's white van was no longer parked in the yard. I had been sure it wouldn't be, but hadn't felt like taking any chances. If the two of them had still been on my property, I would have reversed out of the lane and retreated to park up the road safely out of sight until they departed. After what I had been through with the Shaws I just couldn't have faced them. Or anyone else.

The spare key to Highrise was on the doormat, having obviously been put through the letter box as I'd instructed. And Florrie had been shut in the kitchen, also as instructed. She'd started to bark and cry as soon as I'd begun to unlock the front door, and I then took a few seconds to master the remote control I'd been given, not much bigger than a key fob, in order to deactivate my spanking new burglar alarm system. Indeed, I only just managed to programme the thing into submission before it contacted its monitoring centre, which would cause God knows who to descend on me.

Florrie greeted me with her usual enthusiasm and then began whining pitifully at the back door. Of course, the poor creature must be desperate to get into the garden. I had omitted to give Tom and Eddie any instructions to let Florrie out, and I was quite sure they wouldn't have done so without my say-so. I unlocked and opened the door. Florrie ran straight onto the lawn and crouched down. I shrugged my arms out of my Barbour, then stood with the door open expecting her to return straight away. On such a cold day Florrie rarely spent more time than necessary outside.

Instead she continued to run around the lawn whining. Once or twice she paused, ears pricked as if listening to something. I listened too and could hear nothing. But as a dog's hearing is supposed to be more than three times as sensitive as human hearing I suppose that wasn't surprising.

Ears still pricked, she scampered to the five-bar gate leading into our paddock, then back to me, and back to the gate again. I called her. She ignored me. Instead she wriggled under the gate and into the paddock. I watched as she ran to the old stables just to the left of the gate and began to bark quite ferociously. Then she turned again towards the garden and seemed to bark directly at me, before scurrying back to the stables. I thought possibly a fox had got in there, or that it could be rats disturbing her. Or, Florrie being Florrie, it could even be that her ball had become trapped in there somehow and she couldn't get to it.

'Come in, you stupid creature,' I called.

But Florrie, every muscle quivering, was now sitting bolt upright by the paddock gate looking at the old stables and whimpering. She was behaving very strangely.

'Oh, all right,' I capitulated. 'You win as usual.'

I walked across the lawn, shivering as I'd already removed my coat, and pushed the gate ajar a foot or two. As I approached the stables I thought I could hear something too, a faint crying sound, but pretty much dismissed it as my imagination.

I pulled open the stable door, which took quite a lot of strength as it was one of the few things in and around Highrise that Robert had never bothered to keep in repair. Indeed, he'd been planning to knock the dilapidated old building down and replace it with a summerhouse and perhaps a barbecue area, as it stood in a corner of the paddock that caught the last of the evening sun setting over the moors.

'We could make a sort of secret garden,' he'd said, eyes alight with enthusiasm. I'd loved the idea. Not least because, although the term meant nothing to Robert who, like his son, was no reader, *The Secret Garden*, Frances Hodgson Burnett's tale of rebirth and healing in a beautiful forgotten place, had been one of my favourite books since childhood.

I shook myself. Those memories of a life I knew to be lost for ever just would not stay away. And they did me no good at all. I made myself turn my attention to the matter in hand.

As I stepped into the old stable everything seemed as normal. Inside, there was a defunct lawnmower Robert had said he would try to repair one of these days so that we had a spare, a few other bits of broken machinery, some leftover Delabole slate from when he had made the terrace at the front of the house, some timber left over from the gazebo, and a pile of fairly large pieces of oak, yet to be chopped into burnable size and transported to the log store nearer the house. They were the remains of an old tree, struck by lightning, which Robert had acquired from a neighbouring farmer after offering to pay to have it felled and taken away.

Florrie ran straight behind the oak pile, still whimpering, her tail wagging furiously. I followed her, and as I did so became quite sure that I could hear the faint sounds of some kind of living creature. I proceeded cautiously, afraid of what I might find.

If there was a wild animal in the stable, it must be injured or trapped or it would not have remained there as I approached. And a frightened wounded fox, or perhaps a badger, could be dangerous.

I tried to prepare myself. Nothing, however, could have prepared me for the shock of what I was about to discover behind that woodpile. I stood frozen to the spot for several seconds, unable to believe my own eyes.

A small child, bound hand and foot and apparently barely conscious, lay naked on a piece of soiled blanket.

fourteen

Time stood still for a moment. I doubt it was more than a second or two before I ran to the child. But it felt longer.

I crouched down, registering that this was a little boy. He was whimpering pathetically, his pinched bloodless face stained with grubby tears. Automatically I began to make soothing noises.

'You're all right now, I'll look after you, we'll soon get you back to your mummy,' I said.

But when I touched him I realized he might be far from all right. The child was freezing cold, and I wondered if it was the extreme cold that had rendered him half conscious. His eyes were open but he did not seem to be focusing on anything nor able to comprehend, or perhaps even hear, what I was saying.

I tugged at the binding cord tying his hands and feet together. It was securely knotted and I could not budge it without a knife or a pair of scissors. I looked around the stable. In spite of being half full of bits of old machinery there seemed to be nothing that I could use to free the cord, not without further harming the child.

I would have to carry him into the house before releasing his bonds. I knew I should get him into the warm as quickly as possible because he must surely be suffering from hypothermia.

Wishing I hadn't removed my Barbour in the kitchen, I took off my sweater, wrapped it round him as best I could, picked him up carefully, and pushed myself upright, holding the child close to my body and still muttering soothing remarks to him, even though I feared they were a waste of time.

Florrie kept brushing herself against my legs. I should have been telling her she was a good girl; instead I shooed her away. I was quite frantic. Where on earth had this child come from, and what was he doing lying naked in my stable?

Something else occurred to me. Perhaps the person who had so wickedly dumped this poor little boy there, naked, bound hand and foot, and quite possibly left to die in the cold, was still hiding in the stable or nearby.

I held the boy even more tightly. There seemed to be no sign of any other human presence, and certainly Florrie was giving no indication of such.

I decided not to stick around to find out. Clutching the boy to my upper body, I ran out of the stable without bothering to close the broken door behind me, and through the paddock gate into the garden.

As I ran another thought occurred to me. A thoroughly obvious one. The little boy must surely be the child who had been abducted from his Exeter garden. Little Luke Macintyre. The child half the county was searching for.

I tore across the lawn, barely looking from left to right in my haste to reach the warmth and safety of the house. It could have been that the heat from my flesh, largely in contact with his, as I was now wearing only a bra over the upper part of my body, partially revived the boy because he seemed to regain a degree of consciousness. He began to cry.

As I struggled to hold him more comfortably while still running for the back door, Florrie began to bark again. I glanced at her, and then in the direction in which she set off at a gallop.

Two uniformed figures had appeared at the side entrance to the garden. PC Jacobs and PC Bickerton, their faces displaying a mixture of horror and astonishment beneath their peaked caps, were peering over the top of the gate.

I could only imagine what the scene confronting them must have looked like. A dishevelled woman, half naked from the waist up, clutching a naked child, limbs bound with binder cord. I stopped in my tracks and opened my mouth to speak. No sound came.

PC Jacobs was the first of the three of us to find his voice.

'Open this gate, Mrs Anderson,' he commanded. 'And give me that child.'

Meekly I did what he said. I hurried to the gate, turned the knob on the Yale with one hand while still holding the child in my other arm, and handed the boy over.

It was actually PC Bickerton who took the child.

'You see to her,' he said to Jacobs, referring presumably to me. 'We need to get this child into the warm straight away.'

Jacobs clamped a hand on my shoulder, digging his fingers into my flesh, as if restraining me, as if he expected me to run away. As if I had anywhere to run to. Didn't he realize, I wondered obliquely, that if I'd had anywhere to run to I would have done so already, right after finding my poor dead son, right after discovering that my husband was not the man I'd thought him to be?

I cowered before Jacobs. I was weak with shock and the cold was getting to me too.

My sweater had fallen on the grass just a few feet away. Jacobs half dragged me over to it, bent down, picked it up and handed it to me.

'Cover yourself up,' he ordered gruffly. I did so with pathetic gratitude.

Then still keeping his hand on my shoulder, he steered me into the house through the kitchen door, following in the footsteps of PC Bickerton who had already wrapped the little boy in some towels and my discarded Barbour and placed him on the armchair by the Aga. Bickerton was now calling for backup and the ambulance service on his radio.

The boy had stopped crying and seemed unnaturally still.

'I think we're supposed to try and keep him awake,' I said. 'People with hypothermia just want to sleep. And it's the worst thing for them. I read that somewhere—'

'I reckon you should leave that child to us, you've already done quite enough,' said PC Jacobs.

'What?' I queried.

I turned to look at him, bewildered for just a moment.

The expression on his face told me everything. Light dawned. I supposed it would have been obvious to any onlooker from the beginning. But I wasn't an onlooker. I was directly involved. And in PC Jacobs's eyes, far more directly involved than I actually was.

'Y-you can't believe I had anything to do with this?' I blurted out. 'I just found the little boy in my stables, that's all. Well, my dog did really, she led me to him. I've no idea how he got there.'

He just stared at me.

'You can't believe I'm involved,' I repeated. 'You'd have to be mad to think that.'

'Mrs Anderson, the last time you and I had dealings you swore at me and this time you're suggesting that I'm mad,' said PC Jacobs in a very level tone of voice. 'I might suggest to you that you are not helping your case a great deal.'

As I searched for a suitable reply a kind of moaning sound came from the bundle in the chair. I took an involuntary step towards the child. Immediately PC Jacobs moved forward as if to stop me touching the boy. I rounded on him.

'If we don't help that child, he's going to die,' I said. 'It will take an ambulance a minimum of half an hour to get here from Okehampton. And that's if it leaves straight away and there's no traffic. By then it could be too late. Whatever you think of me, PC Jacobs, I'm a mother. I was once, anyway. That child needs heat and warm milk. There are hot-water bottles and proper blankets in the big cupboard on the landing. Perhaps one of you could fetch them while I warm some milk?'

Neither officer moved nor responded for a moment.

'Let her help, Jim,' said PC Bickerton eventually. 'I'll get the blankets and the bottles.'

PC Jacobs nodded, although he still looked uncertain.

'You just watch her,' said Bickerton over his shoulder as he left the room, taking a kind of control for the first time.

'Don't you worry, I will,' said PC Jacobs, his face set in stone.

I lifted the Barbour a little and rested a finger on the boy's chest. He was still dangerously cold. I thought his heartbeat was slower than normal, and he remained bound hand and foot.

'We have to get these ties off him,' I said, rummaging urgently in a kitchen drawer for scissors.

'I'll do that,' said PC Jacobs, grabbing the scissors from me as if he feared what I might do with them.

Then he set about cutting and untying the little boy's bonds while I took milk from the fridge, poured it into a bowl and put it into the microwave to heat it quickly.

PC Bickerton was quick too with the blankets and the bottles. I took two bottles from him and filled them with water from the hot tap, cooling it to what I judged to be just the right temperature with some from the cold.

'We need to take these coats and bits and pieces off him, wrap, say, one blanket round him, then wrap the bottles inside a second blanket like a cocoon,' I said, not sure where I got that idea from but it sounded like a good one.

PC Bickerton nodded his agreement and began to help me, holding the child while I did the wrapping. PC Jacobs reached forward with one hand to check the temperature of the hot-water bottles. Only after he had felt them carefully did he gesture for me to go ahead.

What did he think I was going to do, for God's sake? I wondered. Scald the little boy to death?

Once we had him securely and warmly wrapped I took the bowl of milk from the microwave, checked its temperature, and did my best to spoon-feed the child just a little of it. Fortunately his lips were already slightly apart and I was able to insert the tip of the spoon inside his mouth quite easily. But at first he made no swallowing motion and I prayed I wouldn't choke him. I tried two or three spoonfuls and could see milk running out of the side of his mouth. I didn't think I was being very successful and guessed I'd better stop. Then suddenly he coughed, and I could have sworn I saw his little Adam's apple move. I reached out to touch his face just as he started to cry again. Tears ran down his cheeks, which I thought were just a little warmer than they had been earlier.

PC Bickerton was crouched by the chair, one arm around the little boy.

I looked across at him.

'I think he's coming back to us,' I said.

PC Bickerton began to smile and so did I. I couldn't help it. Neither of us could help it. There is something wonderful about watching life return to a human being, particularly one so young as this.

Within seconds I realized that Bickerton and I were beaming at each other. At that moment we believed we had done this, that we were responsible for the child's apparent recovery, and it was a good feeling.

Then pandemonium broke loose.

An ambulance, a paramedic on a motorbike, and what felt like half the Devon and Cornwall police force arrived all at once.

It was DS Jarvis who led this medley of assorted medics and police officers into my kitchen. And if anybody had knocked on the front door, I certainly didn't hear them. Jarvis, looking out of breath and out of temper, stood in the doorway for a fraction of a second.

Then he bellowed his first set of instructions.

'Bickerton, Jacobs, you bloody fools, get that woman away from that child.'

Strong arms pulled me upright and away from the little boy, whom, just a moment ago, I'd been so pleased to have helped.

Jarvis strode swiftly across the room and leaned close to the child.

'That's him all right,' he said, as if there had ever really been any doubt. 'That's Luke Macintyre.'

I seemed to be surrounded by police officers of both sexes, in uniform and in plain clothes. And all of them made it quite clear exactly what they thought of me. They half pulled me out of my own kitchen and into the sitting room. It seemed I was not even going to be allowed to remain in the same room as that poor maltreated child.

I realized for the first time, probably, just what terrible trouble I was in. And I had absolutely no idea what I could do about it, or who there was in all the world who might help me. Now, surely, my life was truly over.

It seemed an awfully long time before anyone would speak to me.

'I can explain, you know,' I said to the woman police community support officer who seemed to have been deputed to keep an eye on me, along with another, male, PCSO I could just see standing in the hallway outside the sitting-room door.

What did they think I was going to do now, for goodness' sake? Did they really think I might make a run for it? Did they really think I was that crazy? Yes, actually, they did, I told myself. And that was pretty frightening.

'You'll have to wait for DS Jarvis,' said the woman PCSO. She had a pale elfin face and wispy blonde hair protruded from beneath her cap. She was very pretty. Obliquely, I found myself wondering how she got on with the boys back at the station.

Sexist, stupid, and quite bizarre under the circumstances. I supposed I was no longer really capable of rational thought, so the remains of my brain kept dashing off at tangents.

'He won't be long, I'm sure,' she said.

I nodded, defeated.

I could hear snatches of conversation from the kitchen. All the doors seemed to be standing open. DS Jarvis and PCs Jacobs and Bickerton were talking in loud, clear voices.

'You should have seen her, sarge, tearing across the lawn, half naked, with the little lad in her arms. Gave us quite a turn, I can tell you. Just couldn't take it in for a minute or two.'

That was PC Jacobs, his sharp, rather high-pitched tones, with just the merest hint of a Devon accent, quite unmistakable.

'Ummm. Lucky you came along when you did.'

DS Jarvis. A more modulated, perhaps better educated voice, lower-pitched.

'Yep. It was only a routine follow-up to her call-out. Not that we've ever believed a word about these mystery intruders and all that, have we, Ricky?'

'Well, no. Probably not. But we certainly weren't expecting anything like this, that's for sure.'

That was PC Bickerton speaking. Higher-pitched again, but more thoughtful and measured.

'I wonder where she was planning to take the lad.' DS Jarvis again.

'Or what she was going to do to him, more to the point.' PC Jacobs.

'Look, we don't know that she was going to do anything to him.' Those measured tones of PC Bickerton. 'She told us she just found him in the stable. By chance, like. It's possible she could be telling the truth, you know.'

'Yeah, and pigs might fly.' PC Jacobs.

'She was keen enough to try to revive the boy.'

'That doesn't prove anything.'

'But why would she take a child like that? It doesn't make sense.'

'It does to me, Bickerton.' DS Jarvis again. 'Pretty straightforward, I'd say. She lost her own son and decided to nick somebody else's.'

'In that case, why didn't she look after the child properly? Why on earth would she strip him, tie him up and leave him in a freezing stable?'

DS Jarvis's response was swift. 'Because she's off her trolley, Bickerton. But then, we'd already half guessed that, hadn't we?'

'Yeah, probably thinks she's the Virgin Mary. Soon be

Christmas after all.' Jacobs, laughing snidely at his own joke. Or what he presumably regarded as a joke. I could hardly believe my ears. Even DS Jarvis seemed to think the constable had gone too far.

'That's enough, Jacobs,' he said.

I glanced at the pretty woman PCSO. If she realized that I was listening to every word, she gave no sign. I suspected she might be the sort you get in all walks of life who do what they are told and no more.

At that moment two paramedics carrying a small stretcher holding Luke Macintyre, now wrapped in a silver thermal blanket, went past in the hallway on their way to the front door. And within seconds a trio of blue-suited Scenes of Crime Officers walked by in the other direction.

'I see you buggers have been trampling over everything as usual,' said a strong male voice. 'Now, please everyone, get the fuck out of my crime scene!'

'We did have to ensure the safety of a small child, you arrogant bastard,' said DS Jarvis.

Now I was listening to a row between two different sides of the police force, and it didn't sound like friendly banter to me. I glanced at the pretty PCSO again. As if reading my mind, she turned on her heel and closed the sitting-room door.

Whatever was going on outside was now just an incomprehensible hum. In some ways, in view of what I'd overheard, this could have been regarded as something of a relief. But at least I'd learned exactly what the police attitude to me was. And I had a feeling I was going to need all the knowledge I could acquire if I was going to survive this. Knowledge is strength, Gran used to say.

Just a few minutes later the sitting-room door swung open again and in strode Jarvis with Jacobs and Bickerton at his heel.

My three favourite policemen, though I thought Ricky Bickerton wasn't too bad.

I stood up and braced myself for an onslaught. I'd used the time alone in the sitting room to sort out my thoughts as best I could and to work out what I was going to say.

But I was completely thrown by DS Jarvis's opening remark. It was an absolute corker.

'Can you think of any reason why I shouldn't arrest you, Mrs Anderson?' he enquired.

I just stared at him.

'All right, first of all, where were you on Thursday afternoon?' Jarvis asked.

'I was here. I was teaching in the morning, at Okehampton College. And I got back just after 1.30, I think. I was here for the rest of the day.'

'Were you alone in the house?'

'Yes.'

'And what time did you leave the college?'

'About one. It's around half an hour's drive.'

'So as Luke was taken at approximately 3 p.m. on Thursday you would have had plenty of time to get to Exeter, wouldn't you?'

My head was spinning. I could hardly believe what was happening.

'But I didn't go to Exeter. I didn't abduct the boy. You can't seriously be thinking of arresting me. I haven't done anything.'

'We seem to be hearing that quite a lot from you right now, Mrs Anderson,' Jarvis continued.

'I can't help it that these things keep happening to me. And I can't explain it.'

'Right,' said Jarvis. 'But presumably you can tell me how you came to discover little Luke Macintyre.'

215

'I've already told PCs Jacobs and Bickerton,' I said.

'Yes, and now perhaps you'll be kind enough to tell me,' said the detective sergeant, speaking with deliberately over-emphasized patience. 'I am the officer in charge around here, I believe.'

I ignored the sarcasm and began to relate the whole story again, about Florrie behaving strangely and leading me to the stable, then hearing sounds from behind the woodpile, and the shock of discovering the naked child there.

'What about before that?' asked Jarvis.

'What do you mean before? There was no before.'

'There most certainly was, Mrs Anderson. The medical team have already told me, and it's pretty damned obvious to anyone, isn't it, in this weather, that if little Luke had been in that out-building for three nights, or even for one night, the boy would be dead by now.'

Jarvis paused, as if for dramatic effect.

'But I don't know where he was before,' I said. 'The first time I clapped eyes on the poor child was earlier this afternoon, just before your two constables arrived.'

'Look, it is a medical fact that if the boy had been in that old stable for more than a few hours, and certainly if he'd been there overnight, then he could not have survived. You do accept that, do you not?'

I felt that any answer I gave could only be the wrong one. So I said nothing.

DS Jarvis had no intention of letting me off the hook. 'Come on, Mrs Anderson. I need you to reply to my question.'

'Yes, all right then,' I said. 'Of course, I accept that.'

'In which case, Mrs Anderson, you are very lucky not to be looking at a murder charge, aren't you?'

'But I didn't do—' I began.

'And indeed still might be looking at one, the state that poor child is in.'

'He seemed so much better, though. Surely he is going to be all right, isn't he?' Rather to my surprise, I found that, for a moment anyway, I was every bit as concerned about little Luke Macintyre as I was about myself.

'You never know with hypothermia,' said Jarvis. 'And this is a three-year-old child we're talking about. There's nothing of him. Let's just say you would be prudent, yes prudent, to be anxious about his survival. Very anxious.'

'Of course I'm anxious about the poor little boy's survival,' I said. 'Anyone would be. Particularly a mother.' I half choked on the word. 'But it doesn't mean I had anything to do with what happened to him. I deny that absolutely.'

'Do you, Mrs Anderson?' continued the detective sergeant. 'In which case perhaps you have some idea who may have brought the child here and abandoned him to freeze to death in your stable. And, indeed, who may have been responsible for allegedly entering your house in the middle of the night and then trashing the place?'

'I don't know,' I said. 'Of course I don't know, but . . . but there might be something. There might be someone . . .'

I hesitated. Well, I'd been planning to report Michael Shaw, hadn't I? Just not under such disadvantaged circumstances.

'I learned something earlier today that you should know about,' I continued.

I told him then, to the best of my ability, about Sue Shaw's condition and everything the Shaws had told me.

'So you see, DS Jarvis, Michael Shaw is a man with a temper. He was angry enough to come here and confront my son on the day he died. He could have been responsible for Robbie's death for all I know . . .'

'Mrs Anderson,' DS Jarvis interrupted. 'It is true that the inquest into your son's death has yet to be held, but those of us involved in the case have little or no doubt that he took his own life. And now, thanks to you, it looks as if we know what drove him to do so. Your son had just found out that he'd got his girlfriend pregnant. He was fifteen years old. He couldn't cope, he felt he couldn't go on.'

'And that's it, is it?' I shouted, aware how unwise it was for me to raise my voice, but unable to help myself. 'Are you not going to investigate Michael Shaw?'

'Mrs Anderson, we are conducting an inquiry into, at the very least, the attempted murder of a child. I can assure you that all necessary action will be taken, and that no information we acquire will be overlooked.'

'But don't you see,' I went on, 'if Michael Shaw was angry enough to come storming around here to confront Robbie the way he admits he did, he might have done almost anything to seek revenge against me and my family. Mightn't he? Anything.'

'Yes, well, we will look into what you have told us. But could I ask you, Mrs Anderson, do you really think it is likely that the man would have abducted a child and left it to die to seek revenge against you?'

My head felt as if it might explode.

'I don't know, I don't know,' I cried. 'But it happened. Somebody put that child in my stable. And somebody broke into my house and then trashed the place.'

DS Jarvis sighed. 'Right. So, apart from this Michael Shaw, do you have any thoughts about anyone else who might be responsible?'

'No,' I said. 'Just someone with some sort of enormous

grudge against me, I suppose. And against my husband probably.'

'Really, Mrs Anderson? Don't you think that's just a little self-obsessed? Never mind Michael Shaw, do you really think it's likely that any third party snatched that defenceless child, maltreated him, stripped him naked, bound him hand and foot, and left him in a freezing stable to get at you?'

I met Jarvis's gaze as steadily as I could then looked away. I had no answer. Put like that I had to admit it didn't sound very likely.

'And where is your husband?' Jarvis went on.

'He's away working. On an oil rig in the North Sea.'

'Are you quite sure of that?'

I stared at him. I supposed I was still sure of it, wasn't I?

'Yes,' I said.

'He seems to spend an awful lot of time on oil rigs,' responded Jarvis.

'Well, it is his job,' I snapped. Thinking as I did so that I would never be absolutely certain what Robert was doing ever again.

It occurred to me that this might be the moment to tell Jarvis about Robert, about his having lived a lie for so long, and about my sham of a marriage. I decided against it. I wasn't ready yet. And in any case it seemed obvious that anything I told the police at the moment was just likely to be used as further evidence against me. Further evidence that I was off my rocker.

'I suggest you call your husband and get him home, Mrs Anderson, because I think you're going to need him,' Jarvis continued.

'No, I don't want him here,' I responded, offering no explanation.

'That's your choice. You may wish to call a solicitor then.'

'I don't need a solicitor, either,' I said. 'I am totally innocent of everything you are suggesting. I would never hurt a child, for God's sake. I'm innocent. So I don't need a solicitor.'

'Again, that is your choice, Mrs Anderson.'

Jarvis seemed to stand a little straighter, his expression becoming sterner, and when he spoke again his voice was louder, his delivery more pronounced.

'Marion Anderson, I am arresting you on suspicion of the abduction and attempted murder of Luke Macintyre,' he declared. 'You do not have to say anything. But it may harm your defence if you do not mention when questioned something which you later rely on in court. Anything you do say may be given in evidence.'

I thought my knees were going to give way. Certainly my legs buckled involuntarily. It was the pretty woman PCSO who moved quickly to my side and lent support to my elbow. I very nearly went down. She proved to be a lot stronger than she looked.

I don't know what I had expected after finding the missing Luke Macintyre. And the arrival of the police. But it wasn't this. Never this.

fifteen

It was gone five o'clock before we left Highrise. They took me to Exeter in the back of a patrol car, sandwiched between PC Jacobs and the woman PCSO. The rain was falling steadily again and darkness had already descended on this appropriately dismal November day.

The bells of Blackstone parish church were ringing, presumably to summon evensong, and as we swished our way through the village I saw Gladys Ponsonby Smythe approaching the church, her ample figure clearly illuminated by the lamp which stood alongside the old lychgate. She was wrapped in a shiny green oilskin cape and carrying an armful of autumnal flowers. She had to step back to avoid our spray, and naturally took a good long look at the passing police car. I was pretty sure the lamp provided enough light for her to have spotted that I was inside it.

Our eyes seemed to meet and her mouth dropped open in shock.

At Heavitree Road Police Station I was escorted through the back door to the custody suite, and checked in by the custody sergeant, a sallow-faced man with a hangdog expression. I had to relinquish my personal effects, primarily my handbag which I'd grabbed as I left Highrise, and which contained my wallet, my make-up, my hairbrush and, of course, my mobile phone. I even had to hand over my watch. I was then taken into a cubicle by a woman PC and told to remove my clothes, including my underwear, which were placed in a plastic sack. Afterwards I was given a white paper suit to wear. Then I was photographed and my fingerprints taken. A swab of saliva was extracted from inside my mouth on a disposable spatula in order for my DNA to be obtained.

Processing, the police called it. And it should have been the most humiliating experience of my life, but I was past caring.

The interrogation started as soon as all these procedures had been completed. They call them interviews nowadays, of course. But it felt like an interrogation to me.

I was formally offered legal assistance. I had the right to free independent advice from a duty solicitor, I was told. I declined again. I still had this silly idea in my head that because I was innocent I didn't need any help.

I was questioned by DS Jarvis, and a second detective, new to me, who announced himself, for the interview room video, as Detective Constable John Price. The two men went over the same ground again and again. Once more I was asked how little Luke Macintyre came to be found in my old stable. Once more I said that I had no idea.

Jarvis listed the evidence against me.

'We confidently expect your DNA to be all over the child,' he said at one point.

'Well, of course,' I said. 'I picked the boy up, didn't I? Would you have expected me to leave him just lying there outside, in the state he was in, on a day like this? I was carrying him into the house, into the warm, when your two PCs came along.'

Jarvis grunted. 'We have a team checking out your house and your car right now,' he said. 'If there is any trace of the child in either, we will find it. So why don't you just stop wasting time, and tell us what happened?'

'Look, Constable Bickerton carried little Luke into my kitchen. He and I wrapped him in my towels, warmed him with my hot-water bottles. Of course there are going to be forensic traces of him in my home. There shouldn't be in my car. And if there is anything, then it's been planted. Just like the child himself.'

Even in the state I was in I realized that the evidence they had against me could only be circumstantial. But it was pretty damning all right. And, also, I had no idea what else might turn up. What else this unknown perpetrator who was trying to frame me for this awful crime might have done to further incriminate me.

I was interviewed, on and off, throughout the evening and into the night, for a period stretching over five or six hours, I thought, but I ultimately began to more or less lose track of time. I didn't doubt that care was taken to ensure the necessary breaks demanded by all the rules and formalities of British police procedure, and I was periodically offered tea or coffee and brought food that I couldn't eat. It was, none the less, absolutely gruelling. Which was no doubt the intention. They worked on me in shifts. After Jarvis and Price, the uniformed boys I already knew, Bickerton and Jacobs, had a go. Then Price returned with PC Janet Cox, the woman officer who had tried to give the impression of being my friend when she'd come to Highrise on the day of Robbie's death. She was certainly no longer making any attempt to do that. In fact, she was quite spiky in her approach, and I was rather glad that her stint didn't last long. After what seemed like a relatively short session she was replaced by Jarvis again.

I, of course, had no one to take a shift for me. And when

they eventually told me that the interviews were to be suspended, but I was to be held in police custody overnight and they were taking me to a cell, I felt only relief. Although I was concerned about Florrie. I was told she had already been taken to police kennels. She wouldn't like that, but at least she was safe, I thought. Which was more than I felt myself to be.

However, cells had beds, didn't they? And I so wanted to lie down. I was totally exhausted. But, of course, I had no idea what it was like to be locked in a cell. I'd never broken a law, except the occasional speed limit, in my entire life. Being locked up in a police cell, however, turned out to be the biggest shock of all. After being arrested in the first place that is.

The woman PC who had earlier overseen the removal of my clothes led me to the cell block and into a bleak little room, around eight foot by six, with grubby creamish walls, old graffiti half scrubbed out, and a bare concrete floor. The room was illuminated starkly by one bright light in the middle of the ceiling. The only furniture was a thin plastic-covered mattress laid on a concrete platform. I was handed a single blanket. No pillow. In case I was tempted to suffocate myself? I had no idea.

A lavatory pan with no seat stood in a recessed area directly opposite the cell door which, of course, had a viewing panel built into it. The recessed area had no door. Privacy, I supposed, was one of the first privileges you lost when you found yourself in police custody.

The cell smelt strongly of powerful disinfectant, and I could not prevent myself imagining fleetingly what might have been cleaned up. And how recently.

I sat down, almost involuntarily, on the concrete and plastic bed just as the steel door was slammed shut and I was locked in alone. I was aware, for a moment or two, of a pair of eyes studying me through the viewing panel. Then that was also slammed shut and I heard the unmistakable sound of my escort's footsteps retreating.

It wasn't cold in the cell, but I pulled the thin blanket tightly around me and rolled myself into a foetal position.

I did not weep. I think I was in too great a state of shock for tears. Neither did I sleep. Except perhaps for just an hour or two before dawn, or thereabouts, when I was awakened by the arrival of a breakfast of scrambled egg, which tasted like sawdust, accompanied by two anaemic sausages. I'd thought I was hungry, having eaten nothing since breakfast the previous day, but I couldn't eat it. Apparently all custody units now-adays have stores of instant meals which are microwaved to order. Gone are the days of bacon sandwiches and the like brought to prisoners at police stations either from the canteen or the cafe round the corner. Not that I was at all sure I'd have been able to stomach even a bacon sandwich.

I had no watch so I had little idea really how long I remained in the cell before being escorted from the cell block back to the interview room by a young male PC. But we passed beneath a clock on a corridor wall which told me the time was 8.05 a.m.

'Have to take the scenic route this morning. We've sprung a leak, got plumbers all over the shop,' said the PC.

We passed right by the front office, from which I could hear, in spite of the early hour, the unmistakably familiar strident tones of Gladys Ponsonby Smith. She was demanding from the front office clerk to see the officer in charge of my case.

'I can't believe you have kept Mrs Anderson here overnight like this. I'm sure you have no grounds. I want to see her. Now. Somebody needs to make sure she has a solicitor present – that's her right, as you know – and I need to talk to her so will you please—'

She stopped abruptly as she caught sight of me shuffling glumly along on the other side of the pass door.

'Marion, Marion,' she cried. 'Don't you worry, flower. Gerry has an excellent lawyer friend in Bristol. She'll sort this out for you. We've called her already. She's in court this morning but she'll be here as soon as she can.'

'Th-thank you,' I stumbled.

Having spent just the one ghastly night in a police cell I was not about to protest again that I didn't need or want a solicitor.

'Yes, well, we haven't spent all our working lives in Blackstone, you know,' Gladys continued cheerily. 'I'm a Scouser, me. And a parish in inner-city Liverpool was an eye-opener, I can tell you. Spent half me time bailing out the congregation . . .'

I struggled to find a response. But in any case I was being hustled along by my escort.

However, Gladys was never easily deterred.

'Shall I contact your husband for you?' she asked. 'I understand he's away again—'

'No, no,' I interrupted loudly, finding my voice and shouting over my shoulder. 'I don't want him here. I don't want him.'

Gladys looked momentarily puzzled.

'That's enough, madam,' said the front office clerk wearily. 'We do have procedures to follow, you know—'

'Exactly, and I'm here to make sure you do just that,' boomed Gladys.

Those strident tones followed me down the corridor as she continued to berate the man. 'What kind of procedure is it to keep a woman in custody without a solicitor or anyone at all to advise her, I'd like to know?'

'I can assure you, madam, that Mrs Anderson has been correctly advised of her rights and offered legal assistance, which I understand she turned down—'

'That's not the point,' interrupted Gladys fiercely. 'She's not somebody who's used to this sort of thing, for goodness' sake. And actually I don't believe any of you could really think Mrs Anderson was responsible for the abduction of that child. The whole thing is ridiculous . . .'

Her voice faded as I was escorted further along the corridor to the same sparsely furnished interview room in which I had been questioned the previous evening.

The next interrogation was the most gruelling. This time DS Jarvis was accompanied by PC Janet Cox. I came to the conclusion that the girl must be angling for promotion. There was no longer a hint of the friendly neighbourhood cop I had first met. She was brusque and unforgiving.

'If you really have no explanation for that child being found on your property, then we shall ultimately have no choice but to charge you,' she informed me.

'You must do what you must do,' I told her resignedly. 'I'd never seen the little boy in my life until I found him in our stable.'

'Mrs Anderson, you live in a remote part of Dartmoor. Who do you think would have left the child on your property if it were not you? And why?'

'I have absolutely no idea,' I said. 'How many times am I going to be asked that?'

I honestly thought I was going to break down and cry. It was only because of a stubborn determination not to be worn down by this total injustice, and by dint of sheer willpower, that I managed to maintain a modicum of self-control. Again, I was interviewed on and off by shifts of officers. Then, just before 1 p.m., Gerry Ponsonby Smythe's solicitor friend arrived, and turned out to be not at all what I had expected. Marti Smith was a young-looking woman, thin almost to the point of being anorexic. She had spiky pink hair and wore a leather coat, open over a blinged white shirt, black leggings and black biker leather boots. I wondered vaguely if she'd made the court appearance Gladys had mentioned dressed like that, and what the average judge or magistrate would make of her hairdo.

Anyway, she turned out to be sharp as a needle and tough as her boots. She'd already done her homework and got straight to the point.

'I have little doubt forensics have so far found no evidence at all in Mrs Anderson's home linking her with the child, except in the kitchen where we know the boy was taken in the company of two police officers,' she told Jarvis. 'And neither, I am sure, has any such evidence been found in Mrs Anderson's car. Indeed, as far as I can see you have no case against my client. She told you she found the child in her disused stable, and what evidence there is points only to that.'

'The forensic examinations have not been completed,' responded Jarvis doggedly. 'Also, we are, of course, awaiting DNA results.'

'Yes,' said Marti Smith. 'And that takes days. You may wish to continue with your inquiries, but you cannot keep Mrs Anderson here indefinitely, as you well know, without charging her. You are aware of PACE, I presume, Mr Jarvis? My client will soon have been in custody for twenty-four hours and without the authority of a police superintendent you must then release her. Unless, of course, you are in a position to charge Mrs Anderson, and I don't think you are, Detective Sergeant, are you?'

Jarvis glowered at her. 'No. But your client has been arrested on suspicion of attempted murder, the most serious of offences. I already have our super's authority to extend custody.'

'I'm not happy about that, not happy at all,' said Marti Smith. 'You know very well how flimsy your evidence is.'

'The child was found on Mrs Anderson's property, Miss Smith.'

'Yes, and a couple of years ago now the body of a young woman was found on the Queen's estate at Sandringham. I do not recollect the Queen or any other member of the royal family being charged with her murder.'

DS Jarvis continued to glower at my rather impressive solicitor. I found myself almost smiling. I liked Marti Smith already. How could I help myself?

'Unless we do charge your client or apply for a further custody extension at the magistrates' court she will be released . . .' Jarvis seemed to think for a moment. 'At six o'clock tomorrow morning, exactly thirty-six hours after she was formally taken into custody, and not a minute before.'

'And not a minute afterwards, either, I do so hope, Detective Sergeant,' countered Marti Smith. She was no pushover, that was for sure. Even so, it seemed I was going to spend a second night in custody after all. I tried not to think about it too much or I really would have broken down.

I suddenly remembered Dad. I hadn't returned his Saturday call. Nor Bella's, of course. But that didn't matter so much. Dad would be going frantic. And I couldn't risk him finding out about my arrest from some other source. I asked if I could phone him.

'No,' said DS Jarvis. 'We can't allow that, I'm afraid. But, if you wish, we can phone your father on your behalf to inform him of your whereabouts.'

The thought of that appalled me and would probably be the end of Dad, I reckoned.

Marti Smith saved the day. She offered to call my father as soon as she left the station, to explain everything as best she could, and to tell him that she was sure I would soon be released and able to speak to him myself. It wasn't ideal. But it was certainly better than allowing DS Jarvis, or worse still the now quite disagreeable PC Cox, to call Dad. Anything would be better than that.

Interviews continued, on and off, throughout the rest of that afternoon and evening until finally I was again locked up in the same horrible cell overnight. They roused me early, provided me once more with an inedible breakfast, and took me back to the interview room at about 5.30 a.m. for another session with Jarvis. I wondered if the man ever went off duty.

On the dot of 6 a.m. I was told that I was to be released on police bail and escorted to the custody suite.

'To be processed,' they told me again.

To my surprise and relief Marti Smith, wearing what seemed to be her uniform of leggings, blinged shirt and leather coat, was there waiting for me.

'I didn't expect to see you here at this hour,' I said.

'In court in Exeter today. Just meant an earlier start, that's all,' she said. 'Should make sure I'm not late on parade, anyway.'

The custody sergeant informed me that the clothes I had been wearing when I was arrested would be detained as possible evidence, and handed me a bag containing clothes I had never seen before – underwear, tracksuit trousers, a T-shirt, a thick sweater and a pair of trainers. They were all rather too big for me but I didn't care. I wondered where the clothes had come from but I didn't care much about that either. I had to wear something in order to be able to leave Heavitree Road Police Station, and that was all I did care about.

The sergeant, the same sallow-faced man who had checked me in thirty-six hours previously, also told me that my handbag and its contents had been detained for forensic examination. So, even, had my watch.

'But my money, and my credit cards, they're all in my bag. I have to have them, surely . . .'

The sergeant shook his head morosely. 'I'm afraid you will have to apply for new cards, madam. I am unable to release any of the contents of your bag at the moment.'

I had to sign a receipt for all the items detained and also for other items which had apparently been removed from Highrise, including, of course, my iPad. And my passport, it seemed.

I felt weak and disorientated and was so grateful to Marti Smith for being there to help me through it all.

'Right, before formally granting police bail I will need an address for you, Mrs Anderson,' said the sergeant.

I was perplexed. 'Why, my home, of course,' I said. 'Highrise, Blackstone . . .'

Marti Smith stepped in. 'No, Marion, I'm afraid Highrise is still a crime scene. Look, I know it's not ideal, but Gladys has offered to put you up until the SOCOs have finished.'

I just stared at her. Stupidly perhaps, it hadn't occurred to me that I wouldn't be able to go straight home.

'You may book into a hotel, if you wish, madam,' said the custody sergeant. 'We would accept that.'

I turned to look directly at him. 'Without any cash or credit cards?' I queried sarcastically.

He shrugged, more or less ignoring my inflection.

'It'll have to be Gladys's, bless her,' I said. Actually, the thought of being forced into the company of the vicar's wife and having to listen to her endless garrulous outpourings appalled me, though I knew I was being ungrateful. But anything, anything at all, was better than spending another minute in police custody.

'I'll drive you to Blackstone,' Marti said, when we'd completed all the paperwork.

'But don't you have to be in court?'

'It's not seven o'clock yet,' she replied. 'I've hours to spare and it won't take long to get to Gladys's at this hour.'

Weary, but relieved to be free again, I allowed myself to be led from the station. As much for something to say as anything else I asked Marti if she knew whose clothes I might be wearing. Were they some kind of standard police issue?

She shook her head. 'Gladys told me she'd left clothes for you yesterday,' said Marti. 'Never underestimate that woman. She knows the form when someone's arrested almost as well as I do, and she has a totally practical approach.'

I managed a small smile as we stepped out onto the pavement. But that was when more trouble started.

Half the world seemed to be outside. The news of my arrest had obviously broken with a vengeance. A crowd of locals, apparently furious that I was being released, shouted and screamed abuse at me. Was everyone in this part of Devon an excessively early riser, I wondered? Press photographers half blinded me with a cacophony of flash bulbs; reporters, from newspapers and radio and television stations, called out questions I could not even comprehend in the state I was in, let alone answer.

I suppose it was stupid; I had watched this kind of scene many times on TV news bulletins before, but I had not even thought about anything like it happening to me.

'Just look straight ahead and walk tall,' said Marti Smith. I tried to take her advice. It wasn't easy. At one point I was hit in the side of the face by a rotting orange. Apart from the humiliation, it really hurt. The fruit imploded as it smashed into my cheekbone. Unpleasant brownish juice ran down over my chin. I stumbled as I tried to wipe it away with the back of one hand. A uniformed police officer launched himself into the crowd in search of the offender. But the damage had been done.

Once settled in Marti Smith's convertible Mini Cooper I couldn't hold the tears back.

'How long do you think it will be before I can return to Highrise?' I asked through my sniffles.

'Hopefully not more than a day or two,' Marti replied.

Even after all that had happened I wanted to be in my own home. But I would just have to be patient, it seemed. At least I wouldn't be spending another night in that cell.

Gladys welcomed us warmly at the vicarage and fed us tea and toast in the Formica kitchen. Marti stayed almost an hour before slipping out to her car to fetch a tailored black pin-striped jacket and black court shoes, which she put on in Gladys's downstairs toilet. When she returned to the kitchen her hair, though still pink, had been flattened and slicked neatly back behind her ears. The tailored jacket exposed little more than the white collar of her blinged shirt, and reached almost to her knees. The leggings protruding beneath it, now that Marti's feet were clad in the court shoes instead of biker boots, looked surprisingly conventional. So that's how she does it, I thought, as she left for her appearance at the crown court. She promised to call in later in the day before returning to Bristol. I wondered if she was this attentive to all her clients. I suspected probably not, and that the treatment I was receiving was almost certainly down to Marti Smith's friendship with the Ponsonby Smythes. Something else I had to be grateful to Gladys for.

After Marti had departed I asked Gladys if I could phone Dad, and she left me alone in the kitchen while I did so. He was indeed frantic with worry, though at least it seemed that Marti Smith had broken the news of my arrest to him before he saw it on TV or read about it in a newspaper. He had, however, watched my traumatic release from police custody live on television earlier that morning.

'Terrible, terrible it was, them people throwing things at you,' he said. 'I've been calling Highrise and your mobile ever since. Couldn't get hold of Robert either.'

I explained that my mobile had been detained, I was not yet allowed to return home, and Robert was still somewhere in the North Sea. Predictably, he at once invited me to Hartland, but I told him I hoped to be back home very soon. He wanted to join me there as soon as I was reinstalled, 'to look after you, maid' as he put it. I managed, with some difficulty, to talk my way out of that too.

The whole conversation was extremely fraught, which was no more than I'd expected. Ultimately I informed him that my arrest was just a terrible misunderstanding, and with a confidence I did not really feel assured him that soon things would be resolved.

After the call to Dad I spoke to Gladys about having no credit cards and no cash. I really wasn't functioning properly. I needed her help to apply for replacement cards. She found me phone numbers for Barclays and American Express. My new Connect card and Barclaycard had to be sent to my home address, but I could pick up the AmEx card from the company's Exeter office the following day.

Gladys then offered to drive me into Okehampton so that

I could draw some cash at my local Barclays. Fortunately this was still the kind of branch where the clerks often knew the customers, and I was lucky, albeit a tad embarrassed under the circumstances, to find on duty a woman who had been there so long we were on casual first-name terms, so I didn't have a problem with identification. Curly haired Mavis smiled as I approached the counter, but I saw the colour rise in her cheeks and I'm sure there was more than just a flicker of recognition in her eyes. I wondered if she knew of my arrest. Judging from the commotion outside the police station, it was quite likely that she did.

She made no comment, though, just asked for my postcode, presumably as a cursory security check as I assumed it was on the screen before her. I drew out £500 and was surprised at how much better it made me feel to have money in my pocket.

Gladys and I then made a quick stop at Peacocks, Okehampton's budget lady's clothing store, where I bought some clothes that fitted me: jeans, sweater and a pair of trainers, and some night things. As we walked around the store I thought I noticed a couple of other shoppers stare at me, then look away and whisper to each other. But it could have been my imagination.

During the drive to and from Okehampton, Gladys, true to form, chattered non-stop. I have absolutely no idea what about. But I found I didn't mind as much as I'd thought I might. It meant I barely had to speak. And she asked me no questions, which was an enormous relief.

Back at the vicarage she made a sandwich lunch, which again I could barely eat. The Reverend Gerald joined us, greeting me warmly but in such a way that I suspected he probably had no idea who I was. Afterwards Gladys showed me into a bedroom furnished in shabby G Plan, another legacy from the 1970s when I guessed the vicarage had last had a makeover. Surprisingly, there was a small flat-screen digital TV in one corner of the room.

'You'd probably like some time on your own,' said Gladys, displaying again that innate sensitivity which was so often belied by her manner. She gestured towards the television. 'We have all sorts staying here, and find the TV can be quite a comfort to people. Come and go as you please, anywhere in the house.'

Yes, well, I definitely came into the category of 'all sorts', I thought. But I expressed genuinely felt thanks, and spent most of the rest of the afternoon lying on the bed half dozing and half watching TV, until around 5 p.m. when I heard Gladys calling up the stairs. Marti Smith had returned.

I made my way down to the kitchen. Marti, back in her biker boots and leather coat, was smiling broadly.

'Good news, Marion: the SOCOs have finished at Highrise. I got the call as I was driving over here.'

I was pleased and relieved, even though I had come to the conclusion that staying at the vicarage might not be the ordeal I had feared.

'You're welcome to stay here, of course, but I'm sure you'll want to be in your own home as soon as you can,' said Gladys, full of understanding again. 'I'll drive you, if you like.'

I nodded, and smiled my thanks.

Marti Smith interjected.

'I think I'd better take you, Marion,' she said. 'I would expect there to be press waiting at your home. Could need dealing with.'

There were too. Not as many as there had been at the police station that morning. Just a couple of reporters and photographers and one TV crew, but quite enough to lower me deeper into despair. They were waiting in the yard at the front of the house and surrounded the Mini as we pulled to a halt.

'Just a minute,' said Marti, gesturing for me to stay put.

She got out of the car and addressed the assembled little throng, in a manner far more authoritative than you would somehow expect from so slight a creature with pink hair, introducing herself and telling them she was representing me.

'Mrs Anderson has nothing to say and indeed is legally unable to say anything at this stage,' she said. 'I am sure you all realize that you are on private property. Therefore I must ask you to leave, to make your way up to the top of the lane and wait there. Now skedaddle.'

To my surprise, the group meekly and immediately retreated. Only when they were out of sight did Marti walk around to the passenger side of the car, open the door and invite me to step out.

Then came the worst surprise of all that day.

As the press disappeared up the lane a taxi cab swung into view and pulled up alongside the Mini. Out stepped Robert, his anxious features fully illuminated in the glare of Highrise's security lights.

The very sight of him made me angry all over again, immediately stirring up feelings of distress and apprehension equal to anything that I had experienced during my confinement at Heavitree Road Police Station.

'My darling, whatever has happened?' he asked. 'I couldn't believe it when I heard you'd been arrested. Why on earth didn't you contact me? I'd have come home straight away.'

'Exactly,' I said. 'I didn't want you to come home. Not after what I now know about you. You're not my husband any more.'

'Look, can't we talk?'

'How did you find out I'd been arrested?' I asked.

'It's been on the news,' he said.

Of course it had. Robert would have seen reports of my arrest. I knew well enough that watching television was the number one off-duty activity for the men on the rigs.

'You weren't named,' Robert continued. 'Not in the reports I saw, anyway. They mostly focused on the recovery of the child, but also mentioned that a woman had been arrested at her Dartmoor home in connection with the abduction, and that it was believed she'd recently lost her own son. Naturally, I put two and two together. I called the Farleys and they confirmed it, said they'd heard from the vicar's wife . . .'

Robert carried on talking. I stopped listening. Gladys might be a wonderful woman in many ways, she might be a vicar's wife and a committed Christian, but she was no saint. I would have expected her to be no more able to resist a good gossip than any other human being. And I'd known the village jungle drums would be beating. I just somehow still wasn't prepared for the reality of it at all.

'. . . Anyway, I got a chopper back to the mainland first thing this morning,' I heard Robert say in the background. 'Caught the first available flight to Exeter, and here I am.'

'Yes, but God knows why,' I snapped at him.

'I want to help, of course,' he said, managing to sound quite wounded.

'You know what, Robert, you're the last person I want help from any more.'

He recoiled slightly.

Over his shoulder I could see movement by the farm gate just to the left at the top of the lane. It looked as if the photographers were trying to aim long lenses at us.

'Oh, come in, for God's sake, and let's get it over with,' I commanded him. 'But I warn you, I do not want you here.'

Marti Smith had yet to say a word. Tough as she patently was, it was clear that she had no intention of getting between husband and wife.

'Right, Marion, I'll leave you two to it then,' she said eventually, as I opened the front door. Then she paused. 'You obviously have a lot to discuss.'

That was an understatement, I thought. Though the truth was that I didn't particularly want to discuss anything with Robert. Not yet anyway.

I just nodded.

'I'll call you tomorrow, keep you informed,' she said.

I thanked her, and stepped into the house, pausing to check the new burglar alarm. It had not been activated. Well, the SOCOs who had remained in the house after my arrest wouldn't have known the code. But so much for any police concern for my security, I thought. At least they'd locked up. There was a key on the doormat. They must have used the one that lived on the hook on the kitchen wall and then posted it through the letter box.

Robert followed me into the hallway. I heard his little gasp as he began to notice the sorry amendments to Highrise. The grandfather clock which had stood there so proudly was missing, of course, and there was nothing on the walls which had previously been lined with those lovingly collected paintings and prints. I strode into the kitchen and could hear his footsteps on the flagstones as he followed me. I turned towards him as he stepped through the kitchen door.

His face was a picture. He looked absolutely bewildered. I could see his puzzled gaze taking in the Welsh dresser empty of our wonderful dinner service and the collection of Toby jugs which I had inherited from my gran. The glass-fronted cupboards were also empty, of course, and most of the glass broken.

'My God, whatever has happened here?' he asked, his jaw slack with disbelief.

I had wanted to see his reaction. Although it seemed impossible that he could be involved in any way, not just because of logistics but because I honestly still believed it was not his intention to harm me.

I told him about the intruder in the night and then the trashing of our home.

'Hence the burglar alarm,' I finished. 'At least I reckoned I could put a stop to that kind of thing happening. I hadn't bargained for someone dumping an abducted and abused child in the stables.'

Robert seemed speechless. When he eventually did speak he took me totally by surprise. Again.

'Have you contacted the insurance people?' he asked.

I did a double take.

'I haven't contacted anyone, I didn't even think about insurance,' I said, realizing as I spoke that it might seem rather extraordinary that I hadn't. Perhaps I'd just been too shocked, or perhaps subconsciously I hadn't really wanted to rebuild my home. I wasn't sure.

'Presumably the police gave you a crime number,' Robert continued.

Of course, I thought, PC Bickerton had told me to call to be given one. And wasn't it widely considered to be the only real point in calling the police for a burglary nowadays, so that you had a crime number for your insurance company?

'There is one but I don't know what it is,' I said. 'And do you think we could talk about this another time? I'm on bail for child abduction and attempted murder. I can't really be bothered with an insurance claim.'

'Of course,' he said quickly.

I waved an arm at our desecrated kitchen.

'I don't suppose you have any idea who may have done it?' I enquired casually.

He still didn't speak for a moment or two. I stared at him. He looked away from me. Was there the merest flicker in his eyes of some expression that I couldn't quite work out? I wasn't sure.

'Of course I don't,' he said eventually.

'The first time, when I heard sounds downstairs, I wondered if it might be you,' I told him.

'Me? Why on earth? Why would I steal into my own home in the middle of the night? It is still my home, you know.'

'So you might think,' I said.

He winced.

'Surely you can't hate me that much, Marion?'

'Oh yes, I can.'

He did not really react to that, instead speaking again very quickly, as if something had just occurred to him.

'So that's why you checked if I was really on Jocelyn, because you suspected me of breaking into my own home.'

I made no response.

'I still don't understand why you would think I would do something like that,' he repeated.

'I don't know. Perhaps you wanted to frighten me. Maybe you thought if I was frightened I would need you more and let you properly back into my life.'

Even as I spoke it sounded pretty lame.

'I would never want to frighten you, Marion, not for any reason, ever,' he said.

'But you have frightened me, Robert. You lied to me and deceived me, and you couldn't do anything more frightening than that. All that we had together I now know to be a lie. We've not only lost our son but also the entire foundation of our family life.'

'It wasn't like that . . .' he began.

'Oh yes, it was,' I said. 'Look, I just want you to go. I do not want you here under the same roof as me. Can you not understand that?'

'But I know I can help you, Marion. I want to give you support. And there are practical things I can help with too. I mean, are you sure you have the best possible solicitor? I'll pay, of course—'

'Robert, I am more than satisfied that Marti Smith, the woman you saw, is an excellent solicitor. In any case, it doesn't really matter, because I am innocent of everything I've been accused of. And surely, even in this mad crazy world I suddenly seem to inhabit, innocence must count for something.'

'Well, of course, of course,' he said.

'I do hope so,' I replied.

He took a step towards me, eyes imploring, reaching out with both hands. I took a step back. It wasn't even deliberate. Just the involuntary reaction I now seemed to have to the man I had so loved.

'Look, in any case, it doesn't matter what you've done, whatever you've done,' he said. 'I would understand, after what has happened. Anyone would. I know how overcome by grief you have been, we both have. Then you began to doubt me, in every way. I understand that too. You had good cause. And it was entirely my fault. So if you were responsible for any of this, then I am as much to blame as you.'

Even after all that had happened I found myself mildly shocked.

'I just told you I was innocent,' I said. 'And I cannot believe that you of all people would think any differently. How could you even begin to suspect that I may have had anything to do with abducting a child and letting him half freeze to death?'

'No, of course not, I only wanted you to know I understood, and I only meant . . .' He stumbled over his words, unable to finish the sentence.

'Oh, fuck off, Robert,' I said.

He backed away at once. It was probably only the second time I had ever sworn at him.

'I'm sorry,' he said quickly. 'Of course I know you wouldn't do anything like that. Of course I do. But if you didn't, then who did?'

'Who indeed, Robert?' I repeated. 'I've already asked you that question. You're every bit as likely to know as I am, if not more so.'

'What do you mean by that?'

I sighed. 'I'm not really sure, Robert,' I said. 'I'm not really sure of anything any more. Except that I do not want you here. Just leave, will you.'

He looked shifty.

'And where do you suggest I should go?' he enquired.

'I don't care,' I said. 'As long as you're not here with me.'

'Can I at least take the car?'

'I don't have it, you bloody fool. The police are still crawling all over it, looking for some obscure piece of evidence with which to pin an unspeakable crime on me.'

He looked quite aghast at that.

'I'll call another taxi then,' he said.

'Right. And go and wait in the sitting room, will you. I don't want to have to see you.'

He left the room without another word. About forty-five minutes later I heard a vehicle pull into the yard, presumably a taxi, and the front door open and close.

Robert left without attempting to speak to me again. I locked and bolted the door behind him.

It was almost eight o'clock by then. In a strange flash of practical lucidity I remembered that I had no transport of my own and called American Express to ask them to send my new card to Highrise after all. Then I spent a couple of hours just sitting at the kitchen table staring into space. I didn't dare switch on the TV. I was afraid of seeing the news and of what might be on it. Eventually I set the new alarm system, and took myself off to bed, dosing myself with zolpidem and whisky. Only as I climbed under the duvet did I realize I had made no further enquiries about Florrie. I could have done with her company and the close proximity of her warm furry body. Instead I had thoughtlessly left her to spend another night in kennels. However, I was sure she would forgive me under the circumstances and I would do my best to get her released the following day.

Slightly woozy, I buried my head in the pillows, pathetically grateful for the warmth and comfort of a proper bed, but I slept only fitfully. It seemed like only an hour or so later that there was a loud hammering on the front door. I guessed I must have been asleep then, and awakened by the hammering, as I'd heard no sound of a vehicle pulling into the yard.

I looked at the digital radio on the windowsill. In standby mode its display panel featured an illuminated clock. The time was just before 7 a.m. I got up and walked to the front of the house and peered through the landing window. It was still dark but the security lights had come on. I could see a car parked in the yard, but whoever was banging on the door was standing inside the porch out of my eyeline.

I wondered who would be calling at that hour, and for a moment was anxious that my mystery tormentor may have returned. But I reminded myself that he or she was not in the habit of knocking. Then I heard the rattle of the letter box and a powerful male voice calling out.

'Come on, Mrs Anderson, open up. Now.'

Of course it must be the police, I thought. The car outside was not a marked patrol car, but the voice had that note of accusative authority about it that I was beginning to get used to.

I made my way downstairs, using the remote control fob to deactivate the alarm system, then unlocked and opened the old oak door.

An angry-looking young woman stood on the doorstep flanked by two young men. The woman began to shout at me and one of the young men immediately started taking photographs.

I blinked in bewilderment. Bizarrely, I wondered what I must look like. I was wearing my pyjamas and had merely thrown my dressing gown over my shoulders as I left the bedroom. My hair was all over the place. I knew that I had dark hollows beneath my eyes, in contrast to the deathly pale of the rest of my face. And my cheekbones now jutted out almost as if they were razor blades beneath my skin and might break through at any moment. I never carried much weight, but I had become painfully thin, far thinner even than Marti Smith.

'You're wicked, wicked!' shouted the young woman. 'You're a monster and you should be locked up. What are you doing out on the streets? You should be in jail. They should throw the fucking key away after what you've done. You're a fucking monster, a fucking monster . . .'

And so it went on for what seemed like a very long time while I just stood in the doorway and took it. I think I was still slightly befuddled by my bedtime cocktail of drugs and alcohol. Whatever the cause, I had no way of dealing with this. Fleetingly, I even wished I hadn't sent Robert away.

Eventually I started to function again and tried to close the front door. The second young man, carrying a notebook instead of a camera, stepped forward and looked as if he might be about to push his way into the hall.

'Can't we just have a word, Mrs Anderson?' he enquired. 'Wouldn't you like to respond to Mrs Macintyre, give us your side of the story?'

Light dawned. Mrs Macintyre. The mother of the little boy left tied up in the stable. Of course it was Mrs Macintyre, whom I had seen on television, accompanied, apparently, by representatives of the Great British press.

I found my voice at last.

'No, I wouldn't,' I said.

Then I remembered how Marti Smith had dealt with the press.

'And I should remind you that you are on private property,' I continued as calmly as I could manage. 'I want you to leave. Please leave now.'

Rather to my surprise they backed off almost immediately. Well, I suppose they had got their story. And their pictures.

The young reporter asked over his shoulder if I was quite sure I didn't want to say anything.

'Please leave,' I repeated.

They climbed into their car, manoeuvred a three-point turn in the yard and retreated up the lane.

I had a feeling they may have operated against the law, in more ways than one. But I knew from the Joanna Yeates case in Bristol, when the murdered young woman's innocent land-lord Christopher Jefferies was hounded unmercifully by the press after being wrongly arrested, that a significant flaw in Britain's judicial system is that the laws of sub judice only come fully into force after a suspect has been charged.

In any case what did it matter? I wasn't going to do any-thing about it, was I? I didn't have the strength. I stood watching their tail lights disappear around the bend at the top of the lane. Then I closed and locked the door and slumped against it.

The urge to break down in tears again was almost over-whelming. But I was determined not to let myself. I really had to start fighting back, somehow. I knew what I needed to do. And the first thing was that I could not allow myself the luxury of collapsing in a heap. Not any more.

sixteen

Later that morning, at the more respectable hour of 10 a.m., Gladys Ponsonby Smythe turned up. In spite of the horrors of that dawn visit I remained determined to keep my resolution to find out the whole truth about all that had happened in my life, and the importance of maintaining my strength was pretty obvious. I knew that I had to at least try to eat properly. I also needed to slow up and calm down. I wasn't going to get anywhere rushing around like a headless chicken. If I didn't watch it, I was going to end up in prison for a very long time for an offence I hadn't committed. So I was in the kitchen making myself eat boiled eggs and toasted soldiers when she knocked on the door.

'Do you realize there are photographers wielding cameras with giant lenses at the top of your drive?' Gladys asked.

I confirmed that I did.

'Well, they should be moved on. Do you want me to call the police?'

I shook my head, glad that she knew nothing of my dawn visit from Mrs Macintyre, accompanied by a duo of so-called journalists. I didn't think I could have coped with Gladys's reaction to that.

'Apparently, if they are not actually on my property, there

is nothing I can do about it,' I said. 'And the police don't seem to be my biggest fans right now either. The more pressure I'm put under the better as far as they're concerned, I reckon.'

'Well, we'll see about that,' said Gladys. 'How's Marti Smith shaping up?'

'She seems great,' I said. 'But it's early days. I'm waiting to hear from her about what happens next.'

'Right.'

Gladys seemed, unusually for her, unsure of exactly what to do or say.

I offered her tea or coffee, saw her glance switch to my mercifully undamaged espresso machine, and remembered that she'd never been properly inside Highrise before. Even in its reduced circumstances the old house remained impressive.

'I'd love a cappuccino, chuck,' she said.

'Of course.'

She watched me make the coffee, a double espresso for me, and took a first appreciative sip of her cappuccino before speaking again.

'I really came to see if there was anything I could do to help,' she said. 'Not to drink your coffee. But this is a treat, I must say.'

She took another sip. She may not have bothered with or, for all I knew, been able to afford too many of the niceties of life at home, but she appreciated them all right when abroad, it seemed. I studied her thoughtfully. There could be no more casual dismissals of the few people who were prepared to help me.

'Well, there is something,' I said. 'The police still have my car and they don't seem in any hurry to return it. Florrie's in police kennels somewhere. I don't even know yet what I have to do to get her back, but she's sure to need to be collected. If you could do that, it would be really great. I miss her.'

'Of course I can do that. In fact, just leave the whole thing to me. I'll call the police and check out the form, then I'll pick her up for you as soon as possible.'

Gladys looked delighted to have been asked to perform a task, and I already knew she would do it with speed and efficiency.

'Anything else, luvvie?' she asked. 'Do you need any shopping done?'

I shook my head.

'I'm all right for a bit. Not hungry anyway.'

I gestured at the empty eggshells on my plate.

'Had to really force these down,' I said.

Gladys took another sip of her coffee. 'So you've no idea how long the police will keep your car?'

I shook my head again. 'At least until they've decided whether or not they're going to charge me, I should imagine.'

Gladys grunted. 'Bloody fools,' she said. 'Well, you have to have wheels, don't you, living out here?'

'I suppose so,' I said.

'Do you have a plan?'

Marti Smith was proved right yet again. The vicar's wife was totally practical. Far more intent on ensuring life carried on as it should than gathering in souls.

'Not really. I suppose I thought I'd wait a day or so to see what happened, then rent a car if I need to.'

'You don't want to do that, chuck,' she told me firmly. 'Costs a fortune and you might need every penny you have if the police carry on playing their bloody stupid game.'

She glanced around the kitchen and through the windows providing sweeping views across the garden, towards and beyond the old stable which had been the purveyor of so much grief for me, then out over the moors.

'Owning this house alone will prevent you getting legal aid,' she continued.

I hadn't thought about that. Money had never seemed to be a problem for Robert and me. And Robert had already seemed to indicate that he would be willing to pay my legal fees. But, of course, everyone knew that these fees could be crippling. I also realized that I actually had no idea how our family finances stood. Robert had handled everything. I did now know, however, that my husband was not a highly paid engineering executive in the oil industry, but a glorified labourer, and it was sixteen years previously that he had won the lottery, since when we had lived lavishly in an expensive house and wanted for nothing, and our son's school fees, albeit aided by his swimming scholarship, had been a substantial and largely unexpected expense over the last few years.

'What about Robert?' Gladys asked suddenly. 'Hasn't he come home yet? You're going to need as much help as you can get, and surely that's what husbands are for. Where is the man?'

I pulled a face. 'He came yesterday evening,' I said. 'Just as Marti and I arrived here. I'm afraid I told him to go away.'

'Oh dear.' She looked genuinely distressed for me. And I realized she expected an explanation. After all, absolutely nobody knew the truth about the rift between Robert and me.

'We've been under such stress since Robbie's death,' I said. 'It's my fault really, I just want to be on my own.'

'I see,' she said, looking as if she did anything but see.

'I expect it will all blow over,' I lied. 'But at the moment I'm pretty much on my own. I don't even know where Robert is.'

'I see,' she repeated, then went again into that practical mode in which she was at her most impressive.

'Right. First things first. Wheels will have to be down to me then. Just let me think about it and have a word round the village. I have an idea already. I'll get back to you later today.'

She left straight away, enlivened by her new sense of purpose. One shouldn't mock the Gladys Ponsonby Smythes of this world, I'd come to realize. She really did want to help, and when given the opportunity was extremely effective.

I made myself another double espresso after she'd left and did some more thinking.

I tried to call Sue Shaw again. I had no mobile, of course, but fortunately her number, scribbled on that petrol receipt, was pinned to the cork noticeboard on the wall in the kitchen by the house phone. I thanked the God I'd never believed in for my long-time Luddite habit. But Robbie's girlfriend wasn't answering her phone. Of course, her father could still have control of it.

I considered for a moment calling the landline at the Shaw family home, which I knew from my Internet search was listed on directory enquiries. But while I was still thinking about this the house phone rang and Sue's number flashed onto the screen. I answered eagerly. Unfortunately the caller turned out to be her father.

'I'm sorry about this, Mrs Anderson, but I'm going to have to ask you to stop calling my daughter,' he said. 'She was having a bad enough time dealing with the way your son died and then losing the baby before all this other stuff. I'm sorry, but I really don't want her speaking to you. So please don't call again.'

His manner was courteous and his voice level-pitched, but I suspected at once that it was an effort for him to maintain control.

'I-I only wanted to talk about Robbie,' I stumbled. 'I know we both miss him and—'

'It's a bit late for that, Mrs Anderson,' responded Michael Shaw sharply, his underlying anger quickly getting the better of him. 'Not only did you come to my home uninvited and bully my daughter, but it seems you set the cops on me, not only over how your son died but also over the abduction of that child. Are you out of your mind?'

I mumbled something wimpish. So Jarvis and his team had conducted further inquiries as promised. At the very least it would seem that they had interviewed Michael Shaw. Only at the moment, that did not appear to be helping my case very much.

'What the hell were you thinking of?' Shaw continued, and he was shouting at me now. 'Do you think I'm as barking mad as you are, is that it? Do you think I'd go around snatching innocent children in order to get some sort of perverted revenge on you and your precious son? Don't you fret, Mrs Anderson, anything I want to do or say to you I'll do it direct, only I'm probably too decent a bloke to give you what you really fucking well deserve. You're quite crazy enough to have taken that child, I'm dammed sure of that, and I hope the police throw the fucking book at you. I hope they lock you up and lose the fucking key . . .'

Luke Macintyre's mother had already given me much the same message in much the same language. I couldn't listen to any more of it. In any case there was little point. I ended the call and took a deep, deep breath. I asked myself what else I could expect. Of course Michael Shaw was furious. He would be furious whether or not he was responsible in any way for Robbie's death or Luke Macintyre's abduction. But the latter did seem unlikely, I had to admit. And either way, it seemed clear that the Shaw family were now totally off the radar to me. I had to sort out the whole ghastly mess for myself.

Firstly there were a couple of other phone calls I wanted to make. I never had made that walk on the beach with Bella nor offered an explanation for not doing so. Not, I realized, that I would really need to do that. Bella could hardly have missed the level of media coverage my arrest had attracted. Whether or not she had tried to call me since hearing the news was unknown since the police still had my mobile phone and I hadn't ever given her the Highrise landline number.

I remembered how kind she had been to me on the night of Robbie's death. If anything, I had been plunged into even deeper despair by subsequent events than I had been then. And Bella, for whatever reason, had been the person who gave me some sort of comfort at the start of this dreadful nightmare I was now living. Maybe she really was the nearest thing I had to a friend. Gladys had been kind, too. More than kind. And wonderfully practical and helpful. But she didn't hit the spot the way Bella did.

I so much wanted to call Bella. But, during our first meeting on Exmouth beach, which now seemed so very long ago, I'd plumbed her number straight into my detained mobile, and I had no other record of it. I tried directory enquiries to see if I could get a landline number for her, but I had no proper address, and a not particularly helpful operator could find no listing.

I called Dad again as I'd promised. He still sounded terribly upset, probably not least because I again turned down his offer to drive to Highrise to look after me.

I checked my watch. It was now 11 a.m. I decided that if I hadn't heard from Gladys by two o'clock, I would get a taxi into Okehampton, go to the bank again, draw every last penny out of my joint account with Robert and hire a car regardless.

However, not long after noon I heard two vehicles pull into

the yard. I opened the front door and looked out. Gladys was driving one of them. I saw that she had Florrie in the back.

She coasted to a halt, stepped out of her car into the yard and, smiling broadly, opened one of the rear doors releasing my dog. Florrie demolished the distance between us in one bound then covered me with licks. And hair, of course. None the less, I cuddled her close.

'However did you manage to get her here so quickly?' I asked, while thanking Gladys profusely.

The vicar's wife tapped the side of her prominent nose. 'Not what you know, but who you know, flower,' she said.

Meanwhile a man I couldn't quite place, but whose face looked vaguely familiar, stepped out of the second vehicle, a small, not very new Ford.

Gladys introduced him as Bert Jameson, churchwarden at St Andrew's. The man shook my hand with surprising warmth, I thought, under the circumstances.

'This is Bert's boy's car,' Gladys continued. "Fraid young Charlie likes to put his foot down a bit too much and he's got himself into a spot of bother. Too many points on his licence. Off the road for six months. He and his dad say you're welcome to borrow the car as long as you pay the extra for the insurance. Sorry it's not quite the class of motor you're used to.'

'Oh, Gladys, Bert, thank you so very much,' I said with genuine gratitude. 'It looks like a limo to me, I can tell you.'

I invited them in, offering them both coffee.

'The espresso machine's on standby,' I told Gladys.

'Alas, we can't,' she said. 'We've got a wedding tomorrow morning, and Bert and I have to finish preparing the church.'

I was shamefully rather pleased, even though they were doing me the most enormous favour. I didn't feel up to polite chit-chat. And I reckoned Gladys realized that, understanding so much more about human nature than I'd given her credit for.

Anyway, I wanted to get out of the house that no longer felt like my home. And I decided that as I couldn't phone Bella I might try to pay her a visit. She'd referred to walking home from Bodley School, which narrowed down the territory considerably. As much for something to do as anything else, I thought I would just drive around the area for a bit and see if I could spot her car.

I wrapped a silk scarf around my head and put on a pair of clear glass spectacles, which we'd once been given as part of an advertising campaign by a company promoting designer frames, as some sort of elementary disguise and protection. I thought I could at least prevent any lurking snappers getting a halfway decent shot of me, and also hopefully avoid the sort of public recognition that might lead to another incident like the one outside Heavitree Road Police Station when that rotten orange had been thrown.

I bundled Florrie into the back of Charlie Jameson's elderly Ford, which started at the second attempt, and I trundled up the lane. Flash bulbs half blinded me as I turned left heading towards the Exeter road, past two camera-wielding young men.

The rain was freezing again. The wind bitter off the moors. The two photographers were muffled in big scarves and waterproof gear. Their faces were white and pinched and they looked freezing too. Which pleased me considerably, and was certainly about the only thing that day likely to bring me any pleasure.

I stopped at a petrol station to fill up the tank and bought a packet of boiled sweets. I was pleased that I knew my way to Bodley School as the little Ford had no sat nav.

I drove past the end of the road where I'd once lived, in the little studio flat in a big old Victorian house where Robert and I had first become lovers, and on through Exwick towards Bodley School. I turned onto the leafy street of neat little 1930s semis, very like the Shaws' home in Okehampton, which led directly to Bodley, the street in which I'd somehow assumed Bella would be likely to live. I was hoping to see her car parked outside one of the houses.

I didn't, so I carried on driving, ultimately turning onto the road which ran into the dreaded Bridge Estate, a place we teachers at Bodley, to our shame perhaps, had more or less regarded as a no-go area. I noticed that this road was called Riverview Avenue, and wondered if there could be a more unsuitable name. I was pretty sure I hadn't even known the name of the road when I'd taught at Bodley all those years ago. Yet I was conscious of something niggling at me about Riverview Avenue, a significance which lurked somewhere in the back of my mind that I couldn't quite pull forward.

Looking around me, I was aware that the River Exe could not be far away, but there was certainly no view of it. Neither did there appear to be a single tree along this 'avenue', which became more and more grim as I drove deeper into the Bridge Estate.

Hardly any of the little front gardens looked as if anyone ever paid them any attention. Several of the houses had broken windows. The garages, built in blocks on one side of the avenue, were covered in graffiti.

In the West Country we are spoiled when it comes to places to live and everything, I suppose, is relative. Gladys, ever full of surprises, and hardened by inner-city Liverpool, probably wouldn't have batted an eyelid. But I was shocked. I hadn't realized the Bridge Estate was as bad as this. And I wondered if it had deteriorated since my time teaching close by.

I was even more shocked to spot Bella's Toyota Corolla on the hardstand in front of number 5 Riverview Avenue, right in the most undesirable heart of the estate. A group of rather frightening-looking young men in hoodies were lounging by the row of dilapidated garages opposite, openly smoking suspiciously large and droopy-looking cigarettes.

I coasted past and parked at what I hoped would be just the right distance to give me a decent view of the house without being spotted by anybody going in or out. It was one of the most unkempt in the road. A broken bicycle and an old mattress lay strewn across the little front garden. Two or three tubs bearing dried-out conifers were the only sign of an ill-fated, obviously long ago, attempt at any sort of gardening. The windows were filthy and it looked as if the curtains hanging inside were ragged and dirty.

I couldn't somehow associate this at all with the woman I'd thought I was beginning to get to know, the woman who had seemed so organized and almost professionally kind, like the nurse she'd told me she'd once been, on the night of Robbie's death. Then I had a thought. The car on the hardstand was the right make and colour, of course, but Bella might not be the only person living within walking distance of Bodley School to own such a vehicle. I peered at it more closely. I remembered noticing some time ago that the rear wing on the driver's side of Bella's car had been quite badly dented and the end of the bumper which wrapped partially round the wing twisted upwards at an angle. I always noticed damage to cars. Of course, she could have had it repaired. But apparently not. This vehicle had the same distinctive amendment. It had to be Bella's car. And this had to be her house.

I reflected on my own beautiful home and the impression it must have made on Bella, something which I hadn't given a thought to before. But then, I hadn't expected the contrast to be quite as great. Everything in my life must have looked so perfect and enviable to Bella.

I just couldn't quite bring myself to go and knock on the door, with its peeling yellow paint and the number slightly askew. Instead I sat there looking at the place, thankful all over again for the little old Ford which was now a bonus in more ways than one. My Lexus would have stood out like Joan Collins on a Saga holiday. The Ford fitted in perfectly. Even so, the hoodies paid me rather more attention than I would have liked. I suppose it was because I was a stranger in a strange car in what may have been a rough area but was probably also a tight community. I felt very uncomfortable, but I still sat there for about half an hour just watching, really, though I wasn't sure for what, unless it was for further confirmation that this was Bella's house because I still couldn't quite believe it.

Making myself ignore the attentions of the hoodies, who walked by once or twice staring at me long and hard, I wound down the driver's window. I could hear a dog barking, from within number 5, I was sure. Was it Flash's bark? I couldn't be certain, but if not then the barking dog was certainly the same sort of size as Flash.

I glanced across at the garage marked number 5. The flip-up-and-over door stood half open and, in common with most of the others in the row, did not look as if it would shut properly, let alone lock. All the same, I guessed that most of the residents garaged their cars at night if only in the belief that by putting their vehicles out of sight they would lessen temptation to would-be vandals.

Then my attention was drawn to a drumming sound above my head. To my alarm I realized that one of the hoodies was walking past nonchalantly running his fingertips along the Ford's roof. I nearly swallowed one of my boiled sweets whole. Florrie, always a good traveller, was contentedly curled up on the back seat, but she did manage a noise vaguely resembling a growl, and I was pathetically glad of her presence even though I knew what a big softy she was.

It seemed crazy, but I realized I could be putting myself in danger by just sitting in a parked vehicle on that road. In spite of the Toyota outside and the barking dog I could actually see no sign of inhabitation at number 5. And anyway I no longer had any wish to visit Bella. I really couldn't.

I turned the key in the Ford's ignition. It started on the fourth attempt just as I was beginning to get anxious and the hoodies were beginning to look even more interested.

Visiting Bella had in any case been little more than a displacement activity. There was so much I intended to do. So much I *needed* to do. So many crazy thoughts running through my head. I drove straight to an Internet cafe I'd passed earlier on the road out of Exeter. I now had no computer of any kind at home, and I wanted to check Robert out again, as Anderton and Anderson. Just as I'd done before my arrest, using the iPad I so wished the police had not taken from me.

The results were, of course, exactly the same as before. However, I was perhaps a different person from the woman who had first checked out her husband in this way. I'd been desperate then but was even more so now. I'd been arrested on suspicion of the attempted murder of a child for a start, and that just didn't seem believable. But it had happened all right, and I couldn't help thinking that it was in some way linked to the death of my son and the discoveries I had made about Robert. I studied carefully the names and addresses of, in particular, all the Devon 'Andertons', looking for any sort of clue, anything that might mean something to me now which hadn't before. It was quite an exercise.

When I'd finished I ordered a second coffee. I needed to sit and think for a bit, to assimilate and evaluate the information I had accumulated. After half an hour or so, still pondering my day's activities, I made my way to a mobile phone shop I'd noticed just a block or so away and bought myself a pay-as-you-go phone. Then I drove home via Exeter Waitrose, which, unfortunately from my point of view, stands almost adjacent to Heavitree Road Police Station. I stocked up on provisions other than bacon and eggs and whisky, thinking as I did so that I might soon have to shop somewhere more cheaply. I was too late to catch the bank in Okehampton and empty the joint account as I had earlier planned, but I had transport now and in any case I didn't suppose it mattered much. Unless I could find a way of proving my innocence, any financial difficulties I might face would soon be irrelevant. I would be in jail.

And one thing had become very clear. There was someone out there determined to ensure that I was going to jail.

seventeen

A couple of days later Robert called to say that he was returning to the North Sea. He might as well go and earn some money, he said, as I obviously wanted nothing to do with him.

He told me he was calling from Aberdeen airport, and I could clearly hear airport noises and announcements, even the odd Scottish accent, in the background, which I am sure had been his intention. Just in case I thought he was lying again, I suppose. I didn't ask him where he had been for the three days since I'd turned him away from Highrise. That was irrelevant now. I politely thanked him for telling me. I wanted no more quarrels. They were irrelevant now too.

I had to concentrate on building my strength and learning to deal with all that was happening. I had various plans in my head, but I had to proceed with care. I was already on police bail after all.

I suppose it was almost masochistic of me to buy the newspapers, local and national, every day but I could not resist. In any case I needed to know what was going on and what was being said.

In spite of the dawn offensive on my home by Mrs Macintyre and her insistent press escort, the story of which ran in only one newspaper, presumably the one that had stage-managed the operation, there was not as much coverage of my case as I would have expected. Certainly not as much as there would probably have been before the debacle which had followed the death of Joanna Yeates. But there was enough to upset me quite badly on most days.

I found nothing, however, anything like as sensational as, six days after my release on police bail, a front-page report in the local evening paper, the *Express & Echo*, which was not actually directly connected with my case.

A Mrs Brenda Anderton, aged forty-four, had been killed in a tragic motor accident. Her vehicle, a Toyota Corolla, had been in a head-on collision with a milk tanker on the A377 near Mrs Anderton's Bridge Estate home. An eyewitness said that the car had been travelling at speed before appearing to fly out of control and hurtle onto the wrong side of the road. The police were currently investigating the possibility of mechanical failure. Corollas were among the models recently recalled worldwide by Toyota due to a much-publicized problem with sticking accelerators. The driver of the milk tanker had escaped with minor injuries.

A picture of the dead woman was spread across two columns. And I recognized her at once.

Indeed, I knew her quite well. But I knew her as Mrs Bella Clooney.

There was no doubt about it, even though the report described the woman as having two daughters aged twenty-seven and eleven, rather than a son and daughter aged eleven and twelve, and named her dog, which had apparently died with her in the accident, as Splash, not Flash.

I read the piece through two or three times to make sure of it all. Then I decided to contact Robert at once, while still parked in the car park of the supermarket where I'd bought the newspaper. He had even more explaining to do.

My hands were trembling so much that I had difficulty in punching his number into my new mobile. He might have been out of range in the North Sea, of course, but I suspected not. I was right. He answered his phone straight away. He sounded upset and rather peculiar, which was probably only to be expected under the circumstances, even without the added element of Brenda Anderton's sudden death. But there was another note in his voice too – the glum resignation, perhaps, of someone who suspected that the extraordinary game he had played for so long was finally at an end.

'You've heard the news, I presume?' I began flatly.

'What news?' he responded. Perhaps I had underestimated him. Could he really still be trying to play his cruel game? I reckoned it was more likely that his disingenuousness was just an automatic reaction. The habit of sixteen years must be hard to break.

'I have a copy of the *Express & Echo* here and I've just read the front-page story of a woman called Brenda Anderton who has died suddenly in a motor accident,' I recited as calmly as I could. 'I recognized her picture, of course, but then, you would expect me to, wouldn't you?'

There was a brief silence.

'I see,' he said eventually.

'You'd better come to Highrise as soon as you can, hadn't you?' I continued. 'I think we have rather a lot to talk about.'

'Yes, I know,' he replied. And this time he did sound beaten. 'Where are you?'

'I'm in Exeter. They told me . . .' He paused. 'I, uh, heard last night,' he continued rather obliquely. 'I just got back.'

I was pretty sure he was telling the truth for once. Not just because of that somewhat contrived airport call, but also, as I'd already turned him out of our home, there was little point, surely, in him lying to me now.

'Right. So it won't take you long, will it?'

He mumbled his agreement. I started the engine of the little Ford, which this time obliged at the first attempt, and drove straight back to Highrise where I unpacked the small amount of shopping I'd picked up and fed Florrie her favourite treat – a couple of the disgusting-smelling tripe sticks I'd bought for her. Then I made myself a coffee and sat down at the kitchen table to drink it, with the newspaper spread out in front of me.

I'd confided in the woman I'd known as Bella Clooney, in as much as I'd ever confided in anyone other than, ironically, Robert. She had been the one I had turned to on the night my son died. She had helped me to take a bath. She had seen me naked. The very thought of it turned the blood in my veins to ice.

Robert arrived less than an hour later. I remained sitting at the kitchen table as I heard a vehicle pull up then drive away again. Another taxi, I supposed. It seemed to take him an inordinately long time to reach the front door, perhaps he was trying to think of what he was going to say. I'd put so much of the story together now that in some ways it didn't matter a great deal any more. But that wouldn't be the way he would regard it, and numb though I was, I did have a need to hear his version of events.

Somewhat to my surprise – technically this was still his home too – he knocked on the front door.

'It's not locked,' I called out.

I heard the door open and shut, listened as he made his way along the hallway, and watched wordlessly as he stepped into the kitchen. His face was ashen. Again, his long black hair was unkempt and he needed a shave. There was despair in his eyes. He really didn't look like my Robert at all. But then, he wasn't my Robert any more.

It struck me suddenly that not only did I no longer love him – he had destroyed that in me – but I now hated him. I actually hated him.

I gestured for him to sit down opposite me. I didn't offer him tea or coffee. I didn't say anything, just waited for him to speak.

'I don't know where to begin,' he said. His voice was trembling. So were his hands which he laid flat on the table before him.

'Just tell me the truth, for God's sake,' I said, rather more sharply than I had meant to. After all, I didn't want to put him off his stride. I didn't want to say or do anything to stop him telling me everything. At last.

'I presume that Mrs Brenda Anderton was your wife,' I said. 'And I presume that you were married to her before you married me. No long-lost wife in Australia. Instead, a current second wife, or should I say first, just up the A30 in Exeter.'

He nodded.

'Well, don't you think this might be the time to tell me about it?' I suggested.

He nodded again.

'But where, where do I . . .' He seemed unable to finish formulating the question I knew he was trying to ask.

'Where do you start? At the beginning would be good.'

'Yes.' Robert just stared at me. I could see tears welling up in eyes that full of pleading.

'Please don't try to play the sympathy card,' I snapped at him. 'It's far too late for that. Just get on with it.'

'Yes,' he said again.

I waited. Eventually he did get on with it. Or after a fashion.

'What I told you when you found out I was really Rob Anderton was all true,' he began.

I raised an eyebrow.

'Well, mostly. From the moment I met you I just knew I had to be with you. You were all I wanted in the world. I wanted to be with you and leave everything else behind. I should have told you about Brenda, of course. I should have explained. But I just couldn't. It seemed easier to pretend I was a free agent. To carry on as if neither Brenda, nor our daughters, existed. Then I could be with you, in your world. That was the world I wanted. Your calm, middle-class world; a beautiful home, peace, warmth. Not the crazy place I inhabited with Brenda.'

He spat the last words out, bitterness oozing from every pore of him.

'Brenda is dead, Robert,' I said. 'You seem so bitter. I mean, how do you feel about that? You have a twenty-seven-year-old daughter, it seems. You'd been together that long, far longer than we had. Are you not shocked? Are you not grieving for Brenda?'

'Of course I am, yes. But the whole thing between us had become so dreadful, you see—'

'Other people face up to bad marriages, and to new loves, to changes in their lives,' I interrupted. 'Other people separate and get divorced. They don't just carry on with two families. Two lives. How on earth did you think you could get away with it?'

He shook his head. I spoke again before giving him the chance to.

'But you did get away with it, didn't you, Robert? For sixteen years. And you had a second child with Brenda years after our so-called wedding, years after our son was born. You bastard. My God, you're a piece of work. I want to know how you did it, and why. All of it.'

I knew I was talking too much. I wanted him to do the talking. But I couldn't stop myself.

'It was the job,' he said obscurely. 'Working on the rigs. I realized it might be possible to juggle two families. I became sure I could do it. I told you I worked three weeks on and two weeks off. Actually, after getting my lottery money, I arranged to work two weeks on and three weeks off. That gave me one week out of five to spend with Brenda. I told her I had to work longer than average stints away because we needed the money, for the children, you see. And she accepted that. I didn't think I would be able to pull it off for ever. Definitely not for anything like as long as I did. In the beginning, you see, I had a plan. When Laura was older, I was going to come clean. To get divorced. To tell you both. You and Brenda. Well, that's what I intended, anyway.'

He let the sentence tail off lamely.

'That's a pretty familiar story, isn't it?' I said sarcastically. 'The married man who plans to leave the missus when the children get older. Oh please, Robert.'

'It wasn't like that,' he said. 'You don't understand.'

'Make me,' I snapped.

'You don't realize what a lovely little girl Laura was,' he continued, a faraway look in his eyes. 'Janey is too. Pretty as a picture. Just such a sweet child—'

'Spare me,' I said.

He seemed to pull himself together with a great effort of will.

'I couldn't leave Brenda when Laura was a little girl because of what I knew was going to happen to our child,' he said.

'Laura had juvenile Huntington's. She was diagnosed at eleven. It's rare but certainly not unknown for it to develop that young. You can have no idea what it was like to watch that lovely normal little girl turn into . . .'

He paused, brought his hands up to his face and fleetingly closed his eyes as if shutting out some unwanted picture. I'd half expected some sort of sob story, and been determined to remain unmoved by anything he might tell me. After all, with his track record, how would I even know if he was telling the truth? But surely even Robert would not lie about something like this. I was shocked in spite of myself, and did not trust myself to speak. Instead I waited for him to continue.

'I don't know what you know about Huntington's,' he carried on eventually. 'It's degenerative and incurable. It destroys muscle coordination and ultimately leads to the most serious mental disorder. Worst of all, perhaps, the younger someone gets it, the faster it progresses. It used to be called Huntington's chorea, because . . . well, Laura very quickly began to lose control of her limbs. After a bit she couldn't even feed herself properly. She started to slur her words. And then there was the mental deterioration. My sweet little girl became aggressive and disorientated. She couldn't remember things. I will never forget the first time I went home and she didn't know who I was . . .'

He paused and glanced at me. I guessed that even in the middle of this surely genuinely harrowing part of his story he was wondering if I had picked up on his use of the word 'home'. I had. But I made no comment.

'We'd only learned what was wrong with her a few weeks before I met you,' he went on. 'I will never be able to explain how I felt. I couldn't cope at all. I thought maybe I would just take off somewhere, disappear, never come back. That was one half of me. But I suppose I knew I couldn't just walk out on Laura. Nor on Brenda for that matter. Though God knows she deserved it.'

'What do you mean, deserved it?'

'She never told me there was Huntington's in her family. Even when we found out what was wrong with Laura, she carried on lying to me. She said she hadn't known—'

'So lying is something else that runs in the family,' I interrupted sharply. I knew it was small of me, particularly in view of the story he was finally sharing with me, but I couldn't help myself.

Robert winced.

'Didn't you ever meet Brenda's parents, or any other relatives?' I asked.

He shook his head.

'She always told me that she never even knew who her father was. Her mother brought her up on her own. But she died when Brenda was thirteen and Brenda was put into foster care. She was still with her foster parents when I met her. She was just sixteen and I was nineteen. She was about to start training as a nurse, but all she really wanted to do was get married and have a family. I sort of got carried along with it. She fell pregnant damned near the first time we slept together and that was that really. Before I knew it we were wed.' He paused.

'I seem to have the knack of getting women pregnant straight away,' he said.

'And your son was the same apparently,' I blurted out. 'His girlfriend was pregnant, even though she claims they only had unprotected sex once. He'd only found out the day he . . . he died. I thought at first that was why . . . why he did what he did.'

'B-but we didn't even know he had a girlfriend,' Robert stumbled.

270

He was looking deep into my eyes. For a fleeting moment I even longed for the old closeness. But that was long gone.

'At the funeral, remember? Sue Shaw. I knew that he'd written about her in his diary, but I still thought it was probably innocent. How wrong can you be? Both the men in my life were keeping big secrets from me, it seems.'

'I'm so sorry,' said Robert.

'Save it,' I replied. 'I just want to hear the rest of the story.'

Robert sighed.

'When I met you it really was the way I told you before, Marion,' he said. 'And the bit about the lottery win was true too. The terrible news about my daughter and winning all that money came more or less together. It was enough to drive any man half mad, surely?'

He looked at me pleadingly. I did not respond. He sighed again.

'That day in Exeter, I was just walking around, thinking, trying to work out what to do,' he said. 'What I wanted was to give all the money to Brenda and then just leave. But I don't think I'd ever have been able to bring myself to carry that through. Then along you came. Suddenly I saw this way of having the life I wanted, with you, and still looking after Brenda and Laura. Because Laura had developed the disease so young we knew it was going to be particularly severe, and we also knew that she would end up in care eventually, although Brenda and I decided straight away to keep her at home as long as we could. Well, Brenda did really. She was the one who had to do the caring. I admired her for that if for nothing else . . . she would have made a good nurse, Brenda. She seemed to have a natural talent for it . . .'

Yes, I thought. Didn't she though? I'd experienced that the night of Robbie's death, when, rather chillingly I now thought,

Brenda had provided such proficient help and support. Or so it had seemed. I'd believed she actually had been a nurse. And I'd really believed she was my friend. That was why I'd wanted to see her after I was released from jail. Thinking about it made me feel physically sick.

'And where is Laura now?' I asked. 'I mean, is she still alive? It sounds as if she is from the newspaper report.' I gestured at the *Express & Echo* on the table.

Robert nodded. 'Just about, that's all you can say. She's in a specialist care home, the other side of Exeter. She went there when she was sixteen. And, well, we always felt guilty, felt it was because we put her there that she deteriorated fast, even faster than we'd expected.'

'Do you see her?' I asked.

'I used to. Not any more. She can barely function, and she doesn't know us at all now. I just can't.'

He paused.

'Brenda does, though.' Another pause. 'I mean, did.'

'But you had a second child, for God's sake.' I tapped the newspaper again. 'You and your wife . . .' I put emphasis on the 'w' word. '. . . conceived another child even though you both knew she was a Huntington's carrier. And even though you claim that I was the love of your life, you were patently still having sex with the woman who was really your wife. And, knowing you, rather a lot of it.'

Robert winced again. 'It just seemed to happen,' he said. 'But it wasn't the way it was with you. I mean, how could it be? Sex with you has always been so special. But with Brenda, well, it was kind of automatic really, what we'd always done—'

'Spare me,' I interrupted more forcefully. 'I really don't want to hear the gruesome details of your sex life with another woman.'

He nodded apologetically again.

'But never mind that, and never mind the wicked double life you were leading, wicked to both of us. What about the risks? You and Brenda conceived another child even though you knew he or she would probably develop this awful disease. That's really thoughtless and cruel. I can't believe it.'

This time Robert shook his head.

'I thought Brenda had been sterilized. After we found out about Laura we agreed that's what she'd do. And she told me she'd had the op one time while I was away working.' He glanced at me. I decided not to interrupt again, not to point out that he may have been working, or he may, of course, have been with his other wife. With me.

'But she hadn't had it. She'd been taking the pill. Apart from anything else nobody could possibly have coped with a second child with poor Laura at home the way she was. However, as soon as we accepted that Laura had to go into professional care Brenda stopped taking the pill. I never really understood why. She said she just wanted another child who was normal. But there was little chance of that. When she told me she was pregnant I was horrified. Not only because of what she had done, and the kind of life we might be bringing into the world, but because of you too, of course, and our life.'

'It's not definite, though, is it?' I asked. 'It's not a hundred per cent that the disease is inherited, surely. Mightn't your other daughter be OK?'

'That's what Brenda said. She said there was a fifty per cent chance that Janey would be OK. And it was a chance she'd just had to take.'

'Well, presumably that's still the case. Where is she now, by the way? This eleven-year-old child you never bothered to mention to me.'

273

'She's with a neighbour. And no, it's not the case actually. Janey will get Huntington's. It's just a matter of when. It might not be until she's into her forties – that's the most common time – or she might get the juvenile variety like her sister. But one thing is certain, she will get it.'

'How can you be so sure?'

He wiped a hand across his eyes, wearily.

'When Janey was born I made Brenda have all the tests. She didn't when we'd found out about Laura. In any case predictive tests for Huntington's were pretty new then – they were only developed in 1993 – and Brenda said she wasn't convinced of their accuracy. That we could end up being worried sick for nothing. But after Janey I insisted. She didn't want to, not even then. She said there was no point. That we knew the risks. But I made her, and this time I went to the hospital with her, for the tests and the results. I just had to know exactly what we were facing. The disease is caused by the mutation of the gene called Huntington's. Everyone has two copies. So more often than not a child has a fifty per cent chance of inheriting it. Just like Brenda told me. The only thing is, it turned out that both Brenda's Huntington genes were mutated. That made it a hundred per cent certain that any child she had would develop the disease.'

I thought about what he was saying. 'But Brenda didn't know?'

He shook his head. 'Not until she had the tests, no. I do believe that. You would have to be quite mad to bring a child into the world knowing for sure it was going to get that disease. And she wasn't that. Not then, anyway.'

'What do you mean? Not then?'

'I'd recently been beginning to notice things about Brenda, things other people probably wouldn't, that made me think she was now developing Huntington's. And that her mind was beginning to be affected. Her behaviour was erratic. She could be shaky too, physically, although perhaps again not noticeable to anybody else. Not yet.'

I remembered her shaking and, more specifically, the smashed wine glass and the difficulty she'd had that day on the beach attaching the lead to her dog's collar.

'I suppose I saw things,' I said. 'But only occasionally.'

He nodded. 'That's how it is to begin with.'

I stared at him. I really hadn't expected this.

'Did she know?' I asked. 'Did she know she was getting it?'

'She knew she was going to get it, of course,' he said. 'After the tests showed the double mutation she knew it was inevitable. And she'd reached the optimum age. But sometimes the disease doesn't develop until people are in old age. Sometimes people die before they get it. I did feel guilty about that side of making her have the tests, that she then knew there was no chance at all of her avoiding the damned thing. But she seemed to cope with it extraordinarily well, really. Brenda was very good at going into denial, I think. Very good indeed.'

Wasn't she just? I thought, reflecting on all the times we had spent together. Brenda knowing full well who I was and my relationship with her husband. Me totally unaware of who she really was.

What had she been hoping to achieve? And had she achieved it with Robbie's death? It was my belief that she had.

I'd thought I had guessed most of Robert's story. But I hadn't dreamed of anything like this. For a fleeting second I felt a wave of sympathy towards the man I'd once so loved. I quickly cast it aside.

He had deceived me to a devastating degree. He deserved no sympathy at all. Not from me or from anyone.

'You could have told me,' I said. 'You should have told me. We could have worked something out together. That's what people do.'

He shook his head quite violently.

'No. Don't you see? I wanted another life. I needed another life. I loved my daughters but couldn't cope with them being all there was for me. I couldn't cope with just watching Laura deteriorate and then waiting for little Janey to develop this terrible illness. Just watching and waiting. I was afraid I would end up as mad as them. And I suppose in a way I did.'

'But you brought it on yourself,' I said. 'I mean, what did you think, for God's sake, when you came back the night Robbie died and there was Brenda, your wife, in our kitchen? What did you think, Robert?'

'I didn't know what to think. But it was obvious that you didn't know who she was, and all I wanted was to keep things that way for as long as I could. That's why I had to leave you the next day. I had to go and see Brenda. To find out what was going on. To try, somehow, to square things with her. Don't you see?'

'Oh, I see all manner of things now, Robert. All manner of things. But what did you say to each other? What did she tell you, and what load of rubbish did you tell her?'

'I told her more or less the truth,' he said. I almost smiled at the use of the phrase 'more or less'. I feared that was probably the best he would ever be able to do with the truth.

'She told me about meeting you on Exmouth beach by chance, seeing Robbie, and being struck at once by how like me he was. Then how she talked to you and found out about your husband Robert and so on. She said she pretended to be someone else simply so that she could get close to you, see how you lived, find out more about our life together.'

'And did she tell you how she felt when she found out about me?'

'She said she was devastated, of course. But she decided not to confront me at least until she'd found out more. And she still didn't want to risk losing me altogether, it seemed.'

'But can't you imagine the effect it must have had on her seeing the near-perfect life we had together?' I asked. 'Imagine comparing the life you had with me, here at Highrise, with her life, her hellish life surely, looking after a dying daughter, knowing both she and her second child would go the same awful way, and living in that dreadful house I assume you shared . . .'

I stopped abruptly.

He shook his head very slightly as if trying to clear it. 'You went to the house? To Riverview Avenue?'

'Not exactly,' I said, and I told him about my aborted visit to the home of the woman I knew as Bella Clooney.

Robert did a kind of double take. 'My God,' he said. 'You only told me she was called Bella. I'm sure of it. If you'd ever mentioned that the surname of the woman you met on the beach was Clooney, I don't know, but I may just have wondered—'

'What are you talking about?' I interrupted, irritated that he seemed to be going off at some sort of a tangent.

'Brenda was crazy about George Clooney. Obsessed almost. She had DVDs of all his movies, the complete boxed set of *ER*, and she played them all the time—'

'Can we get back to what we were talking about, please?' I interrupted again.

He nodded. Then did another double take. 'My God, what would have happened if you had knocked on the door, I wonder, gone into the house . . .'

His voice tailed off.

'Indeed,' I said. 'It was the day after I was released by the police. And you were there then, with Brenda, weren't you? I presume you went to her after I kicked you out. You might have answered the door to me. Wouldn't that have been interesting?'

He looked startled. 'Yes, I didn't think of that. Yes, I suppose I was staying there then.'

'And, even if you hadn't been in the house, I could easily have noticed signs of your presence, seen photos of you about the place,' I continued. 'Or did you do your best to prevent there being any of you with her too?'

He looked down at his hands.

'You'd certainly have seen more pictures of George Clooney,' he muttered.

I ignored that.

'I didn't have to wait long to see Brenda's picture in the paper, though, did I?' I went on. 'To see her name in print.'

He made no comment.

'So, getting back to your story, how did you attempt to "square things with her" as you put it?' I asked.

'Well, I just promised her I wouldn't change anything, I wouldn't leave her, I would always look after her and the girls, as long as . . .'

He broke off.

'As long as what?'

'As long as she let my life with you continue. As long as she never attempted to tell you the truth. We could all carry on just as we had done. All she had to do was accept it and not tell anyone. Particularly not you.'

'And you thought she was prepared to go along with that?'

'She told me she would. She told me she'd been more afraid

of my leaving her, abandoning her, as she put it, than anything else. She was angry, of course. But she said she realized she had been partly responsible for everything because she hadn't been honest with me from the start about the Huntington's. So she said yes, she would go along with it.'

I studied him carefully.

'You still don't get it, do you?' I asked.

'Get what?' he replied.

'Don't you see? Bella or Brenda has been responsible for everything. Breaking in here so mysteriously in the middle of the night, with keys I assume she somehow stole or copied from you; wrecking the place; snatching little Luke Macintyre specifically for the purpose, I don't doubt, of trying to incriminate me. I'm sure she was responsible for Robbie's death too. Quite sure of it. It was her revenge, on you, on all three of us in this family. And she'd been planning it, or something like it, for months . . . all that time I thought she was my new best friend, she was . . .' I paused, searching for the right word. 'She was grooming us, me and Robbie. And she was guilty of incitement to suicide at the very least. She had to be.'

Robert's eyes closed, then opened again, rapidly, several times. His head rocked on his shoulders. He looked as if he might pass out. I knew this must all have occurred to him. How could it not have? But from his reaction I wondered if he honestly still didn't believe it.

'No,' he said forcefully.

I was right. Obviously the man was capable of remaining just as much in denial as his wife had been.

'No. Don't blame Brenda. She wouldn't have done that. She was not a bad woman. She was a good woman. A Christian. A churchgoer . . .'

Of course she had been, I thought. And neither had there been anything wrong with Gladys Ponsonby Smythe's memory.

'You too, it seems, you hypocrite,' I interrupted. 'You did sing in that church choir, obviously.'

He shot me a trapped look. I didn't push the point. It was irrelevant anyway.

'Since when did you believe going to church prevents people committing evil?' I asked. 'Or maybe your opinions about religion were lies too. Brenda did it, Robert, how can you doubt it? One way or another, she killed our boy.'

'No, no!' he cried, his voice high pitched, verging on the hysterical. 'She couldn't have done that. I'm to blame. It's all my stupid greedy arrogant fault. How could I have thought that I would get away with my idiotic double life without some terrible disaster sooner or later?'

His lower lip dropped, leaving his mouth gaping half open. His eyes, staring at me now, were full of tears. His hands were trembling. And still he was kidding himself about so much.

I wondered again how I could have lived with Robert for so long without realizing how intrinsically weak he was.

'You fool,' I said. 'You pathetic bloody fool.'

His eyes remained fixed on me, pleading again, though I wasn't sure for what. Sympathy? Understanding? Or just for me to still love him. That would be it, of course. He was desperate for me to still love him. It was all he had left.

I didn't, though. I really didn't love him at all now. I had already admitted to myself how I felt about him. Now I just wanted to tell him, to hurt him as much as I could. I didn't think I would ever be able to hurt him as much as he had hurt me, but I could try.

'Yes, Robert,' I said. 'It is all your fault. You are to blame for our son's death. And I hate you for it. I hate you with all my heart.'

He recoiled from me, leaning back in his chair as if I had hit him.

I could see what a terrible blow I had delivered with those words. And I'm afraid I felt the nearest sensation to real pleasure that I'd experienced since the nightmare began.

eighteen

He left shortly afterwards. I assumed he was once again staying in that grim house he'd shared with his first wife, his real wife. The house I had so nearly visited.

Robert had wondered, with some alarm, I'd thought, what might have happened if I'd knocked on the door and been invited in. If Robert had been there, then the game, his wicked game, would have been up, of course. At once. But if not, the woman I'd known as Bella would surely have feared that I would quickly become aware of the strange and cruel deception she had so effectively accomplished, or even that I was already aware of it. And I believed her to have been capable of terrible things. So just what might she have done?

The thought made me shiver. DC Jarvis's business card remained pinned to the kitchen noticeboard, though his manner towards me made it seem unlikely that I would ever want to call him again. What I had heard that morning changed everything. I called his mobile.

Rather to my surprise, again, he answered straight away. I was almost taken aback, and uncertain where to begin. But surely he had to listen now.

I started by telling him about the story in the *Express & Echo*, and how it had made me realize immediately that my husband must have been leading an extraordinary double life. I explained that Brenda Anderton had been known to me as Bella Clooney, and that she had insinuated her way into my life, the life of our little family.

'I feel sure she's been responsible for everything that's happened to me: the night-time intruder, the trashing of the house, probably even the kidnapping of that poor little boy,' I went on. 'And I also believe she was involved somehow in Robbie's suicide. I don't know how, and Robert still claims she couldn't have been, but—'

'Mrs Anderson, is your husband with you?' Jarvis interrupted.

'The man I thought was my husband, you mean,' I remarked unnecessarily.

'Please, Mrs Anderson. Is he with you?'

'No. I called him when I saw the story in the paper and he came right over. I made him tell me everything, though knowing what I now do about him it's anybody's guess whether he did or not . . .'

'But he's not with you now?'

'No. He left about ten minutes ago. I called you more or less straight after he'd gone.'

'Right. Stay in your house, Mrs Anderson. Lock the doors and do not let anyone in, except me and DC Price. We'll be right over.'

It seemed Jarvis had listened to me for once. I couldn't resist a jibe.

'So you are taking me seriously at last, are you, Detective Sergeant?' I asked.

He did not rise to the bait.

'Please, Mrs Anderson, do exactly as I have told you,' he said. 'You could be in real danger.'

We ended the call. I considered his parting remark. I'd kind of assumed that any danger I might be in had departed with the death of Brenda Anderton. DS Jarvis obviously did not think so. Other than her there was surely only Robert who might, for whatever crazy reason, want to harm me. I believed that Robert still loved me. In as much as he ever had, I reflected grimly. Could a man who really loved a woman deceive her the way he had me? I had no answer to that. I only knew that I could not have behaved that way to someone I loved. Even the practicalities of it would have been beyond me. There was no way I could have successfully maintained such a deception while appearing to share my life with someone in the way Robert had.

DS Jarvis and DC Price arrived forty-five minutes later. They had wasted no time in getting to me. Indeed, they roared into the yard at Highrise with lights flashing and the siren attached to the roof of their silver saloon car still wailing, which I thought might not have been totally necessary.

While waiting for them I'd lit the fire in the sitting room. I don't know why, really. In my other, now so distant seeming life we lit the fire frequently in winter and always on the rare occasions that we had visitors. Maybe some part of my sub-conscious was still seeking normality. Not that there was anything, surely, that could be regarded as remotely normal in the company of two police detectives wishing to question you about the double life of your bigamous husband and the death of his other wife.

The fire was blazing by the time I led the two men into the now so rarely used room. They each sat in one of the big armchairs on either side of the grand old fireplace, Price leaning forward, in that way open fires invariably invite, to warm his hands. I sat very upright, perched on the edge of one end of the smaller of the two sofas. I almost didn't want to be comfortable.

Jarvis was serious and thoughtful, displaying a side of him I hadn't seen before. His questioning was meticulous and incisive. His manner towards me had changed significantly. It occurred to me that he'd previously been so sure that I was an unhinged woman responsible for the crimes she claimed had been committed against her, and therefore also for the kidnap of Luke Macintyre, that he hadn't really considered any alternative. Nor, probably, had he overseen a satisfactorily thorough investigation. I wondered if that was what he was thinking himself, and if he now regretted it.

He asked me to go over again what I had told him on the phone, occasionally prompting me for more detail, or clarification of a certain point, but otherwise listening carefully and quietly.

Only when I had pretty much finished did he begin to ask more questions of his own. The first was an obvious one.

'I wonder, Mrs Anderson, if you have any idea how Brenda or Bella found out about you and Robbie? How did she first discover that her husband had another family and was leading a double life?'

I was ready with the answer. I stood up and walked across to the little Victorian Davenport desk which stood by the window, lifted its lid and removed from it a photograph of Robert and Robbie which I'd put there, when the Farleys and I were clearing up the house, largely because I could not bear to look at it any more. It was one of the few Robert had ever allowed of either me or our son with him, and the last one ever taken, on a beautiful evening in the garden at the end of the previous summer. Their faces, glowing in amber light, beamed at me from within a simple wooden frame. Father and son, so unmistakably father and son. The shrubs and trees which formed a backdrop already displayed more than a hint of autumn colour. Sycamores, that much maligned species of tree, lined much of the perimeter of our garden, and their angular leaves had just begun to turn. There was winter jasmine in bud. Autumn crocuses sprouted purple, white and yellow. Ours was a garden for all seasons. I held the photograph still and studied it for just a few seconds. We had been so happy then, hadn't we? Surely we had. Now all I felt as I looked at my two men together was the pain of what was to come.

I handed the photograph to DS Jarvis. There was no glass within its frame, of course. That had been smashed into smithereens when the photo had been swept to the floor in the wanton destruction wreaked on the day Bella/Brenda – and there now could surely be no doubt that it had been her – entered my home and trashed the place.

The policeman looked down at the image then up at me.

'Wow!' he said.

'Yes,' I responded. 'They could be clones, couldn't they?'

'They're quite remarkably alike, that's for certain,' said DS Jarvis, as he passed the photograph to DC Price.

I felt the enormity of my loss hit me again. My special men. Gone for ever. Both of them. Robert was still alive. But really he may as well not be, as far as I was concerned anyway.

'So you think that casual meeting of dog walkers on Exmouth beach wasn't really that at all? You think Brenda Anderton arranged it, in order to begin to get to know you, to get close to you and your son?'

I shook my head.

'No. When we met on the beach I honestly don't believe she

had any idea either I or Robbie existed. Any more than I had any idea about her. Robert was too clever for both of us as far as that was concerned.'

'Then do you believe it was pure coincidence that you both decided to walk your dogs on Exmouth beach on the same day and at the same time?'

'Yes.'

'Was it something you often did?'

'No. Nor her, I shouldn't think. Robbie and I were only there because we'd had to go shopping in Exeter and Brenda didn't have the sort of lifestyle that gave her a lot of leisure time, that's for sure.'

'So, it was just chance, catastrophic chance as it turned out?' Jarvis sounded doubtful.

'Yes.' I said. 'Coincidences do happen, you know, Detective Sergeant.'

'Indeed,' said Jarvis. 'They're just not something detectives are very fond of. But it seems you are probably right about this one. So exactly what happened on the beach?'

'From the moment Bella – I mean Brenda – spotted Robbie, I reckon she just had to approach us, to find out who he was. Robert said she told him that, in as much as you can believe a word Robert says about anything. But I believe absolutely that she would have been suspicious straight away. More than that – shocked, I should imagine. I mean the resemblance is so striking. It would have been a total Boris Becker moment, wouldn't it? You couldn't really doubt Robbie's parentage for a minute.' I paused, reflecting briefly again on a wonderful young life now lost for ever.

'We used to joke about it. Robert, Robbie and me. Robert always said he'd been going to ask me to have a DNA test when I claimed to have got pregnant the very first night we were together, but as soon Robbie was born he'd realized there was no point.' I paused again.

'How did Brenda make the approach?' asked Jarvis.

'She threw her dog's ball straight at us, deliberately I now realize, contriving a minor incident if you like, making it seem perfectly natural to start a conversation with me. It's what dog walkers do. And, of course, I was totally and blissfully unaware of any hidden agenda.'

'You think she already had an agenda.'

'Well, she would have known about Robbie, just known, at once. I feel sure of it. And, understandably, she wanted to talk to me, to find out exactly what was going on. I don't think she would even have considered to begin with that Robert had married me. That he had built another family, and managed to lead a double life, to keep two families going for so long, each without any knowledge of the existence of the other.'

'I still can't quite understand how he got away with it,' said Jarvis.

'Robert was a master of deception, no doubt about that,' I said. 'But luck must have been with him, mustn't it? His two families didn't live that far apart. We didn't go to Exeter often – and Robert never did, come to think of it – but Robbie and I had been shopping there that very day we finally met Brenda. A chance meeting could, surely, have happened long before it did.'

'So Brenda Anderton questioned you, did she? About your son, your husband, and so on?'

'Well, yes, looking back that was exactly what she did. But she was very gentle about it, made it seem like normal conversation. I don't expect it took her long, though, to know she was dead right about Robbie's parentage. And it would have been apparent that I was married to my son's father.' I realized what I had said and added: 'Or thought I was.'

'The level of Robert's deception would have quickly become clear to Brenda, then,' mused Jarvis.

'Yes, which I've no doubt was as much of a shock to her as it was, eventually, to me.'

The detective looked thoughtful. 'She thought quickly, didn't she? Gave you a false name, and so on.'

'Yes. I suppose she was afraid that I might mention our meeting to Robert. I'm not sure that I would have thought so quickly, though. I mean, I don't know if it was deliberate or not, but she chose to call herself Bella, which is vaguely similar to Brenda. It's what Robert did too, only he went further, using a last name that was damned near the same apart from one letter. They say that people who adopt false identities are quite often found out because they don't respond to their names properly. And that it's easier if the names are similar. Is that right in your experience, DS Jarvis?'

'It probably is, yes. But there aren't many people capable of maintaining a false identity, a double life, the way your husband did, that's for certain.'

'Thank God for that,' I said. And I meant it from the bottom of my heart. The hurt and distress caused by such enormous deception could never fully be understood by anyone who had not experienced it. I wouldn't wish it on any human being.

'Bella – I mean Brenda – did the same thing with her dog's name,' I went on. 'She called him Flash; turns out he was really called Splash. Dogs respond to sounds really, not actual words. So Splash and Flash would sound much the same to a dog and it would therefore respond to either as if it were the name it had been taught. Did you know that, DS Jarvis?'

Jarvis nodded. 'I've heard it,' he said. 'Though I have a dog that appears not to know her name or the sound of it. Always tearing off in the opposite direction . . .'

I smiled and glanced down at Florrie, her head resting on my knee, her tail wagging occasionally, eyes not quite open, not quite shut. She was a real comfort to me, even in such dire circumstances. More than that I rather envied her: well fed and well loved, unaware of the horrors of the last few weeks. She might be missing the presence of her masters, but they say dogs have little concept of time. That's why they will just sit and wait for their owners to return, even when they have been abandoned. But a loved and well looked after dog has a pretty good life, I thought. An uncomplicated life, that was for sure. At that moment, and not for the first time since the death of my beloved son, I rather wished I was a dog.

My mind had wandered. I could hear that DS Jarvis was still speaking, but only in the distance. I made myself concentrate. I still had enough desire for self preservation to want very much to be released from police bail and to no longer be suspected of a dreadful crime. I knew this was my opportunity to provide the information that could make this happen sooner rather than later. I needed to grasp it.

'So after that first meeting how did things develop?' DS Jarvis was asking.

I explained that it was Bella who'd suggested a second dog walk together, instigated our swapping phone numbers, and made sure to arrange further meetings.

'So she took the initiative, did she?' queried Jarvis.

'Yes,' I agreed. 'I also realize now how she always managed to turn any conversation she was having back to me and my family. She must have learned so much about us. She certainly had the knack of doing that without raising any suspicions. And I was someone who wasn't used to talking about myself to strangers.'

The detective sergeant proceeded to press me on every detail

I could remember in my dealings with Bella, and he took a note of all our meetings. Not surprisingly he was particularly intrigued by what had happened on the night of Robbie's death, when I had – and it so made my flesh crawl now – turned to Bella for company and comfort, and then Robert had walked into Highrise to find the two women in his life together.

'How on earth did he react to that?' asked DS Jarvis.

I tried to answer him truthfully and accurately. Bizarrely, it was very hard for me to remember. I suppose at the time all I had been thinking about was the death of my son and then the relief, albeit so fleeting as things turned out, of at least having my husband home to share my grief with.

'I suppose he just looked stunned,' I said. 'But then I would have expected him to be stunned that night, and at the time I certainly didn't think it had anything to do with Brenda's presence. He said something like "What the hell is she doing here?" But I didn't think anything of that either, really. He never liked visitors much. And one thing there is no doubt about is how much Robert adored Robbie. Being the kind of man he is . . .'

I paused. 'I suppose I should say the kind of man I once thought him to be. Well, I would have expected him to want to be alone with his wife. The mother of the son who meant so much to him. His reaction didn't surprise me.'

'And Brenda Anderton? How did she react? They must both have known, husband and wife, that their various games were up. She'd been stalking you and Robbie, hadn't she? That's what it amounted to.'

He glanced at me as if waiting for a response. I hadn't thought of it that way, but of course that is exactly what she had done.

I nodded. Jarvis continued.

'Robert must have realized, at the very least, when he saw

her here, that Brenda knew about his double life. There could have been no doubt in his mind about that, surely?'

Again, I had difficulty remembering.

'He told me that today, but on the night she just left, and I really wasn't aware of anything strange,' I said. 'She left more or less straight away after Robert arrived. I remember apologizing to her, for Robert's rudeness, I suppose.' I half laughed. 'Deeply engrained English courtesy even in such circumstances. She said something like "Of course you need to be on your own now." And she just went.'

'But sooner or later there must have been a confrontation between them, presumably? Yet things carried on much the same for you, in as much as they could, after the death of your son.'

I told him that Robert had admitted to me that he'd gone straight to see Brenda the next day and how she'd agreed to put up with his double life, put up with almost anything, as long as he didn't leave her or the girls. She'd even continue the deception.

'But, of course, he didn't know what it seems she must already have been planning, did he? That the death of your son was not enough. She was determined to destroy you completely.'

I nodded. Then realized what Jarvis had said.

'Does that mean you also now believe she had something to do with Robbie's death?'

DS Jarvis stared me directly in the eye, something he had never really done before. Perhaps he had never been able to bring himself to look directly into the eyes of a woman he thought was mad.

'We have no way of knowing that for certain, Mrs Anderson, do we? At least, not at the moment. But I can assure you that we will be thoroughly re-investigating that matter along with the abduction of Luke Macintyre and the break-ins and destruction of your home.'

This time I knew I could trust him to do so. I felt mightily relieved. I didn't think I cared very much about myself any more, and I was somewhat surprised by how much I wanted those criminal charges against me dropped. But now surely that would happen, and hopefully in the not too distant future.

Price, who had been keeping in the background while his superior officer did most of the questioning, shuffled forward in his chair and leaned towards me.

'Mrs Anderson, do you know where we could locate your husband right now?' he asked. 'Do you know where he is living?'

'Well, yes, of course,' I said straight away, mildly surprised that they hadn't grasped what I felt to be obvious. 'At the home on the Bridge Estate that he shared with Brenda. He returned from the North Sea after being told the news of her death, as you're aware, and I presume he is looking after his younger daughter there as we speak. And I know, well, as much as you ever know anything with Robert, that he was there with his other family after he came home when I was arrested, until going back to work just two or three days ago. He phoned me from the airport . . .'

I told them about hearing the airport noises, the flight calls and so on.

I saw Jarvis and Price exchange meaningful looks. It seemed I had presented another possibility to them, one that now probably seemed quite obvious too, and one which this time they took swiftly on board.

'We will also be conducting further investigations into the motor incident that caused Mrs Brenda Anderton's death,' said Jarvis.

I noted the choice of word. Motor incident. The newspaper report had called it an accident.

DC Price interjected again.

'Mrs Anderson, do you happen to know if your husband has any mechanical knowledge of motor cars at all?' he asked.

'Oh yes,' I said. 'He's a very good car mechanic. It's what he used to do before he went on the rigs. He's always looked after all our vehicles . . .'

I stopped in mid-sentence. Jarvis and Price exchanged an even more meaningful look.

It was Jarvis who spoke next. And his expression was sombre.

'Mrs Anderson, if your husband had come to believe, as we know you do, that his first wife was in some way responsible for your son's death, whether or not she in fact was, how do you think he would have reacted to that?' he asked.

'I don't know,' I stumbled. 'He told me he couldn't believe she would ever do anything like that. Even if you accepted the other things she really must have done, the kidnap, and the house trashing and so on, he couldn't believe she would have deliberately brought about Robbie's death. At least that's what he said. Of course, I have finally learned not to accept as truth anything he says, really.'

Jarvis nodded. 'So let's say he suspected her, nothing more than that. And he must have, surely. What do you think he might have done?'

It was pretty clear where he was leading. I didn't know quite what to say.

'What do you think Robert may have been capable of?' Jarvis persisted.

I took a few seconds before I answered.

'He worshipped Robbie,' I said. 'I think, I honestly think, that he could have been capable of anything, anything at all.'

nineteen

DS Jarvis, again accompanied by DC Price, returned to High-rise the very next day just before 5 p.m. They gave me no advance warning so I entertained them in the kitchen, but this time I did offer them some refreshment, something I had omitted to do the previous afternoon.

I made them the cappuccinos they requested and piled short-bread biscuits onto a plate while they began to tell me of the considerable progress which had been made in the last twenty-four hours or so.

It seemed that Brenda Anderton's home had been searched from top to bottom by Scenes of Crime Officers and substantial evidence found indicating that Luke Macintyre had been there.

'There were fingerprints and bits of hair and other DNA evidence that we're pretty sure will prove to have come from the boy, though we have to wait for the DNA results,' Jarvis told me. 'Same in the woman's car. Seems clear she snatched him from his garden and then kept him at her own home before bringing him here in an attempt to frame you. Just as you thought.'

He paused. I didn't say anything. All I felt was relief. This surely proved that I had nothing whatsoever to do with Luke Macintyre's abduction.

'And we found his clothes in her dirty washing basket,' Jarvis went on. 'It's bizarre. She'd made no attempt to conceal them, just put them there with her own and her daughter's clothes as if he were one of the family and she was preparing to do his washing. Her husband, Robert, like you said, was almost certainly at the house he shared with Brenda after you sent him away until going back to the North Sea. He could have found them—'

I interrupted, half smiling in spite of everything. 'Not Robert,' I said. 'He always had strict ideas about the demarcation between a man's job and a woman's. He didn't do washing.'

Jarvis inclined his head in acknowledgement. 'It kind of indicates that she at first may have treated Luke almost like one of her family. Although we now know she gave the child drugs, presumably to keep him quiet and docile, every sign in the house shows that she was looking after Luke reasonably well. And yet then she apparently left him more or less naked in your shed on a freezing cold day. Doesn't make any sense.'

I shrugged. 'Of course it doesn't make any sense. The woman had a terrible hereditary disease which seriously affects mental health and on top of that she discovered her husband had bigamously married another woman, leading a privileged life with her and fathering a healthy child, something she could never have. I thought you believed that people can simply be mad, DS Jarvis? I think Brenda Anderton was driven mad.'

DS Jarvis ignored the jibe, if it even registered, and spoke quietly. 'Yes, I think that probably is about the sum of it,' he said.

'It doesn't excuse what she's done, though,' I said. 'Not to that poor little boy or to me.'

'No, it doesn't,' said Jarvis. 'I just regret that she is no longer with us to stand trial. We might have found out the truth about all kinds of things.'

I nodded.

'And how is Luke Macintyre? Is he going to be all right?'

'Looks like it, thankfully. We're told he's recovering well. Physically, at any rate. There are psychological implications, of course, even though he's so young.'

'And what about me, Detective Sergeant? Do I still have to stand trial?'

Jarvis shook his head. 'That's really what I came to see you about, Mrs Anderson. Obviously no charges will be made against you and you are therefore released unconditionally from police bail. There's some paperwork, just a formality . . .'

I felt the relief wash over me. It was like a warm bath, cleansing and restoring, when you feel dirty and vaguely unwell.

'Thank God,' I said.

DS Jarvis looked down at his coffee cup, while fiddling with the cuff on one of his jacket sleeves. I remembered him doing exactly the same on the night Robbie had died. Obviously something of a nervous tick when he didn't feel entirely comfortable.

'I'm only sorry we got it all so wrong,' he said.

I glanced at him in surprise, and so, I thought, did DC Price. I somehow didn't think Jarvis was a man who would often apologize for anything.

I had previously been furious with the detective sergeant, and the police in general. They hadn't listened, not any of them really, and they had made little or no effort to move beyond their original crass assumptions. In my opinion they had not appeared to even attempt to conduct anything resembling a proper investigation.

But I saw no point in being anything other than conciliatory. Not at this stage. I was hoping they might reveal far more about their inquiries, not just concerning the abduction of Luke Macintyre and the break-ins at Highrise, which directly affected me, but also Brenda Anderton's death. And most importantly of all, I wanted them to investigate Robbie's death properly, and was even hoping they may already have begun to do so.

'I can see how it must have looked,' I said mildly.

'Yes, well, I suppose we just have to move on,' muttered Jarvis ambiguously, still fiddling with his sleeve.

He emptied his coffee cup and brushed the froth from his upper lip, resembling fleetingly rather more the gawky schoolboy I suspected he would once have been than a hard-nosed detective.

'There's something you may like to know,' Jarvis continued, just a tad tentatively, as if he weren't sure whether he should share it with me but was going to anyway. 'We have CCTV footage of Brenda Anderton's car travelling through the speed-restricted roadworks area of the A30 on the morning of your son's death. She took the Blackstone turning, and definitely could have been heading for Highrise. In fact, the coincidence seems too great for her to have been going anywhere else.'

I gasped.

'It looks like she could well have been involved. Your son was at an impressionable age and his circumstances made him highly vulnerable. We can only assume that you are probably right, Mrs Anderson, and that Brenda deliberately revealed to Robbie the truth about his father in, doubtless, the most blunt and unpleasant manner. That could perhaps have been enough to push him to do something he never otherwise would have contemplated, to take his own life . . .'

I just stared at him. I was afraid I might break down

and weep again, for the first time in days. Jarvis continued to speak.

'The problem is, Mrs Anderson, now Brenda Anderton is also dead, I fear we will never be able to prove it.'

My mind was buzzing. 'That CCTV footage is good enough for me,' I said. 'I feel I now know what happened. What is it judges tell juries? They must reach a verdict beyond any reasonable doubt. I know what happened, all right, beyond any reasonable doubt.'

But, of course, I could only imagine what actually took place in Robbie's room between Brenda Anderton and my son. I could only imagine how Robbie had felt. And that was the part of it all that really devastated me. More than anything. My beautiful boy being told something that was so totally destructive to him that he no longer wished to continue living.

I felt tears pricking at the very thought of it and blinked them away ferociously. There were still things I wanted to know and DS Jarvis seemed, from what I knew of him anyway, in an unusually receptive and helpful mood. Perhaps he was under his own pressure, I thought obliquely. Maybe the great and the good of the Devon and Cornwall Constabulary feared that I might sue them.

I wasn't sure if it would be remotely possible, but the thought had a certain appeal even in the state I was in. I had questions to ask first, though. I needed to know all the facts possible.

'What about Brenda Anderton's death?' I asked. 'You told me you were re-investigating that? Have you found anything out? Do you now have reason to believe her death was suspicious?'

Jarvis turned towards me, his face expressionless.

'I'm afraid I cannot really talk about that, beyond

confirming that our investigations are ongoing,' he said formally.

I pushed him as much as I could but got no further. Indeed, he almost reverted to type – at least to the way I'd summed up when we first met on the day that Robbie had died. On the worst day of my life.

The two officers left a few minutes later. Jarvis repeated his instruction of the previous day for me to stay inside and keep all my doors and windows locked, and told me to make sure I set the alarm when I went to bed. I could only assume that he still suspected Robert of all kinds of things I really didn't want to think about. Who else could he think might want to harm me now that Brenda was dead?

'I'll get Jacobs and Bickerton to continue to keep an eye right through the night,' he said. 'This is their patch and, if you ask me, they don't usually have enough on, it's that peaceful round here. A bit of extra duty will do them no harm at all. So don't panic if you hear an engine or see lights approaching. It'll be the boys in blue looking out for you.'

He paused, then added almost inaudibly: 'I hope.'

I had good ears. 'So do I,' I said.

He grinned. 'Don't worry,' he went on. 'I'll make sure they stay on red alert. And if you have any cause for anxiety, dial 999 at once. Don't mess about. I'll also make sure it's known everywhere that you're top priority.'

I nodded. A little boy had to be kidnapped and a woman, whatever she might have done, had to die before I was given any priority at all, I thought. But I said nothing.

The next morning Gladys arrived shortly after nine, holding a delicious-looking gooey cake before her. I answered the door in my dressing gown, Florrie at my feet.

'Don't worry, I didn't make it,' she said, by way of greeting, 'Mrs Simmons, specially for you. Sticky toffee. Best she does, I reckon.'

I smiled my gratitude.

'Hope I'm not too early,' Gladys continued. 'Just wanted to bring the cake round and tell you how thrilled we all are that the police have finally come to their senses.'

I thanked her and invited her in, wondering yet again at the efficiency of the village jungle drums.

She insisted on making coffee and cutting into the sticky toffee cake – 'nothing better to start the day with, flower' – while I got dressed. During which time I remembered my manners.

'I just want to thank you so much for your support and all you did when I was arrested,' I said. 'I don't think I've done so before, not properly, and that's very wrong of me. You've been terrific. Really.'

'Don't worry about that, Marion, you've had one or two other things to think about,' Gladys replied. She looked slightly embarrassed, but pleased, I thought.

'I'm just glad it's all worked out,' she added.

I thanked her again, thinking, none the less, that it was a little premature to refer to anything having 'worked out'.

'I suppose so,' I said mildly. 'But you and I both know I will always be that woman whose son killed himself, and who was then arrested for abducting a little boy. Mud sticks in small communities. And Dartmoor mud sticks like nothing else I know.'

'Oh, goodness,' countered Gladys, reaching out a hand to touch my arm. 'You mustn't think like that, luvvie. The ones who just gossip will soon move on to something else, and the rest of them . . . well, I know a lot of people who just want to help you. Really.'

I managed a weak smile. I wondered how much, if anything at all, she knew yet about Robert's double life and the role Brenda Anderton may have played in events. In any case she and the rest of the village would learn about it sooner or later for sure. I thought I probably owed Gladys the courtesy of giving her a summary of events myself, but I just didn't feel up to it.

I studied her in silence. She smiled back at me warmly, and began to make light small talk. She asked me no questions about anything. Not for the first time I became aware how much more sensitive she was than she appeared to be. And I was quite surprised to realize what a comfort her presence was. Gladys Ponsonby Smythe really was an unusually kind and strong woman. She didn't overstay her welcome either, leaving right after we'd finished our coffee and cake.

'Take care if you go out,' she said. 'The vultures are still gathered at the top of your lane.'

I'd assumed they would be. Even if they knew that I was no longer a police suspect they would presumably be looking for a quote on that and a picture to go with it.

However, I was going out. I was pretty sure neither DS Jarvis nor his colleagues would approve of what I was planning to do, but I didn't care.

When Gladys had left I gave Florrie her breakfast – a scant handful of dried food – and shut her in the kitchen. I put on a warm coat and my fluffy boots, set the alarm excluding the kitchen, locked up, and left the house. Then I climbed into the little Ford and roared up the lane as if I were Jenson Button and it was a Formula One racing car. Well, I certainly drove as fast as speedster Charlie Jameson had ever driven on such a surface, I was quite sure. If not faster. When I got to the top I did not slow down, instead swinging the car onto the public road at full throttle, causing it to slide sideways for quite some way, so that mud and muck splashed all over the gathered group of vultures, as Gladys had so accurately described them. They scattered in various directions, several of them jumping into the hedge in order to escape me and my speeding vehicle. I only just managed to maintain any kind of control and narrowly avoided ending up in the hedge myself. It would have been worth it even if I had. Indeed, it gave me such pleasure to watch the panic of those who had so diligently added to my distress that I felt almost in high spirits as I slowed to a more sensible pace and proceeded on my journey.

I was heading for that grim Exeter council estate again. The place where Brenda had lived; the house she had shared with Robert, when he wasn't with me or in the North Sea; the other home he had kept going for so many years. The other home which was such a far cry from Highrise. The place where I assumed Robert now was, with his younger daughter.

It took me the best part of an hour to reach the inappropriately named Riverview Avenue. I drove slowly by number 5, and parked a little way up the road behind a white transit van, almost mimicking my first visit to the street. But this time, thankfully, there were no threatening hoodies gathered by the garages.

There was also no sign of any police activity or any of the paraphernalia of a crime scene around the house. I could only assume that the police had completed their search – and, come to think of it, that was what Jarvis had indicated – and that the house was no longer a crime scene. Indeed, had it been so I would definitely have had a wasted journey because presumably Robert and his child would not have been allowed to be there.

There was a window slightly ajar on the first floor which

hopefully indicated that somebody was in residence. And surely it must be Robert. For reasons I couldn't quite explain to myself I wanted to see him in this other environment. Just a glimpse would do. I had driven to the grim Bridge Estate entirely for that purpose.

I waited for about forty-five minutes. Then the door to number 5 opened, and Robert, as unshaven and dishevelled-looking as now seemed to be his habit, stepped outside and seemed to be sorting some newspapers and bottles into recycling bins.

His clothes looked as if he'd slept in them. I hoped he wouldn't notice me watching him, and was glad that I was driving a car he wouldn't recognize and had been able to park behind the transit van. However, he seemed almost curiously intent on his task. A movement behind him caught my eye. A little girl, presumably Janey, had appeared in the doorway. She seemed quite small for her age, and young, both in looks and behaviour. But then I only really had Robbie to compare her with. And he had always been tall and rather grown-up. She was jumping on and off the doorstep, up and down, up and down, laughing like children do, as if she didn't have a care in the world. Maybe Robert had so far managed to keep at least the worst of it all from her. She must surely have known that her mother had brought a little boy into the house, and I wondered how Brenda would have explained that. I also wondered if the girl even realized fully that her mother was dead. Whatever she knew at the moment, and however much she was being protected, she could not be kept in the dark for long, that was for certain. Just as she surely could not be kept in the dark for long concerning the terrible illness which lurked within her lithe young body.

In stark contrast to her father, and the sorry state of their house, little Janey was immaculately turned out. She wore a pristine cream tracksuit jacket, clean jeans and those trainers all the kids like which light up at the heel when you stamp on them.

She had very black hair and pale opaque skin. Just like her father. And just like the half-brother she had never known. Robert's genes must be powerful, I thought. His daughter, like our son, was the image of him. No wonder Brenda had avoided my meeting her, and made up her story about a son and daughter as a kind of further camouflage, I suppose, in case of anything I might mention to Robert. Anyway, if I had ever met Janey before, I would have at once spotted the resemblance to the man I'd thought was my husband. Another Boris Becker moment.

Robert finished his recycling, straightened up and went back into the house, ushering the child in before him. I watched as the door shut behind them, unsure really what I was feeling. And I was so wrapped up in my own muddled thoughts that I didn't spot the police patrol car until it pulled up right outside number 5.

Two uniformed officers, both men, and a woman in plain clothes whom I presumed to be CID, none of them among the considerable number of officers I had recently encountered, stepped out and approached the front door.

After just a few seconds the door opened and Robert appeared again. I could see him clearly. He did not register surprise; more resignation tinged with dismay really. It was almost as if he had been expecting this visit. And I suppose he probably had.

Like me, he would have known that, at the very least, the investigation into Brenda's sudden death was still ongoing. And, like me, he must surely have thought he would be the prime suspect.

He opened the door wider, and stepped to one side, allowing the three officers to pass through. Then the door shut again.

I waited. After half an hour or so, Robert, wearing a coat now, appeared again at the door with the child I presumed to be Janey. He was carrying a small rucksack. I recognized it as the one he always had with him when he travelled between home and the oil rig. Or when I'd assumed he'd been travelling to a rig. I thought the little girl now looked confused and ill at ease. Robert put the rucksack down on the doorstep and took hold of her hand, bending over slightly to talk to her, as if trying to reassure her. He led her down the garden path and out through the gate onto the pavement, turning right – fortunately in the direction away from me – as I really did not want him to see me, then up the garden path of a house two doors away.

An almost cliché-like motherly sort of woman, full-bosomed and smiley, welcomed the two of them, and made a big fuss of the child, before leading her inside.

Robert, head down, shuffling his feet, returned to his own house, though it still seemed odd for me to regard it as such. I noticed then that one of the male uniformed police officers was standing in the porch. He had presumably been watching Robert's activities. They stood there together for just a moment or two before being joined by the other two officers. Robert stepped into the porch, to lock the front door, it seemed, and to pick up his rucksack. The smaller of the two uniformed men led the way to the patrol car, unlocked it, and climbed into the driver's seat. The second uniformed officer and the woman waited for Robert, then proceeded to walk on either side of him towards the car.

As they stepped onto the pavement two male photographers with cameras and another man and a woman, presumably reporters, came tearing out of a house opposite.

The police officers indicated that they should keep their distance, and the reporters satisfied themselves with shouting questions at Robert and his police escort, all of which remained unanswered, while the photographers rattled off their snaps from several feet away. I suspected they had already taken plenty of shots from a window across the road from Robert's. I'd heard about journalists paying householders to use rooms in their house as a vantage point from which to keep watch on targets. The press had probably been watching 5 Riverview Avenue ever since it became public knowledge that the house was the subject of a major search.

The whole incident only lasted a matter of seconds. Very swiftly Robert was ushered into the back of the patrol car where he sat with an officer on either side of him. I watched the car set off up the road and the journalists retreat.

I hoped I could be forgiven for feeling a kind of vicarious satisfaction. Whatever the outcome, and whatever truth might be revealed, I found myself hoping that Robert suffered the same level of fear and humiliation that I had experienced. After all, as he had admitted himself, if one person was to blame for everything, it had to be him. Not his poor sick wife, driven mad by a combination of disease and despair, both probably as terrible as each other. Not her, nor anyone else, like the bullying father of Robbie's poor young girlfriend.

Just him. Robert. The man I had married in good faith and devoted my entire life to.

twenty

The following afternoon DS Jarvis phoned to say that Robert had been charged with the murder of his wife. His legal wife.

'We're just about to release a press statement. I didn't want you to see it on the news,' he said.

Bizarrely, I reflected on his new-found sensitivity before the enormity of his words hit me. It had been obvious this might happen since my first conversation with Jarvis and Price three days earlier. None the less, I found myself totally shocked. I was standing by the kitchen table. I sat down with a bump.

Nothing that Robert had said had given any indication he was likely to confess to killing his wife. Indeed, he had still been half protesting her innocence of any wrongdoing and insistent that she was not involved in Robbie's death.

'So what happened?' I asked. 'Everybody seemed so sure Brenda Anderton's death was an accident.'

'That was when we had no reason to believe anyone may have wanted to kill her,' said Jarvis. 'The kind of woman she appeared to be, a married mother going about her business, did not suggest there was anything suspicious about her death. So the investigation proceeded on that basis. But after what you told us, about your husband's double life and Brenda Anderton's stalking of you and your son, we had the car re-examined

309

by forensics. And we called in your husband for interview and subsequently arrested and charged him.'

'Has he admitted it then?' I asked.

'Look, I can't go into details,' he said. 'But let's just say we have found evidence to indicate that this was no accident. We know the car had been tampered with, and in such a way that it could only have been done by someone with expert knowledge. And we already know from you that he is an accomplished motor mechanic.'

It had all happened so fast. I had been aware of the effect of what I had earlier told the police. I had seen the reactions of Jarvis and Price. Yet I was shocked rigid. My mouth felt dry. I had no words.

The months leading up to Robert's trial at Exeter Crown Court in March the following year passed in a kind of limbo. I was barely able to even think about my shattered life, let alone attempt to rebuild it.

My car and all the rest of my personal possessions, including everything that had been detained at Heavitree Road Police Station, were returned to me. So was the hard drive of Robbie's Mac, no longer any good to me, and his phone, which I eagerly checked out.

There were records of the call Sue Shaw had told me she'd made to Robbie on the day he died, and of several attempts he'd made to call her back. He'd also sent her a text – *We must talk* – making no specific reference to the immense news Sue had given him. If he had mentioned her pregnancy, presumably the police would have picked up on it. Even taking into account the lack of any real interest that they'd displayed at the time, I thought wryly.

I also heard from DS Jarvis that DNA extracted from the

sample of excrement removed from Highrise matched that of Brenda Anderton.

'We can't try a dead woman,' he said. 'I just thought you'd like to know.'

I thanked him. But I'd known that anyway, of course.

I pretty much locked myself away inside Highrise. Actually, I didn't have a lot of choice. The financial problems I had half expected kicked in just before Christmas, a couple of weeks after Robert's arrest.

The first indication came when I tried to pay for one of my regular Waitrose shops with my American Express card and it was declined. My Barclaycard was also declined. But my Barclays Connect card, my debit card linked to the joint account in Robert's and my name, was, however, and much to my relief, accepted.

I had gone into denial about my finances – I'd known full well that I should make enquiries into my financial situation and I had done nothing about it. In the distant-seeming days when all had apparently been well with my family, I had known little or nothing about our financial affairs except that our household bills were paid by direct debit or standing order from our Barclays joint account. The statements for this account arrived at Highrise regularly and I sometimes gave them a cursory glance, if Robert was not at home, before putting them into a drawer of the desk in the study to await his return.

I knew that Robert had another Barclays account solely in his name into which his Amaco salary was paid. Robbie's school fees and other larger or irregular expenditures, like the purchase of a new car, were paid for directly out of this account, from which a substantial monthly amount was transferred to our joint account. It was the way Robert had liked to handle things, and I'd had no reason to question him.

Robert had always been vague about his Amaco salary, but had indicated that it was into six figures annually, and that level of income would have been necessary to fund our lifestyle. He'd said the precise amount varied according to the hours he put in, and also whether or not bonuses were paid. Again, I never pressed him because we always appeared to have more than enough for our needs. It now seemed obvious, however, that the bulk of the transferred sums must have come from his lottery win. Certainly no rigger would be likely to earn that sort of money and, unknown to me, Robert had been supporting a second family.

I drove home far too fast, rushed into the sitting room, and removed all the remaining joint account bank statements from the desk drawer. The most recent had arrived since Robert's arrest and I'd not even opened it. I tore the envelope apart. It showed an overdraft of £1,615 and 10p. And I had never seen the account overdrawn before.

I checked the 'money in' column. During November and so far in December there had been no transfer at all from the R. Anderson account. Then I checked the 'money out' column. There were no payments to either Barclaycard or American Express, and it suddenly occurred to me that I didn't think any such payment had ever been made from this account. I could only assume that our credit card bills had been paid from Robert's sole account, or even from some other one I knew nothing about, and that this account was no longer in funds.

It suddenly struck me that I had never seen a statement for the R. Anderson account. I rifled through every drawer in the desk, and had another quick look anywhere in the house that it seemed likely the statements might be kept. But I knew I would find nothing. After all, I had searched thoroughly enough already, looking for anything in the name of Rob Anderton and any paperwork connected to Robert's lottery win. I found myself wondering about that too, suddenly. Had he really won the lottery? The money to fund us, his second family, must have come from somewhere. But perhaps he'd robbed a bank. That thought was not a serious one. At first. But when I considered it further, well, who could guess what R. Anderton/Anderson might have been capable of doing in order to live out his lie?

Robert and I were Barclays Premier customers. That meant, unusually in the modern age, that we had access to a personal bank manager for whom we had a mobile phone number. I remembered that his details were also stored in the office desk drawer along with the joint account statements. I found the necessary paperwork and dialled the number, for the first time ever. After all, Robert dealt with all that kind of thing. I was connected to a recorded message, but at least it had been recorded by the man himself, one George Lindsay. I left my name and number. Rather to my surprise, less than a couple of hours later, he returned my call.

I asked him the current balance of our joint account and was told it was now £2,540 and 32p overdrawn.

'But you have an overdraft limit of £5,000,' he said.

Yes, I thought, *and it looks like that is all I now have.*

'I wonder if you could also give me the balance of my husband's sole account,' I said.

There was a brief silence before George Lindsay replied.

'I'm sorry, Mrs Anderson. As your name is not on that account I am not able to give you that information.'

I thought fast. Faster than I had for some time.

'Mr Lindsay, I'm sure you must be aware, are you not, of my circumstances, of all that has happened to my family, and that my husband is in prison awaiting trial?'

'Well, yes, of course I am, and I am very sorry for your—'

'Yes, Mr Lindsay,' I interrupted. 'Of course you are, it's been all over the media, hasn't it? So, therefore, if I were to ask you to indicate if it was likely to be possible for any moneys to be transferred from that R. Anderson account into our joint account in the near future, could you not do so?'

There was a slightly longer silence this time before George Lindsay spoke again. He spoke with a distinct North Devon accent, something I always found reassuring, probably for no other reason than having been brought up there.

'I think I can do that, Mrs Anderson,' he said. 'And no, it is not likely to be possible. Certainly not for as long as your husband remains in prison and unable to deal with his affairs.'

'Thank you, Mr Lindsay,' I said. 'I have just one other question. Will that overdraft limit still be honoured?'

'I see no reason why not,' said George Lindsay, whom I was quite sure could see any number of reasons why not.

Thank God for that, I thought. And thank God too, I reckoned, for George Lindsay. I hadn't known that banks still employed human beings. His days had to be numbered, surely.

I realized what I should do next was contact Robert in prison. But I had no wish to, even though he had given every indication of wishing to stay in close contact. I'd already received several letters from him, which I hadn't opened, and there had even been phone calls I'd left to the answer machine, deleting the messages before even listening to them. In any case I suspected that he would be unable to help even if he wanted to. It was pretty clear that, with devastating timing, his money had run out.

Of course, if Brenda had not discovered his double life and so cruelly set about destroying part of it, it was possible that Robert would have found a way around his financial problems, a way of carrying on with his extraordinary deception. After all, he had proved himself to have the most inventive of minds, that was sure.

I called Mrs Rowlands and asked her about the possibility of returning to my teaching work. She told me she was sorry but she'd actually just hired another full-time staff member, long overdue, she said. She'd been friendly enough and expressed what I thought was genuine concern about my predicament, and I expected it was probably true about the new full-time teacher. But I somehow doubted she would have wanted me back anyway. In addition to having a husband who never really was my husband awaiting prosecution for murder, I had been arrested on suspicion of the abduction and attempted murder of a child. Not something any headmistress would want her school associated with if she could avoid it. All charges against me may have been dropped, but such matters are never forgotten. Mud sticks, and Dartmoor mud sticks particularly well, I'd told Gladys Ponsonby Smythe. It was the truth.

Ultimately I reckoned the best thing for me to do was to try to live on that joint account overdraft until Robert's trial. I realized I was merely putting off the inevitable, and sooner or later the financial mess I was in would have to be dealt with along with everything else. But there was a case for at least waiting until I knew what was going to happen to Robert. That was what I told myself anyway.

Having made that decision, I turned Highrise into a kind of Hitler's Bunker, in which I existed in a trance-like state, cut off as much as possible from the outside world.

I could no longer afford to heat the place properly, so I more or less lived in the kitchen, feeding the Aga from the vast store of logs Robert and Robbie had amassed before the nightmare began. Not only had we regularly culled the abundant sycamores and ash on our land, but there was also that old oak that Robert had acquired and behind a pile of which I had found little Luke Macintyre naked and half dead. Only I tried not to think about that any more.

Anyway, this long-burning, non-spitting stuff was supposed to be our best wood, to be burned only in the inglenook in the sitting room. But during those few months waiting for Robert's trial I burned 'best wood' in the range along with whatever else came to hand, every morning loading logs into a wheelbarrow and pushing it straight into the kitchen.

I couldn't afford to buy the malt whisky I had been numbing my senses with since Robbie's death, but that, I was forced to admit, might not have been such a bad thing. And there was plenty of wine in Robert's wine store. Enough to last one person several months, I thought, even at the rate I seemed to be going through it.

I spent much of each day huddled up in the big old leather armchair pulled close to the stove, Florrie half straddling my lap. Sometimes I watched TV on the little portable I had set up the day after Highrise had been trashed, and sometimes I tried to read. But I didn't seem able to take much in.

I dreamed of Robbie sometimes. And of Robert too, though I didn't want to. Occasionally I thought about sex with him. It was hard to so abruptly lose a good sex life. And also to know that, whatever happened, you would never want to have sex with that person again. I even fantasized about sex with some anonymous fit young man, as a kind of ultimate diversion. But there wasn't much chance of that as long as I remained in the back of beyond. In any case, I was far from ready for a new lover.

I could not stop myself reliving the past, the good and the bad, wondering if things really had been as good as I'd thought, and just how I had managed to remain so unsuspecting for so long. I remembered driving Robert to and from the local airports. I imagine Brenda had done the same. Presumably sometimes I had dropped Robert off, assuming that he was flying to Aberdeen, only for him to have been picked up by Brenda. And the other way round. And surely that had involved risk of discovery. But Robert had never let me go into the terminal, even when I picked him up, in order to avoid the hassle and unnecessary expense of parking, he'd said. At each airport he'd found a tucked-away place for me to park and wait. Just as he had for Brenda, I assumed. And, in any case, I guess that after sixteen years of getting away with an extraordinary deception you must begin to believe you will never be found out. I certainly had never come close to finding him out until Robbie died. I felt such a fool. And sometimes almost as angry with myself as with Robert.

As winter deepened and the nights grew bitingly cold I moved the smallest of the two sitting-room sofas into the kitchen and even slept there through the hours of darkness.

Gladys and Tom Farley were regular visitors, although, perhaps to my shame, I rarely invited them in. They brought boxes of food and provisions which apparently the entire village contributed to. I had no idea how they knew that I had money problems on top of everything else – perhaps my living only in the kitchen had been a clue – but they certainly seemed to have guessed it and I was deeply touched by their kindness. However, I could not cope with their company and was always somewhat relieved once they had left.

Florrie was my greatest comfort. She never left my side, and everything about her indicated, to me at least, that she somehow understood the depth of my misery. I know every dog owner says this, but I honestly believe it to be true.

Christmas came and went, and I might not have noticed it were it not for my little band of supporters. Gladys brought me a special box of Christmas goodies: chocolates, nuts, a pudding, some mince pies, clotted cream, and an oven-ready pheasant.

'Even a turkey crown's too big for one,' she'd said in her businesslike way.

She'd begged me to join the Reverend Gerald and her for lunch at the vicarage, promising: 'You needn't worry, luvvie, it won't be a religious affair. Once the morning service is over Gerry and I just get stuck in to eating and drinking far too much like everyone else. And if you feel like you want to contribute something, I did hear that husband of yours kept rather a good wine cellar . . .'

I managed a smile for, I thought, the first time since Robert's arrest. But I declined the invitation none the less.

'I'm just no kind of company,' I said. 'And I'd honestly rather be alone, Christmas Day or not, until this is all over.'

I sent her on her way clutching a couple of bottles of Robert's finest claret as a seasonal gift, which I hoped would make me seem slightly less ungracious.

Tom Farley stopped by with a tiny beautifully iced Christmas cake, made by his wife, he said, and he too invited me to Christmas dinner.

'The missus says you'd be ever so welcome and to tell you all men are bastards,' he recited deadpan.

I managed my second smile in a long time. But I turned him down as gently as I could, gave him some wine too, and sent my love and thanks to his wife.

'Tell her she's dead right,' I said. 'And when all this is over and I feel more up to it I'll pop round one day for a cup of tea and we can discuss the matter further.'

He went off chuckling. At least I'd managed not to offend him.

Dad, of course, also invited me for Christmas.

'Or I could come to you, maid,' he said.

But this time I think he really did understand my reasons for wanting to be alone. Or maybe at heart he didn't really want to have to cope with me. Either way, he made little protest when I declined.

He called me on Christmas morning before setting off to spend the day with one of his dart-player pals from the pub. I'd known he wouldn't have to be alone. Dad was far too popular in his village for that.

We wished each other Happy Christmas, like you do, which seemed rather surreal under the circumstances. In my case, anyway.

Then I set about obediently roasting the pheasant Gladys had given me, along with accompanying roast potatoes and Brussels sprouts for which I'd foraged in the sorry remains of our vegetable garden. I made gravy and even bread sauce. I found an unopened – and unbroken – jar of redcurrant jelly at the back of a cupboard and ladled some into a silver dish. I put the pudding on to steam and scooped the cream into another silver dish. I selected a bottle of the St Emilion Grand Cru 2000, which I knew had been a favourite of Robert's, and opened it early to let it breathe. I laid the kitchen table with our best cutlery and one silver goblet. Then I cut the pheasant in half with my poultry shears, placing one half on an anonymous new white plate, and surrounding it with vegetables. I poured gravy over it and added a generous dollop of bread sauce.

I set my plate on the table, poured some of the wine, and stepped back to admire my handiwork. It looked great. I knew the pheasant was moist and tender from the way it had sliced open; the roast potatoes were golden and crunchy-looking; the sprouts just right, still firm and crisp. I liked my food. Well, once upon a time I'd liked my food. I stepped forward to take my single place, almost eagerly at first.

And then it hit me. My single place. The previous Christmas my entire little family had been happy and together for the celebration, it being Robert's turn for Christmas leave. Or so he'd told me. We'd set the table in the formal dining room as we always did on special occasions, with the best cutlery, of course, but also the crystal glasses and the wonderful old dinner service now smashed to bits by his mad first wife.

We'd begun the festive day as usual, with coffee and croissants followed by a glass of champagne. Robert had been in fine humour and had thoroughly embarrassed Robbie with an energetic rendition of Tom Jones's 'Sex Bomb', directed at me. He'd had to appease our son with a glass of Buck's Fizz. Then, in front of a blazing fire in the sitting room, we'd opened our presents, which had been stacked beneath the tall Christmas tree in the bay window.

As usual in the good old days I'd roasted a goose, which I'd served the traditional English way: with apple sauce and sage and onion stuffing. Robert carved the goose at the table. We all agreed it was much more interesting than turkey, tucked in accordingly, and when we'd finished marvelled at just how much of it we'd managed to put away, accompanied, of course, by copious quantities of carefully chosen claret.

Last year I'd made the pudding myself a couple of months in advance, and we'd all stirred it for luck. We'd had brandy butter as well as clotted cream and finished off the champagne. Then we'd pretty much dozed away the rest of the day in front of the fire in the sitting room, with the TV switched on but its content only fleetingly entering our sated consciousnesses.

I could see it all so clearly inside my head, almost as if it were yesterday rather than a whole year ago. There I was, so secure in the company of my family, cosseted, I thought, by the love of a wonderful husband, excited by all that the future might hold for a clever, attractive son.

That woman, without a real worry in the world, no longer appeared to have been me at all. Last Christmas now seemed almost like some wicked practical joke. Indeed, my whole life with my husband and my poor dead son seemed like a wicked practical joke.

The tears I'd tried so hard to keep away were pricking again. The big house, which I had always thought to be the most wonderful home in the world, filled with warmth and love, felt cold and empty. I felt cold and empty. These were feelings that had begun the day Robbie died and I feared they would never leave me.

I picked up the plate of food I had so carefully prepared and emptied the lot into the bin. Then I threw the horrid white dish, somehow such a stark reminder of all that I had lost, human and mineral, into the sink with such force that it broke in half. Another wanton piece of destruction in a life already ruined.

I felt sick. I just couldn't eat a thing. I drank the St Emilion, though. And then I opened a second bottle, desperately seeking oblivion again, my only hope of any rest.

twenty-one

The trial began on Monday the 26th of March 2012. Nearly four months after Robert's arrest, and almost exactly two months before Robbie would have celebrated his sixteenth birthday. I had been asked to give evidence against Robert. Because I was not his legal wife I could have been compelled to do so. I needed no such compulsion. I wanted him brought to justice.

The prosecution called me as their first witness.

'To set the scene, as it were,' the Crown Prosecution Service barrister, Pam Cotton, had said a little obliquely. But I thought I understood pretty much what she meant and although I'd only met her once before, earlier that day in the court's witness support room, she'd briefed me well enough on what was required.

Thirty-something Pam Cotton was very black and very beautiful. In fact almost disconcertingly so, because at a glance she resembled a Hollywood actress playing the part of a barrister rather more than a working brief. She was a rare Marlene Dietrich-like creature who wore suits so severely tailored that they were quite masculine in cut, and yet somehow contrived to make her appear all the more feminine.

I'd walked with her across the main lobby of the court after our earlier meeting and had noticed heads turning. It was

322

obvious that men could not take their eyes off her. I wondered whether this was an advantage or a disadvantage in her profession. Probably a bit of both, I thought.

Regardless of any of that, the woman had a brain like a bacon slicer.

I was the one in the witness box, but Pam, as she'd instructed me to address her out of court, was the one in control of every bit of evidence I gave. Briefly she took me through my marriage to Robert, the marriage that had turned out to be such a sham, from the moment we met, through the birth of Robbie, right up to his death, and asked me to tell the court how I had returned home from an ordinary day at school to make the discovery that our son appeared to have hanged himself.

I swear I could feel Robert's eyes burning into me from where he stood in the dock towards the rear of the courtroom. I made myself not look at him.

'Before your son died, did you ever have any suspicions that all might not be as it seemed in your marriage, Mrs Anderson?' Pam Cotton asked.

I replied that I had not. 'Indeed, I'd considered myself to be very fortunate,' I said. 'I seemed to have everything: a loving husband, a fine son and a beautiful home.'

'And after Robbie's death, when were your suspicions first raised?'

I told her how I had tried to get in touch with Robert to tell him about Robbie, how the Amaco personnel people had appeared not to know of a Robert Anderson, and how they had first mentioned the name Rob Anderton to me. And I explained how I had come to realize that derrickman Rob Anderton and senior drilling engineer Robert Anderson were probably one and the same.

'Did you confront your husband with this?' asked Pam.

I nodded. The red-robed judge, Sir Charles Montague, who looked rather younger than a stereotypical idea of a Justice of Her Majesty's High Court, his face tanned beneath his judicial wig as if he'd recently been on a good holiday, coughed and frowned in my direction.

'Could you please give an audible answer, Mrs Anderson, for the court record,' he said.

'Yes, I did confront my husband.'

'And how did he respond?'

I told the court how Robert had tried to explain it all away, using his desire to leave his past behind and start a new life with me as an excuse for everything.

'And at this stage what did he tell you about his marital status?'

'He told me that he was probably still married to another woman, and that was partly why he'd assumed a false name, but that his wife had left him and disappeared to Australia and he'd absolutely no idea where she was or how to find her. Neither could he, therefore, even be certain that she was alive.'

'I see,' Pam Cotton allowed herself a dramatic pause. 'Perhaps you would now tell the court, Mrs Anderson, how you came to meet and, it seemed, become friends with the woman you knew as Mrs Bella Clooney.'

I told the first dog-walking story, and related how we'd exchanged phone numbers and began to meet quite regularly for walks.

'But you were never invited to the home of Mrs Bella Clooney?'

'I wasn't, no.' There seemed to be no need to mention my uninvited visits. After all, I had never actually crossed the threshold of number 5 Riverview Avenue.

'And did your husband ever meet her in your company?'

'Yes. The night Robbie died. The police wanted me to find someone to be with me. I think it's routine, isn't it? We never had many friends, as a family. We always seemed to be enough for each other . . .'

The memories flooded over me again and for a moment I lost my thread. I opened my mouth to speak again, but no words came.

'Are you able to continue, Mrs Anderson, or would you prefer to take a break?' asked the judge kindly.

I nodded. 'Yes, but c-could I have a glass of water?' I stumbled eventually.

This was duly provided. I took a deep drink and did my best to pull myself together, aware that I was standing unnaturally straight, as if the physical act of doing so might in some way prop me up emotionally. I was wearing the same ancient navy suit I'd worn to both Gran's and Robbie's funerals, and I'd lost so much more weight that it was falling off me now, as were all my clothes. But I hadn't any spare cash to spend on a new outfit, and in any case, I'd no wish to splash out on anything new for this particular occasion. Neither had I been to a hairdresser since before Robbie's death, and my hair, displaying prominent iron-grey roots, was now well below collar length and had lost much of the curly bounce Robert had always professed to love so much. I knew my face was haggard and drawn. I thought I looked like a victim, all right, and suspected that suited rather well the purposes of the prosecution barrister. Certainly the contrast between my lacklustre appearance and her confident glamour could not have been much greater.

'Are you ready to continue now, Mrs Anderson?' asked the judge, again quite kindly.

I said I was. But actually I had no idea what I'd been saying. Pam Cotton stepped in.

'Mrs Anderson, I asked you if your husband ever met the woman you knew as Bella Clooney in your company.'

'Yes,' I said, finding my voice and some of my brains again. 'I phoned her the night Robbie died and she came over to be with me. She was still there when Robert got home from the rig, earlier than he'd led me to expect.'

'And how did they respond to each other?'

I told her how Robert had been quite rude but I'd understood that was because he was in shock and would have hated any outsider to be there. Bella had seemed to behave normally.

'But, of course, I didn't know her very well. Not at all, as it turned out . . .'

Pam moved on from there to ask how I'd eventually discovered that Bella Clooney was actually Brenda Anderton and that we shared a husband. I told her, as I had the police, about seeing the newspaper story after she'd died, and how I'd recognized her from her picture.

'You had no doubt that Brenda Anderton and Bella Clooney were the same woman?'

'None at all,' I said.

She took me through my second confrontation with Robert and I related how he'd finally admitted everything to me.

'And what about Mrs Anderton's death, did you discuss that?'

'I suppose so,' I said, 'I know it's dreadful but I was more interested in what he'd done to me . . .'

I paused again.

'Rather than what he might have done to her,' I added.

'"Rather than what he might have done to her",' Pam repeated. 'What do you mean by that exactly, Mrs Anderson?'

I thought for a moment before replying.

'I'm not quite sure,' I said. 'I mean, I don't think I suspected him of anything then. I don't think it occurred to me. Not until after I'd called the police anyway. Actually, not until after the police came round and questioned me about it all.'

'And then?'

'Then, well, I began to wonder, yes. I still found it hard to believe that he could have been responsible for his wife's death. But I did know he had been with her, staying at the house they had together, their home, just a day or two before the accident.' I paused. 'Or whatever it was.'

'I see.' Pam stared at me for a few seconds, then turned her back to me and walked towards the jury box.

She still had her back to me when she asked her next question.

'Mrs Anderson, perhaps you would tell the court if your husband knows anything at all about motor cars?'

'Yes, he does,' I responded honestly, again telling her what I had told the police.

'Robert always serviced our vehicles himself and just took them to a garage for their MOTs. He also seemed able to carry out most repairs unless they required specialist equipment. He'd been a professional car mechanic before going to work on the rigs, and he was very good at it.'

As the significance of what I'd said sank in, an audible gasp reverberated around the courtroom.

'No further questions,' said Pam Cotton, returning to her seat.

I was then cross-examined by Robert's defence barrister, Mr Joshua Small, a sharp-featured little man whose stature matched his name. It was not a pleasant experience. His very first question was aggressive, and designed, I was quite sure, to shake any confidence I might have.

'Mrs Anderson, do you really expect the court to believe that you shared your life with a man for sixteen years, and had a son by him, and yet you had no idea at all that he had another life, another wife and another family?'

However, this was a question I was ready for, because it was one I had asked myself so often.

'You can believe what you like,' I snapped. 'But I am telling the truth, and that's all I can do. I trusted Robert absolutely and had no idea that he was leading a double life, no idea at all until after our son died.'

The defence barrister, who had what I found to be a disconcerting habit of standing with his head tilted backwards and slightly to one side, gave a small snort of disbelief.

'He must have been extremely convincing,' Mr Small responded. 'Indeed, rather more convincing than most people would consider possible. Would you accept that to be the case, Mrs Anderton?'

'I don't know what "most people" might think,' I said. 'But if you're asking me if Robert was a good liar, then the answer is a resounding yes. Indeed, he was a far better liar than I would have thought possible. Far better.'

Another little gasp could be heard in the courtroom. It was only later that I realized just how significant that remark must have seemed. At the time I merely I thought I'd dealt with the first barrage rather well, and I probably had, because Mr Joshua Small seemed to tone down his aggression after that and only asked me a couple of more innocuous questions.

After I'd finished giving my evidence I was able to watch the rest of the proceedings from the public gallery. I was fortunate to have been called first because, painful though I knew the experience would be, I did not wish to miss a moment of Robert's trial. My father had said he was too distressed to see his supposed son-in-law, who he had been extremely fond of, in court. And I'd managed to fend off Gladys. So I was alone in the gallery, but actually much preferred it that way.

There followed evidence from the young police officer who had been first on the scene when Bella was killed. He explained how her vehicle was found on the wrong side of the road having collided with a milk tanker, as I'd read in the paper.

'We believe Mrs Anderton was killed instantly,' he told the court.

DS Jarvis then gave his evidence. He was coolly professional, and somehow more articulate than I would have expected, as he summarized the police case against Robert. He spoke of Robert having both motive and opportunity, just as he had explained it to me.

And he told the court that Scenes of Crime Officers had found a set of overalls belonging to Robert, which he apparently kept in the garage of 5 Riverview Avenue, and forensic examination had revealed clinging to the overalls small particles of accelerator cable.

'Were forensics able to establish precisely where these particles had come from?' asked Pam Cotton.

'Yes, ma'am,' replied Jarvis. 'From the damaged cable of Brenda Anderton's Toyota.'

Pam Cotton emphasized the point as usual by repeating it, then began to take DS Jarvis through other aspects of Brenda Anderton's life.

'Is it true, Detective Sergeant, that, following the death of Brenda Anderton, you have now closed your investigation into the abduction of Luke Macintyre?' she asked.

Jarvis agreed that was so.

An expert witness in automotive forensics, Mr Maxwell Brown, a man approaching retirement, I thought, with rather more white hair in his bushy eyebrows than on his head, was then called to the stand. He had apparently been brought in from Bristol to give a second opinion after the initial examination of Brenda's car.

Pam Cotton made quite a performance of establishing that Brown was considered to be the foremost in his field. He stood even more upright than I had done in the witness box, shoulders thrust back, like a soldier at attention, while she asked him to explain what he believed had caused Brenda Anderton's fatal accident. At first he appeared to reiterate the theory which I'd initially read in the *Express & Echo*.

'Following a thorough investigation of Mrs Anderton's vehicle, assisted by the original Devon County Constabulary team, I am quite certain that the accelerator pedal jammed,' he said. 'Mrs Anderton was unable to decrease her speed, so in an attempt to do so she switched off the engine. It was this that ultimately had fatal consequences because she was, of course, then unable to steer, the electronic steering system having been disabled. And it was at this point that her car swung across the A377 into the path of an oncoming milk tanker.'

'Have you been able to establish the speed at which Mrs Anderton's car may have been travelling when it collided with the tanker?' Pam Cotton asked.

'Probably between seventy and eighty miles per hour,' replied Brown.

'And you feel certain that she was simply unable to slow down.'

'Yes. All the evidence points to that.'

'So, could you please, Mr Brown, tell the court what caused the accelerator pedal to jam?'

'Yes, indeed. Strands within the accelerator cable had been cut, so that it was only a matter of time before the cable would split fully into two halves, thus rendering it impossible for the driver to control the throttle.'

'You said the strands within the accelerator pedal had been cut, Mr Brown?' Pam continued. 'Do you mean deliberately cut?'

'Yes, indeed.'

'And there is no doubt about that.'

'No, none at all.'

'Is it possible to say when this damage might have occurred.'

'Not exactly. It would depend largely on how much mileage the deceased had covered in her car. Not all the strands had been cut, and the intention was presumably that the rest of them would break after a period of time when the strain on them became too great, which would have been most likely to occur when the vehicle was travelling at a higher speed.'

'So, is it possible for you to state, Mr Brown, whether or not the damage to the accelerator cable could have been executed, say, as much as three or four days before the incident which led to Mrs Anderton's death?'

'Oh yes, easily, depending on the subsequent mileage, of course.'

'Thank you very much, Mr Brown, no more questions,' said Pam after another of her dramatic pauses.

I realized that she was trying to establish early on in the jury's minds a timescale confirmed by an expert, so that they would later more easily accept that Robert would have had the opportunity to sabotage Brenda's car even though he was in the middle of the North Sea when she died.

Mr Joshua Small was on his feet at once to cross-examine.

'Mrs Anderton's vehicle was a Toyota Corolla, was it not, Mr Brown? It is well known that many of these vehicles were recalled three years ago due to alleged problems with accelerator pedals sticking, so could not this fatal collision have been a tragic accident?'

'No. Absolutely not. The strands within the accelerator cable had definitely been cut. The problem with the Corollas, as with other Toyotas, involved strands breaking due to wear and tear. And it was actually later models than Mrs Anderton's which were recalled by Toyota.'

'And yet the Devon County Constabulary and their forensic unit at first accepted that this fatal collision was an accident, did they not?'

'I believe so, yes.'

'And was it not only after DS Jarvis interviewed Mrs Marion Anderson and was told of Rob Anderton's double life, and all that entailed, that the car was re-examined?'

'Yes, that was the case.'

'So surely the fact that these strands had been cut and not just broken due to wear and tear could not have been that obvious?'

'Pretty obvious, in my opinion.'

'But not, it would appear, in the opinion of the forensics experts who examined the car the first time round?'

'Apparently not. No.'

'And surely the fact that the accelerator function of these particular cars has been so suspect must still give rise to some doubt?'

'Not in my opinion, no.'

'Mr Brown, could I ask you when you actually inspected this vehicle yourself?'

'When I was asked to do so by the police, a few days after Mrs Anderton's death, because of concerns relating to the initial examination of the car.'

'So, not until after you had actually been given cause to

doubt that the mechanical damage had been caused accidentally?'

'Well, no, but—'

'So it would seem reasonable to refer to the opinion of those who first examined the car, and who did not already have a hidden agenda, would it not?'

'I had no hidden agenda,' blustered Maxwell Brown. 'I was asked to examine the car in order to give a second opinion. I am now relating my findings to this court to the best of my ability, and I do object—'

'Yes, indeed, Mr Brown,' the barrister interrupted thunderously. 'I am quite sure you do object. But it is the duty of this court to explore all aspects of this case, and as far as I can see you at least were never in a position to conduct your investigation into the condition of Mrs Anderton's car in as independent a manner as might have been desired. No further questions, My Lord.'

Robert was the first witness to be called by the defence. I suppose Mr Small QC was relying on his apparent plausibility, but I may have already partially scuppered that with the jury. Even so, Robert seemed to be his usual calm and credible self, to start with at least. It seemed hard to believe he could be capable of murder.

Unlike me, far from having lost weight, Robert looked considerably heavier than when I had last seen him. He had the beginnings of a double chin and his belly strained against the confines of his light-grey double-breasted suit, a suit I had never seen before. I was vaguely aware that a prison diet was supposed to be high in both stodge and fat, and I assumed this was the cause of his weight gain. After all, Robert had been remanded in custody for almost four months. His hair, cut shorter than usual, was still coal-black, though.

Mr Small began by establishing that Robert had been away on a North Sea oil platform at the time of his wife's death.

'I'd gone back to work two days before,' said Robert. 'Then I returned to Exeter after learning that Brenda had been killed.'

'When you were in Exeter with your wife Brenda would you normally also have driven the car in which she died?'

'Yes, sir,' said Robert.

'And so, had that car been tampered with in any way you too could have been at risk, as well as your wife?'

'Yes, sir,' said Robert again.

Pam Cotton was on her feet as he spoke.

'Objection, My Lord. Counsel is grossly leading the witness.'

The judge half smiled at Joshua Small. 'Come along now, Mr Small,' he interjected mildly.

'I apologize, My Lord,' said the defence barrister, pausing briefly before asking his next question.

'Would anyone else have also been at risk, Mr Anderton?' he asked.

'Well, yes, of course. My younger daughter Janey. And I would never do anything that might harm Janey.'

Joshua Small then asked Robert about the double life he had led, which Robert admitted with humility.

'I am ashamed now of what I did and the way I lived,' he said. 'I believe that I was responsible for the chain of events that have led to all the terrible things which have happened to . . .' He paused, perhaps searching for words. 'To both my families,' he concluded.

Mr Small asked him if he could explain to the court why he had embarked on his extraordinary double life in the first place. And Robert began to relate the same story that he had told me, concerning the legacy of Huntington's and his inability to cope with its inevitable effect on his wife and daughters.

'I just wanted to escape from it all,' he said. 'I know it was weak of me, but I am not a strong man. Yet I could not bring myself to leave my wife and the poor sick child we had together brought into the world. When I learned that Brenda was expecting another child I felt betrayed by her, and yet all the more bound to her side. And even less able to reveal the truth about my double life to either Brenda or to Marion.'

Pam Cotton began her cross-examination by addressing the question of logistics, which she had already set up in her questioning of Maxwell Brown.

'Would you agree, as already indicated by one of the country's leading experts in motor forensics, that your whereabouts at the time of the incident which claimed your wife Brenda's life is irrelevant, Mr Anderton?' she enquired.

'I don't know what you mean,' Robert replied.

'But I think you do, Mr Anderton. As an accomplished mechanic you would be perfectly able to cut through a cable in such a way that it would continue to function for some miles after receiving your attentions, would you not?'

Mr Small began to rise to his feet, but Robert answered so quickly and forcefully that he lowered himself back in his chair without raising the objection he had seemed to be preparing for.

'I didn't touch the car,' said Robert.

'That's as may be, Mr Anderton, but you must then at least accept that the cable could have been cut in such a way by a person or persons unknown.'

'I suppose so,' Robert muttered grudgingly.

'Yes. And, of course, if you knew that damage had been done you would then presumably have been able to avoid driving the vehicle again before going back to work in the North Sea, would you not?'

'But I didn't know—'

'All right, Mr Anderton,' Pam Cotton interrupted. 'Can we just agree that, with your prolonged absences, your wife Brenda would have been the principal driver of the Toyota?'

'I suppose so, yes. But my daughter, Janey, was often with her. I have said already, I'd never do anything to put Janey in danger.'

'I was coming to that, Mr Anderton,' said Pam easily. 'You have already told the court about the dreadful illness which your eleven-year-old daughter will ultimately develop and how difficult you found it to cope with that, have you not?'

Robert agreed that he had.

'So, might it not be possible, Mr Anderton, that you may have been prepared to leave to chance the possibility of your daughter being in the motor car with her mother when the accelerator cable finally split, and indeed her survival, rather more than you would have done were she a well child?'

Pam spoke slowly and deliberately, clearly selecting her words with great care.

Robert, who must surely have been extremely disturbed if not infuriated by this line of questioning, kept his voice level and his manner respectful.

'I would never do, and have never done anything that might harm Janey,' he repeated. 'Nor any of my children.'

In spite of everything I could feel a certain pervading sympathy for him in the court. But then, Robert had always been good at manipulating emotion.

Pam Cotton, however, moved on swiftly to deal with that too.

'Mr Anderton, you have painted a picture of your actions which seems to me to have little relation to the bitter truth, which is that you maintained a cruel charade for sixteen years regardless of the feelings of either of the women in your life. Is that not the case?'

'It's not how I saw it,' muttered Robert so quietly that he was asked by the judge to repeat his reply and to speak up.

'I'm sure it isn't,' responded the prosecution barrister. 'But wouldn't you accept that many men and women have to deal with serious illness within their families? Do you really feel that justifies the course of action you chose to take?'

Robert's aura of humble self-confidence began to desert him. He looked up at the high ceiling of the courtroom as if seeking inspiration. In the end his reply was just one word.

'No,' he said.

'No,' repeated Pam. 'You admit that you have been responsible for unleashing a terrible and tragic sequence of events. Can the illness within your family be regarded as justification for any of that?'

'No,' replied Robert again.

'No,' repeated Pam again.

'And yet you went to quite extraordinary lengths over an astonishing period of time, for sixteen years, in order to keep the existence of your two families secret from each other, did you not?'

'Yes.' Robert seemed to have more or less run out of words. And even at that moment I could not stop myself reflecting that that, at least, made a change.

'So when this double life of yours started to unravel following the death of your son, were you not afraid that your first wife would eventually expose your activities, which were, of course, criminal, and all that remained of your fragile house of cards would collapse, probably leading to legal action against you?'

'Well, yes, I was afraid of that, obviously.'

'Obviously,' interrupted Pam Cotton. 'And just how far were you prepared to go to protect your unusual lifestyle, Mr Anderton?'

'Well, I don't know really . . .' stumbled Robert.

'Surely you went at least as far as to threaten your wife Brenda if she exposed your activities to Marion? Surely you did that?'

'Well, yes. I suppose so. But I only threatened that I would leave her. That's all.'

'Are you quite sure of that, Mr Anderton?'

'Yes. Absolutely. I am not a violent man. I wouldn't make any other kind of threat.'

'So, there is no question that you would even have considered murdering your wife in order to protect your double life?'

'No. Of course not. I didn't consider it and I didn't do it.'

'But just how far would you go to wreak revenge against someone you may hold responsible for the death of your beloved son?'

Robert looked startled, shaken even, by this new approach. 'I don't know what you mean,' he said.

'I think you do, Mr Anderton. I think you do—'

'No.' Robert interrupted the barrister this time. 'I told you. I blame myself for Robbie's death. I blame myself because of the crazy lifestyles I imposed on both my families.'

'You blame yourself,' Pam repeated. It seemed to be a habit with her, if not all barristers, to emphasize almost every significant point by repeating it.

'Yes, I blame myself,' said Robert again.

Pam stared at him hard.

'No, Mr Anderton,' she barked. 'That is not the truth, is it? Isn't the truth that you had reason to strongly suspect that your wife Brenda had in some way been responsible for Robbie's death. Very good reason indeed.'

Another of those gasps went round the courtroom.

Robert seemed not to know what to say.

'I don't know, I-I just didn't know, I couldn't believe that . . .' he stumbled.

'But I think you did believe it, Mr Anderton,' Pam Cotton continued. 'Certainly your second wife, Marion, the woman you married bigamously, the woman you said was the love of your life, she believed that Brenda was responsible for Robbie's death, didn't she?'

'Well, yes. She was quite sure of it, from the moment she recognized Brenda's photograph in the paper after – after the accident. But I c-could never believe that Brenda would have done such a thing, not even when she told me . . .'

Robert stopped abruptly in mid-sentence, as if he had only just realized exactly what he was saying. But it was too late. Pam Cotton pounced.

'When she told you what, Mr Anderton?'

'Nothing, nothing.'

'C'mon, Mr Anderton. I am sure the jury is already guessing what you were about to say. The entire court is ahead of you now. Would you please tell us what your wife said? What she told you about Robbie's death?'

'I uh, I can't. It was too awful,' Robert said.

'Oh yes, you can, Mr Anderton. Oh yes, you can. You were about to say "when she told me that she had induced Robbie to kill himself", or words to that effect, were you not, Mr Anderton?'

'Objection, My Lord,' cried Joshua Small.

The judge leaned forward.

'You will not put words in the defendant's mouth, Mrs Cotton,' he commanded.

'I'm so sorry, My Lord,' said the prosecution barrister, looking anything but.

'You do not have to answer that question if you do not wish to, Mr Anderton,' the judge continued.

Robert didn't seem to hear him. But neither did he speak. His shoulders drooped. I could see from his body language that he was close to tears.

Pam Cotton had no mercy.

'Just tell the court what your wife said, Mr Anderton,' she repeated loudly.

The judge cleared his throat and looked as if he might inter-ject again. But he didn't. Perhaps he wanted to know what Brenda Anderton had said to Robbie as much as the rest of the court. And maybe he also thought the court should be told.

Robert looked as if he might fall over.

'Yes,' he said. It was almost inaudible.

'Would you please speak up, Mr Anderton,' instructed the barrister.

Robert nodded.

'She told me she had been to see Robbie on the d-day he died,' he began falteringly. 'She said she knew the day of the week Marion taught at Okehampton College, she knew he would be alone studying for his mocks. He invited her into the house. After all, he knew her, knew her as Bella Clooney. She told him who she really was, and that his father had lived a double life full of lies and duplicity. She said it was easy to convince Robbie that his life wasn't worth living, that he might as well end it, that she would help him, make it easy for him . . .'

Robert stopped abruptly. He looked grey and drawn, as if he were about to break down.

I hadn't expected that. Robert, even at his most vulnerable, had proven himself over many years to be so controlled.

I just stared at him. My worst fears were being realized. But it didn't seem quite right somehow. Pieces of the jigsaw were still missing, I felt sure. There had to be something more. After all, Robbie was an intelligent and well-adjusted boy. He would have realized that nothing Brenda had said actually meant he didn't have a father, however crazy, who loved him. And he still had me. He still had his mother. Surely that would have counted for something.

Pam Cotton waited a few seconds, for Robert to continue perhaps. But when he did not she piled on the pressure.

'Your son was fit and healthy, just fifteen years old with his whole life in front of him. He was clever and talented, that rare mix of an academic and a sportsman, was he not?'

'Yes,' muttered Robert.

'So come on, Mr Anderton. Come on. What else did your wife say to him? What on earth did she say to him, to make him want to take his own life, to take his own life straight away, without even confronting you, or speaking to his mother? What did Brenda say to your son, Mr Anderton?'

Robert's eyes seemed focused on some unseen point in the middle distance. It was almost as if he were somewhere else, perhaps back with Brenda listening to the terrible revelations she'd made concerning the death of our beloved Robbie. Never mind a pin, it was as if you could have heard a piece of thread drop in that courtroom.

'Why don't you tell us exactly what Brenda said to him, Mr Anderton?' Pam Cotton repeated. 'All of it. Because you know, don't you? Brenda told you, didn't she?'

Robert nodded in a vague sort of way. His voice when he spoke again seemed to come from a long way off.

'She said she wanted me to share Robbie's pain, to understand why he felt his entire life had been destroyed . . .'

'Yes, Mr Anderton. But what did she say to him?'

'She said – she said she told him about the Huntington's, and about his older half-sister who already had the full-blown disease and was unable to function as a human being any more. She told him how we were just waiting for Janey, for his younger half-sister, to become ill too. We didn't know when it would happen, but we knew it would happen sometime, because in their cases the disease was carried one hundred per cent . . . there was no chance, not even a slight chance, that Janey might not get it . . . she told him all of that . . .'

Robert paused again. He was holding on to the front of the witness box for support. He looked absolutely defeated.

'Go on, please go on, Mr Anderton,' said Pam, much more gently now.

'Everything she said was true, it was all true, except for one thing . . .'

Yet again he seemed unable to continue. Yet again Pam encouraged him, her voice quite soft, cajoling almost.

'Please tell us what that one thing was, Mr Anderton,' she coaxed.

Robert was still holding on to the witness box. He looked down at his hands so that I could no longer see his face. His voice was weak and strained, but the words were clear enough. Frighteningly, shockingly clear.

'She told him that I was the carrier. That I was the one who carried the deformed Huntington's gene, not her. She said she'd told Robbie that he too would get Huntington's, that it was a hundred per cent certain. And so, and so . . . would any children he fathered.'

Even Pam Cotton seemed stunned.

'She told him that you were the carrier of Huntington's,' she repeated, stressing the point as usual, but I thought she was just operating on autopilot.

I remembered once reading that barristers are reluctant to ask questions in court to which they do not know the answer. There was no way Pam Cotton had second-guessed that piece of evidence. And neither had I. Nor anyone else it seemed. This time it was not a strangled gasp which could be heard in the courtroom, but more of a loud and sustained rumble.

I could not at first quite take in what I was hearing. However, Pam Cotton swiftly gathered herself together and began to speak again, determined, it seemed, to clarify every aspect of Robert's devastating evidence.

'And did she say how your son responded to that terrible news?'

'She told me that h-he broke down, and said at once that he couldn't carry on. That . . . that he didn't want to carry on.'

'Indeed. And, of course, not only did your son believe himself to be the recipient of quite terrible news about his own health and his own future, but he'd just learned that he was about to become a father himself, had he not?'

'Yes,' said Robert.

'And he presumably would therefore have believed that he would be passing on this awful disease to his own child, is that not so?'

'Yes,' said Robert again.

'Did your wife, did Brenda, know that Robbie was about to father a child?'

'Not when she went to Highrise that day. She said, she said . . .'

Robert looked even more as if he were about to collapse. But he didn't.

'She said that was a bonus,' he continued after a brief pause. 'A bonus, for God's sake. She said Robbie told her about the baby right away. About how he'd just learned that he was going to have a child and, of course, yes, he then believed he was going to pass on a terrible disease to that child. She said it was easy after that, easy to convince him, or let him convince himself, she put it to me, that he'd rather die than face what he then believed the future to hold. And easy, she said, easy to help him do it.'

'So how exactly did your wife say she helped your son to kill himself?'

'She told me she suggested hanging, because it was quick and rarely failed, and he just meekly accepted what she said. He was broken, just broken. My poor boy . . .'

Robert wiped tears away from his eyes with one hand.

'Just repeat what she told you,' encouraged Pam Cotton. 'Just tell the court exactly how Brenda said she helped your son to take his own life.'

Robert nodded, and took a big gulp of air.

'She . . . she said she helped him move his desk below the big beam that ran across the ceiling of his room, then sent him to find a length of rope, and helped him rig it all up. Then . . . then she just . . . just watched him do it. That's what she said. She stood there and watched him climb on the desk, put the rope around his neck, tighten it, and jump. She stood there and watched him choke to death. Our wonderful boy. Then she left, went home as if nothing had happened.'

Robert's voice was high-pitched now, almost hysterical. His shoulders were heaving. Tears were pouring down his cheeks.

I had always been so certain that Robbie had not killed himself, or not unaided anyway. And I'd been so sure, from the moment I discovered who and what she really was, that Brenda

Anderton was the one responsible for his death. But I hadn't actually come close to imagining anything like this, to guessing the terrible lie which had made Robbie not want to live any more. I didn't want to think about what he must have been feeling, what he must have been going through on the day he died. I realized there were tears running down my cheeks too.

The judge coughed and again looked as if he were about to speak, perhaps to ask Robert if he were able to carry on. Even defendants in a murder trial are treated with that sort of courtesy in an English courtroom.

Pam Cotton, however, was in full flow. She made sure she didn't give the judge time to interject before firing off her next question.

'And so you believed that you then knew the truth about the death of your only son, and that your legal wife was responsible for it,' she barked. 'You therefore decided to wreak the ultimate revenge. You decided to kill her, did you not? You decided to kill your wife Brenda. Is that not the case, Mr Anderton?'

Robert's jaw dropped. It was as if he had not considered at all the impact of what he had just told the court. He stopped weeping as if a switch had been thrown.

'No, no!' he cried. 'I hated Brenda then, of course I did, but I'm not a murderer. I would never kill anyone, not even her, not even after what she'd told me she'd done. In any case, I could never really believe she'd done it. Not to Robbie. He'd never hurt anyone—'

'Oh come on, Mr Anderton. You idolized your only son, ironically your only healthy child. Your wife Brenda told you she helped him to die. Encouraged him to kill himself. You must have felt this justified taking her life too. Didn't you, Mr

Anderton? Isn't that what happened, Mr Anderton? You murdered your wife in revenge for the death of your son, did you not?'

'No, no,' said Robert more quietly. 'I told you, when I thought about it, I didn't even believe her. Not really. I thought she was just trying to hurt me, to make me suffer too. I certainly never planned to hurt her. I didn't kill her. I didn't.'

But Robert was no longer at all convincing. Not only had he proven himself to be a most accomplished liar over the years, which my evidence alone had made clear, but also his own evidence had been muddled throughout to the point of being totally contradictory.

'No further questions, My Lord,' said Pam Cotton.

The court seemed curiously silent. Then the judge glanced towards Joshua Small.

'Do you wish to re-examine, Mr Small?' he asked.

The defence barrister, apparently as stunned as all the rest of us and quite clearly previously unaware of the evidence his client had just given, climbed to his feet.

'I do, My Lord,' he said, without any real certainty, I felt.

He turned to Robert.

'Mr Anderton, how could your wife possibly have known that she would be able to persuade your son to kill himself?' he asked.

'I don't know,' Robert muttered.

'In confronting Robbie and exposing her real identity to him she surely risked ending her entire charade without necessarily wreaking any significant revenge against you at all. So what would she have done if your son had not proved so susceptible? What would she have done if he had simply picked up the phone to call his mother?'

Robert looked down at his hands and said nothing.

'You must answer the question, Mr Anderton,' instructed the judge.

Robert looked up.

'Brenda told me she had been prepared to kill him if necessary.' His voice was barely more than a whisper but the court was so quiet there was no need for the judge to ask him to speak up.

Joshua Small QC seemed to turn rather pale. Rather desperately, I felt, he sought some sort of recovery.

'Mrs Anderton planned to kill a fit and athletic teenage boy. How exactly?'

Robert looked appealingly towards the judge. Sir Charles Montague merely stared at him.

'She told me she had taken a carving knife with her,' Robert said, again in almost a whisper. 'From the kitchen . . . it was in her handbag. She always carried quite a big bag . . .'

His voice, already so tiny, faded away.

A kind of embarrassed titter reverberated around the court. In spite of the awfulness of Robert's latest revelation, I understood. There was something almost surreally comical about the concept of this middle-aged woman seeking out Robbie at Highrise with a carving knife concealed in her handbag.

Joshua Small was no longer at all the super-confident QC of earlier in the day. You could just see how much he regretted having asked that question. He really was a man in a hole unable to stop digging.

'But did you really think your wife would have been capable of using a knife on Robbie?' he blustered on.

'No, of course not,' said Robert, his voice louder and stronger. 'I'm sure she couldn't have.'

Small ended his re-examination, and did his best to continue with the case for the defence, which, it seemed to me, had been more or less totally scuppered by Robert's performance. The defence barrister had been left with damned near nowhere to go.

He called, as had doubtless been his intention before Robert's outburst, one of the Devon and Cornwall Constabulary forensic team who had initially examined Brenda Anderton's car.

From the beginning John Parsons, a big man in his early forties, looked as if he'd rather be almost anywhere other than Exeter Crown Court that morning. He stumbled over his words and was clearly ill at ease. After all, he must already have been well aware that he and his colleagues had missed something rather important when they'd first examined the Toyota. The little matter of deliberate sabotage had totally escaped them.

However, Mr Small pushed his point gamely.

'Is it significant that any question of these strands being deliberately cut only arose after the police learned that there may actually be people – indeed, they came to believe, one person in particular – with reason to want Mrs Anderton dead?'

'I suppose so, yes.'

'And does the history of the accelerator system of Toyota Corollas continue to cast an element of doubt on this?'

'I'm not sure I understand, sir,' said John Parsons.

'I am asking you if the possibility that the death of Mrs Anderton was due to a tragic accident caused by mechanical failure might indeed remain,' continued Small.

John Parsons finally grasped that he was being thrown a professional lifeline.

'Oh yes,' he said. 'Of course. Absolutely.'

But it was clear that his evidence was having little effect on the jury or anyone else in the courtroom. This was technical stuff. And it paled into insignificance compared with the excitement provoked by Robert's appearance in the witness box, which the press were later to widely describe as having offered 'scenes of the highest possible drama' and a 'spectacular courtroom revelation'.

In any case Pam Cotton put paid to it in one brief onslaught.

'Obviously the original forensic team can be totally forgiven for allowing their initial opinion to be coloured by the unfortunate recent history of certain Toyota motor cars,' she said. 'And furthermore there was initially no reason at all to even consider, really, the possibility of suspicious circumstances surrounding the death of Mrs Anderton. But, Mr Parsons, when you were asked to re-examine the vehicle, along with a more experienced man, the UK's acknowledged leader in the field, and in a more thorough and detailed way, was it not then abundantly clear to you and your team that strands of the accelerator cable of Mrs Anderton's vehicle had been deliberately cut?'

Parsons coloured slightly. 'Well, not entirely,' he said.

'C'mon now, Mr Parsons,' Pam Cotton persisted. Another of her favourite phrases. 'Come on, now. Surely you were then able to tell whether or not the threads had been deliberately cut? So, were they?'

'Yes. They must have been, I suppose.'

'You suppose, Mr Parsons? Surely you must now accept beyond any reasonable doubt that the damage to the vehicle's accelerator cable was not caused by mechanical failure?'

'Well, yes,' Parsons agreed with obvious reluctance, looking more uncomfortable than ever.

'And so you must therefore accept that the cable threads were cut by someone wishing to harm Mrs Brenda Anderton, do you not?'

John Parsons glanced pleadingly at the judge, who in turn fixed a disapproving look on Pam Cotton.

'The witness cannot possibly be in a position to answer that question, Mrs Cotton,' he said.

'Of course not, My Lord, I do apologize,' the barrister responded, again looking almost anything but apologetic.

'No further questions,' she added, once more taking her seat.

Ultimately the cases for both prosecution and defence, including the opening and closing statements of both barristers, took eleven days to complete. On the twelfth day Sir Charles Montague sent the jury to deliberate their verdict.

They took less than four hours. And their decision was unanimous, the foreman told the court. Guilty. Robert had been found unanimously guilty of murdering his first and only legal wife.

Still protesting his innocence, the man I had once so loved, the husband who had never really been mine, was sentenced to life imprisonment, with a recommendation from the judge that he serve a minimum of fifteen years.

As I left the court, hurrying past the press gathered on the forecourt, I did experience a certain sense of satisfaction. The woman directly responsible for my son's death was herself dead, and the man I now held indirectly responsible for the entire tragedy had been jailed for life for her murder.

They had both got no less than they deserved and I felt no compassion for either of them. Not any more. It wasn't enough, of course, because nothing could bring my beloved Robbie back.

But at least a kind of justice had been achieved.

twenty-two

I retreated into Highrise again, into what had once been the comforting womb provided by my beautiful home. Although this time only for a few days. I had already planned what I would do if Robert was convicted, in theory anyway, but I did not yet know if it would be possible.

I remained devastated by all that had happened and would for the rest of my life. However, in a way, I had done my grieving. For my son, for the life I had once lived, and indeed for the man I had once loved. In order to survive I had to move on, at least to the best of my ability. And if I were to have any chance of doing so, I could not stay at Highrise long term. Not only did I no longer have the money or the will to maintain the place, but the home I'd once thought so perfect was now just a constant reminder of the sham of my marriage and the tragic loss of my son. Although, of course, I really needed no reminder.

I also had to remember that I was not yet quite forty. I would celebrate my fortieth birthday later that year – to use the accepted term, even though I felt as if no celebration of any kind would ever be part of my life again. Unless I were to follow in the footsteps of my dearest boy, I could reasonably expect to live another thirty, even forty years. And I had already rejected suicide. That would be the ultimate defeat. I wasn't going to allow my supposed husband and his wicked wife to defeat me in anything. Not any more. Robert's shocking court-room revelation of how Brenda had used our son like some worthless puppet in order to execute the worst possible revenge on his father and me had made me even more determined about that. To me, Brenda Anderton was quite simply a murderer, every bit as much as was Robert, who had now paid the proper price for her actions. I wasn't going to allow myself to become another of her victims.

But, somewhat bizarrely, I needed Robert's help before I could move on.

Once the trial was over I finally opened the letters he had sent me. It seemed strange to take them from the back of the kitchen cupboard, into which I had flung them immediately upon receipt so that they would be out of sight, and to know that I was touching what he had touched. It would once have been unthinkable for me to have left unseen any word at all from this man. But I had done so for months. And there they all were. Twenty of them. Every one had remained unread and unanswered, but he hadn't given up writing them.

I checked the dates of the postmarks as best I could and ripped open the first, which he had sent me right after he was arrested. Its content was predictable. This was a letter full of guilt and remorse concerning his double life and the way in which he had bigamously married me, and his grief and even greater sense of guilt over Robbie's death. It also protested his innocence of any involvement in Brenda's death. He had written:

I just want you to know that you did not marry a murderer on top of everything else that I have been. I also want you

to know that I love you as much as ever – that was always
the only true and honest thing about me probably. I cannot
expect you to still feel the same way about me. I just hope
that you can bring yourself to visit me while I am on
remand and allow me at least to try to explain.

I tossed the letter angrily to one side. I was surprised that I
could still feel this level of anger towards Robert, but I most
certainly did. The letter just emphasized to me the fantasy world
in which, I now knew, he had always existed. Ever since he'd
met me anyway.

For a start, he had never married me. He'd committed
bigamy with me. How could he, even in the wildest imaginings
of his twisted mind, have thought that I could bear to visit him,
let alone want to? Finally, what on earth did he mean by his
plea to be allowed to 'try to explain'? How could anyone, even
plausibly ingenuous Robert, explain away what he had done?
The calculated callous way in which he had conducted his
double life over such a long period, and the terrible consequences of his actions, could never be explained. Not to me
anyway.

The contents of the letter were exactly what I had expected,
which is why I hadn't opened it or any of the others. I was
fairly certain the rest of them would be merely more of the
same, but I opened them just in case, and glanced quickly
through.

One of the quite early letters contained information about
our financial situation. Robert said he wanted me to have access
to what funds remained. He told me that the lottery money
had been kept in an off-shore savings account and included the
account details and his access code. He also gave me the access
codes for his R. Anderson account and an R. Anderton account

I didn't know about. The address for all three accounts was the same – 240a Airport Road, Bristol – and meant nothing to me. This certainly explained why no incriminating correspondence concerning any of these accounts arrived either at Highrise or, presumably, at the Exeter property he'd shared with Brenda. But did Robert have yet another home, I wondered? The man really was a box of tricks.

I kicked myself for not having opened any of the letters earlier as this information may have made life easier for me. Then I read on. He explained that 240a Airport Road, presumably conveniently situated close to the airport he regularly flew in and out of, was just an accommodation address, saying: 'It probably wouldn't be possible to open a bank account with an accommodation address nowadays. But sixteen years ago, and with a little creativity, you could do it.'

Well, he could do it, anyway, I thought wryly. And I could only imagine just how 'creative' he had been. Then I got to the important bit.

Unfortunately I fear there is very little money left anywhere. Of course, as a rigger my wages from Amaco stopped just as soon as I stopped turning up for work. I'd thought that the lottery money, even after we bought Highrise, would be enough to last us the rest of our lives, Marion. It was just over a million pounds. But low interest rates and Robbie's school fees, even with his scholarship, meant that for some time now I have been eating into the capital which I'd set aside to provide an income. I'd planned to deal with it. I'd thought I might perhaps try to raise a mortgage on Highrise. But I just never quite got round to it. I suppose I didn't want to face reality. I'm so very sorry, Marion . . .

I tossed the letter to one side. He didn't want to face reality. He was sorry. Nothing new there then. And how dare he in any way blame our poor dead son for anything. Robbie wouldn't have minded if his father had said he couldn't afford to send him to Kelly. He would have understood. He had been that kind of boy.

It occurred to me that I hadn't known before the alleged amount of Robert's lottery win. I'd not even bothered to ask him. After all, by the time I'd learned about it I'd been pretty sure there wouldn't be much of it left. I thought about our lifestyle for a moment. Robert must have spent several thousand pounds every year on fine wine alone. Looking back, it had become almost an obsession, and I knew that some of the bottles he'd acquired had cost over £100 each. Our cars were always luxury models bought new as Robert said he didn't want either of us driving vehicles that may have been misused by someone else. Our latest, the top of the range Lexus hybrid with all its extras, had cost over £50,000. Then there was the upkeep of Highrise, not to mention its initial purchase. Even without the fall in interest rates it seemed to me rather more surprising that the cash had lasted as long as it did than that it had now run out.

Another letter asked if I would try to visit his daughter, Janey, who was in local authority care and had apparently been placed with a foster family. Not for the first time I marvelled at the man's cheek. There was no question of my visiting Janey. While, of course, I felt dreadfully sorry for the poor child, an innocent caught up in all of this, I could not get involved with her in even the most spurious of ways. I was still having enough trouble coming to terms with my own situation.

The most recently received letter had been written soon after Robert's conviction. He had been returned to Exeter, a local prison which took male prisoners on remand from all over Devon and Cornwall, but was now awaiting transfer. He might even be sent to Dartmoor, he said, if he was considered low risk enough for a category C establishment. The irony of him possibly being locked up in the middle of the moor he'd so loved to roam, often with our poor dead son, was not lost on me.

Predictably the bulk of the letter was another outpouring of self-pity, full of his despair at the prospect of spending fifteen years in prison: 'without you being there for me. Locked up in some dreadful place and I now know that my life is over, and that is made all the worse by the knowledge that I brought this all about myself.'

Yes, I thought, *and our son's life is over because of you too.*

He still maintained, however, that he was innocent of the murder of his wife Brenda. That he had been wrongly convicted. He wrote:

The car crash must have been an accident – it's the only explanation. That accelerator cable must have split because of wear and tear, because of a mechanical fault, and all those so-called experts have got it wrong. I didn't touch it, I swear to you, Marion. And I have instructed my solicitor to see what can be done to obtain proof of that. Then we can appeal. That is my only hope . . .

I skimmed over most of the rest of it. Just more of the same. Yet again he begged me to visit: 'It would mean everything to me. I don't expect you to love me any more, but just to know that you didn't totally hate me would give me some will to live, and to fight on to prove my innocence.'

I bundled up all the letters again and put them back in the cupboard.

Then I considered what to do next. I found that I rather wanted to speak to Pam Cotton. She hadn't been at all what I had expected in a barrister, not out of court anyway. After Robert's conviction she and my solicitor Marti Smith had insisted on taking me for a drink in a pub near the court. For them I think it had been something of a celebration at getting the right result. For me it had been more of wake really. Pam had been kind to me, her star witness as she referred to me. Albeit after quite a few drinks had been consumed, she had even given me her mobile number and told me not to be afraid to call if there was ever anything she could help me with. I called. And she answered straight away.

I cut to the chase.

'I-I just wanted to ask you . . . Robert has never admitted that he killed Brenda; do you believe there is any chance at all that he might be innocent?'

'No chance at all,' replied the barrister at once. 'Guilty as hell. And rightly found to be so by twelve people of average ignorance.'

'What?'

'Herbert Spencer's definition of a jury,' she said. And she chuckled.

I didn't. I wasn't in the mood for any sort of attempt at humour.

'But wouldn't you have expected him to confess, to confess in court?' I continued. 'I mean after breaking down the way he did and revealing all that stuff that Brenda had told him?'

I could hear a sort of harrumphing sound down the phone. 'No chance of that, either,' she said. 'I've been at the bar for almost twelve years and I've never yet experienced a Perry Mason moment. They never confess. The evidence Robert gave about Brenda is about as good as it gets. But all he told the court was what she'd said she had done. Even though he seemed to more or less break down he still wouldn't admit what he had done. And that's par for the course.'

'I see,' I said, but I still felt, and I suppose sounded, uncomfortable.

'What's brought this on, Marion?' Pam asked. 'You're not still carrying a torch for the man, are you?'

In spite of myself I managed a hollow laugh. 'No,' I said. 'I certainly am not. It's just that, well, he's been sending me letters I've not opened. Until now. And even in the last one, which only arrived yesterday, he's still protesting his innocence. I mean, is that normal?'

'I should say,' responded Pam. 'You must know the old adage. There's not a guilty prisoner in any jail in all the land.'

I ended the call and thanked her. I certainly wasn't going to share with her what I intended to do next. I called Marti Smith, my solicitor, and asked if she could advise me on the technicalities of arranging to visit Robert. I knew that as he was no longer on remand I would need a visiting order which had to be approved by him, not that, from the tone of his letters, I thought there would be a problem with that.

'And there's something else I need you to do for me first, some paperwork I need you to deal with,' I told Marti.

Less than two weeks later I found myself on my way to Exeter Prison, the imposing Victorian-built penitentiary situated quite centrally in the lovely old county town. I was not looking forward to seeing Robert again, and in such a place, but it had to be done.

I passed through security, enduring the indignity of a body search, which brought back unwelcome memories of my own brush with the law. The prison officer who searched my bag removed the sheaf of paperwork I had with me and glanced at me curiously.

I explained that these were legal papers I needed Robert to sign.

'Did you know you could have arranged a legal visit in a private room with your solicitor present?' he enquired.

I nodded. 'I didn't want to make it too formal,' I said.

The officer removed my pen from my bag and then replaced it.

'All right,' he said. 'But if your husband agrees to sign, then I'd like you to indicate that to us before handing him a pen. For your own safety and his.'

I agreed, wondering at this new world where even a pen could be regarded as some kind of weapon. Although maybe the officer was watching his back as much as anything else, because Robert had presumably already had plenty of access to a pen in order to write to me, before and after his conviction.

He was waiting at a small table in a big room, along with a number of other prisoners already with visitors. He looked as if he may have put on even more weight. His complexion was now quite unhealthily pallid, and he seemed to be sweating. His hair was still short and, I thought, perhaps just beginning at last to turn grey at the temples. He stood up and half smiled as I walked towards him and for one awful moment I was afraid he was going to lean across the table and attempt to kiss me. But I think he saw the expression on my face. Anyway, he sat down again smartly. I sat down opposite him.

He spoke first.

'I can't tell you what it means to me that you've come here,' he said. 'When I was told that you'd applied for a visiting order it was the first good news I'd had in months—'

I interrupted him then. There was no point in stringing him along.

'Don't get your hopes up, Robert,' I told him coldly. 'I have come to see you for one reason and one reason only. I need your cooperation. It appears we have run out of funds and I no longer have any income at all. I have to sell Highrise and I can't do it without you. Not easily anyway.'

I slammed the necessary paperwork down on the table.

There had definitely been hope in his eyes when I'd walked into that room. I saw it fade as I spoke.

'Not Highrise?' It was a question rather than a statement.

I nodded. 'I have no choice. We have no choice.'

With resignation, and without saying anything else, he looked down and began to read the papers before him.

'You maintain ownership of one half of the property,' I told him. 'This document just gives me the right to dispose of the place and its contents as I see fit. Your share will be put in trust for you until your release.'

He glanced up at me.

'Do you think that makes any difference to me?' he asked. 'Now?'

I shrugged. 'I just wanted you to know I wasn't trying to take anything from you. I don't want to take anything from you. I don't want to touch anything of yours ever again.'

I spat out the last words in spite of knowing I shouldn't. After all, I was there to persuade Robert to do my bidding, not to vent my latent fury on him for its own sake.

He did not reply. Instead he looked down again at the papers on the table. I noticed that his hands were trembling. I waited.

I'd thought about asking Marti Smith to approach him. Or, as I assumed would be the correct procedure, to ask for the approach to be made by Robert's solicitor. But I'd known I would stand a better chance of getting what I wanted in the least problematic way if I went to visit Robert and asked him directly. It was an uncomfortable thing to do. But I had been fairly confident of the feelings he still held towards me. And of his tremendous sense of guilt. And actually I still was. In spite of my outburst.

Eventually, after what seemed like a very long time, he looked up at me again.

'Is this what you really want, Marion?' he asked.

'Yes,' I said.

'But think of the memories? Do you really want to leave Highrise? I mean, maybe I will appeal successfully. There is nothing standing in the way of us having a life together now. Perhaps we could rebuild our life? Is that out of the question, Marion?'

For a moment or two I was speechless. Then it was like the waters breaking, as words and thoughts I had barely voiced even to myself poured out of me.

'Do you ever listen to yourself, Robert?' I stormed at him. 'You're crazy. Mad. Crazy. Do you honestly think any woman in her right mind could countenance a future with a man who's done to her what you've done to me? Our son is dead because of you. We don't have a home. We certainly don't have the slimmest hope of any life together ever. Even if I were stupid enough to consider such a thing, neither of us have the means to keep Highrise going. How could you have thought that your lottery money was going to last for ever? It was a miracle you kept all those ridiculous balls in the air for as long as you did. I have a mountain of bills to pay. I have no money even to refill the oil tank. It may be April but every room in the house is still freezing except the kitchen and that's where I've existed all winter. Since your

361

arrest I've barely been able to feed myself, or the fucking dog. And I wouldn't have been able to do so at all without the generosity of the vicar's wife, of all people, and others in the village, the neighbours you never wanted anything to do with. You're a fucking maniac, Robert. A total fucking maniac and I was too blind to see it. Our poor fucking son had to die before I could see it. Then I saw it all right. Now I fucking see it. So just sign these fucking papers, will you, and then that will be the end of everything . . .'

I stopped abruptly, suddenly aware both of my use of language and that my voice had risen until I was shouting at virtually the top of it. The room around us had fallen almost silent. The same prison officer who had earlier searched my bag was walking purposefully towards us. He stopped walking when I stopped shouting.

Robert merely stared at me. His eyes blank and yet filled with pain. His jaw slack. I wondered if he really was crazy. I thought he must be to have done what he did. Sometimes I wondered if I too were crazy. Driven that way by this madman before me.

I glanced towards the prison officer and made a show of taking my pen from my bag. The officer stepped forwards, again. Watchful. I placed the pen on the table alongside the legal papers. Without another word Robert picked it up and signed in each of the places Marti Smith had marked.

That was it. He had with those few signatures given me the right to sell Highrise, to walk away from the place and from him for ever.

I half snatched the papers from him, shuffling them into some sort of order as I stood up, swung round and prepared to leave. Then he spoke once more.

'Will you come and visit again?' he asked, almost plaintively.

'Will you? If only to tell me how you've got on, and if you've sold the place?'

I could barely believe my ears. I turned round to look at him one last time. His eyes were pleading. His lips were trembling as well as his hands. I didn't give a damn.

'Your solicitor can do that,' I said, my voice deliberately expressionless. 'I never want to see you again as long as I live.'

I began to walk across the visiting room to the exit. As I did so I could hear a kind of strangled wail. It hardly sounded like Robert, more like the anguished cry of a wild animal. But I knew it was him.

I did not look back.

When I arrived home, or rather to the place I now thought of as having once been my home, I took the signed papers from my bag and flipped through. I felt no sense of triumph. This really did mark the end of it all. The end of an era. The end of a lifetime. I felt mostly sorrow. But I also experienced perhaps just a glimmer of hope for some kind of future, something I knew I had now denied Robert even more than Exeter Crown Court had.

I did want to start again, if it were to prove to be possible. I would never stop grieving for Robbie. But I was damned if I was going to grieve for his father too, and let that man destroy whatever might be left for me.

I called an estate agent that very afternoon in order to put Highrise on the market. And I called Marti Smith to tell her Robert had signed. Then I set about giving the place a massive spring clean and generally making it as presentable as I could in order to sell. The next day I planned to tidy the garden, particularly at the front, where visitors first arrived at the property. I needed to get out fast, I really did. And I was prepared to do anything necessary in order for that to happen, including ensuring that the price was right.

Ultimately, and thankfully, the old house sold surprisingly easily. Or perhaps not that surprisingly. I put it on the market for more than £50,000 less than the price suggested by our major local estate agent, and ultimately agreed to sell for almost £100,000 less than his estimate. Ironically, it was Robert who had always said, when I'd gone to car boot sales or markets, that everything has a price, and everything will sell at the right price.

I was more readily prepared to accept a low offer for Highrise because the prospective buyer was, unusually, neither in a chain nor in need of a mortgage. I just wanted to get out of the place as quickly as possible, and he just wanted to move himself and his family in as quickly as possible.

At around the same time the inquest into Robbie's death was eventually held in the North Devon market town of Barnstaple. It was a curious affair. I attended with my father. Dad had offered to accompany me, and for the first time since the nightmare had begun I did not turn him away.

I wasn't required to give evidence and did not have to be at the hearing. But I wanted, indeed, needed to be there to witness the final chapter in my son's tragic story,

The coroner for Exeter and Greater Devon, Dr Elspeth Hunt, had been supplied with written reports from the ambulance service and from the Scenes of Crime Officers. DS Jarvis was the principal witness.

He briefly outlined how he had been called to Highrise on the night of Robbie's death and had found my son hanging from a beam in his room.

'My first reaction and that of the paramedics and other police officers called to the scene was that this was a case of tragic suicide,' said Jarvis. 'However, subsequent events have led us to believe that there was probably a third party involved.'

'Indeed, Mr Jarvis,' agreed the coroner. 'And the involvement of this third party is something that has recently become a matter of record in another court, has it not?'

'Yes, madam. However, the third party concerned is deceased and we are unable to take our investigations into the death of Robbie Anderson any further.'

'So I understand. You are speaking of Mrs Brenda Anderton, are you not, whose husband, Robbie Anderson's father, was recently convicted of her murder?'

'Yes, madam.'

'And you were quite right, Mr Jarvis, to be reticent about naming a person who can neither answer the allegations made against her nor be brought to trial. However, I think it is important for this court, the sole task of which is to ascertain the cause of Robbie Anderson's death, to be able to place on record that all known aspects of this case have been considered.'

'Yes, madam,' said DS Jarvis again.

'And so, also for the record, Mr Jarvis, can you confirm that no other person is being investigated regarding the death of Robbie Anderson?'

'I can, madam. In fact, our investigation into the young man's death has now been closed.'

Within just over an hour the coroner announced her verdict on the ending of fifteen years of bright and promising life.

'Under the complex circumstances of this case, and because there is insufficient evidence to come to any other conclusion, I am delivering an open verdict,' said Dr Hunt.

I had been ready for that, of course. DS Jarvis had already indicated that there could really be no other ruling, and both he and my solicitor, Marti Smith, had explained the legal situation to me.

The coroner then went on to offer her sympathy to Robbie's family.

'I can only imagine what this fine young man's parents have been through following his tragic death,' she said. 'This really is the kind of case I would like never to come my way again.'

She did not mention further that one half of Robbie's parentage was in prison. As I left the court, my arm through Dad's, I did feel hurt that in the annals of law the circumstances of my son's death would never be fully explained nor recorded.

None the less, I also, finally, felt a sense of closure.

The sale of Highrise was completed in mid-June, just over six weeks after my accepting the buyer's offer. Everything went extremely smoothly. But I suppose it does when you're damned near giving a house away.

I didn't care. In fact, I didn't give a damn. I just wanted to leave the place and never see it again. And I would still have enough money to begin to rebuild my life. I didn't know how long it might take me, or even if ultimately I would find the will to do so, but I was going to give it a good try.

During that six-week period I called in a clearance firm and accepted another doubtless derisory sum to clear Highrise of most of its remaining furniture and decorative pieces, all of Robert and Robbie's clothes which were still there, and indeed most of my own clothes and personal possessions.

Then I spent a sizeable chunk of the proceeds on a new hairdo. I wanted to change everything about myself, and my full head of curly brown hair was probably my most distinctive feature. It was a big thing for me to do. My hair had been much the same since my teens, except for the grey roots. I determined to do it in style, so I took the train to London and splashed out on the full works at Vidal Sassoon's Mayfair salon. I wanted a totally different look. I had my hair straightened and went for a very short geometric cut, typical Sassoon, and a full white-blonde peroxide dip. I then took a cab to John Lewis in Oxford Street and bought myself a black leather jacket, black leggings and a couple of those cotton print dresses everyone seemed to be wearing that you put on over leggings. I had a long way to go before adopting Marti Smith's unique sharpness of style, but I had to admit to myself that my clothes shopping was somewhat influenced by my solicitor. More than anything, I wanted to look modern. After all, I was finally about to leave behind what had been, even in the very good days, a kind of time-warp existence, and project myself into the modern world.

I discarded the dated nearly black trouser suit that I'd worn in order to travel to London and left John Lewis wearing the leather jacket I'd purchased over one of the print dresses and the leggings. I couldn't help looking at myself in every mirror I passed, if only to check that the woman in the reflection really was me. I seemed to be well on the way to at least looking like a different person, and it was only by more or less becoming a different person that I thought I would ever have a chance of moving on from the enormity of all that I had lost.

I thought I was getting there, although the day that would have been Robbie's sixteenth birthday, the 28th of May, was predictably black. But I coped. Just about.

I even threw a little farewell party for the people who had been so kind to me: Gladys and the Reverend Gerald, the Farleys, the Jamesons and Marti Smith. I'd also invited Pam Cotton, but she'd been in Truro prosecuting a crooked Cornish county councillor. At least, Pam said he was crooked. Seriously so.

The rest of us drank all that remained of Robert's wine and got quite squiffy. Well, I did, anyway. And Gladys too. She wobbled on her feet a bit and looked rather weepy as she enveloped me in a great big hug and said: 'You will come and visit, won't you, Marion? We're going to miss you, you know.'

I promised that I would, but had no intention of doing so.

When I left Highrise Farm a couple of days later I needed only a couple of medium-sized suitcases to carry what was left of my personal possessions. On one of the wettest and windiest days of the worst June on record I loaded the cases onto the back seat of the Lexus, my only legacy, really, of all those years with Robert. Then I loaded Florrie into the rear compartment behind her doggie guard, started the engine, and drove dry-eyed and without a backward glance up the lane away from the place I had so loved, from the place that had once been my wonderful dream home, and from a life I had also thought to be wonderful.

I suppose I surprised myself a little. But I had, of course, already wept so many tears that there were probably none left. Highrise represented only misery now. It reminded me only of great tragedy and great loss.

Suddenly I found that I couldn't wait to put it behind me once and for all.

I hoped eventually that I might be able to return to teaching as a career, albeit after some retraining, perhaps in a place where I was not known. Meanwhile I thought I might travel for a bit, visiting places I had never been to, which held no memories for me of my other lost life.

But first I had arranged to visit my father for a couple of weeks. It was a long time since I'd actually stayed in the old cottage attached to the little garage he still ran part-time on the outskirts of Hartland. And even longer since I'd been inside the garage where I knew I would find him once I'd realized he wasn't in the house.

He was down in the inspection pit working on an old MGB roadster. He'd seen me a couple of times since I'd acquired my peroxide-blonde geometric hairdo, so he'd already got over the shock. Well, got over it enough to no longer mention it, anyway. He came to the edge of the pit and peered up at me.

'Don't suppose you can give me a hand, maid?' he asked. 'Young Jim Hickson, you know, lives with his mam up by the church, needs to get to Bude tomorrow 'bout a new job. Bleddy young fool's never learned how to look after an MG exhaust. Drives everywhere fast as he can whatever the state of the road and he's really scuppered it this time.'

I bent down so that I could clearly see the end of the B's exhaust pipe hanging at a terminal angle.

'Needs a whole new system, of course, but I'm damned if I can get the parts in time,' Dad went on. 'Two or three days, they say, so I'm just going to have to patch 'er up . . .'

He was a lovely man, my dad, kind, trustworthy, always trying to help people. It was just like him to be putting himself out for a neighbour, a young man I knew he had seen grow up. If only I could have married a man like him, I thought to myself, not for the first time.

I straightened up and smiled down at him.

'So it's the old bean-can trick is it?'

'It sure is,' he said. 'Fiddly bleddy job, too, and 'twould be a damn sight easier with two pairs of hands.'

'I'm not sure I'd be much help,' I remarked casually.

'Oh yes, you would.'

'I don't think so,' I persisted.

'Come on, maid.' It was Dad's turn to persist. 'When you worked with me as a slip of a girl you were a better mechanic than any boy. You should have carried on with it, you know. You were a natural. You won't have forgotten, I'm sure of it.'

I studied him carefully for a few seconds. I didn't know how closely my father had followed Robert's trial, if at all in view of the distress I knew it had caused him, nor how fully some of the less dramatic evidence, the technical stuff, had been reported in the press. But Dad's entire concentration appeared focused on the task confronting him. There certainly seemed to be no edge to his remarks.

I relaxed. 'All right,' I said. 'I'll do my best. Got any spare overalls?'

Dad climbed up out of the pit.

'I'll find you some, and I'll fetch a can,' he said, beaming at me. 'Still my right-hand girl, eh?'

He disappeared into the cottage. The bean-can trick, as it's known, involves vertically slicing open a tin can, cutting out a strip, and fastening it around a blown or broken exhaust pipe. It could only ever be a temporary job, but with a bit of luck, would get young Jim Hickson to Bude and back.

While I waited for Dad to return I rummaged around the garage looking for a couple of jubilee clips with which to secure the makeshift repair.

During what I now regarded as my long sham of a marriage to Robert I'd left the whole of the early part of my life behind me and never talked about my perhaps unlikely knowledge in certain areas. Nor would I have been sure, then, how much I'd retained. In any case, Robert had believed in a pretty clear demarcation in our roles. He'd been the man and the engineer. He'd looked after our vehicles and everything mechanical and technical. He'd not had the vaguest idea that I might also have been capable of doing so.

But my father knew me well. I had indeed forgotten very

little from those long ago days working alongside him in his garage.

I'd realized that as soon as I'd started my deadly work on Brenda Anderton's car.

extracts reading groups
competitions books new
discounts extracts extracts
competitions
books new events reading groups
events books
extracts
new titles reading groups
interviews events
events extracts
discounts
new books events
events new interviews
discounts extracts discounts
www.panmacmillan.com
extracts events reading groups
competitions books extracts new
books